SLASH OR PASS

TW/CW:

Explicit sexual scenes (consensual)
Murder
Gore
Blood
Mentions of Sexual Assault & Rape

Thalia Sanchez is known for writing slasher romances. She began writing at the early age of thirteen and soon discovered she wanted to be an author in the future. Thalia has a degree in film and another in Creative Writing. She was born and raised in Puerto Rico, where she lives with her dogs and cat. When she's not writing, you can find her studying, reading, and rewatching her comfort movies.

SLASH OR PASS

THALIA SANCHEZ

HEADLINE
ETERNAL

Copyright © Thalia Sanchez 2026

The right of Thalia Sanchez to be identified as the Author of the
Work has been asserted by her in accordance with the Copyright,
Designs and Patents Act 1988.

First published in 2026 by Headline Eternal
An imprint of Headline Publishing Group Limited

1

Apart from any use permitted under UK copyright law, this publication
may only be reproduced, stored, or transmitted, in any form, or by
any means, with prior permission in writing of the publishers or,
in the case of reprographic production, in accordance with the terms
of licences issued by the Copyright Licensing Agency.

Cataloguing in Publication Data is available from the British Library

Paperback ISBN 978 1 0354 3472 5

Typeset in 11.4/15.67pt Baskerville MT Std by
Six Red Marbles UK, Thetford, Norfolk

Printed and bound in Great Britain by Clays Ltd, Elcograf S.p.A.

Headline's policy is to use papers that are natural, renewable and recyclable
products and made from wood grown in well-managed forests and other
controlled sources. The logging and manufacturing processes are expected
to conform to the environmental regulations of the country of origin.

Headline Publishing Group Limited
An Hachette UK Company
Carmelite House
50 Victoria Embankment
London EC4Y 0DZ

The authorised representative in the EEA is Hachette Ireland,
8 Castlecourt Centre, Dublin 15, D15 XTP3, Ireland (email: info@hbgi.ie)

www.headline.co.uk
www.hachette.co.uk
www.headlineeternal.com

To the older sisters (especially mine)

Chapter 1

A BLOODCURDLING SCREAM SHATTERS THE MORNING stillness. Loud enough to wake everyone in the sorority. The first thought to cross my mind isn't to find out what's happening outside. No, my first thought is, *I need a screamer like that for the final assignment of my Advanced Cinematography class.* Lungs with that capacity don't come around often, especially not ones carrying a specific aura.

If there's something I've learned in the years I've been studying film at Westbrook College, it's that anyone can scream, but not everyone can convey the true essence of horror.

And that girl screaming like a banshee outside is exactly what I need.

I've already used all my contacts from previous projects, both for school and personal, and held auditions at the auditorium. So far, nothing matches what I'm hearing.

It's not like a lot of people are willing to work with you now.

I jump from my seat, leaving behind the half-eaten bowl of Cheerios, and I rush out along with the other Kappas to find my perfect scream queen. My bare feet slap against the floor tiles. I know I should probably run upstairs to find my slippers, but I can't miss this. What if I wait and she's gone when I go to find her?

This can't wait.

By the time I make it outside, there's a group of people gathered around the main fountain in the roundabout. A mix of frat guys and sorority girls have begun to crowd the area, making it impossible for me to see what's happening. Murmurs become loud and the shrieks of my missing scream queen cut through them, creating a dissonance. Whoever is screaming is clearly in a serious amount of shock.

"Excuse me," I say, elbowing people as I make my way through the crowd, trying to catch the conversations around me.

"Where's my emergency whistle? I never leave without my emergency whistle!"

"Lavender, the emergency whistle is for alive people; the guy is clearly dead," someone responds.

Lavender—she might be a Sigma, but I don't recognize her—lets out a shocked gasp that transforms into a sob. *Why is she crying?*

It doesn't seem like she knows the dead person.

"How will the cops find him then?"

Two girls next to Lavender begin to softly pat her back in an effort to calm her down, explaining they should call 911 instead.

"Does anyone know who it is?" someone asks.

"Glenn, you know everyone. Can you see if he's one of us?"

Us. He means another frat guy. Someone I've probably seen around on campus or at parties. A person we might have been in class with. Realization begins to settle in my limbs, stopping me in my tracks. For a moment, I become paralyzed by the news. A person died today.

The screams were full of horror because someone found a dead body.

My stomach churns with embarrassment and nerves. Have I truly become so desensitized to horror that I no longer consider a scream a call for help? My first thought . . . *Jesús.* What's wrong with me?

"No way," the guy, Glenn, replies instantly. "I'm not going anywhere near *that*."

"I'll check," another guy offers, and while I can't see the owner of the voice, I recognize it.

Danny Singh.

Inevitably, like the main character of a cheesy chick-flick, I feel my breath hitch, getting stuck somewhere in my throat. Pure heat makes its way to my cheeks, even though the sun hasn't fully warmed up yet. My body betrays me, and I can't help but stare down at my bare feet on the gravel to find a distraction to prevent me from looking at him.

I haven't talked to Danny in days, possibly more than a week now. Not after The Incident.

"Don't dead bodies have diseases? You could get, like, rabies or something from getting too close," a girl supplies, her voice thick with concern.

"I'm pretty sure it doesn't work like that, Paris, but I'll take it into consideration, okay?" he says in a calm and even tone.

Danny always knows what to say and how to calm people around him. His aura exudes peace and trustworthiness. That's why he's the president of Delta Phi. There's probably not a single person on campus who doesn't like Danny.

Including me. Especially me.

Ignoring the way his voice makes my stomach flutter, I attempt to swallow through the dryness in my mouth. I need to get it together. As much as a big part of me wants to run away and continue my plan to avoid Danny until graduation day arrives, my feet remain locked to the ground. Aware I won't move until he confirms if we know the victim, I stay still, hidden among a row of girls.

"Is it one of us?" the guy presses again.

"No, not anymore," Danny states, but there's a secondary layer to his tone, something he isn't quite saying and doesn't know how to reveal. "It's Brian . . . Brian Manders."

Hearing the name knocks the air out of my lungs.

Cold sweat spreads over my body. A trace of tingles makes my fingers shake.

I push everyone out of the way to get a better look. A wave of nausea rolls through my stomach, but I don't allow the bile to rise. Instead, I stay still, staring at the gory scene in front of me. I've seen plenty of horror movies, from slashers to splatter films, to the point where barely anything fazes me anymore.

But this? This was a murder done with pure hatred and anger.

Brian's mutilated corpse hangs from the statue in the middle of the fountain. His arms twisted in an unnatural position. Blood drips into the water, pooling around the center like a red shadow. Deep cuts slash through his face, making him barely recognizable. But it's not the wounds on his face or the position of his body that make me want to bend over and hurl. No, it's the way he's been gutted like a fish. His intestines hang from his abdomen like ropes, reaching his feet. On his chest, the killer has used Brian's own blood to spell out one word: *rapist*.

"Mabel." I vaguely hear Danny call out my name, but it's barely white noise in the back of my brain. I'm unable to stop staring at Brian's dead body. The violence lures me in, keeping me in a locked trance as if it were hypnotizing me. A warm hand touches my shoulder, and I jump, startled until I realize it's Danny. His soft caress pulls me in, but it's not enough to get me to break free from the spell.

"Please, take a step back," Danny urges in a gentle tone.

His fingers delicately touch my jaw and turn my gaze from the body to look at him instead. Worry swims in the warm caramel of his irises, grounding me to reality by spreading a flush of comfort through my veins.

I blink, suddenly too aware of what's happening. It's not the fact that Danny is touching me, his thumb drawing invisible circles over the fabric of my T-shirt. I had approached the fountain. I'm not sure why. I simply . . . did.

Rising tension cramps my lungs.

What the hell was I thinking?

"That's it," Danny praises, offering me one of his radiant smiles. But I've spent too much time observing him in the past to not know it's forced. There's a slight tremble making the corners of his lips waver. It's not real. Danny's real smile is blinding and breathtaking. "Keep looking at me, Mabs." Without breaking eye contact, he lures me into him, gently shielding me with his arms. "Don't look at him. Focus on me."

But while I try to keep my gaze locked on his, the murmurs are distracting.

Somehow, me approaching the body like a horror freak has caused a stir. Everyone is staring at me, including the only two people I want to protect from this view. Behind Danny, I see the beautiful light brown curls of my sister's hair as she rushes up with my best friend.

The world seems to shift on its axis. Although every cell in my body doesn't want me to, I take a step back from Danny's touch. Giving in to his initial request to step away from the fountain, I run to stop Carmen and Cerys from getting closer. The first person I reach is my best friend and I wrap her in my arms, shielding her from seeing this gnarly scene.

The murmurs grow around us, so loud it's deafening.

"What happened?" Cerys asks, with a small tremble in her voice. "Who is it?"

My heart constricts in my chest.

"It's Brian," I announce. I'm surprised my voice doesn't break with the fear of what's to come. "Someone murdered him."

And it's only then I realize I'm hugging the person who will become the prime suspect: my best friend.

Because, a few months ago, Brian Manders raped her.

Chapter 2

One year later

TEXTING LITTLE SISTERS IS LIKE BEING GHOSTED, SEEING as they both have one outcome: no response. Annoyance prickles along my skin, right under the layer of sweat pooling at the back of my neck, as I send Carmen another angry message. I stare at the delivery confirmation and wait fifteen seconds. Then, thirty more.

Come on, Carmen.

No response.

A groan vibrates in the back of my throat, threatening to spill free, but I don't allow it. Instead, I shove my phone in my back pocket. Fine. If she plans to ignore my messages, I'll just have to find her. Carmen might think she's being sneaky, but I know her better than she knows herself. I know all her preferred hangout spots and secret hideouts. Westbrook College might have a big campus, but it's not that big. I'll find her before the day is over.

It's not like I have another choice.

The pink folded envelope becomes heavy in my backpack. For a split second, it almost feels as if I am carrying a bag of bricks, when it's merely paper. Although, deep down, I'm aware it's not just a piece of paper. No, it's a dreadful reminder of why I desperately need to get a hold of my sister, why I've decided to return to Westbrook after leaving last year with no intention of ever returning.

Using the back of my hand, I wipe the pearls of sweat gathering at my hairline, and take a moment to breathe, dropping my backpack onto a bench. Memories flood my brain, but I do my best to keep them at bay, focusing my mind on simple tasks. I remove my jacket and push it into my backpack. Tie my hair into a high ponytail to prevent it from getting frizzier with the humidity than it already is.

Clearly, I've chosen the worst day to walk all over campus. It might be mid-February, but the Florida sun can be unforgiving..

I glance around, hoping to catch a glimpse of my sister, but all my eyes catch are clingy, loved-up couples and a bunch of rose-colored flyers stapled all over campus. I ignore the first and focus on the latter. They're promoting a Valentine's Day event in the Kappa house.

Anxiety bubbles in the pit of my stomach.

I know what I have to do, yet I don't feel confident in my options. I wish I could find Carmen right now and drag her ass to a plane far away from this nightmare of a place, but the universe won't have my back on this one. If there's one thing I've gotten accustomed to, it's Murphy's Law.

What can go wrong, will go wrong.

And it's my worst fear.

I check my phone one last time and sigh. Still no response from Carmen, which leaves me no choice but to go straight to the source: Kappa house.

My old home.

It takes me fifteen minutes to walk across campus to Greek Row. With every step I take, my heart beats faster. The nerves crawl up my system, heightening my senses. I'm hyperaware of every person walking by me, of every corner of the buildings, of the replaced water fountain in the roundabout where Brian Manders's body was found last year.

The image of his gutted body is still engraved on my brain. Maybe if I were a special effects make-up artist, I would find that image more inspiring than I do working as an Assistant Director for BSIX Studios.

I shake my head and walk to the main entrance of Kappa house. The doors are wide open, and inside, the Kappas are preparing for the party, decorating the place and organizing even the tiniest details. I prepare for cold and aloof reactions to my presence in the house. After all, when I left here I was public enemy number 1.

When Brian's body was found, the police investigation led to Cerys, and while she provided an iron-clad alibi for the crime, everyone was still pointing the finger at her. They didn't need to find the real culprit when they had already made up their minds, especially when Brian's rich daddy was leading a witch hunt against my best friend. The harassment took over her life. They practically drove her to leave campus and lose all her professional opportunities. Cerys had always been a spectacular student who dreamed of becoming an attorney. Yet with Senator Manders' influence wrecking her reputation, having a 4.0 GPA and a spotless CV were worthless. She wouldn't even get into the weakest of law schools.

I always stood by her side.

Cerys *is* innocent, and I have no doubt about it.

"Mabel!" The loud chirp makes me jump, but it's not the yell that catches me off guard. It's the fact that it sounds . . . happy? Could they really be glad to see me after everything that went down? "Girl, what are you doing here?"

I barely get a chance to brace myself before I'm almost tackled by Leighton. Last year, she was one of the new pledges of Kappa. She was always sweet and had a bright smile.

A few other girls also share hellos and smiles.

It's so jarring, like no one even remembers why I left in the first place.

Behind Leighton, I spot Bethan, and I bite the inside of my cheek to stop the sourness from showing on my face, although I don't doubt she can feel the intensity emanating from my glare. Bethan used to be one of Cerys' closest friends, as they both come from the same town. While I wasn't too tight with her and she was a year younger, we used to hang out a lot. Until she decided Cerys was lying about Brian abusing her and didn't care to even defend her when things got rough. She was never a real friend to Cerys.

Regardless of my reaction, Bethan blinks and smiles welcomingly, pushing her perfectly styled auburn hair over her shoulder.

"Mabel, it's good to see you," she greets me, politely. "Carmen mentioned you were working in LA."

I nod. "Yes, I am."

"I always knew you would make it to Hollywood." She places a manicured hand on my arm, and I subtly take a step back. If she notices my rejection, she doesn't comment on it. Her broad smile remains the same. "What are you doing here?"

"I missed Carmen too much and had some free time between productions," I say nonchalantly. The lie comes out effortlessly. I might not work as an actress, but I've written enough scripts to know how to come up with lines on the spot. "Have you seen her? I want to surprise her."

"Oh, I haven't! But you can wait in her room. I'm sure she'll turn up soon. We have the V-Day party tonight. You should stay around for it. It'll be a perfect night." Bethan beams and clasps her hands together. "You know the way to the sophomore rooms. Please, make yourself at home."

I pass by her and go up the stairs to find Carmen's room. While I haven't been here since I moved out, I know where her room is located thanks to my stalking skills. She has posted enough photos on the gram for me to know her room is the only one that has a direct view of the fountain. I got assigned the same one back in my sophomore year.

Going unnoticed by the other Kappas proves to be an impossible task. The girls keep trying to make small talk. It feels like I walked straight into an alternate universe where everyone is suddenly friends with me. I've always joked that being part of a sorority was almost like being part of a cult, but it doesn't seem so funny now when they've collectively decided to forget all about last year.

When I'm almost at my sister's room, I bump into the first sign of unpleasantness. Relief washes over my body. Finally, a natural reaction to my presence in the house. Sophia, Zelda and Elodie are a mix I expected to happen—up to a certain point.

Sophia and Zelda were always mean girls, the epitome of the sorority cliché. Hypocritical, superficial and shallow. I would feel bad about describing them in such an ill-spirited way, when girls should be supporting girls, but they're the first ones to break the code. I remember them pointing their fingers at Cerys, calling her all sorts of names and making her existence in the house a pure living hell.

However, Elodie? I'm surprised she's clung on to the evil twins. When she was a pledge, Kappa appointed me as her big sister, and while I can't say we were the best of friends, we always had a polite and friendly relationship. Elodie always carried herself with kindness, being a friend to everyone.

"You're not welcome here, Mabel," Zelda says now, crossing her arms over her stomach.

"You and your little liar friend cost us the Greek Cup, breaking our winning streak of a decade. Our legacy, if you even care."

"Clearly, she doesn't care, Soph. She always ruined the vibe."

I roll my eyes.

"Right, because rape and murder are always a party booster around here." Sarcasm drips from my tone.

Sophia and Zelda purse their lips and disregard my comment, strutting down the hall. However, Elodie stays behind, giving me an apologetic smile.

"I'm sorry. They're a bit . . ."

"Bitchy?" I supply.

The corners of her mouth twitch. She's fighting a laugh.

"I wouldn't use that word, but sure," she accepts. "It's good to see you, Mabby."

She leaves me alone and I manage to make it to my sister's room without any other issues. Her room is a mess of clothes sprawled all over the place, make-up spilled over her dresser, and an unmade bed.

Oddly enough, I find her mess comforting.

Out of the two of us, she has always been the messy one. Maybe because I always indulged her, taking care of her as if she were my own child. Our parents weren't bad by any means. I value how they both worked multiple jobs to provide for us and sustain our household. It hasn't always been easy for them, considering they moved across an ocean with us when we were little. But that also meant they were too busy and tired to be overly present in our lives. Since I was the oldest, I always put Carmen's needs above my own. She needed a role model, a person who could take care of her.

And I've always been that person.

On her nightstand, I find a photo of us as kids, and I can't help but smile. She can ignore me all she wants, but she has me near her when she sleeps.

"What are you doing here?"

I turn around on my heel and face Carmen, standing with her hand on the door handle. Judging by her slightly widened eyes, she's clearly stunned to see me. A frown wrinkles her forehead. Her lips are pressed together into a thin line, the same way they always do when she's unhappy.

Tough shit, sis.

I scrutinize her with squinted eyes, checking if she's truly in one piece. Carmen has her curly hair pushed back from her face, presenting her flawless skin. She wears a short black skirt and a blue crop top that contrasts perfectly with her light brown skin. In her right hand, she holds her phone, confirming my suspicion that the little brat has been avoiding me.

But my muscles still release some of the tightness I've felt since I got the pink envelope.

She's okay.

"I don't pay your phone bill for you to ignore me when I text you, Carmen Lucía." I use her middle name because, while it annoys her, it makes her fall in line. It's something I've always done since I started taking care of her.

Carmen rolls her eyes and turns to close the door.

"Aren't you being a little dramatic? I was busy. You didn't need to fly all the way from LA just because I missed one text, Jesus."

"One text? Try thirty."

"Whatever," she mumbles, and walks past me to lay her things on the bed. "Did you come to scold me, or did you want something?"

"I'm worried about you," I confess.

"Because I didn't answer your texts? *Psycho alert*," she singsongs. "No wonder you never got a boyfriend."

I disregard her words and dig into my backpack, pulling out the pink envelope. The edges have started to peel from my constant touch through the flight, but it's still in one piece for her to see. I pull out the contents, revealing the folded letter. Handing it to her, she unfolds it without bothering to fake interest. Her expression falters for a split second. Short enough that it wouldn't be noticeable to the average person, but enough for me to know she's been taken aback.

It's a single photograph of her, taken from outside her window while she was getting changed. Her underwear covered the essentials, but it was enough to make me concerned, even without the red writing scribbled over it. Someone had been stalking my sister, and she hadn't noticed. But the cherry on top is the two words written over the image. *She's next.*

"Dude, you're such a creep," she whistles under her breath. "When did you even take this?"

"Me? I didn't take anything. Someone sent this to me," I argue. "Carmen, you have a stalker."

She snorts and shoves the photo back into my hands.

"Now you're being overdramatic."

"Overdramatic?" I echo, aghast. "This room is on the second floor. It's not easy to spot from outside, yet someone managed to take this *intimate* pic of you. What do you call that?"

She shrugs.

"I don't know what you want me to say, Mabel. Yes, it's a bit creepy that someone took a photo, but what do you want me to do? College is full of creeps."

I dig my teeth into my bottom lip.

"I want you to come stay in LA with me for a few weeks until we can disregard this threat."

"Threat?" she croaks out. "C'mon."

"What do you think the message means? *She's next?*" I snap. I refuse to let her brush this off as if it were nothing, because it's not *nothing*. "Carmen, I believe this message came from the killer."

Her dark brows shoot up high on her forehead. "The killer?"

"Brian's killer."

Her expression transforms from slight amusement to anger.

"Now you've truly lost it," she spits out. "Maybe you should take a break from working on shitty horror movies and think about what you're really doing here."

"Shitty horror movies?"

I almost want to laugh bitterly, I feel it simmering in my system along with my own anger.

Carmen has always had a spitfire mouth, but I've never been the target of her ruthless tongue. Until now. It stings right in my chest, and my heart speeds up, pumping hot blood through my burning veins. I want to understand where she's coming from, but I can't make sense of it. Yes, I've been exposed to horror. I spent my college years creating short horror films for class and I *loved* every single second of it. They're what got me my current job at BSIX. Pride doesn't even begin to cover what I feel for my accomplishment because being able to work alongside important horror figures while being so young in the industry is a big deal.

Yet she's minimizing my labor only because she doesn't like what I'm implying here.

I might be a hardcore fan, but this entire scenario is one step away from becoming a slasher film. And while they can be fun to watch and create, I can't say I would want to live it, especially when my sister appears to be the next target.

My eyes travel across the room to the window, where I can spot the statue in the fountain where the killer hung Brian's body.

It might only be a matter of time before the next body shows up, and I don't want it to be Carmen.

Bile rises in my esophagus, and I swallow it down.

"Listen, let's leave the screaming match for another time. I don't like the idea of someone stalking and threatening you. That's all."

"You're being silly. This is clearly just a prank or something." She shrugs again, and there's something about the way her muscles stiffen that makes me wary of her words.

"A prank?"

"Yes, *señorita*. A prank." She opens her nightstand drawer and pulls out another pink envelope. "I received this some time ago and I ignored it, like any sane person would do."

I snatch the envelope from her hands, pulling out a photo. However, this time the object of the photo isn't my sister. It's me. Very similar angle, taken from a distance when I was still a student here at Westbrook and a Kappa. I'm wearing a wet Kappa shirt and some shorts. This was taken last year.

Someone has been watching me since last year.

"You ignored this?" I hold it at her eye level. "Are you insane?"

"You're being stupid, Mabel. I know how your mind works; you always let yourself get carried away by these silly horror plots, but this isn't a movie. This is real life, and you could absolutely ruin mine."

"I'm not trying to ruin your life, I'm trying to save it," I correct her. "I've always kept you safe."

Carmen glares at me.

"It's not your job to keep me safe. You're not my mother," she snaps back. "As much as you would like to be, you're not."

I take a step back as if she slapped me. She might as well have punched me in the gut. It would've hurt less because, right now, my ribs ache and my lungs are constricting. It feels like the oxygen has completely abandoned my body with no intention of returning.

Her words *hurt*. They hurt more than anything I've ever experienced before.

Carmen's right, I'm not her mother. I haven't pretended to ever be her mother, but I have taken care of her. I've worked my ass off to help her pay for acting lessons so she could completely focus on her studies. Growing up too fast to ensure she had the life I didn't get to have. Supporting her dreams meant more to me than she could ever realize. I doubt she'll ever know. I've never expected her to be grateful, but the way she stomps on my effort like it's worthless ignites a flame of anger.

"I'll stop acting like it when you stop behaving like a child."

I regret the words the second they come out of my lips. My wounded pride only wanted her to feel as hurt as she'd made me.

"Get the hell out of my room," she mutters through gritted teeth. "Mabel, I mean it. Get the hell out!"

Nodding, I swallow back all the words I still haven't said, and push both letters into my backpack before leaving her room. No longer having the energy to fight her on this, I might need to take a step back and re-evaluate my approach to get her to a safe place. While I'm angrier than I've ever been with her, I won't let her be killed.

I would rather die than live a day knowing she's gone.

Keeping my head down, I rush out of the Kappa house. I'm so caught up with my thoughts and trying to get out of there fast that I don't notice the barrier of human flesh standing in my way. It's solid and unyielding, almost knocking me on my ass if it weren't for the strong hands holding on to me.

"Whoa, easy there."

That voice.

No, it can't be him. Perhaps I am losing my mind, because there's no way he's standing in front of me. He shouldn't be on campus. The last time I saw him, he was walking across the stage to receive his diploma. We didn't even talk. Our interaction consisted of one long glance before leaving.

Slowly, I raise my gaze to his face and, when I'm greeted by soft, caramel-colored eyes, I confirm it's him.

Danny.

Chapter 3

DANNY ALWAYS HAD PUPPY EYES. IT'S PROBABLY WHY I considered him to be half golden retriever and half man. I remember the first time I saw them. Although we lived in Greek Row for years, I saw him for the first time at the library. It's such a cliché, but I swear I lost my ability to speak properly when he set his gaze on me, and something in me melted a little.

Then he smiled, and I knew a guy like that would be dangerous. Not because he's a bad person. No, the Danny I know—the guy who promoted mental health services on campus, volunteered to be the designated driver at parties—wouldn't hurt a fly.

He's dangerous because he makes me vulnerable. And being vulnerable means he has the capacity to hurt me.

Underneath my layers of protection, I have a fragile ego

and, as my grandmother would say, *un corazón de pollo*—a chicken's heart. Tender and soft. Yeah, getting too close to Danny could leave me scarred and broken, and I don't know how to handle that. I can barely handle looking at him after The Incident.

He continues to stare deep into my eyes, and I spot a flicker of relief swimming in his irises as they roam my face. I can't tell if he's trying to make sure I'm okay or if he's glad to see me. Is he glad to see me? A foreign sensation flutters in my stomach. *Am I?* Glad to see him?

"Are you okay?" he asks, letting go of my shoulders.

I had almost forgotten I slammed into him.

Almost being the key word, because the phantom of his touch on my arms still tingles over my skin. I fight the need to shudder.

"Yeah," I mumble and then cough to clear my throat. *Get it together, Mabs.* "What are you doing here?"

Danny chuckles a little, shaking his head. There's a sense of awkwardness lingering in his stance, which is unusual for him, as he always carries his body with confidence. He seems almost nervous.

"I should be asking you that question," he retorts. "You're the last person I expected to see here."

"I came to visit Carmen," I respond, and my words come off strained and more hostile than I intended them to. "If anything, I would say it's weirder to see *you*."

Danny cocks his head and arches a brow.

"I didn't say seeing you was weird. It's surprising," he clarifies, trying to clear up the misunderstanding. "It's great to see you."

I ignore the way my heart does a flip at his words.

He's being polite, I can tell. But I would be lying if I said the feeling isn't mutual. After my argument with Carmen, Danny is a sight for sore eyes.

"So what are you doing here?" I inquire, shifting the subject.

"It's complicated, but it's a good thing you're here," he says, before pressing his lips together. A slight wrinkle creases his forehead and his stance becomes tighter. More serious. "We need to talk. It's important."

Nothing of what he just said sounds good. If anything, it's the opposite because he's being ominous and secretive about it.

"Okay."

"*Really* important," he emphasizes. "And private."

"Okay," I repeat, because I don't trust my voice around him.

Danny's fingers grab mine for half a second, and then he drops his hand by his side, as if I were made of fire. I try to not let it bother me so much. Physical touch has never been my forte. There's not an actual reason why it should matter if Danny dropped my hand. I should be glad he did it, because we're currently on awkward terms.

Once upon a time, Danny had become a close friend, someone I could trust. Beyond any lingering crush I had on him, I always valued that he took the time to listen and care about me. Not many people in the Greek life understood my personality, but he did.

Then, he ruined it.

Or I did.

It doesn't really matter.

"Where do you want to go to talk?" He puts his hands in his pockets as he speaks, almost like he's trying to get a grip on himself. "I would prefer it if people didn't see us . . ."

I frown and my spine straightens.

What the hell is that supposed to mean?

"Ashamed of being seen together?"

Danny seems to catch on and his eyes widen with regret.

"What? No, no, no. I didn't mean it like that," he assures me and sighs. "The topic is . . . sensitive."

"I have no preference whatsoever," I say. "You choose."

He nods in agreement and leads me to the pool house behind Delta, which I'm grateful for because I would rather not go in there. Danny might've kicked out Brian when Cerys accused him of rape, but too many guys supported him. I don't trust anyone who defends a rapist.

"How have you been?" he asks as we cross the backyard around the pool to reach the pool house.

I raise my brows. "Making small talk now?"

He gifts me a lopsided smile and scratches the back of his neck.

"I know you hate it, but indulge me."

"Okay, then," I accept, cringing internally for saying *okay* for the hundredth time since we started talking. I lose my words whenever I'm around him. "I've been good. Got a nice job opportunity working at BSIX. I rent a room in LA because the cost of living is insane, but I manage."

"BSIX, huh?" he muses. "Seems like we both went after the big leagues."

His comment piques my interest and I tilt my head slightly to the side. When I left Westbrook, I did my best to stay away from everything that reminded me of the past, only keeping in touch with Carmen—who ignored me half of the time—and Cerys every once in a while. But Danny? My wounded pride wouldn't allow me to stay in contact with him. No matter how much I missed him sometimes.

"Big leagues?" I dare to say in a soft whisper, partly ashamed I had to ask in the first place. "Did you end up following baseball after all?"

He lifts his hand in front of us and tilts it. "More or less. I got into law school, and I've decided I want to pursue sports law. Close enough, right?"

"What does your dad say about that?"

Danny's laugh rumbles and I'm suddenly transported to last year, when we used to climb to Kappa's rooftop and talk for hours while we shared *nankhatai* that his grandmother would send him. I've always felt like Danny laughs like a child, the corners of his eyes creasing and his head tilting back, letting the cackles rip through the air. A shiver trails down my spine, and I feel the tug of yearning squeezing my insides. My knees turn to jelly and my mouth dries. It should be embarrassing to admit that something so simple as a laugh can disrupt my collected system, almost sending it into overdrive.

Dangerous.

The alarm beeps in the back of my brain, giving me a bitter reminder. Why is it that he has so much power over me, yet he doesn't acknowledge it? Well, maybe it's more like he doesn't want it.

Last year, before Brian's murder happened, he chipped away all the boundaries I had around my heart to protect it and I let him into my soul. What started as a little crush became much more with every deep conversation, with every moment we shared together. All the times we avoided cleaning after a party to go to the rooftop to gaze at the stars and talk. I would get too cold, and he would lend me his hoodie that always carried the scent of his cologne. I remember every inside joke, and the way he would save his biggest and most radiant smiles for me. He even started carrying green apple gummies because he knew they were my favorite. It was easy to fall for him.

Because Danny wasn't just a good guy, he had a beautiful soul. *Has* a beautiful soul, and I liked him. I thought, for a deluded second, that he felt the same way about me, so I made a move and kissed him. If I close my eyes and wander to that moment, I can almost feel the warmth of his soft lips over mine. For a second, I swear he let out a little moan before he kissed me back.

But I surely must've heard wrong, because apparently the idea of kissing me wasn't so appealing. Or maybe I'm just a terrible kisser. After those seconds of pure bliss, he grabbed my arms and pulled away before mumbling words I will never forget: *This isn't right.*

It was over before it even truly began.

I had been drinking and partying a lot, but I remember every detail about that night. The memory of it haunts me.

"Oh, I'm hoping to find out soon enough."

"You haven't told him?"

"Telling Papa I won't pursue corporate law?" He shakes his head with a hint of humor. It vanishes quickly as his eyes turn somber for a second. "No. I haven't told anyone."

"Oh," I mumble, the sound escaping me as my brain struggles to process the meaning of his words.

He hasn't told anyone, yet he told *me*.

My throat closes and I blink rapidly, because for a moment it feels as if we're the same people we were last year. Two friends confiding in each other, expressing dreams that were far too scary to say in the daylight. It gets harder to breathe the more I dwell on it.

I want to say I'm happy for him, that I'm grateful he still trusts me enough to share this with me. But all I can think about is how I've lost a friend because I was stupid enough to develop feelings for him. Now, we're nothing but strangers and his confession is just a weird reminder of that because, as a stranger, I don't know what to say.

Maybe, in the future, when I'm not tormented by the past and I have better control over my emotions, I could reach out and thank him for trusting me with this news. I would hug him. But, right now, it feels like he's only telling me because, after we're done here, we're probably not going to see each other ever again.

Danny coughs awkwardly and scratches the back of his neck again, something that has become a nervous tic for him. We've run out of things to talk about, and we both know it.

We enter the pool house. It's practically a shed, small and packed with pool tools and floaties used for parties. It's big enough to walk a few feet inside the place without bumping into each other, and that helps me concentrate, because the last thing I want is to be in a tight space with him. The more time I spend with Danny, the more vulnerable I become. My attraction to him is a weakness.

While Danny peeks out the door to check that we're completely alone, I allow myself to truly take in how much he's changed in the past year. Danny has always been tall and lean. He has put on a little bit of weight, but it looks great on him. His chest and arms look fuller under his gray shirt. I don't let my eyes go below the waist. I'm afraid the sight of his thighs will trigger more dangerous memories, so I stay at eye level. His face has always been a safe place.

Or maybe not, because when his eyes focus on me, warmth spreads through my insides.

I blink rapidly to fight off the effect he has on me and try to focus on the new things I catch about him, like the slight shadow growing on his jaw. Is he growing a beard or did he forget to shave? In contrast, his dark brown hair is shorter, buzzed on the sides and slightly longer on top. It's a clean cut, showing off his slightly pointy ears that I've always found adorable. His appearance fits well for law school.

"I'm sorry I'm taking up so much of your time," he starts off. "And for being so sketchy about everything. I just . . . I don't know what to do."

The seriousness of his tone sends a shock of worry through my skin.

"What's wrong?"

He pulls out a pink envelope from his back pocket. My heart drops into the pit of my stomach, dragging me down with it. I haven't seen the contents, but I'm sure it holds another threatening photo. Slowly, Danny takes out a picture, unfolds it and reveals it to me. It's similar to the one my sister got: a candid shot of me, but this time, Cerys is in it too. It wasn't taken the same day as the one Carmen received. No, this was from the night Cerys' nightmare began. I recognize her blue crop top because it's what I stared at while she got her rape kit done.

Nausea almost overpowers me, and I press the back of my hand against my mouth. Goosebumps erupt over my skin. I inhale deeply, willing the bile to settle in my stomach.

Finally, when the memories of that night stop invading my brain, I read the threat.

Come back or they're next.

"I'm sorry if this is too much, Mabel," he says, placing a hand on my shoulder. Comfort coils in me under the warmth of his palm. "But I don't know what to do. I showed it to the police, but they brushed it off. They didn't take it seriously. Seems like these types of letters are way too common. They dusted it for prints but found nothing."

My stomach twists painfully, anxiety stabbing me.

"I got one, too. It's why I came back," I reveal as I grab it from the backpack and hand it to him along with Carmen's. "My sister got the other one."

Danny takes his time to evaluate both photos, alternating between them. He frowns with concern and his mouth twists.

"Do you have any theories?" he asks. "They seem to be from the same person."

I wrinkle my nose and pace around the pool house to find the right words. Unsure of what to say after my conversation with my sister.

"Carmen thinks it's far-fetched, but I think it might be the killer."

"The killer?" he arches a brow.

"Brian's killer."

His expression dims. "I hate to say this, but I'm with you on that one."

For the first time, I wish he had told me the opposite. Maybe I wanted Carmen to be right. Somehow, it seems easier to think I'm being paranoid than to believe we might have a killer threatening the lives of the people I care about. I don't want to carry this worry with me. I've already carried guilt with me throughout the last year.

Confusion swells in my brain.

"Why do *you* think so?" I ask, turning to face him. "That it's the same killer, I mean."

He glances around like the answer is obvious. "I'm not the horror fan here, but I'm pretty sure only one person we know got murdered last year, and it's one we were all close to, one way or another."

"No, I get that, but why send us the photos? We have nothing to do with what happened to Brian."

This is what doesn't make sense to me. The only photograph with a link to Brian is the one of Cerys, but she hasn't been around. If they wanted her . . . why threaten Carmen or me? Why send Danny a threat too? There's a big blur; a gap I can't fill no matter how hard I try. I wrack my brains for the one vital detail that could help us solve this before it turns into a nightmare. For some reason, the killer has dragged us back to this place. Me by putting a target on my sister's back. Danny by threatening two of his old friends.

Why?

We haven't done anything.

There are more things I *didn't* do than things I did.

"I don't know, Mabel. I wish I did, but I don't."

I groan in frustration.

"If the killer got rid of Brian, why go after any of us? Including Cerys. It doesn't make sense. I'm missing something important here and I don't know what."

"You'll figure it out. You always do." His eyes soften as he says the words. The curves of his mouth tilt into a light smile, like he hasn't been surer about anything else in the world. "Stop beating yourself up for it."

I snort. "Oh, I'm sure I'll figure it out like every final girl does: after the killer manages to kill almost everyone and does the big reveal with a villainous speech," I mutter bitterly. Running my fingers through the dark strands of my ponytail, I bite my inner cheek. This is the part of the movie where people yell at the screen because the characters are making dumb choices. "There's just one big chunk missing. I refuse to let this bastard harm the people I care about."

Yet . . .

What if, after everything, it's just one big prank that the Deltas are pulling to mess with Cerys and me? It's possible. It could be a ploy to make me waste money for nothing.

"What if we're wrong?"

Danny presses his lips into a thin line.

"If we're wrong, then it would be the best possible outcome. But I don't think we are."

Deep down, I agree, and I can't ease the bundle of anxiety and fear creating havoc in my stomach.

"Mabel," he calls softly. His hand delicately wraps around my wrist, the tips of his fingers caress my skin. He's not forcefully grabbing me. No, his touch grounds me, allowing my brain to calm the panic coursing through my body. I lift my gaze to meet his caramel eyes, comforting and supportive. *Damn him*. "I don't think we're wrong either."

Nervousness, both from uncertainty and Danny's warm touch, drags a pattern along my spine. A shaky sigh sneaks past my lips as I focus on the tingles spreading through my skin as Danny continues to caress me. There's something in the gentle way he touches me that makes me wonder, for the tiniest second, if I wasn't imagining things when I kissed him. It's the sense of familiarity in his touch, the comfort it brings, that leaves me trying to figure out if it means something more.

"What are we going to do?" I ask, once my heart no longer feels like it wants to jump out of my mouth.

Danny's fingers graze the length of my jaw as he cups my chin delicately.

And, shit, my heart lumps in my throat again. I lose my ability to breathe and my mouth goes dry. The lines of our former friendship blur the more he touches my skin.

"Focus on what we can control."

"That sounds a lot like waiting around for something to happen."

"Sometimes it's all we can do," he acknowledges, keeping his calm throughout this. I envy him. I wish I could sit around and take one thing at a time, but my brain won't let me. Knowing everything I know about horror and slashers, I fear the worst. It's not in my nature to be laidback and collected. "You should keep an eye on Carmen while I focus on keeping Cerys safe at the party."

"Cerys? She's here?!" My voice raises in pitch, the panic returning.

"I called her after I got the letter. She told me she got one too."

My blood feels like it's stopped flowing and my knees seem to get heavier as reality sets in. Knowing what it means, I feel the dread begin to form in my body, stabbing every inch of my skin. Everything is in place for horror to ensue.

A gory introductory murder? Check.

Compelling group of friends? Check.

A stalker threatening their lives? Check.

A party where things can get out of control? Double check.

And just like that, the recipe for a slasher plot is complete.

It's about to become a bloody valentine.

Chapter 4

DANNY'S PRESENCE IS BARELY A BLUR IN THE BACKGROUND as my brain struggles to slam the brakes on the multiple scenarios flooding my mind. Cerys being back at Westbrook changes everything. Not only because it means I have another person to worry about when there's a killer threatening us, but also because it gives a motive. She has become a pariah in this place, constantly linked to and blamed for last year's dreadful event.

While I don't understand why the killer wants us back, I can tell it's a bad omen. Cerys' return to Westbrook is a guarantee of upcoming chaos and trouble. But I'm missing a big chunk of the motive. Is this all related to Brian and Cerys, or is there another reason?

Blinking rapidly, physically forcing the thoughts to back away from the front of my brain, I focus on Danny. His shoulders are rigid as he observes me, the slight squint of his eyes showing his concern.

"When did she get here?" I ask, holding on to his wrist. I don't bother hiding the demanding undertone as my fingers tighten their grip. I *need* to know the details of her arrival because it might give me the information I need to put the puzzle together. Focusing on the mystery is easier than sitting with what's truly bothering me. She never told me any of this. "Why would she come back to this place?"

Why didn't she tell me? I want to add, but the words die on the tip of my tongue. I can guess why, and it's itching under my skin. *This* is what I'm struggling with, because the truth is more painful than I'm willing to admit. Though *painful* might not be the correct word to describe it.

Embarrassing.

Yes, it's embarrassing how terrible I've been at keeping in touch with everyone from this place. I've never been good at letting people take care of me. It's always easier for me to hide what I'm feeling than relying on my friends. The last time Cerys and I spoke was a few weeks ago when she called me. Guilt gnaws on my bones. I should've tried harder to prevent my life in LA from overcrowding my time. After everything we went through together last year, everything she went through alone, it's the least I could've done for her. But it was easier to let the city consume me and make me forget every awful thing that happened in this place. All the mistreatment Cerys endured—and me by association—the constant fighting to prove her innocence, her final breakdown before she decided to leave. To forget my friendship with Cerys, and the kiss with Danny, ever happened.

It was all too much.

But it still hurts to know she didn't trust me.

There's a painful and bitter realization coating the surface of my tongue. While I've been happier and thriving in LA, I miss the friendships I had here. I miss hanging out with Cerys and being her biggest confidante. She was pure light and joy, and I was her shadow. I liked having that contrast in our friendship. My sister has been miles away from me, constantly ignoring me. And Danny... I don't even want to think about what I lost with him.

It all makes me too aware of the fact that I've been lonely.

It stings deep in my soul.

Instinctively, wanting to protect myself from becoming too vulnerable, I drop my gaze to the ground. I bite the inside of my cheek, hard enough to taste blood.

"Whatever you're thinking, you're wrong," Danny determines.

I'm taken aback by the decisiveness in his voice. How can he be so sure of what I'm thinking and his conviction to prove me otherwise? He has no idea.

"You don't know what I'm thinking."

I recoil defensively, crossing my arms over my stomach, almost building a shield around me. A part of me needs to physically put a barrier between us, to feel like I'm being protected and not attacked.

Danny arches a brow and steps closer to me.

My breath almost hitches, and I hold it in to prevent smelling his cologne. Danny's fingers find their way to my chin again. Although his touch is soft and lingering, it carries enough strength to force me to stare deep into his warm and caring eyes.

Inevitably, my insides start to melt, debilitating my knees, but I stand with straight shoulders and my arms firmly in place around me. Maybe if I stay still enough, I'll be able to remain unaffected by him.

"You don't think I can read you?" he asks, tilting his head slightly. "We might not talk to each other, but you're as expressive as you were when we were close friends. Whenever you're having a bad train of thought or dislike something, you show it here," he points out, softly pressing his index finger between my brows where my forehead is wrinkled. His touch smooths it with a caress before it travels to the edge of my mouth, near the corner of my lips. "And here too."

My throat goes dry. I'm unable to swallow or utter any words to contradict what he's saying. I'm too caught up by the fact that he's touching me this freely, as if he knew exactly what it took to disarm me with just one touch. How can he know my body so well, and still reject me? Am I being delusional again?

Too many thoughts cloud my brain. The scent of his cologne overpowers my senses with how close he is.

It's not the first time he's been this close—he's hugged me before—but it's the first time since the kiss. I don't know if he has realized that I can feel the warmth of his breath brushing my face. I can barely contain the way my heart speeds up.

"*Daniel . . .*" His name spills from my lips in a featherlight whisper, almost hoping to lure him back to me like a desperate siren trying to keep him under a spell.

But the moment has passed. He clears his throat and pulls back, as if he caught himself touching a display item that has a *Do not touch* sign next to it. His hand drops to his side as he shakes his head like he's snapping out of the moment. He scratches the back of his neck again.

He's nervous.

His lips tremble ever so slightly as he struggles to find the words.

"I . . . I went to find her after the police did nothing with my claim, and she had just received her letter. I would've tried to find you, but . . ."

He lets the rest of his statement linger in the air between us. The atmosphere grows thick and heavy, making it harder to breathe in the closeness of the pool house. I know exactly what he means by his silence. It's louder than screams. *We weren't on speaking terms.* We're no longer friends. He inferred it before, but it stings to have the confirmation so out in the open when, for a moment, I forgot about it.

His touch has a powerful effect on me. I grow weak.

"Right," I say curtly. Before things can continue getting even more awkward and stiff, I choose to guide the topic back to our immediate concern. The reason we're here in the first place. "What did her letter say? Do you have it?"

His face contorts into a grimace. "I have a photo," he says reluctantly, and in his eyes I see a silent plea to let the topic drop.

"Show me."

"It's a little disturbing."

"Show me," I demand again, extending my hand.

With a sigh, Danny reaches for his phone and taps on the

screen until he produces the photo of the letter. He gently drops the phone in my palm, and I turn it over to examine it. The overview is simple, but there's something different about this one.

Unlike the others, it's not a candid shot. It's not a personal picture either. No, this one is cut out straight from the yearbook Kappa does at the end of the school year, specifically the one from when we were in junior year. The photo was taken at a rush party. In it, I'm standing next to Cerys and Bethan. Sitting on the floor, Carmen is in front of me, her dazzling smile immediately catching my attention. She was barely a potential new member there. We all look extremely different than we do now—happier, more innocent. I would smile at the memory if it weren't for the daunting detail that made Danny hesitant to show it to me.

Everyone's eyes are crossed out, but Cerys' eyes are completely cut out from the photograph. We all look hollow inside. It looks like a prop made for a weird movie about a cult or something. It's creepy. There's no other way to put it.

A shiver runs down my spine.

"*Every death will be your fault if you don't return.*" I read out loud the message scribbled in the corner.

My stomach constricts.

Everyone else's letters were cryptic and threatening without crossing the line of graphic. But they took liberties with Cerys. Probably because she has already received so much hate in the past that it wouldn't have been taken seriously if it didn't stand out from the sea of abuse she got last year after Brian's death.

"Now you know why she came back," he states.

"This is crazy."

I give him the phone back, unable to stare at it any longer.

"I didn't want her to, but there was no stopping her. You know Cerys better than anyone. It doesn't matter how much they hated her here, she would rather die than let anyone be harmed. So, I figured it was better if I came here with her."

I nod, understanding his point. Cerys might be a pariah in Westbrook, but she could easily become a martyr.

"Someone has to have her back. She's too good for any of this to be happening."

"Yes, she is," he confirms.

Although Cerys has been pushed around and dragged through the mud, her heart is admirable and kind. It doesn't matter how much everyone in that photo mistreated her, she wouldn't let anyone come to harm if she could help it. I understand her reasoning, even if I don't share it. I've always been more selfish than she could ever be. Hell, if it hadn't been because someone threatened Carmen, I wouldn't be caught dead in this place. If I were Cerys, I wouldn't let myself be affected by it. But I get why she is. It's in her nature.

Yet it doesn't help ease the terror crawling under my skin.

"I have a bad feeling about this."

Danny rubs his palms together anxiously.

"Best case scenario, nothing happens, and we just spend our night at a party." He puts it in simple terms, offering me a tight-lipped smile.

I roll my eyes.

His enthusiasm is as fake as mine, but I appreciate it

because it almost makes me laugh. It's possible we're both being delusional in this. I doubt it, but there's always a possibility.

"Worst case scenario, we all die because we couldn't do the smart thing," I retort with a huff.

"And what is the smart thing?"

"Run away before danger materializes."

"You're the horror movie connoisseur," he says. "Does running away ever work out?"

I sigh. "No. We would get murdered on a lonely road. One of us might survive if they made it until dawn. Severely maimed, though."

He looks at his watch. "Considering it's barely past noon, there's not a lot of hope for us."

"Definitely not."

A sigh escapes him. He sounds defeated. His shoulders deflate, almost making him appear shorter. The joke is over. Time to return to our reality, as skewed as it is.

"What are you going to do?"

I wish I could say I'm hopping on a plane and getting the hell away from here as soon as possible, but Carmen isn't buying my fear. Since she won't be going anywhere, there's nowhere else I can be.

"What do you think I should do?"

"Not die on a lonely road," he responds, his tone jokey, although there's a crease at the corner of his mouth that lets me know there's actual concern behind his words.

The way he phrases it makes me smile.

He doesn't think I should leave. Temptation curls into my veins, almost pushing me to ask if he *wants* me to. There's a difference between him thinking I should stay and him wanting me to. The weakest part of me hopes for the latter.

I swallow the question and say instead, "Is that so?"

"The alternative is surviving severely maimed."

A snort escapes past my defenses. My heart aches. *Ay*, I've missed him.

"Sounds like we'll be going to that party, then."

Chapter 5

GREEK ROW PARTIES TEND TO BE OVERWHELMINGLY PACKED, the crowd overflowing into the backyard and loitering around the common areas of the houses. Especially when it comes to big events like the one they're having tonight. The Valentine's Day party is the one that everyone wants to attend, even though you must purchase a ticket in order to get in. It's pure madness.

It also means that this stupid plan of keeping an eye on Carmen and Cerys is complicated. The urge to force them to leave campus before the party even starts lingers in my system, but still I find myself standing in line in front of Kappa's main doors, waiting to buy my entrance to a night that promises mayhem and disaster.

There are two tables, one on each side of the door, where some of the Kappas are selling the tickets and giving out wristbands. Through the open doors, I can see pink neon lights shining, creating a tunnel leading to the backyard where the party takes place. Usually, sorority parties tend to be outside because no one wants the hassle of having people sneaking into their rooms, especially when it comes to drunken idiots wanting to find a place to hook up. The last thing you want is to go to your room and find a random couple fucking on your bedsheets when you're dead tired.

At least that's how Kappa's policy works. Parties are contained in the backyard unless the weather conditions don't allow it. But if you don't count the hurricane season, the weather here is typically nice. Like today, even though it's mid-February and winter isn't over yet. The night is chilly, but not cold enough to need layers and layers of clothing, which means I'm comfortable standing outside in just my jeans and a long-sleeved green shirt.

"Next!"

The line moves forward and I'm glad it's my turn. Glancing around to check if there's anything suspicious, I take two steps and stand in front of the table covered with a pink cloth. There are four boxes of colored wristbands, and each box is labeled with a description. From what I've gathered, the party is a take on a stop light party: the green bracelet means you're ready to date; the pink one means you only want a one-night stand; the red one means you're taken. And the white one means you're up for anything.

I consider my choices and look up to the girls manning the entry desk, only to see the two people who can't stand my presence: Sophia and Zelda.

Increíble.

"Oh, it's you," Zelda mumbles with disdain. "We're sold out."

I glance at the full boxes of wristbands.

"Really?"

"Tickets sold out a week ago," Sophia chips in. "Guess you can't ruin this party now."

"I'm a Kappa alumna; I don't need a ticket."

Lying to them is almost too easy. Mainly because there are too many sorority rules regarding alumni and legacies. A lot of crap, if you ask me, but it surely comes in handy when you deliver the words with confidence.

"Mabel, I know you like to impress everyone with your Spanish, but it has no effect on me. I took Spanish in high school," Sophia announces and purses her lips.

What on earth is she on? I haven't... Then I catch on to what she means, and I blink in shock.

"Alumna is Latin," I mumble in response.

Sophia rolls her eyes.

"My point stands. You're not invited."

"You're wrong," I point out. "Bethan invited me."

Zelda gasps. "She did not!"

"Why would we believe a liar like you?" Sophia retorts, with a faint squint of her eyes.

"Why don't we call her? We'll see who ends up being called a liar." I arch a brow, daring her to tell me otherwise.

Both Sophia and Zelda stay silent.

Something I learned while being a Kappa is that the girls who are overly committed to the sorority have a deep dread of breaking the rules or destroying their reputation in front of figures of power. Bethan becoming president of the Kappas puts her at the top of the pyramid, and while Sophia and Zelda can't stand me, their fear of being seen as troublemakers is something they can't allow.

I won this round, and I can't help but preen a little, raising my chin in triumph.

"Mabel!" Leighton calls out to me, as excited as she was earlier today. Her blonde hair is curled up with a little braid hanging at the side of her face.

Next to her, Elodie smiles timidly, glancing at Zelda and Sophia from the corner of her eye. Almost like she's too scared to contradict them, but still being the nice girl she's always been. "It's so lovely to see you again. I'm glad you stayed!"

Leighton gives me another hug, and I suppress the need to push her off, only because being mean would get me kicked out of here. I can't afford to lose my access to Kappa when I'm trying to keep an eye on Carmen and Cerys tonight. There's too much at risk, so I let her hug me for an uncomfortable ten seconds before she lets go and Elodie steps closer.

She seems to defy Sophia and Zelda and moves to the table asking, "What color do you want tonight, Mabel?"

"Oooh, pick green!" Leighton encourages. "Wait, unless you have a beau back in LA. I condemn cheating. Last month, Patrick—you remember Patrick, right?—he cheated on Courtney with a Sigma, and it was devastating for her. All the Kappas swore to never allow cheating. Girls have to stick together." She nods and lifts a hand to her face, pressing her index and middle finger against her lips before holding them in front of me.

My brows knit together. What on earth am I supposed to do now? After being clear of the Greek life for a year, every interaction I've had today seems alien. To think I once lived here and inhabited the same space as these girls is a haze in my mind. Though, to be fair to myself, I only ever applied here because Carmen pressured me. She wanted to have insider information for when she finally got to join Kappa, so I dutifully did it because there's nothing I wouldn't do for her. Although, I must admit, not everything about living here was terrible. I had great moments with the girls. I met some amazing people through the Greek life, so I can't really antagonize all of them.

As ridiculous and stereotypical as they might be, I can't fully hate the Kappas. Well, as long as I don't count how mean and terrible they were to Cerys.

Elodie raises her brows at me expectantly.

Que jodienda.

A lie prickles the tip of my tongue, yet I can't force it out of my mouth. They would never know it's a lie. All my personal social media is private, and I made sure to remove anyone who wasn't from the inner circle, so it's not like they would know the truth: that I come home from work and binge-watch silly romcoms because that's the only source of romance in my life. Besides, I'm only here for a brief time. Lying is the best scenario for my plans. Faking a relationship could mean I wouldn't be approached by people tonight, but it also means Danny might see it and get the wrong idea. Not that that matters. He has no romantic interest in me and I'm sure as hell not looking for romance tonight. Especially not with someone who already made it clear that wouldn't happen.

But still . . .

"No beau. And no cheating," I say, kissing my fingers and pressing them against Leighton's in complicity.

"Mabel being unable to keep a man, what a shocker," I hear Sophia say to Zelda in a stage whisper. There's no hiding that she intended for me to hear it.

I bite the inside of my cheek, suppressing the urge to flip her off.

Instead, I turn to Elodie and decide that taking advantage of the fact that she's being nice to me is helpful. I seek her advice by saying, "I don't know what to choose, if I'm honest."

She clasps her hands together over her chest, beaming gleefully while presenting the options to me.

"It's never too late to meet the love of your life," she reminds me, pointing at the green ones. "You could never go wrong with a hook-up. We all need to blow off some steam sometimes," she suggests, lingering on the pink ones. "And if you're unsure, white is always a smart move."

I give the colors a once-over, considering my options.

Green, pink, white.

Available, down to fuck, not sure.

Finding a date was never part of my plan when I decided to travel here. No, I just wanted to grab my sister and run like hell. But as the hours pass by and nothing seems to happen, my paranoia has simmered down. Everything around here seems normal. *Too* normal. Almost as if a force from above cast a mindwipe spell and made everyone forget about last year. If it weren't for the letters still tucked in my backpack, I wouldn't think there was any reason to worry.

The obvious choice would've been red, but not only did I just admit to being as chronically single as I was when I was here, but it will also limit my interactions with people all night.

Yet I can't bring myself to choose pink either.

The thought of having random frat guys approach me at this party makes nausea roll in my stomach. No, I don't want a random hook-up. Not with the history linked to this place, and certainly not when I know I won't go through with it. There's only been one person with whom I could see myself taking that step, and the chances of that happening are incredibly slim, so . . .

White is tempting, but it could still make guys get the wrong idea about what I'm trying to do here. My brain briefly drifts back to Danny's nearness at the pool house. I can almost feel my blood pressure rise when I recall the way he softly caressed my face.

I lose control when it comes to him.

Danny disarms me.

"Green." The word slips out before I can change my mind. "I want the green one."

It's for the best, I try to convince myself. It's the best option to make Carmen not suspect much about what I'm doing. She was livid earlier and, unless I have an excuse to be here, she might talk to Bethan and have me removed from the party altogether. I can almost hear her throwing another fit because I'm lingering creepily in the background, micromanaging her life instead of getting a life of my own. And if I had chosen red, she would've been the first one to call me out on my chronically single status.

Deep down, I'm aware this is all bullshit I'm feeding

myself so that I don't have to think about the real reason that pushed me to choose the green band.

"Atta girl!" Leighton exclaims, nudging me with a bright smile. "Have a blast!"

Elodie grabs a green band and wraps it around my left wrist.

"Have fun, Mabby," she wishes me, with one of her warm smiles.

"Thanks," I mumble.

The paper wristband feels a bit tight as I walk into the house, wrapping itself around my wrist like a manacle. *Have I made the right choice?* Dipping my body into the pink neon lights of the tunnel that leads to the backyard, I look around at the decorations. The Kappas have outdone themselves. The tunnel is made of red cardboard cut to give the guests the illusion that they're walking through hearts. I feel like I'm entering a new reality.

The backyard has also been transformed. Love seats are spread around the place, along with photobooths and decorated places to take photos with friends. Drinking stations are situated in each corner. Everything is covered by an explosion of neon pink, white and red. Everything is on theme with Valentine's Day. And I don't know how, but they've managed to get a chocolate fountain with a massive Cupid statue on top.

I can't deny that they know how to throw a great themed party.

With every step I take, merging with the crowd, doubts scratch my skin, making me feel uncomfortable. What am I doing?

Tugging my sleeve over the wristband, I take a deep breath and will my heart to slow its frantic beats. My body doesn't get the message that this is just a regular party, like all the ones I've been to before. Even though I'm here to make sure my sister and my friend aren't in any danger, I can't help but think about all the possibilities I just signed myself up for by choosing green. It's like I'm holding a sign over my head that screams *Available to everyone!*

If Carmen was actually talking to me, she would make a joke about how no one would approach me even if I had the sign. She would then sweeten the comment by adding that no one here is worthy of me either way.

Thinking about my sister and her snarky attitude makes me smile and gives me the strength I need to straighten my back and dive into the sea of people, some of whom are already mingling, looking for other available people to get their fill of the night. To no one's surprise, I spot Delta and other frat guys wearing pink wristbands. There's rarely anyone wearing red wristbands.

A few girls approach me to say their hellos and make small talk. My jaw hurts from faking smiles, face muscles twitching as I try to blend in and search for my sister and Cerys. The minutes drag by slowly as I drift around. Although the temperature has dropped considerably, I welcome the light breeze of the night. It makes my drill of wandering the backyard more comfortable. I don't need to worry about unnecessary heat or sweating.

Around twenty minutes later, I spot Carmen talking with a few of her friends. She looks beautiful. I might be biased, but my sister has grown into a stunning woman. Her curls fall softly down her back, meeting the beginning of her light pink dress. The color contrasts perfectly with her light brown skin. Around her wrist, she wears a white band, which makes me buzz with curiosity.

Is she up for anything?

The big sister in me wants to question her about her choices and demand that she's careful, but I also know Carmen is more than capable of taking care of herself around people. She might pass on a written threat, but her snark is sharper than a butcher's knife.

"Hello, may I have your attention, please?" Bethan's melodic voice takes over the backyard as she climbs onto a table, holding a microphone in front of her red lips. "Thank you so much for coming here tonight and being part of our 'Smash or Pass' event." She pauses as people hoot and cheer her on. "So here are the rules. For the next two hours, a buzzer will go off every fifteen minutes. For the first fifteen, you must talk to someone you don't know, and when the buzzer goes off, you can decide if you'll smash . . . or pass."

"Smash me, baby!" a guy yells at her.

Bethan's smile remains intact, but I catch the slight twitch of annoyance in her green eyes.

"You'll have eight chances to be struck by Cupid. But if it doesn't happen for you, remember that the afterparty event will be held at Theta's house across the street, and you all know what that means: a night of debauchery." She winks complicitly. "Let the games begin!"

The crowd claps for her and I join them as the first buzzer sounds. Almost instantly, I see the people look around to find their chosen targets, and I try to keep a low profile until I feel a tap on my shoulder.

Ay no.

Biting the inside of my cheek, I turn on my heel, only to meet familiar blue eyes.

Chapter 6

"HI, STRANGER."

All the fight I had gathered in my system dissolves into fumes as I welcome the proximity of my friend Aidan. After spending the day faking smiles and making conversation with people I don't care about, it's thrilling to finally stumble upon someone I'm actually glad to see. Relief spreads through my limbs, softening my stance.

Aidan takes a step forward and, before I can process it, he comes at me full force and wraps me in his arms, squeezing me into a tight hug. Joyous laughter bubbles from my lips as he lifts me from the ground a couple of inches, spinning me around. The movement is fast, and my brain struggles to process what's happening amidst the blur surrounding me. I think I catch a glimpse of Danny in the crowd.

Once Aidan sets me on the floor again, I shift my

position, so I can get a better look at Danny. He's standing barely a few meters away from Cerys. The sight of her makes a desert spread down my throat.

My friend looks stunning as always, but also so different from the girl she used to be. Her hair is shorter, the blonde locks barely scratching the fabric covering her shoulders. Once upon a time, Cerys used to be like a bright light in a crowd. Now, her glow has dimmed. Life has been rough on her. You can see her stance has grown closed within itself; her confidence broken.

Returning my attention to Danny, I'm taken aback by the fact that he's staring back at me, his eyes shadowed by his frowning brows.

A shudder spreads down my spine. I turn away from Danny and meet Aidan's happy smile. I give his arm a squeeze before letting go, taking a step back.

"What are you doing here?" I ask him, knowing parties aren't really his scene. "Looking for love?" I tease.

The last time I saw Aidan was when I visited his father during the late summer to pick up the recommendation letter that he personally wrote for me to work at BSIX. Unlike me, Aidan is the definition of a nepo baby. Though I'd argue he has the talent to back up his nepotism status, *and* he's going through the hoops and loops of learning the art by getting his degree. Aidan's father, Aaron Ledger, is someone I consider a legend in the horror genre. Named one of the most influential figures in the zombie subgenre by multiple film critics. He won three of the big five Academy Awards for his film *Gray Matter*, and it completely redefined the genre in the nineties.

He's a complete badass, but also one of the humblest

people I've met in the industry. Two years ago, he taught me and Aidan multiple techniques for using practical effects instead of relying on CGI—which was something we couldn't otherwise have done, given our severe lack of resources and funding.

"Well, never say never on the love thing," Aidan responds with a boyish grin.

"Come on, why are you really here?" I press, knowing it can't be that, or at least not completely.

"You want the truth?" he questions. He's piqued my interest, so I nod effusively. "I joined Delta this year."

Okay, I wasn't expecting *that*.

Things have changed a lot around here, because it's almost out of character for Aidan to join a fraternity, especially in his senior year. Surely he knows better than to pledge, considering how much shit I've talked about it. Hell, he witnessed first-hand the torture I went through during my last couple of months at Westbrook. Why would he do that?

"You . . . joined . . . a frat?" I pronounce slowly. The words taste surreal on the tip of my tongue.

Aidan laughs.

"I know, I know," he says, raising his hands in front of him as if he were waving a white flag. "I promise it's a much better place than it was last year. The trash was taken out when you left."

"I won't hold my breath about it," I mumble. "But I'm guessing you had an ulterior motive for it?"

"Dad told me I need to broaden my horizons and socialize more, especially since you're not here anymore. So, you could say he sort of twisted my arm. And I figured living here was a nicer experience than the dorms."

I wrinkle my nose. I hate to agree with him, but I've heard all the horror stories about living in the dorms. Sadly, although the people here aren't the best, Greek Row has better living conditions.

"What is he giving you in return?" I inquire, crossing my arms.

Aidan flashes me a smile. "He told me he would do five calls on my behalf from his list of B-list actors for my final short."

Nepotism doing its job.

"Wow."

"See why I willingly joined?"

"I definitely understand it better now," I admit.

"Maybe you would like to assist me?" he offers. "It would be just like old times. I hope to start pre-production around spring break."

"It would be quite the change in our dynamic."

Since I was ahead of him in my studies, usually he would be my AD—assistant director—while I directed. It would be a different experience to be the AD for him when I know how bossy I can get during productions.

"Would it be that bad? I'd say I handled you bossing me around quite well."

A laugh spills free from me.

"Oh, please. You loved it."

Aidan's eyes darken for a split second as he sucks his bottom lip to hold back a smile. The dimples in his cheeks give him away, even when he tries to hide it.

I tilt my head slightly, taking a good look at him for the first time tonight, noticing how he's changed in the past year. Aidan has always been a good-looking guy. Not the type who's fawned over by many, but he's always been cute and geeky in an endearing way. His brown hair is longer than it was last year—he used to have a buzzcut—and the strands have gained the slightest wave on the tips. A constellation of freckles adorns his face, giving him a boyish appeal along with his dimples. His build has always been skinny, but not lanky. His torso is proportionate and balanced. Slim, but fit enough to carry a boom mic without getting tired every thirty seconds—we always joked that the only workout film students had to worry about was being able to hold the pole over our heads without ruining any takes because we got tired after fifteen seconds.

He's cute.

When did he get cute?

"Oh, I definitely did." Aidan clicks his tongue. For a second, he gives me a once-over. "There's something oddly attractive about a pretty woman commanding your every move."

My smile wavers as my body tenses slightly, completely caught off guard by his admission. Holy shit. Is he flirting? I thought we were joking around as we always did, but this seems different. Charged with an undertone I can't quite decipher.

Before I can stop myself, my gaze moves an inch to the side, focusing on Danny in the background. He remains in the same spot as he was, but now he's engaged in a conversation with a girl. From this angle, I can't tell who it is. I can see she's a petite blonde, and considering we're at a sorority party, that covers at least half of Greek Row.

A twinge of jealousy awakens and churns in my stomach. Suddenly, I desperately want a drink so I can put out the fire. I bite the inside of my cheek and tell myself I need to stop this, just as Danny's eyes find me again. Then, he does something I'd almost forgotten about. He taps twice under his chin and once on the chest.

My mouth dries. Back when we used to be close, Danny spent a while trying to teach me some of the baseball signals his coach used. That one specifically meant *hit and run*, but it ended up turning into our way of checking in on each other at parties.

I'm so taken aback that I don't return the signal to let him know everything's fine. I just stare and frown.

For the first time, I see Danny's puppy look harden as his jaw twitches visibly.

"Earth to Mabel," Aidan calls, moving his hand in front of my face to catch my attention. "I lost you there for a second."

I clear my throat and shake my head to brush Danny away from my thoughts. I shouldn't care if he's flirting with someone else and taking advantage of the night. It's none of my business.

"Sorry. I got distracted looking for Carmen," I lie. "We had an argument earlier."

"Little Carmen still driving you nuts?"

Driving me nuts? That's quite the euphemism. Her decisions and behavior lately leave a lot to be desired, but there's only so much I can do as her sister. Especially when I live across the country. I have to bite my tongue and wait for her to need me, because as much as I still see her as the little girl who used to sneak into Mami's closet to try on her heels, Carmen's an adult now. I need to trust her choices. Although that doesn't mean I won't worry and hang around until she's ready to confide in me.

"You have no idea."

"Is that why you're here and not in LA?" Aidan asks, piecing it together.

Should I tell him the truth about the letters and the threats?

Other than Danny, Aidan is probably the only person who would believe me. After all, he was one of the few who believed and supported me when Cerys dropped out and I had to finish my degree. If it hadn't been for him, I probably wouldn't have been able to complete the assignments. Especially as Danny was no longer in the picture.

But the words get stuck in my throat. They refuse to climb the rest of the way and spill from my lips.

"Something along those lines." I sigh. "You know how she can be."

"I know, but she's as strongheaded as her sister," he says. "It's a good thing, Mabel. You've given her all the tools she needs for the future."

I press my lips into a thin line. "I'm not sure about that."

Aidan places a hand on my shoulder, squeezing it lightly to give me some support and reassurance.

"I've been keeping an eye on her for you, Mabel. That's one of the reasons why I chose to join Delta instead of staying in the dorms," he confesses, taking a more serious note. "I know how much she means to you. You worry about her, but trust me, you have nothing to sweat over. She's one of the strongest girls I've ever met."

His words hit the spot because I find myself struggling not to cry. Blinking tears away and unable to speak because there's a lump in my throat.

"Thank you," I whisper.

"Of course. She's like a little sister to me too."

I don't have the heart to tell him that Carmen would eat him alive if she heard him saying that. She can barely handle me calling her my little sister, let alone having someone like Aidan doing it as well. So I simply change the subject and ask him what his short film is about.

The minutes pass by too quickly as he talks, because the next thing I know, the buzzer goes off and Aidan looks at me, expectantly.

"So . . . smash or pass?"

Now there's no hiding that he's flirting with me. I don't know how I feel about it. Aidan is a cute guy and clearly is interested in me, but my obnoxious heart can't forget about Danny. His hold remains lassoed around it, holding me hostage.

Inevitably, I look for Danny in the crowd again. I find him almost immediately. Though he's moved a few meters from his original position, he's still focused on me and my companion. There's no sight of the petite blonde he was talking to earlier, and I assume she must've gotten away when the buzzer went off. I guess it was a *pass*.

"I . . ."

"Are you guys smashing or passing?" a black-haired girl

cuts me off. She's staring directly into Aidan's eyes, slightly pushing out her chest to get his attention. I spend too long forming a word, and it's all she needs because she grabs his arm and drags him with her. "Perfect, my turn!"

Aidan's eyes widen, completely blindsided by the girl.

"I'll see you later!" I tell him, chuckling at the absurdity of the interaction.

I can't say I'm not relieved by the interruption, because I wasn't sure how to respond. While I want to continue catching up with Aidan, I don't think I have it in me to lead him on. Nor do I want him to get the wrong idea. Primarily because he's been a close friend, but also because my first instinct when he asked was to check Danny's reaction.

The last thing I want is to give him false hope. It'd be unfair on him.

Considering I'm free to do as I please now, I decide to find Cerys. I spot her in a corner talking to Bethan. My friend keeps her brows arched as she listens attentively to what the other girl is saying. I can't hear her words, but it must be something important by the way Bethan's eyes are glistening with unshed tears. While I want nothing more than to run to Cerys and hug her, they seem to be caught in a deep conversation, so I opt for grabbing a drink in the meantime. I don't want to interrupt them.

I approach one of the drink stations and ask for a bottle of water with the cap on.

"I'm surprised to see you here."

Turning my head, I frown at the guy standing next to me. I don't recognize him. He's tall, probably around Danny's height, with sandy blond hair and a perfect smile that makes him look like a Ken doll. He's wearing a white polo shirt, khaki pants and a gold watch that's probably too expensive for a party like this. Everything about his cocky stance and attitude screams that he's one of those guys who can get away with whatever they want because his daddy pays for it.

A guy like Brian Manders.

I clench my jaw and ignore his comment, focusing on the bottle of water.

He laughs. "You have quite the attitude."

"Do I even know you?"

"Maybe you will after I'm done with you," he says and then he leans in closer to me. "I always thought Brian wasted his time with that blonde girl. You were much hotter."

The blood freezes in my veins. Pure disbelief lodges in my system as the initial wave of shock courses through my body. Did I hear him right? Has my paranoia gotten out of hand? Because there's no fucking way he dared to make that comment.

Who even is he? I don't remember him, but he clearly knows me.

"What the fuck did you just say?"

If he dares to repeat what he said, I'll wreck his perfect nose so that he can't look in a mirror without remembering me. My fingers clench into a tight fist, making sure I don't stick my thumb into my palm. My dad might've been too busy with work most of the time, but he taught me how to throw a punch. I'm ready to do whatever it takes to defend myself.

To my disappointment, the guy just shakes his head mockingly and pushes his body away from the station.

I fight the urge to go after him and beat his audacity to a pulp, but I know how easy it is to get on the wrong side of everyone around here. Tonight is not the night for me to lose my temper.

Saliva turns thick and sour in my mouth. I uncap the bottle, making sure that I've broken the seal, and take a long gulp. Every muscle in my body is tight and hard with accumulated unease. What is wrong with men and their privilege? Why do they think they can mock someone's sexual assault and infer they would've preferred it had happened to you instead? It's not funny, nor a compliment. It's insulting, infuriating and demeaning. Is that how they see us? Like a warmer fleshlight with legs? My chest aches.

"Hey, are you okay?" Danny's voice somehow manages to both relax and annoy me. I can't even shit on the male gender in peace without the universe reminding me that he's the opposite of everything I hate about men. It's almost as if God created him as an apology for giving the male of the species infinite amounts of audacity. "Was he bothering you?"

I tighten my jaw. "Do you know him?"

Danny tilts his head. "He seems familiar, but the name escapes me. What did he do?"

A long sigh abandons me.

"Nothing. He made a distasteful comment about Cerys and now he's on my shit list," I mumble.

"I can find out his name for you," he offers.

I consider it for a moment. But I end up shaking my head. "It's not worth it."

"Let me know if you change your mind." The part of me that was enraged with men begins to melt at his feet. Why does he have to be so darn sweet and perfect all the time? Isn't it tiring for him? "Are you having fun tonight?"

I arch a brow at him. Is this his version of making small talk?

"I'm not really here to have fun, remember?"

The sides of his jaw contract as he grinds his molars together. Is there something bothering him? Aside from the obvious concerns of the letters.

"You looked like you were having fun with the guy I saw you with."

"The asshole from just now?" I spit out.

"No, the one that hugged you and made a scene."

I scoff, almost choking on my saliva. Surprise jolts through my spine at the hint of bitterness in his words. Throughout our friendship, he's always been a laidback guy. Never interrogated me about my friends or any of the guys in my life. Why is he doing it now?

"A scene?"

"You know what I mean," he says.

Do I? Because if I didn't know better, I would say he's jealous. And there's no way in hell he's jealous of Aidan . . . right?

"I'm not sure I do." I cross my arms defensively. "Besides, does it matter that I was having fun with Aidan? We've been friends for ages."

Why am I even explaining myself? It's not relevant and, frankly, it's none of his business. He shouldn't be questioning me about it when he was flirting with a girl before.

"Is that his name?"

"You've met him before. He was always filming with me, used to hang out with me at the fountain?" I jog his memory.

Danny shrugs. "Can't say it rings a bell." There's something in his voice that makes me believe he's lying, but I can't call him out on it. Maybe it's the crinkle in his left eye. "He must've not left an impression." I gape at him. He's being completely unrecognizable. Where is this behavior coming from? Just hours ago, he was being the sweet and kind guy I've always known. This is a new facet of him. After a moment of silence, he says, "Oh, wait, I think I do remember."

"Yeah."

"He's into you," he points out casually, though there's nothing casual about his tense expression.

"I gathered that," I confess, snorting. "But he's just a friend."

Danny's eyes scan my face as if he were trying to catch a hint that I'm not being truthful. But I'm not hiding anything. Aidan is nothing more than a friend and that won't change regardless of how he might feel about me.

"Just a friend," he repeats, his voice straining like he's forcing the words out of his mouth.

"Yup. Like I was to you." The words roll off my tongue before I can do anything to hold them back.

"What do you mean?" Danny questions as he turns briefly to ask for a soda.

Like me, he's taking the sober route tonight.

"Nothing," I mutter quickly. "Why aren't you taking advantage of the night?" Changing the subject is such a cop-out, but I find myself too close to an edge I can't back away from. It's too revealing. "Find a girl to talk to before the buzzer goes off again?"

Danny moves his head to the side. "Who says I'm not doing that already?"

My heart races at his unexpected response.

He shoves his hand into his pocket, pulls something out, and gestures for me to take it.

I frown as I grab the small Ziplock bag. It's full of green apple gummies. There would have been other flavors in the bag, but Danny has taken the time to pick out the ones I like best.

"Those are still your favorite, right?" he asks, his brows arching like he's begging for a hint of validation.

I end up taking a step back, hoping the distance will give me some perspective. Are my feelings clouding my judgment or did he mean what I think he meant? The gentle flirting and bringing me my favorite candy are confusing.

I look up from the candy to stare deep into Danny's eyes. They've softened around the edges now that we're not discussing Aidan and he's solely focused on me. I hope to find the answer I desperately seek in his gaze, but what I see there only makes the hazy confusion thicken between us. There's a layer of intensity in his pupils, mixing with flashes of memories of The Incident. When I chose to kiss him on an alcohol-induced impulse. It's the same kind of gaze, the same level of yearning swimming in the honey of his irises.

What does it all mean? Because he can't use the same gaze he had when he rejected me to flirt with me tonight. It doesn't work that way.

Or maybe I'm the problem and he can't figure out what he wants because there's something wrong with me. I'm aware of my flaws. My personality comes off as rude and blunt, as I've had to wear thick layers of protection to avoid being hurt by the world. I'm avoidant. My flight or fight instinct constantly leans towards the former rather than the latter.

And physically... Well, I wouldn't consider myself ugly, but I don't even know what his preferences are. For all I know, his type is the girl he was talking to earlier. She was petite and blonde. Everything I'm not.

So why is he doing this?

"Do you think I'm ugly?"

This is not what I meant to say. Honestly, it might be the worst possible conversation starter, but it still opens the door to the conversation we need to have. This is my way of jumping off the edge I was hanging on to. I want to know the truth.

I've run away from it for far too long.

By now, it's no longer just curiosity; it's a need. A need to understand why he's giving me mixed signals, like a stoplight that has all its lights flashing at the same time. The mixture of red, yellow and green becomes a dizzying and confusing mess. How should I act when I'm unsure of how to proceed? Do I stop my advances, proceed with caution, press the pedal on the gas and carry on? Maybe not the latter.

The last time I threw myself at him, it all went wrong. I lost a friend.

"What?" Danny blinks, confusion permeating his expression.

"You heard me," I say, not daring to form the question again. "It's fine if you think I am. It's nothing personal and it won't ruin my life." *Though it might hurt my ego.* "I just need to know."

Danny's shoulders drop an inch as his eyes roam over my face, his head tilting slightly to the side. He appears to be taken aback by the conversation, like he can't fully piece together where this is coming from.

I stand awkwardly in front of him as he inspects my looks, making up his mind. Insecurity creeps into my brain. Is he trying to figure out a gentle way to say I'm not pretty enough for him?

"No, Mabel, I don't think you're ugly," he says a moment later. "In fact, I think you're quite beautiful."

His words make my heart flutter and heat rush to my cheeks. I push through the symptoms of my lovesick soul. This is the first time I've felt brave enough to confront him about The Incident. Maybe because we might not see each other again after tonight, living as we do on opposite sides of the country. Or maybe it's the influence of the party with its hearts and romance, forcing me to face one of the biggest regrets I have. This is my chance to let it go completely. I can't move on and find someone else when I have this uncertainty haunting me and holding me back. That much became clear when Aidan was flirting with me, and I couldn't even *try* because I was too focused on Danny.

He's going to keep on holding me back.

I push the candy into the back pocket of my jeans and arm myself with all the courage I can summon to articulate the next question.

"Am I a bad kisser, then?"

Chapter 7

DANNY CHOKES ON HIS DRINK, SPITTING HALF OF IT OVER the white fabric of his T-shirt. Amber drops slide down his chin, hitting the floor as he leans forward, trying to avoid getting more soda down the front of his shirt. Coughing loudly, he wipes his chin with the back of his hand.

"Excuse me?"

His reaction knocks a brick of confidence from me, but it's too late to back down. I collect every ounce of courage left in my cells and straighten my back. This is the first, and possibly only, time I've felt the urge to confront him about The Incident. If I shy away and tell him to forget I ever mentioned it, I'll never get my answers. I'll be boarding a plane to LA soon and going far away from him.

So this is it.

It's now or never.

Besides, if I'm a bad kisser, I would welcome the feedback. If only for the benefit of my future partner. Knowing I need more guidance in that area could prove to be beneficial. I don't have a lot of experience, but I consider myself a quick learner. Receiving criticism is crucial to my learning process.

"Last year, we shared a moment. I kissed you, and from what I can tell, you absolutely hated it. Considering you say you find me somewhat attractive—"

"Beautiful," Danny corrects. "I said you're beautiful, Mabel."

I gulp.

"Yeah, well, considering you've said it's not that, then my next theory is that you think I'm a bad kisser," I conclude, offering my explanation in simple terms. Tackling the subject directly is easier than tiptoeing around it. "If I am, I would like to know. Please."

I wince at myself for adding *please* at the end. Being polite isn't something I should be concerned with right now. I know Abuela would probably clutch her rosary at the way I'm talking to him. Or perhaps she lost all faith in me from the moment I pulled Danny in for a kiss last year.

Danny's demeanor changes entirely. His shoulders grow stiffer, tightening under his shirt, and he suddenly seems taller. The curve of his lips flattens into a thin line. A cloud of emotion covers his honey eyes, and his real feelings. I haven't witnessed him look so serious in a very long time.

Mala mía.

This was a terrible idea. I shouldn't have said anything or even thought about bringing the topic up when I'm not prepared to face the consequences of my actions. I guess that has always been a problem; I tend to act without having a back-up plan for dealing with the consequences. There's a thin line between believing you can handle a truth and actually being ready for it. But, goddammit, I want to move on.

I can't keep holding a lit candle for Danny when there's doubt lingering in the back of my brain.

"Mabel..."

"I can handle it," I lie, faking a smile to go along with the faux confidence in my voice. "You can just rip the Band-Aid off and we'll never talk about it again."

This last part isn't a complete lie because I'll never talk to *him* again. Besides, what is there to lie about? It wouldn't make a difference. We didn't stay in touch after that moment either way.

Danny scrubs his eyes with his left hand and then scratches the back of his neck.

Great. I've made him uncomfortable.

"I don't think we should have this conversation," he says in a lower voice, the octave vibrating under my ribcage. "Not right now."

I raise my brows. Frustration clogs my airways.

"When then?" I press, sounding choked. Desperate. "We've been avoiding it for so long. I want to know, Danny. *Please.*"

He glances around, avoiding my eyes at all costs. I follow his gaze in an attempt to discover what he's looking for. No one is taking any notice of us. People are too focused on flirting with each other before the buzzer goes off again. Even Cerys and Bethan seem to be locked in their conversation.

"Maybe not here," he gives in.

"Why not?"

"It's too public," he states.

His words hit me in the gut, leaving me breathless for a second.

"You don't want to be seen with me," I conclude after a beat.

Danny rolls his eyes, annoyance printed boldly in the small action.

Whoa, where did that come from? The initial confusion has faded from his expression, and it's replaced by a mix of frustration and a slight blush on his cheeks. I can't decipher if they're red from anger or embarrassment. Or both. I would feel bad about putting him in an awkward position if it weren't for the fact that he seems to be uncomfortable at being seen with me.

His nostrils flare slightly. This is a different side to him, a new flavor of Danny to add to the mix.

"Why do you always assume I don't want to be seen with you?" he snaps, roughly gritting the words out. "I find it quite insulting. I've always been nothing but proud of you and our friendship. If anything, you're the one who's always avoided me in public."

I take a step back. "Me? Are you serious?"

Danny takes a deep breath and pinches the bridge of his nose, closing his eyes for a few seconds. When he finally looks at me, his irises have softened around the edges. They're silently pleading.

"Mabs," he says my name softly, almost as if he were caressing it with his lips. "I don't want to talk about this in public because it's a private matter. It's not due to shame. I just want to respect you and our privacy." His explanation is clear, and it makes perfect sense. I can see the logic behind his reasoning, and I appreciate it. "Let's find somewhere we can talk about this, okay? Preferably before the buzzer goes off."

He might've been a seer in another life because as soon as he finishes talking, the buzzer goes off again, silencing the crowd. But although people start moving around us, Danny's gaze stays locked on my face, awaiting my response.

Before someone appears to drag Danny away like they did with Aidan, I move. For the first time in forever, I seek his touch and grab a hold of his arm, right over his green wristband. His arm is warm and the skin of my palm tingles with the urge to move higher where I can squeeze his muscles.

Danny's sight drops to the spot where our limbs are connected. I almost expect him to pull away from me because his behavior was so serious just a minute ago, but he doesn't. He just . . . waits.

I examine our surroundings, spotting the people I care about. Cerys is still talking to Bethan, both disregarding the event. Carmen is standing with a guy I don't recognize, but she seems to be into it. Her posture is relaxed and she's smiling and batting her lashes at him.

An idea sparks in my mind.

"I think I know somewhere we can go."

Without letting go of me, he gestures to the entrance—or exit, in this case—with his head.

"Lead the way."

I try not to think about the fact that we'll have to go through the love tunnel together as we abandon the backyard.

It's almost poetic to think I'll go through it with Danny before he inevitably shuts me off. I inhale deeply, hoping to find some courage for what's to come. My expectations are sprawling, with no sense of direction or what to prepare myself for. The only thing I'm sure of is that I'll have a bruised ego.

As much as I want to be mad at my sister for consistently leaving her bedroom door unlocked, I'm thankful when I twist the doorknob and it gives in without protest from the lock. The door opens smoothly, and I step to the side to let Danny in. In silence, I wait for him to walk past me. I make the mistake of breathing as he does, and the woodsy scent of his cologne makes my knees grow weak. A shiver runs down my spine.

Looking for a distraction, I shut the door with trembling hands and examine the state of Carmen's room. This was the only place I could think of for what he wanted. It's the perfect spot to have a conversation without being interrupted or seen. I also appreciate the silence. The music is barely a murmur in the background, not nearly loud enough to make us raise our voices, which I think covers Danny's request for privacy.

I don't think Carmen will come here any time soon. She was always one of the last ones to leave a Kappa party, so I doubt this will be the exception to her rule. Knowing her, when it finishes she'll head directly to the afterparty. Not that it will make any difference—I doubt this will take more than a handful of minutes.

This is Danny's way of letting me down gently, making sure I don't suffer any public humiliation. He's too much of a gentleman for that.

I ignore the mess that Carmen left behind when she was getting ready, judging by all the makeup and clothes spilled over the bed. Instead, I focus on the possibilities. The gears in my brain start working on what other reasons there are for Danny not wanting me back. Other than me being a terrible kisser, which is something fixable. Even if I were bad at it, he could've taught me. He used to be a tutor, so he's patient and has teaching experience. So . . . what else? It's not a matter of beauty. Or at least that's what he said.

"So, *am* I a bad kisser?" I repeat my question as I seek something to keep my hands occupied. A way to channel the bundle of nerves.

Danny rolls his eyes once again.

"It's not about that."

I pull out the bag of candy and set it on Carmen's nightstand. I turn around and grab a dress from the bed and fold it. I can't keep looking at him when he's being difficult. Why won't he say what he needs to say and get it over with?

"That's not good enough. Why won't you tell me?"

As I organize Carmen's stuff, I come to a sudden realization.

Cerys.

Not only did they spend time together when she was recovering from the massive hate from Westbrook and Greek Row, but they came back here together. He talks about her as if they were close friends. He went to find her first, so it must've been because they keep in touch. What if there was more to it?

They could've been growing closer while I've been away. She knew about my crush on him, but I kept the details of The Incident under wraps, which means she might think it was merely something innocent. It could explain why Cerys decided to stop reaching out to me as well.

Acid sizzles in my stomach. The thought of Danny having romantic feelings for my best friend makes me nauseous. The walls of my stomach constrict painfully, forcing bile to rise in my esophagus. I hold my breath and squeeze the dress between my fingers, regaining some control.

"What do you want to hear from me?" he asks, pleadingly.

"I don't know," I confess. "I don't know what I want to hear from you, but I know I've been wracking my brain trying to figure out *why*. So, if it's not the kissing and you don't think I'm ugly, then . . . do you have feelings for her?"

"For whom?"

I know I'm being unclear, but it's so hard for me to even say it.

Cerys is my best friend regardless of our lack of communication. Our bond can't be measured by something so trivial as the passing of time. But it will hurt me deeply if he has feelings for her, and she for him. I would want them to be happy, but for that I would have to remove myself from the equation all together.

"Do you have feelings for . . ." The words get stuck in the back of my throat.

"For whom?" Danny presses. "Look at me," he demands.

I bite the inside of my cheek until I start to taste the familiar metallic flavor of blood. Slowly, I turn to face him.

"For Cerys."

Danny shakes his head in complete disbelief, blinking as if I just slapped him. His reaction makes me confused, and I can't help but frown.

"Are you joking?" he asks.

"No, I'm very serious."

Why does he act like it's such a ridiculous question? Cerys came back to this place *with him*. Am I missing something here?

"This is crazy," he mumbles. "You can't be serious. That makes no sense." He rubs his forehead. The blush on his cheeks returns with a fury. Air comes out of him in small but audible puffs as he grows more frustrated with me.

I lick my lips before I explain.

"It does to me. I've been trying to figure out for ages the reason why you rejected me that night. You could barely look me in the eye afterward, so I'm wondering if you rejected me because you've been in love with Cerys the entire time." I gulp my emotions down. "Trust me, I get it if you are. She's a lovable person. She's the best person I've ever met, aside from Carmen."

Danny frowns. His stance grows awkward, his body tense. Uncomfortable. He scratches the back of his neck again.

"No, Mabel, I don't have feelings for Cerys. How could you think that?"

I dig my nails into the palms of my hands, hoping the small scratches will help me stay focused.

"Aside from the obvious, the biggest clue is that you went to see her first when you got the letter. You came here together. She seems comfortable with you, enough to return to this hellhole. Should I go on?"

"We're friends," he states. "We kept in touch after she dropped out. I sent her contacts so she could get the therapy she needed during that time. I helped her find resources so she can complete her degree online and still build a competitive and compelling CV for law school. I'm practically her mentor." With every word, he sounds more irritated, verging on angry. "That's all."

"You've talked to her more than to me."

"I wonder why," he spits out, sarcasm dripping from his words.

"Don't use that tone with me."

He tilts his head. "You're asking a bunch of ridiculous questions. Accusing me of having feelings for a good friend is outrageous, Mabel."

Anger flashes through my system, spreading a hot wave across my nerve points. The corners of my eyes start seeing red.

"Outrageous?" I echo his words. "Outrageous was the way you completely cut me off without giving me a reason. You were supposed to be my friend, and I get that I ruined our friendship. But do you know how much it's fucked with my head? You bailed on me. I haven't even been able to accept a coffee date with co-workers because I can't stop thinking about how much I messed up with you."

"Mabel—"

"I get it," I interrupt him, holding a hand up as I step closer. Danny's stands there, chest heaving with every rapid breath he takes. "You've never felt anything for me and that's the cold hard truth. But there's no reason for you to preach honesty and transparency and then give me the cold shoulder.

You could've talked to me about it and explained it to me. God, we were friends before that happened. Why couldn't you still be my friend?"

"Because I've never seen you as a friend!"

His expression crumbles a split second after he explodes, immediately regretting the words. Brows arching softly over his brown eyes.

My heart falls to the pit of my stomach.

Have I been so delusional as to think he at least saw me as a friend? I was sure we'd had a connection. Every moment we spent on the rooftop, the long conversations, the inside jokes. The secret smiles. There *was* something.

Now I feel stupid and ashamed. The truth stabs into my chest, digging itself deep in my soul. It *hurts*. My breathing shallow, I'm unable to hide the emotion that overwhelms me.

"Oh."

Danny sighs, letting his shoulders drop in defeat. "I didn't mean it like that. Why do you always assume the worst of me?"

I swallow, forcing the pain down my throat where it meets the ache in my stomach.

"Look at my history in this place, Danny," I say, pointing around me. "When Cerys dropped out, I was utterly alone. I stayed here until the end, despite all the bad memories and the hatred. You have no idea how mean people were to me in those months. If it weren't for Aidan, I would've probably lost my mind, because even Carmen merged with the crowd of people telling me I was a lost cause for defending Cerys. They all said I was a liar. I was everyone's enemy, even though I had done absolutely nothing but defend my friend. It fucking hurt to go through everything alone, and I have a thick skin; I wouldn't have survived in this place if I didn't. But you . . . you left along with the rest, Danny." My eyes sting but I try to keep the emotions at bay, holding back from showing how vulnerable and raw I feel saying this. "Don't forget that."

Danny's lips quiver as he tries to find the words. He struggles for what seems like forever, the seconds stretching between us.

"I didn't . . . I didn't leave you."

I scoff a laugh.

"Oh, really? Where were you then?"

"Mabel, *you* stopped talking to *me*," he reminds me.

"What did you expect me to do? I kissed you and you ran away. There's only so much my ego can take."

"It's not what you think."

"Then tell me what to think—not once have you given me a reason!" I exclaim, running a hand through my hair, tugging on the strands to release the rising frustration in my body. "All I know is it happened, and then afterward you never tried to fix things either."

"Because I was ashamed of myself!" he yells. He lets out a defeated groan, mumbling a curse under his breath as he rubs a hand over his forehead. "Mabel, you were drunk the night we kissed. You were so drunk, and part of me was aware of it when you got closer. I could smell it on you, and I didn't stop you," he explains, lowering his voice. Almost driven by an impulse, he steps closer to me, shortening the distance between us. "I could've stopped you," he whispers.

We're so close that his words tingle on my face. The warmth of his breath makes me want to sigh. I'm overpowered by the tension tightening around us, wrapping us together and pushing us even closer. Our chests almost brush with every breath we take, and, instinctively, I begin to match my breathing with his. Only centimeters separate us now and I'm too tempted to touch him. My hands ache with the need to feel him, to pull him in and dig my fingers into his hair.

"Why didn't you?" I ask.

I need him to say it and be clear about what he means. I refuse to move an inch if he's not open about what he wants. Reading between the lines has caused me a lifetime of heartache. It's not what I want this time. It doesn't matter that it would be almost too easy to kiss him right now. If he can't say how he feels, I'll walk away from him. I deserve better.

Danny's hand brushes mine, the featherlight movement causing goosebumps to erupt all over me. I flex my fingers, wanting to reach for him, but I don't, and he doesn't make any attempt to intertwine our hands. Instead, he reaches higher, slowly drawing an invisible path that goes from the back of my hand to my shoulder.

I shudder and a ragged sigh slips past my lips.

"Danny . . ."

"I couldn't resist you," he whispers. With care, he pushes my hair away, exposing the skin of my neck where his touch finally stops. His fingers rest at the nape of my neck, cradling my face. "I've never been able to, and you . . . You have no idea how much I've wanted to repeat that moment. I've thought about touching you every night since we talked for the first time. You've been in my mind ever since, making me want you, driving me crazy. And when you kissed me . . ."

His thumb finds my lips, parting them with a subtle touch.

Desire curls in my body, making me feverish. Pure need rumbles in my bones, heating under my skin.

"When I kissed you . . .?"

He huffs, leaning in to rest his forehead against my own. His nose rubbing mine as he breathes rapidly.

"When you kissed me, I thought I was dreaming," he says, closing his eyes. "But you were drunk, and I was taking advantage of you. That's why I pulled away. I've never thought you were ugly, never believed you were a bad kisser, nor did I have feelings for Cerys. All this time, I've been crazy about you."

Oh God.

My heart skips a beat before speeding up so fast I fear it might burst out of my chest. I hope I'm not the one dreaming here. It would ruin me if it were, because this moment, right here, with him whispering his confession to me, is everything I've ever dreamed of.

"You have?"

He nods.

"But I valued our friendship and didn't want to be that guy who only becomes friends with a girl to ruin it by having feelings for her. Then, I was too ashamed of myself for not stopping you sooner. I didn't want that kiss to be a drunken impulse. I hated myself for waiting until you had already kissed me to stop it from going any further. The next day, you couldn't even look me in the eye, and Mabel, I couldn't live with myself, knowing I lost you because of those seconds where I lost perspective."

My sweet Danny, beating himself up for something that was never his fault. Always the gentleman I've known him to be, caring more about my well-being than he cares about himself. All this time . . . We've wasted all this time because of a stupid misunderstanding.

"It wasn't a drunken impulse," I tell him. "I was aware of my actions, the alcohol just gave me the confidence I was lacking. I'd wanted to kiss you for too long before I actually did it."

Danny pulls his head back to meet my eyes, searching for the truth in them. "You did?"

I nod. "I did," I reaffirm, and even as my survival instinct screams at me to run away before he can do something to hurt me, I add, "I still do."

His brows perk up. "You do?"

"Of course. Do *you* want to kiss me?"

He groans. "That shouldn't even be a question."

"Are you going to wait around for me to make the first move again?" I question, arching a brow inquiringly.

"Oh, shut up," he mumbles.

Before I have the chance to say anything else, he closes the distance between us.

After a year of causing both of us unnecessary pain, Danny finally kisses me.

Chapter 8

THE WORLD EVAPORATES AROUND ME AS DANNY'S LIPS meet mine. I forget everything I've felt prior to this moment. The party, the letters, the interactions tonight—everything fades into nothing when I give in to him. An invisible string seems to tie our bodies together, lacing our souls as we connect in a way we haven't done before.

The kiss starts out light and sweet, the pressure warm and inviting. He gives me a short peck at first, then another and another, lingering a bit longer each time, letting me get used to the sensation. Nights of yearning pile together, spilling free with every second we spend discovering each other. I completely melt against him, receiving his kisses, my mouth ready to meet his every time, eager for more.

Danny seems to read my body and he deepens the kiss, sucking on my bottom lip and gently biting it. I moan, the sound vibrating against our mouths. I wrap my hands around his neck, pressing myself against his torso. I feel him guide his free hand to my waist, where he rests it on my lower back, making me arch into him.

The passion radiating off his body gives me the confidence to try something new. I drag the tip of my tongue over the seam of his lips, and he rewards me by whimpering. It ignites a fire in my blood, fueled by desire.

Holy shit.

Is this what being kissed by Danny feels like? Because I might've been wrong about my assessment. He's not a golden retriever right now. He's a passionate kisser, putting everything he has into the way his lips dance against mine. He's devouring me like a starved man receiving his first meal in a very long time.

His hand on my neck tangles in my hair. I gasp, shocked at the way he pulls it ever so slightly, holding me in place as his tongue dives into my mouth. Every cell in my body screams for more. The temperature under my skin making everything feel hot. A coil of arousal twirls in my lower abdomen. I crave him. The pressure builds in the apex of my thighs, and I'm taken aback by the foreign sensation of needing to feel some friction.

I suck on his tongue, and he groans, parting from me.

"How can you think you're a bad kisser?" he says softly. His hands caress my cheeks as he looks at me like I'm a treasure he just found. "You're perfect."

"That's your feedback?"

He hums. "I'm not sure."

I tilt my head back.

"Not sure?"

A grin curves his mouth.

"Can I have another go?" he asks, teasingly. "Just to make sure, of course." His expression is serious, but I catch the playful undertone.

I roll my eyes.

"Come here," I mumble and pull him in for another kiss.

I expect the feeling to die down from the first explosion of sensations I experienced the second he kissed me for the first time, but it doesn't. The fireworks blast inside me, every thought in my brain disappears into nothing, and the heat spreads through my veins. This time, we don't bother with the pecks but immediately find a slow but passionate rhythm that makes me shiver.

"Danny," I moan.

He grins and bites my lip, leaving a sting behind.

"What is it?" he asks gently.

"I..." How can I express that I just want to jump his bones without being so blunt about it? Blood rushes to my cheeks and I can almost feel the heat emanating from them. "I need..." I struggle to find the words.

"What do you need, baby?"

A longing sigh abandons me at his sweet pet name. I never thought I would be the type of girl to grow weak at the knees by being called something as trivial as "baby", but here I am, melting into his embrace and kissing him again. I grow bolder each time, getting familiar with the shape of his mouth and the softness of his lips.

"More," I whisper, and nibble on his bottom lip, trying it out for the first time. "I need you."

He groans, and it vibrates directly to my core.

"How much more?"

Everything, I want to say.

I'm not thinking straight. Hell, I'm not thinking at all, but I know that if he asks for it, I will give him everything he wants. There's not an inch of my body he doesn't already own. Although the idea of being so intimate with someone is terrifying, I trust Danny to not shatter me. If there's any guy in the world I can trust with my body, it's him. I might regret this if it turns sour, but my brain can't focus on anything other than feeling his skin against mine.

My thighs tighten in anticipation.

Driven by desire, I choose to show him without breaking eye contact. I move his hand on my back and lower it so that he's touching my butt instead. His pupils dilate and his hand immediately squeezes, grabbing a handful of my ass. My breath hitches.

"Just this?" he asks, giving my butt cheek another pinch before he lets it go. His brings his hand to my stomach then ventures higher, tracing a path between us until he meets my chest. There's an unspoken request lingering between us. "Or more?"

"More," I confirm.

I'm wearing the green wristband, but I might as well be flashing a green light at him. He can do whatever he wants with me. I belong to him as much as he wants to own me.

Danny slides his hand over my chest, lightly squeezing one of my breasts over the layers of clothing. The fabric is getting in between us and I'm desperate to feel his heat pressing against my bare skin. I don't get the chance to beg for more because Danny kisses me again, erasing my thoughts. He takes the lead, moving my body backward, guiding me until the backs of my knees meet the edge of the bed.

Oh.

Oh.

"More?" he checks in.

I nod enthusiastically.

To prove my point, I grab the hem of my shirt and pull it over my head. Danny's jaw drops in surprise, and I lift my chin, smug that I managed to shock him. I might be inexperienced, but I do know how to make a statement. We've been so bad at saying how we feel, so now I stick to the first rule of scriptwriting: show, don't tell.

"Well?" I quip as I let my shirt fall to the ground.

Part of me wishes I was wearing more attractive underwear than my plain black bra, but he doesn't seem bothered by the lack of sexy lingerie. Instead, it's quite the opposite, Danny chews on his bottom lip as he takes in the view. Pupils dilated, breathing labored, expression undone. There's no denying he likes what he sees.

"You're perfect," he repeats. Boldly, he hooks two fingers on the middle of my bra and yanks me toward him. Caressing my naked skin, he makes his way to my back and finds the clasp. His touch is lingering on it, silently asking for permission. "I can't get enough of you. I don't think I'll ever be satisfied."

"Do it," I encourage him, referring to the clasp.

He doesn't wait to be told twice.

Immediately, Danny undoes the clasp and leans into my neck where he rubs his lips on the sensitive skin. Gently, he nibbles on it, and I moan. Shivering, I bury my fingers in his hair, which he takes as an invitation to suck on the curve of my neck. I don't even care if he leaves a mark. It feels too good to stop.

I help him remove my bra and he squeezes my breasts again, this time skin to skin. My nipples harden and he pinches them, evoking a visceral reaction from me. They're more sensitive than I was expecting. It doesn't feel nearly as good when I've touched myself in the past. His touch is solely focused on my boobs, but I feel the tugs and twists south. The pleasure tingles along my skin, concentrating on the spot between my legs. Now I understand why people lose their minds for sex, because he's merely teasing me and I'm ready to combust.

Closing my eyes, I concentrate on the pleasure I get from him kissing my neck and playing with my nipples. The instinct to get friction where I need it the most is strong. Even if I rock my hips against him, it doesn't give me the release I desperately seek. Instead, I grow needier when I feel his hard dick against me.

God, he's so hard.

Danny's kisses go lower, and I let out a loud moan when I feel his lips wrap around my nipple. I cover my mouth with my hand, ashamed of the wanton noise that came out of me.

"No, baby, I want to hear you," he says, and he sucks on my nipple again. "I want to know I'm making you feel as good as you deserve. You're so beautiful."

I bite my bottom lip, hoping it will muffle the noise so it's not as loud.

He switches our positions before he sits on the mattress. Sliding his hands to the back of my thighs, he guides me to straddle him. I spread my legs and press myself directly over his hard dick. With a hand on my hip and the other on my ass, Danny helps me rock against him.

Sparks of pleasure dance behind my eyelids.

"I want to make you come," Danny says. "Please, can I make you come?"

The heat in my cheeks intensifies, spreading down my neck.

My thoughts come back to me in a rush. There's a bigger pressure in his question. Insecurity drills a hole in my arousal. What if I'm not able to? I've never done it with a partner, only in the comfort of my room, sheltered by the bed covers where I'm completely safe. But he's looking at me with pleading eyes, and I'm scared I won't be able to reach a climax. I don't want to disappoint him. Yet I don't want to fake an orgasm just for his sake either.

"Hey," he says, bringing me out of my thoughts. His forehead creases with concern. "I just want to make you feel good. I don't mean to pressure you into doing something you're not ready for."

I lick my lips, attempting to gather my thoughts.

"It's not that," I mumble. "What if I don't . . ."

"Don't what?" he prompts me to finish my question.

There's something in the gentleness of his tone that melts all of my barriers. His attentive eyes focus on me, and he rubs my skin with the pad of his thumb, drawing soothing circles while he waits patiently for me to answer. I've never been with anyone who has cared so much about me, keeping things clear and comfortable. It makes me feel safe.

I take a deep breath and stare at the ceiling for a second. The back of my throat itches. A light sting glosses over my eyes as I try to pull myself together. When it doesn't feel like I'm going to lose it, I glance at him, finding his sweet caramel eyes focused on me. It gives me the security I need to respond with honesty.

"If I don't come."

Relief washes over Danny's expression.

"Mabel, it's okay if you don't, but you have to communicate with me. Tell me if you like what I'm doing, so I can do better. I just want you to enjoy it. If you come, I'll be a happy man. If you don't," he leans in until his lips brush my ear, "I'll try harder next time."

"Next time, huh?"

"Do you think this is a one-time thing? Because it isn't for me. I've wanted you for too long, baby. I'm going to need more."

"Okay," I accept with a nod.

Danny raises his brows. "Okay, what?"

"Are you going to make me say it?"

"Yes, Mabel, I want you to say it. Your consent is the most important part of this. I need to know you want this as much as I do," he explains, his words dripping seriousness.

A thousand butterflies flutter in my stomach. "Make me . . ."

"Where are your manners? You once said Puerto Rican

households made sure to teach their kids manners," he jokes.

"What would your grandmother say about your filthy tongue?"

Danny's cheeks acquire a red hue that spreads across his face, and I want to laugh at how cute it is.

"Don't bring Dadi into this," he mumbles. "Not when I have your sweet tits in front of my mouth."

"I want you to make me come," I say, running my fingers through the hair at the nape of his neck.

Danny closes his eyes for a fraction of a second, enjoying the sensation of my nails on his scalp. The tint on his cheeks hasn't disappeared entirely, but I'm not sure if he's still embarrassed about my mentioning his grandmother or if he's turned on. Judging by the bulge softly beating between my thighs, I'd say it's the latter.

"Manners," he reminds me.

"Please," I add, rolling my eyes.

"Please what?"

"Please, make me come."

"That's what I like to hear."

Danny lifts me from his lap and sets me on the bed, climbing on top of me without letting his body weight crush me. Under him, I'm suddenly conscious of the way my chest rises and falls with every breath. I'm completely overpowered by him, yet I've never felt safer.

Focused on the request, Danny starts kissing his way south, starting at the spot on my neck where my pulse beats hardest. Then, moving slowly to the valley between my breasts, he takes a moment to suck on each nipple before he continues his journey down my belly. The slight stubble on his jaw scratches my skin, and I wriggle at the sensation.

"I'm okay," I assure him when he stops for a second.

Danny continues until his fingers rest on the hem of my pants. He looks up at me, intensity swimming in his eyes as he silently asks for permission.

"More?"

I nod. "More."

His fingers unbutton my jeans and undo the fly, revealing a hint of my plain pink panties. There's nothing special about them, nor sexy. They're just simple bikini-style underwear with no design to them or lace. I make a mental note to invest in sexier underwear when I get back to LA. I need to be ready for the next time I end up having Danny staring at them.

But Danny doesn't care about them because he pulls on the fabric of my jeans, yanking them off with a minor struggle as he has to remove my shoes to slide them off. He stares at my almost naked body. Biting his lip, he lets a hand wander over my bare thighs. Delicately, he spreads them, and moans at the sight.

"Fuck," he whispers under his breath. "You're so wet, you're soaking through your panties," he points out, dragging a single finger over my core, earning a moan from me. I squeeze my eyes shut, trying not to think about how obviously I want him. "Look at me, baby." My body reacts to the command, and I meet his gaze. "Can I get a taste?"

"Yes."

His hands settle on my hips, and he drags me to the edge of the bed, kneeling between my thighs. First, he presses a kiss on my mound; I tremble in response. Then, he licks me through the cotton fabric, and I lose my ability to speak.

Fuck.

The sensation intensifies when Danny anchors two fingers on my panties and pulls them to the side, completely exposing me to him. The flesh wet and pulsating, needing the friction as much as my lungs need my next breath. His tongue trails across my slit, starting at the bottom and going up to find the spot where I'm most sensitive. Wrapping his lips around my clit, he sucks on it, his tongue swirling as he does.

Dark blotches appear in my vision. My hands fly to his hair, holding his head in place as I moan, rocking my hips against his face. Every ounce of insecurity and doubt abandons my body. I can just *feel*. Pleasure builds in my core, spreading across my limbs, growing stronger each time he sweeps his tongue over my clit, alternating between licking and sucking.

"Don't stop, please," I beg. Danny obeys, staying with the same pattern and speed as I inch closer to the edge. Heat spots tingle on my chest. I hold on to the bed covers, bunching the sheets between my fingers as I fall over the edge, shattering into a million pieces. Bliss swims through me. Hips trembling and grinding against Danny's face as I ride each wave of pleasure coursing through my body. "Holy shit," I whisper, my soul returning to me.

My thighs shake uncontrollably, and I gasp for air.

"You're so beautiful when you come," Danny says in complete awe. "From one to ten, how much do I need to improve?"

I sit up, laughing.

"That was—"

"What the fuck?!" Carmen's voice makes me jump, and Danny stands, shielding my almost naked body with his frame as I spot my little sister standing in the doorway.

Chapter 9

CARMEN'S PRESENCE MAKES MY BLOOD GO FROM SCALDING hot to ice cold in the span of a second. It freezes me to the spot, slowing the world around me. The bliss from my orgasm disappears, replaced by the embarrassment of being caught in a compromising position. I try to hide my naked state behind Danny's figure to preserve some sense of dignity, although I wouldn't say there's much left to save. My little sister already saw me with my legs spread open while Danny knelt between them, his face buried in my thighs.

A hot flush concentrates in my head, burning and itching in my scalp. My limbs shake, and I attempt to gather my thoughts and get a grip. As ashamed as I am, I know this was my fault. I brought Danny here, encouraged him to kiss me, and then some more. Well, I can't really take all the blame for what happened; he was the one who persuaded me by telling me he wanted to make me come. A shudder travels down my back at the memory.

But I don't get a chance to sit and enjoy the moment, not with my sister standing only a few meters away.

"Turn around!" I yell at Carmen.

For once she obeys, but I think it mostly has to do with the fact that she doesn't want to stare at my boobs any longer. She turns on her heel and faces the half-open door, her hands rolled into tight fists. Oh no. I recognize that tremble in her stance—she's fuming.

"I'm giving you one minute to get dressed before I lose my shit," she grits out. To make a point, she starts counting the seconds out loud.

What was I thinking when I let my guard down enough to allow Danny to . . . Yeah, I think it's pretty clear that I wasn't thinking at all. I lost all train of thought when he kissed me, and it went too fast from there. Control slipped from my fingers until it was completely out of reach. Did I want to get it back? No, I didn't. Even when it ends up with my sister catching us at the end, I would still repeat it. It gave me the clarity I so desperately needed.

While it wasn't what I traveled here for, it's surely the highlight of the trip.

I glance at Danny, noticing the blush extending down the collar of his shirt. The tips of his ears are bright red as he helps me gather my clothes. The nerves and anxiety make me pull on my shirt before I even find my bra. My brain is focused on covering my body as fast as possible before Carmen turns and sees me naked . . . again.

"Here," Danny whispers, handing me the bra.

Part of me wants to laugh at the awkward gesture. If Carmen weren't waiting here, I would be laughing at the ridiculousness of the situation. But since she's here, embarrassment drills into my system, making me shy and clumsy. It also speeds up my thoughts, pushing me closer to the edge of spiraling. Hundreds of questions flash in my brain, and I wish we had more time to discuss what just happened. There are questions I wish I had asked before I decided to take off my shirt because, now, I crave another type of clarity. Something very different to how it was with The Incident.

What are we?

God, I want to cringe at myself.

I shouldn't be asking that after letting him go down on me, but I didn't think it mattered in the moment. Minutes ago, I had been too high on the thrill of him liking me to consider the logistics. Would we be able to handle a relationship with the major distance between us? I can't simply drop my life in LA, my job and career, because a guy suddenly decides he wants me in his life. And I can't ask him to choose me either. He has his own dreams and goals to achieve, so we're down to just two options: try to continue this despite the long distance, or rip the Band-Aid off and let it die before it begins.

I'm getting ahead of myself. After all, just because he went down on me, that doesn't mean he plans on seeing me as anything other than a good lay until the itch is scratched. Everything he said could've been in the heat of the moment.

There's too much to discuss, but everything is overshadowed by Carmen's presence in the room. If it had been anyone else, someone random from the sorority, maybe I wouldn't care as much because I would be able to follow Danny outside and have a conversation.

But since it's Carmen, it changes everything.

Considering how we argued earlier today, it's safe to say I owe it to her to explain what just happened and what she walked in on. Including the fact that I fooled around with Danny on her bed.

With trembling hands, I grab the bra, sticking it into the back pocket of my jeans. I'll deal with it later when I don't have the pressure of getting dressed in front of my sister. Even if it means my nipples will be on display through my shirt.

It's not like she didn't see them a minute ago.

"I'm sorry," I mumble at Danny.

He shakes his head.

"You have nothing to be sorry for," he assures me, caressing my chin with tenderness. His lips curve into a slight smile. "Can we talk after?"

After I finish talking to Carmen, he means.

Part of me is grateful that he knows me well enough to understand I need to have a conversation with her before we can sit and discuss our relationship. If there even is one. He might decide he doesn't want to engage in this after tonight. We have very different lives.

Stop, I tell myself. I close my eyes for a split second, realizing I'm indulging in self-sabotage.

This is Danny. It's not a random man I just met. Danny is the guy who turned a horrible place into a safe haven.

That guy wouldn't play with me the way my insecurities do. Our circumstances aren't as dire as my brain seems to think.

"Time's up!" Carmen exclaims, bringing me back to reality. I have more important business to handle before Danny and I get another shot. "You better be decent now or I swear to God..."

"Later," I say to Danny.

He nods in agreement.

Carmen clears her throat, claiming our attention, and I take a second to look at her. She has her arms crossed over her chest, nostrils flaring as she breathes. Her plump lips are pursed. Pure anger swims in her eyes as she stares at us.

"I can't believe you two," she starts, her teeth biting the words as they come out of her mouth. She rests her hands on her hips, her elbows framing her figure in pointed directions. "Is this how two grown-up and professional adults behave? Is this the example you're setting?" With each word, a drop of mild annoyance spreads in my chest. She's borrowing a card from our mother, using the same tone to scold us. Suddenly, I'm fifteen, getting reprimanded for any slight misdemeanor. "Don't you dare roll your eyes at me, Mabel Marie."

Oh, now she's using my middle name as well.

My cheeks burn, the embarrassment mixing with the irritation.

"You're overreacting."

The comment clearly makes things worse because Carmen's eye twitches as she lets out a sardonic laugh.

"Overreacting?!" she practically shrieks. "You were naked on my fucking bed! I left my clean clothes there and you decided to hook up with this himbo..."

"Himbo?" Danny tilts his head. He sounds mildly offended.

"You shut up." She points at him with her index finger. "I'm going to talk to my sister now, *in private*, and I swear if I find out you took advantage of her, you'll pay for it."

"Carmen," I reprimand her.

Her head snaps at me.

"No, you don't get to use that tone with me either. You're walking on very thin ice, Mabel. Trust me, the last thing you want is to test me."

Danny shoots me a look. "It's fine, Mabs," he says softly. He leans in and presses a kiss on my temple. It makes my heart flutter and gives me hope that our future conversation will be a good one, not like my insecurities are making me think. "I'll let you talk."

Carmen keeps her gaze locked on Danny as he crosses the room and heads to the door, giving her an apologetic smile as he passes her and sneaks out. She remains glaring at him until he disappears, and then she fixes her death glare on me. The intensity rolling off her is enough to make me want to shrink away to nothing.

While I've always been the caregiver in this sisterhood, Carmen always had a meaner streak. Sharp tongue, grudge holding, hurtful and judgmental glares. I've rarely been the target of them, but I'd be lying if I said it didn't intimidate me all the same, because I know my sister can jump to her own conclusions and stick to them regardless of what I have to say about it. Considering that she has already strayed too far from me, it terrifies me to think my actions tonight might drive a bigger wedge into our relationship.

More than my baby sister, Carmen is the person I love the most in the entire world; she's my best friend. I wouldn't be half the person I am if it weren't for her presence in my life.

I don't want to lose her.

I can lose everyone in the world but her.

So, I choose to take the initiative.

"I'm sorry you had to witness that," I say, rubbing my palms on my arms.

"So, you're not sorry that you did it?"

I sigh.

The situation is more complicated to explain. There were a lot of feelings of yearning and anticipation between Danny and me. A bunch of miscommunications that were hurting us like a thorn in our feet, unable to take a step without remembering what we let go unfinished.

"No, I'm not," I admit frankly. She's already seen me in a vulnerable position, so I can speak of this with nothing but the truth. "This wasn't something I planned to do, let alone in your room. It wasn't to get back at you for our argument either."

She scoffs. "Yeah right."

"It wasn't," I insist as I approach her. Her back straightens, arming herself, appearing to keep me at bay. "Danny . . . you know he's a complicated subject for me. I saw him earlier, after our argument, and we talked for a bit. It made me remember everything I felt for him. Then we saw each other at the event and things progressed from there. We only came to your room so that we could talk in private."

"Is 'talking' code for 'screwing' in LA?" she retorts.

Regardless of her snark, her posture relaxes a little bit. My apology seems to be getting through to her.

I press my lips together, holding back a laugh.

"No, I meant actual talking. We had unfinished business to discuss."

Her brows raise.

"Well, it doesn't seem like the business was anywhere near done." She gives me a pointed look.

I catch the hidden double meaning in her words, and I stare at her, feeling the corner of my lips twitch until I can't hold it anymore. Laughter bubbles out of me in a contagious giggle.

Carmen's tough act cracks, and her shoulders shake with every cackle abandoning her. Laughing with her is easy because, once we start, we can't seem to stop. Once my shoulders stop shaking from laughter and silence begins to settle between us, I stare at her. The hotness I felt before reduces into a welcoming and familiar warmth. Comfortable and safe.

"Come here," I motion her to the bed so we can sit.

Her face wrinkles with disgust.

"Um, no, thanks. I won't be subjecting this dress to all the filth you guys did," she says, turning her nose up. "I'll stay right here." Rolling my eyes, I grab her arm and pull her with me to the bed. "Ew!"

I bark out a laugh, falling back on the mattress. The bed moves under my weight, swaying for a second. Reluctantly, Carmen lets her weight drop on the bed next to me. I prop myself up with my elbows to get a look at her.

"Don't be a baby."

"I get to be a baby. You guys are fucking nasty," she complains. "I can't believe you were about to fuck him on my bed.

Were you just going to do it and then leave as if it never happened? Dragging your ass on my sheets, leaving behind sweat and lord knows what else?"

I snort. "Oh, cut me some slack. Aren't you glad I'm getting some?"

"Not on my bed!" she declares. "But, yes, I am glad you're finally getting some. The years of repressed sexual tension had you turning into a raging bitch."

My jaw slackens. "Respect me, *pendeja*," I reprimand her, though my tone doesn't carry the same seriousness it should.

I would be lying if I said Danny's oral skills didn't help me relieve some stress and tension. My body feels relaxed, muscles loosened. I'm floating above the clouds with glee.

"You're going to wash those sheets. This isn't a joke, I won't let you go back to LA until you do," she establishes, and then shudders as if she got hit with a jolt of disgust. "I'm never going to be able to unsee that image."

"Stop it." I dig an elbow into her ribs.

She whines dramatically.

I barely nudged her, so I roll my eyes.

"It was nasty, Mabby." Carmen fakes a gag. "I still can't believe it."

Humming, I ponder on her comment because I can't believe it either.

"Honestly, this wasn't on my bingo card when I traveled here," I admit.

That's an understatement. The last thing I expected was to bump into Danny today. Hell, I never would've guessed he'd ever come back to Westbrook after graduation. I expected him to be long gone from here, focusing on his grad studies, or working with his father. But it was like fate wanted us to come together today and confront our issues.

And do more.

A *lot* more.

"Right, you came because of *that* thing." Annoyance drips from her voice.

Defeat washes over me. I wish she could understand where I'm coming from, but it's not easy to put into words when we have such different perspectives. It's not about my paranoia or the mindset of being a horror freak. It's about the fact that she might get hurt.

If there's someone out there looking to hurt her, I don't know what I would do.

"Carmen, *that thing* is concerning," I begin to explain. "I know I worry a lot about you, but that's all I know. It has nothing to do with me trying to be Mami or thinking I can do a better job at protecting you. It doesn't even have anything to do with me not trusting you to keep yourself safe. I worry because I'm your big sister, and I know you've been acting out recently. I don't know what it is or if it has to do with what happened last year with Cerys and Brian, but you've been different, and I worry."

"Mabel . . ."

"This is something you're never going to be able to experience or understand. For you, all your life I've been there, checking your every move, guiding you, babysitting you. But, for me, it's different, I chose to do those things because I've loved you since the day you were born. I was barely a toddler when Mami *y* Papi brought you home, but I remember getting to hold you when you were a baby. I've always wanted you to be safe, and even though you're an adult now, sometimes I still see you as that little baby and I get scared that the world will somehow harm you."

Carmen's eyes well with unshed tears, red rimming the edges as she looks at me.

"I love you, Mabby," she whispers. "I'm sorry that I'm such a brat and I give you so many headaches. I know you worry about me, but—"

"Shh ... it's fine," I tell her when her voice breaks, wrapping my arms around her frame to hold her tight. A faint scent of alcohol comes off her body, and my concern for her increases. It's not like her to get so emotional. Her chest heaves with a shudder, and I rub circles on her back. "I get it. I can be a little intense, and I'm sorry too. I would lose my mind if anyone hurt you."

She lets out a choked noise, a sob mixed with something I can't decipher.

"I'm sorry I said that stuff today," she repeats. "I know I can't understand what being an older sister is like, but I also know I've always been spoiled by you. It's not fair of me to do that."

"It's okay," I brush it off. While her words hurt earlier, I'm aware we both said things we now regret. I know she does, so I don't intend to punish her for it. We've spent too long being apart in the past months to dwell on things that were said in the heat of the moment. "I know you don't truly mean it."

"No, I don't," she agrees. "I just ... I've had a lot going on."

"But, Carmen," I beg for her attention, softly lifting her from my chest so I can examine her face. Tears edge her brown eyes, crystalizing them. "I know something's wrong. If anyone hurt you, you can tell me. I promise, you can trust me; you can tell me anything. I'm here for you."

Her eyes soften and her lips tremble.

"Mabel, I—"

For a moment, I think she's about to confess what's been driving her away from me, but then her phone buzzes on her lap and her gaze drops to look at the screen. It's merely a second, yet it's enough for me to tell the spell is broken. Carmen's brows knit together, and she unlocks her phone screen to show me the message she just received.

It's from Bethan.

SOS. I need you and Mabel to meet me at Theta's in 10.

Another message arrives.

ASAP.

I frown.

There's one rule of Kappa that I've never taken lightly, and it's the use of the SOS. It doesn't matter who uses it, the moment it's invoked, you have to drop everything and go to the person who sent it. It means they're in desperate need of help.

Worry sets in my stomach again, making me nauseous.

The last time I saw Bethan before I came up here with Danny, she was talking to Cerys. What if something happened to them while Danny and I were too busy being horny? Oh God. We completely lost all perspective on what we came here to do in the first place. We were supposed to keep an eye on them to make sure they were safe.

"We have to go," Carmen announces, motioning to stand up.

"Wait." I grab her arm, stopping her from standing. I

want her to feel like she can confide in me about anything. "You wanted to tell me something."

She shakes her head, disregarding the topic. Her protective mask is back in place and there's nothing that will sway her. I've seen it too often when we were growing up.

"It's nothing."

"Carmen."

She rolls her eyes. "Don't start again, please. We just kissed and made up. Let's not have another unnecessary argument."

My heart deflates at her tone, but I let it pass only because Bethan's message has made me uneasy.

"Will you tell me later?" I ask Carmen.

Reluctantly, she agrees to my request, and we leave the room together. Anxiety solidifies in my stomach, making me feel as if I've swallowed a ball of nerves. I have a bad feeling about this, but I keep it contained because Carmen would simply say it's my paranoia. It only takes us a few minutes to get out of Kappa and, before I can process it, we're passing by the fountain where they found Brian's body.

My feet stop moving altogether and I stay locked in the memory of that morning. If I close my eyes, I'm sure I'll be able to picture his mutilated body hanging off the statue, gutted and with the accusation written on his torso. It's been weeks, perhaps months, since I've thought about that morning. The morbid part of me was too transfixed by the image until Danny pulled me away. It's odd to witness real death and then carry on playing pretend in movies. Every time I see some gnarly blood splatter on set, I compare it to Brian's body, and I use it for reference.

Am I a bit sick for that? Possibly.

Yet it's a different thing to think about his death when miles away than to stand in front of where his body was found and ponder what he looked like. I hate that he was killed before Cerys had the opportunity to clear her reputation. While it means he doesn't get to hurt anyone else, it sucks that it ruined her life, even though she had nothing to do with it.

"Are you coming or what?" Carmen puts a hand on her hip, staring at me impatiently.

I blink, snapping out of my trance.

"Yeah," I mumble, forcing my legs to take one step and then another.

The rest of the way to Theta goes by in the blink of an eye. The front door is ajar, and we sneak in through it. Pink neon fairy lights glow from the archways, guiding a path from the foyer to the main hall and the grand stairs at the far end that lead to the bedrooms. A projector is nailed to one of the walls, flashing the beginning of a romantic comedy that I've seen too many times. If it weren't for the sound of voices coming from the living room, I'd say the house was empty. Everyone else seems to be in Kappa for the event or have gone out on dates.

After all, it's Valentine's Day.

Although the house is prettily decorated in a lighthearted spirit, there's an underlying feeling I can't quite shake from my body. Something bad will happen, I'm sure of it. I don't like how the text sounded nor what it implies, and considering the threatening letters I forgot about during my moment with Danny, I'm almost certain this is where things will start to go downhill. I've studied the art of filmmaking and worked in horror long enough to know this is the part where the audience experiences the beginning of the second act.

Where the conflict hits and everything goes to shit.

Or maybe my paranoia has gotten the better of me and I'm presenting symptoms of impending doom. It's possible I might need to schedule an appointment with a therapist after I return home because this isn't healthy behavior. Coming back here, remembering what I experienced in Westbrook, has pushed me over the edge. I'm beginning to understand why Carmen is so annoyed at me for worrying too much about her well-being.

I shouldn't be so paranoid and freaked out over a text message, but I am.

Something about it doesn't feel quite right.

Walking into the living room, I'm surprised by the small crowd of people that are already here.

Apparently, Carmen and I weren't the only ones Bethan texted, because behind her I spot Leighton and Elodie. Sitting on a couch with two guys I don't recognize are Zelda and Sophia. Across from them, I recognize Seth, sprawled over the couch with a red cup in his hand. His presence irritates me the most because he was Brian's best friend. I spent a long time hearing him defend his disgusting buddy. Next to him, there's another guy I vaguely remember from Delta. Was his name Ollie? I think it might be Ollie, short for Oliver. I don't know him, other than by sight.

Danny and Cerys are standing in a corner near the electric fireplace.

And in the darkest part of the room, I spot the guy that approached me at the event. His gaze locks on Carmen and me, and I can't shake away the bad vibes he gives off. Especially after the off-handed comment he made about him telling Brian he should've gone for me instead of Cerys.

I grab Carmen's hand and pull her with me toward Cerys and Danny, ignoring her protests.

"Hey, what's going on?" I ask them.

Cerys' expression changes from a frown to a bright smile. Her eyes light up with an excited gleam, and before I can process it, she hugs me tightly. Instantly, I relax into her hug, allowing the familiarity to help soothe my nerves. If she can stand here with all these people who made her life hell and still manage to smile, I can do it too.

For her.

"It's so good to see you," she whispers in my ear. A pang of pain spreads along my chest. I've been such a bad friend to this gentle soul. She deserves better than this. Better than me. "We have so much to talk about."

Instinctively, my eyes dart to Danny behind her. He's watching our interaction closely with a small smile. I notice his hair is messier than it was earlier, probably from my fingers grabbing it as he licked me less than an hour ago. I wonder if he can still taste me on his tongue.

Oh, Cerys, you have no idea how much we have to talk about.

I make a note to update her on everything that's happened, both in LA and tonight, after this is over. I know I haven't been a good friend to Cerys. But I badly want to rekindle our friendship because she's been a pivotal part of my life. And my introduction to Danny too.

Carmen takes the opportunity to sneak out of my hold.

"What are you doing here?" she questions Cerys with a

frown. "And you," she motions at Danny, "am I going to be forced to see you everywhere now? Wasn't it enough to find you going down on my sister?"

I cringe at my sister's bluntness and loud voice. Not only does it carry across a room thanks to her theater training, but Mami used to say that Carmen was born with a megaphone in her vocal cords because her regular tone is louder than the average. It does wonders for her career, but it's hell when she's not actively trying to be discreet.

Like now.

Cerys' blue eyes open wide and her jaw drops.

Danny's face acquires a darker hue. The tips of his ears pinkening and almost matching the shade of the lights from the foyer.

"I feel like I missed a chapter here."

"I'm going to kill you," I grit out at Carmen. "Have some discretion."

My sister rolls her eyes. "It was disgusting," she tells Cerys.

My best friend smirks at me, enjoying the revelation.

"Stop talking," I beg Carmen. "But what *are* you doing here?" My question is directed mostly at Cerys, since I'm guessing Danny is here because he wanted to keep an eye on her. Especially if she was going to be summoned into an empty frat house.

It reeks of bad news.

Cerys and Danny exchange a look.

"Well, that's the thing," Danny starts, scratching the back of his neck. "Shortly after I left Carmen's room, I received a message from Cerys asking me to meet her here. And she got a text from you."

I frown.

Why would I send her a text to meet her here, of all places? It makes no sense. I wouldn't ask her to come to Theta house. If I had wanted to speak to her in private, I would've asked her to go to Carmen's room. Here? No, it wouldn't have happened. Never. But it doesn't matter, because I didn't send anyone a text. I haven't touched my phone since I went to the Kappa event.

"From me? We're here because Bethan texted us."

This scenario is all wrong. The theory I had built with the letters begins to morph with the texts. They're not threats, but they have a clear intention to bring us all here, together. There's no reasonable explanation this, especially when these groups of people don't have much in common.

And if the pattern repeats for everyone else, if none of them sent the texts, then who did?

The ball of anxiety in my stomach begins to roll around the walls.

Something isn't adding up.

"Guys, you gotta be careful with that duo there. They'll start making up lies about you that will get you killed." Seth's voice carries through the living room, reaching us in our corner. He's talking to the guys sitting next to Sophia and Zelda, but it's clear he meant for us to hear. "What are they even doing back here?"

Cerys' body stiffens and she shrinks into herself, taking a step back to almost hide behind Danny's broader frame. It breaks my heart that she has to constantly make herself appear less to avoid the hateful confrontations. I don't know how she manages to survive in so many hostile environments and still remain the sweet person she is. Lord knows I would've lost the plot a long time ago.

Her reaction triggers the protective instinct in me.

"Oh, shut up," I snap at Seth.

If I could erase someone from this place, it would be him. I can tolerate Sophia and Zelda and their bitchy comments, but Seth? He makes my blood boil with rage every time he dares to open his mouth. Because I know he's going to spew some hatred to idolize his trash friend.

"No, he has a point, what are you all doing here? Didn't half of you, like, graduate already?" Sophia chips in. "It's kind of creepy to hang out at our parties."

I hate to admit she has a point. Danny and I graduated last year, and Cerys would've been close to it as well if she hadn't dropped out. We're officially those people who peaked in college and continue to hang around campus, trying to get a shred of the high and thrill we experienced during those years. The losers.

At least that's what it looks like from their perspective.

We wouldn't be here at all if the person who sent us the letters hadn't twisted our arms with threats.

"Let's not start an argument," Bethan cuts in, lifting her hands. "Is this why you told us to come here? To make Kappa's guests uncomfortable?"

I'm shocked that she has chosen to step up for Cerys and me. I guess their serious conversation had more weight than I was expecting it to. Maybe Bethan has done some inner work during the past year and realized her mistakes. It doesn't absolve her from completely abandoning Cerys when she needed her the most, but it's a step in the right direction. At the end of the day, it's up to Cerys to decide if Bethan has earned her forgiveness or not.

Seth smiles. "I didn't tell you to come here, sweetheart."

"Wait, what?" She tilts her head with confusion and spins around to look at everyone. "Who told you all to come here?"

Everyone says a different name in response.

Uncertainty grows in my system, spreading through every limb. This doesn't feel right. With every second I spend standing here, my instinct to flee grows. Maybe I should've convinced Carmen to flee this place when we still had the chance. Even if it meant we could be stuck on a road somewhere. I wouldn't say I have some sixth sense when something's wrong, but after everything I've been through, I've developed the ability to pick up on when certain situations promise danger.

And this is one of them.

The blond guy is still staring at me, not engaging with the conversation unfolding before us. He's solely focused on me, and it makes the hairs at the nape of my neck stand up, a wave of goosebumps erupting down my spine.

I don't like this.

"We should go, guys," I suggest, only loud enough for Cerys, Danny and Carmen to hear.

The last thing I need is for someone else to catch the urge to go. Not when we can be followed out of here. God, now I don't know what to do. Every option seems to come with risks I don't want to face. If we stay here, it promises danger. But if we leave, danger might still be looming behind us.

What to do when every option seems daunting? Not even my horror knowledge can help me here because, for instance, the characters probably wouldn't even acknowledge something is sketchy. Not until the conflict hits and Act Two begins.

I bite the edge of my nail to release some of the increasing tension coiled in my body. The relief I got from Danny earlier is gone, leaving only the memory. But it's not enough to help me forget the anxiety rattling my system, keeping me alert.

"Well, it's clear that one of us has to be lying," Bethan points out, crossing her arms. "There's no way we would all be here if no one sent the texts."

"Come on, Beth. You don't have to act like you don't know who gathered us here. There's only one big liar in here," Seth says, pointing at Cerys, and then looking at me and flaring his nostrils. "Well, maybe two."

"Oh no," Cerys whispers, closing her eyes.

It doesn't take a genius to see she regrets ever coming back to Westbrook. No matter how much she fades into the background, someone always wants to make her life a living hell. I hate that Brian's death only made that worse for her. She doesn't get to experience a level of peace that should come with his death, because no one can clear her name. The justice system failed her before, and it continues to do so over and over again.

The only way she could get the chance for a shred of justice is if the real killer showed up and owned their actions.

"Cerys, why don't you tell us why we're here?" Seth stands up and motions her to walk to the center of the room. She remains hidden behind Danny, avoiding Seth's attempts to lure her into an unsafe and exposed position. "Or better yet, why don't you tell us why *you* are here? It's surprising given the crybaby act you pulled last year. I know you managed to fool the police into thinking you didn't kill Brian, but you don't fool us here. We all know murderers come back to revisit the crime scene."

"Watch what you say, asshole," Danny steps in, his chest puffing out.

"Or what?" Seth dares him with a shrug. "What will you do about it? Make us talk about our little feelings?" he mocks. The guys next to Zelda and Sophia laugh at his remark. "Oh, I get it. Did she let you tap it? I admit she has a nice piece of ass, but . . ." He pauses. "I'd be careful if I were you. She might've returned to kill you the same way she killed Brian."

His comment triggers everyone in the room. Danny takes a step forward, and I'm sure he's going to punch Seth by the way his right fist begins to rear back, but Cerys catches his arm in time. It's surprising how her small frame can have the strength to make him pull back.

Bethan's voice screams for everyone to calm down as the two guys that were next to Zelda and Sophia jump to their feet, ready to defend Seth.

It's all a mess.

My heart races in my chest. I turn to check on Carmen standing next to me, but she has retreated a few meters away.

And just as I think things can't get any worse, the lights go out.

Chapter 10

A SCREAM CUTS THROUGH THE DARKNESS, FOLLOWED BY a thud, and I flinch. Instinctively, my hand reaches for the person next to me, and I relax slightly when I recognize Danny's touch meeting mine. In the midst of the chaos, he came to find me. His fingers intertwine with mine as he gives me a comforting squeeze that acts like a protective blanket around my terrified heart.

"Oops, sorry. I dropped my phone," the screamer excuses herself, and I recognize the voice as Leighton's.

Relief washes over me, and I let out a long sigh. My lungs relax with the breath, deflating along with the adrenaline coursing through my system.

"It's fine," Danny speaks up, and he gives my hand a reassuring squeeze. While he's jumping right into his leading role, he's silently offering me his vote of confidence. One thing about Danny is that, no matter the situation, he always slips into the leading role. He's always been good at working with people and guiding them, which is something not easily cultivated in the Greek Row environment. It's often a competition masquerading as siblinghood. However, Danny does it naturally, giving his best to those around him, even in the stickiest of scenarios, like the one we're in now. "It's just a blackout."

Although his tone is strong and convincing, I notice a subtle waver in his voice. Is he lying? I think he is, and I can guess why. Danny, Cerys and I came back to Westbrook because we received threatening letters; then there were the texts asking us to come here, and now, with the lights, it's all too much of a coincidence. We're stuck in a perfect horror scenario.

I feel a twinge of pain behind my ribs when I realize how tonight's events got twisted from what they were supposed to be. Danny and I failed Cerys and Carmen. Instead of taking care of them like we had agreed to, making sure they didn't get themselves into any trouble tonight, we ended up hooking up. Then, we willingly brought them to this place, when we should've caught on that it was a trap.

We were stupid.

"Actually, it's not a blackout," Carmen points out. "You can hear the party outside."

I close my eyes and focus. Behind all the rustling and our heavy breaths, you can hear the background hum of the music coming from Kappa's house. The statement falls into the pit of my stomach, dragging it to the soles of my feet. If the rest of Greek Row has electricity, it means someone shut the main lines here.

The house was tampered with.

This can't be a coincidence.

The feeling of impending doom returns to me, drilling into my bones.

I shouldn't have come here in the first place.

Danny's hand abandons mine and I hear his footsteps move to my right. A second later, the flicking noise of the light switch echoes in the house. He's testing the lights, but nothing turns on.

We would be in total darkness if it weren't for the faint pink fairy lights taped up in the hall. But they're barely any source of illumination when the house is drowned in shadows. The space is too big to be lit by small bulbs. If anything, the faint pink glow makes the scenario seem even creepier.

Leighton turns on her phone's flashlight, brightening the room.

"Right, I'm out of here," one guy says, stomping out to the hall. I step back, feeling the flat wall behind my back, and lean against it, hoping to find some balance. Anxiety spreads in my brain, tingling down my body, and it increases when I hear the doorknob rattling. He returns a moment later, yelling, "What the fuck? Did you lock the door when you came in?"

The question is directed toward Carmen and me.

After all, we were the last ones to show up to this place. Everyone was already here, so I can understand how suspicious it looks. Locking the door behind us would've been easy, but they're missing an important factor here. How could we have known that everyone was gathered there? We had no way of making sure everyone had responded immediately to our summons.

I shouldn't even be wasting time on their stupid theories. I should be focusing my attention on trying to solve this mystery before anything bad happens. It's only a matter of time before the other shoe drops.

"Of course not," Carmen responds curtly. "Why would we do that?"

"We can't leave? What about the back door?" Sophia asks, her voice slightly wavering. More rattling follows and I hear people attempting to budge the door open. "Or the windows?"

"No point even trying." Bethan crushes the idea before anyone moves. "We struck a deal with Theta about having a completely closed afterparty, so we would have only one entrance and closing the others to prevent non-Greeks from sneaking in. And they like to put on the storm shutters for their parties."

"Shit, the noise," I mumble under my breath.

I had forgotten that Theta house is well known for their incredibly loud parties. To prevent getting shut down by the police, they would put on storm shutters. It drowns out the noise coming from the house, plus it prevents drunk kids from getting wild ideas. One time, I saw one of the frats try to throw their mattresses from the second floor, so it seemed like a reasonable precaution.

Now? It only makes the paranoia in me spike.

We're trapped in here with no way out.

If the shutters weren't locked in place, we could crack a window open and sneak out. Instead, we're stuck. I'm not sure if there's a way to escape through the shutters. It would take a lot of effort and tools I'm pretty sure we don't have.

"I'm going to see if I can find some flashlights," Danny announces, once again taking the lead.

"How do you know they have any?" Elodie questions with a shake in her voice.

"Every house on Greek Row is required to keep flashlights in the house," Danny responds, his voice soothing.

Maybe it's my horror fanatic coming out, but it unnerves me that he's volunteering to venture into the darkness to find flashlights. I understand we *need* them. But it's always when people start to split up that bad things happen. I'm not prepared to lose him when I just got him, when we've finally found each other. We haven't even begun to establish a relationship, and now I'm scared to death something will happen to him if he goes alone.

"I'll go with you," I chip in, even though I know that volunteering to go into a dark part of a house isn't the correct move.

It never is.

There are rules in every horror movie scenario. Key points to ensure your survival, no matter what or who you're facing. One of them is to never volunteer to go anywhere, *especially* just before things begin to go downhill, like they are now. This is usually the part when the audience yell at the people on the screen not to make that decision.

Yet I'm doing it because maybe, if I go with him, things won't go downhill at all. Maybe two negatives can turn into a positive, or however that math rule works. It's possible that this just ends up being a movie I've created in my mind, another of my scripts where I've self-inserted myself as a character.

Right?

God, I hope so, because I'm not prepared to handle the opposite.

Danny grabs both of my hands, lifts them to his lips, and presses a kiss on each of them. I can barely see his eyes with the dim glow of the pink lights, but they're staring deep into mine. What I find in his puppy gaze isn't the reassurance I'm looking for.

I frown.

What's going on? Is he about to reject me?

"No, you stay here, Mabs," he says in a soft but firm voice. "I'll go with one of the guys."

The V between my brows deepens to the point where I swear they touch each other.

One of the guys?

Why would he go with one of the guys when just a few minutes ago they were about to come to blows? It doesn't seem like a logical choice. He can't be thinking straight.

"What? Why?" I question immediately, clutching his hands so he doesn't get to rush away before we've had a chance to discuss this.

I need one more minute to think about this.

It's such a rash decision.

Danny wets his lips and subtly tilts his head toward Carmen and Cerys. He's trying to say something without putting it into words. It takes me a second, but I get what he means. He's telling me to stay here with my sister and my friend—in case anything happens.

The *just in case* attitude makes my stomach constrict painfully.

Reluctantly, I let his hands slip away from mine. He calls out to Ollie—probably the best option he has—so they can go together. He uses the excuse that he will need someone to help him raid the closets or perhaps a storage room, and they disappear down the hall seconds later, their voices fading with each step they take going farther away.

"Can anyone call someone to get us out of here?" I ask, forcing myself to be the spokesperson now Danny has left.

We can't simply sit and do nothing. We have to get out of here as soon as possible, and the only way to do it is to ensure someone speaks up and guides the group. It doesn't matter that in a few hours the house will be plagued with college students looking to party. A lot can happen in a few hours. After all, the best slasher movies have a runtime of an hour and a half. The shorter the better. It raises the stakes, and it assures the audience that the bloodshed will be quick.

From nowhere, the image of Brian's butchered body flashes into my brain. How long did it take for him to die? His senator father never allowed the records of his autopsy to be revealed to the public, but I saw the body firsthand. If the wounds were inflicted quickly, it wouldn't have taken him too long to bleed out.

The shudder running down my back jolts me back to reality.

I need to stop thinking about blood when I'm on the edge of having a panic attack over being in a potentially dangerous situation.

"Anyone?" I insist, watching the multiple screens light up in the darkness.

"I can't," Elodie mumbles. "I have no service."

Someone scoffs.

"I keep telling you to switch from that shitty company. You never have service," Zelda retorts, and then lets out a loud *oh*. "That's weird."

"What's weird?" I press.

This isn't the time to be cryptic. Can't they just get to the point?

With every second, I find myself closer to the edge of hysterics. I can hear a giant clock ticking at the back of my brain, like a bomb about to go off and blow us to pieces.

"I don't have service either."

My hands move to find my own phone, and I see that not only do I not have phone service, but my battery is running dangerously low. I spent a lot of my time texting Carmen before I found her, and then I forgot to find a place to charge my phone while I waited for the party to begin. What was I thinking? This is such a rookie move.

I was hoping I wouldn't be in this position, I remind myself. Because it's the truth. The entire day I've been trying to convince myself that nothing is wrong, and I'm caught up in delusional scenarios. No one in their right mind would consider this a reality. It seems even stupider when put into words. *Oh, yeah, I received a threatening letter, went to a party, hooked up with my crush, only to end up trapped in a stupid frat house with people I would rather not be with.*

Not one soul in the world would believe this.

I'm not even sure I do.

"Wait, no one has phone service?" Bethan asks, her voice pitching. Worry is present in her words. "Oh God, they said this would happen," she laments, pacing around the room. Her breath shortens and becomes louder, hitching with panic.

"What do you mean?" Cerys asks her. She's the only one daring to press her when she's in this chaotic state. "Beth, what do you mean?"

Bethan lets out a small whimper. "I got this letter a few days ago, telling me to quit being president of Kappa or bad things would happen to my friends. They sent me a photo of the chapter; we all had our eyes cut out. I thought it was a sick joke. It had to be, right? What was I supposed to do? Quit because some random person decided to play psycho?" Her voice cracks, both from fear and emotion. "I'm sorry. I didn't mean to put us in danger."

I hold my breath with this new information.

Bethan received a letter. Similar to the one Cerys received, but with a clearer threat. Hers had a motivation—to make her quit her role. This keeps getting more and more confusing with every letter.

What does Bethan have to do with any of this? What does the role of president of Kappa have to do with the rest of the letters? She hasn't done anything *that* impactful. Yes, she made the questionable choice to shun Cerys when she needed her the most, but that seems like an isolated event that has no impact on anyone else. It doesn't seem to have a correlation with Cerys because people praised her for it. Even then, I wouldn't say she's a terrible president. Bethan isn't my favorite person in the world—forgiveness doesn't come easy to me—but she's an adequate enough leader for Kappa.

Again, what is her role in this?

What is the sender's motivation for doing all this? Nothing seems to make sense.

"You too?" Cerys voices my thought.

"What do you mean? Has anyone else received a letter?" Bethan inquires. She suddenly stops pacing.

"Yeah," I admit, hugging myself. "Cerys, Carmen and I."

And Danny, I think, but I don't expose him when he's not here to volunteer that piece of information himself. Cerys knows about this too, but she doesn't tell them either.

At my side, Carmen lets out a low groan. She still doesn't want to believe in this conspiracy, even when it's right in front of her. By now, it's too much information thrown together to not mean something.

"I got a letter too," Leighton sheepishly admits. "It freaked me out. All of our eyes were cut out from the photo. But it told me not to say anything."

Sophia, Zelda and Elodie join her, admitting they also got letters and were too scared to share them with anyone, even among themselves. Whatever their letters said, it caused enough fear to make them stay quiet about it when they're not renowned for being good secret-keepers.

The guys remain silent, watching this unfold between us.

If they received letters, they choose not to mention it, which makes me assume they didn't get anything at all. It means Danny was the only guy to receive a threat. Maybe because of his emotional connection to Cerys and me. It's possible he could've been used as a pawn to bring Cerys back, like they used Carmen to bring me here.

All the Kappa girls and a guy from Delta.

What is the connection here?

Being unable to put the puzzle together makes my teeth hurt and my stomach twist.

"Who sent the letters?" Bethan voices what we're all thinking.

Carmen pinches my ribs. She's telling me not to even think about mentioning my theory, but I disregard her. At this point, my madness doesn't seem too far-fetched.

"I think it was the killer," I speak up, even though my voice trembles. "Brian's killer."

"Hold on," Seth steps in, alerted by my statement. "We all know Cerys killed Brian. So that means she sent all of you bitches those letters and then tricked us into walking into her trap."

"Whoa, who even said that?" Carmen surprises me with how she turns on Seth. Her tone is laced with anger, almost sounding dangerous with the way her words slither out of her mouth. Her sharp tongue carving the words, daring him to say anything else.

"For the last time, I didn't kill anyone!" Cerys exclaims, frustrated with the accusation. "Why would I kill him when I know I would be the only suspect?"

"Well, you've always been crazy," Seth says back.

"Already lying about how he abused you, when we all know he wouldn't have done that. Hell, he wouldn't even have touched you if you'd been begging for it. Or maybe that's it. You begged him to give it to you, and when he said no, you decided to destroy his reputation."

Acid slides down my throat, fueling the fire boiling my blood. How fucking dare he? Brian was a nasty piece of shit whose reputation wasn't even harmed by Cerys' accusation, no matter that the rape kit she got had traces of his DNA. He carried on with his life, probably drugging other girls. It's nauseating to hear Seth defend him. He always idolized Brian. I worry it's because he also likes to roofie girls and rape them when they're unable to defend themselves. Seth is as disgusting as his buddy used to be, and I hate that men like him get to walk the earth, facing no consequences for their actions.

They keep getting away with it.

My body reacts before my mind catches up with it. I step toward Seth, standing in the middle of the living room, and I slap him. Hard. The clap of my palm hitting his skin cracks in the darkness like a whip, and he recoils.

"You crazy bitch!" he seethes. "You're just as fucked-up as your friend. I wouldn't be surprised if you killed him together!"

All hell breaks loose.

He leans in, fists tights at his sides, and I fear he'll hit or push me. But I don't move out of his path.

Maybe I want him to hit me, so I have an excuse to harm him. I'm sure it wouldn't do any good, but it would feel amazing to unleash all my rage on him. Make him pay for his friend's sins. Or his. I have no doubt he has skeletons in his closet, but he keeps getting away with it. Someone who idolizes a rapist is most likely a rapist too.

Maybe it's my impulsive thoughts feeding me a narrative where I see some benefit in causing harm. I take a step forward with my chin high.

Bring it on, bitch.

I feel hands grabbing both of my shoulders, and it takes me a second to process that it's two different people reacting to protect me. Carmen and Cerys pull me back. The group starts arguing. I hear Carmen's voice telling Seth she will cut off his balls and make him choke on them if he dares to touch me; Sophia and Zelda accuse Cerys and I of being weird psychos, and Leighton begs everyone to stop fighting.

A loud scream pierces the atmosphere, making all my hair stand on end. It wasn't a scream telling us to stop fighting. No, there was pure horror and pain in it. Guttural and visceral. The scream is the bell announcing danger's arrival.

Everyone stops, turning in the direction of the noise. The back of my brain blasts an alarm, the warning present: something bad is approaching fast.

I hold my breath, bracing myself for what's to come. For the other shoe to drop.

Someone switches their phone's flashlight on, and by the slight movement, I recognize her as Zelda. When she switches it to the source of the scream, my heart stops beating.

The scene in front of my eyes almost makes me heave. Because the scream came from Elodie. Her eyes are widened, mouth hanging open, lips stained red. Her hands grab her chest where blood spills from between her fingers, making a spattering sound as it pools around her feet.

A figure stands behind her. Tall and covered from head to toe in black clothing, except for the face that's covered by a mask. It looks porcelain, resembling a statue, or perhaps a cherub—it's Cupid. They're wearing a Cupid's mask. And then, as if motivated by the attention around him, Cupid pulls out the knife from Elodie's back and plunges it directly in her chest, causing a mouthful of blood to projectile out of her. Spraying the people closest to her.

My body feels as if it is made of stone, limbs too heavy to move as Cupid kills Elodie. Tears sting behind my eyelids, but I can't stop watching as her body spasms and she bleeds out in front of us, life abandoning her. Someone killed Elodie and we're all just staring, unable to do anything to help her. A trapped breath collides with the sob erupting from my chest, choking me. Shock washes over me like a cold wave.

Everything I thought today, when I was theorizing that the letters promised mayhem and a bloody valentine, has come true. I wasn't being crazy or paranoid or too caught up in the possibility of a horror movie plot, because every suspicion has become a reality.

Loud shrieks buzz in my ears, and it's only by the vibrations in my chest that I realize I've joined them too. Cupid tilts their head and withdraws the knife, throwing Elodie's dead body to the ground. The thud of her weight hitting the floor booms in my body. Cupid is getting rid of the victim to find a new one. I can't allow it to be my sister or best friend. I grab their hands and pull them with me. I'm not sure where we're headed, I just know it has to be far from Cupid's reach.

We almost bump into the people around us as everyone scatters, running from the killer in the room. The rush of steps has slowed down, and it seems like the killer has decided to follow targets closer to them before chasing after us. I slow the pace as we slide into a dark room. My eyes are adjusting to the darkness, my senses heightened by the adrenaline, and I can make out the outline of a table. This must be the main dining hall. Gesturing at the girls to follow me, we run to the other side of the room, lowering to the ground in case Cupid decides to check if there's someone here. That way, at least it looks like the space is empty.

"Wait, wait," Carmen says once we're successfully hidden and can have a moment to think. "We need to defend ourselves."

"How?" Cerys asks, baffled at Carmen's suggestion. "That guy has a fucking knife!"

"Would you rather we scream and hide?"

"Yes!" Cerys exclaims. "You're literally five-foot-two and a theater kid. We stand no fucking chance, are you insane?" Slouching against a wall, she gasps for air as she starts sobbing. "Oh my God. This is my fault," she laments. "My letter—"

"We have no time for this!" Carmen cuts her off. "Let's hurry to the kitchen, see if we can find a knife or something."

I close my eyes, holding the bridge of my nose as I think.

Carmen is right. We can't run around the house completely defenseless when there's a killer chasing us, especially when said killer has trapped us inside this stupid house. God, I can't believe I'm in a near-death experience in a stupid frat house of all places.

This has to be one of the most pathetic horror scenarios

I've ever witnessed. Cinematically speaking, it would make a horrible film. The entire thing would be poorly lit. Not even a dark theater would help the viewer see what's happening or who's dying.

"What do you think?" Cerys turns to me, expecting guidance.

I arch my brows. "Why are you asking *me*?"

"You're kind of an expert at this."

"An expert?" I echo, aghast.

"You work on horror movies!" she reminds me.

"*Movies*, not real-life psychos!" I snap back.

But as much as I hate to admit it, she is right.

My experience might not be related to handling cold-blooded killers, but I've studied them for horror. When it comes to writing, I know the formula around a good slasher film, and I'm well aware of the rules on how to survive them.

No matter what, don't run up the stairs when you can escape through the front door.

A bit difficult to achieve considering we're trapped inside this house, but we can switch it to not put ourselves at unnecessary risk when we know we can't fight the killer. In the best-case scenario, we manage to hide until we're rescued.

No usage of alcohol or drugs.

It's a good thing I foresaw this night turning skewed because I've remained sober the entire time. However, this can't be said for my sister. When I hugged her back in her room, I smelled the alcohol oozing from her body.

Don't go anywhere alone, or volunteer to go anywhere; you'll be the first one to die.

Volunteer . . .

A lump forms in my throat and my heart falls to the pit of my stomach when a memory sparks in my brain. I had been so caught up in the panic of escaping the killer that I completely forgot about the fact that Danny volunteered to go find the flashlights.

He doesn't know Elodie has been murdered, let alone that there's a killer in the house.

But there's another fact clogging my airways.

We were all screaming, and yet he didn't return.

He didn't make it back.

Chapter 11

THE POSSIBILITY THAT SOMETHING DREADFUL MIGHT'VE happened to Danny sinks deep in me, scratching my bones and paralyzing my muscles. Time slows around me, dragging into nothingness. For a long second, I stay still as a new scenario builds in my brain. One that makes a wave of nausea roll in my stomach, almost pushing me forward with a dry heave. I press my tongue to the roof of my mouth as I inhale through my nose. We've been thinking Elodie was the first person to die tonight, but it might've been . . .

I shake my head, refusing to consider it.

No, there's no way Danny could've died. He was probably lost around the house when he heard the screams and then had to go into hiding like we did. Yes, that sounds like a better outcome. I'm not ready to think about anything other than a positive outcome. I *have* to think positively, because the alternative is to accept death as an absolute.

I'm not ready to die tonight.

Whenever people die young, the elders always comment on how they were barely getting started in life and had so much left to do and experience. I didn't actually think about it until now. I'm barely getting my career started. I haven't gotten to write a full-length script, direct the idea, see the film on the big screen. I don't own a house. Hell, I haven't even started paying off my student loans. There's so much of life I want to experience.

I can't die tonight.

And I sure as hell don't want the people that I love to die either.

If anything happens to Carmen or Cerys or Danny . . . I might lose my mind. I don't have the sanity to survive in a world without any of them. This last year, I've barely been a person. Surviving, but not thriving. If I lost them, I wouldn't even try to focus on other aspects of my life.

I would just . . . give up.

"Mabel." Carmen shakes my shoulder, pulling me back to reality. Her voice is firm, and it reminds me I don't have time to dwell on the possibilities of a future. I must focus on what I'm currently experiencing. "What do you think we should do?"

My sister's face is void of emotion. Where I expect to find fear, I find a mask of strength covering her features. In this moment of panic, she's risen above it, becoming the pillar and keeping me steady. Shock rattles through me. Since when has my little sister become such a strong woman?

But she shouldn't have to be the strong one.

I take a deep breath, push away all the anxiety in my body, and lock *in*.

We're being chased by a killer, yes, but I have enough experience to get us out of this. I might not be the final girl of this plot, but I can survive. Or I can get the people I care about to safety.

What was the question?

Right.

They're asking me what to do.

I consider the options.

We can't stay hidden here the rest of the night until the killer shows up for us, or we get rescued, whatever happens first. But we shouldn't venture around carelessly either.

I rub my forehead with my index finger as I try to remember the layout of this place. Usually, Greek Row houses tend to mirror each other in architecture, so it means it should be close enough to Kappa's. But I also tended to avoid spending time in houses where guys like Brian used to hang out. I think some houses got some remodeling done, but I'm unsure if it was something big or just some touch-ups.

If it wasn't anything major and they didn't change the overall layout of the house, if we're in the main dining hall, it shouldn't be hard to find the kitchen. Only a room or two over. In there, we could find some weapons to defend ourselves when Cupid comes for us.

Having a weapon would increase our odds of survival. Better than running around blindly, not knowing what to expect.

"Kitchen," I mumble. "We should go to the kitchen." Carmen's original plan.

This doesn't mean we're going to hunt down Cupid ourselves because, like Cerys said, Carmen is barely five-foot-two and a theater kid. I'm two inches taller, but it's not really like it would make any difference. The killer was taller than Elodie by at least a foot, and with the way they manhandled her dead body, I'd say none of us have the strength to face them.

"Good, that's good," Carmen agrees, bobbing her head.

"Wait, guys," Cerys halts us before we can even move. "How do we know the killer isn't going to—" Her words get interrupted by a loud, guttural scream.

Another victim.

"We gotta move. Now!" I say, pushing them to their feet.

Moving cautiously, but determinedly, we begin our journey through the house. Although it's easier said than done, considering Carmen is wearing platform shoes and they make a noise every time she steps. It doesn't matter how light she tries to tread on the floor, it echoes against the walls, alerting everyone in a three-mile radius about our position.

"Take them off," I whisper the order.

She doesn't have a choice here. It's too loud. Besides, if we have to run again, her shoes will slow her down. I know Carmen is balanced and way more coordinated than I could ever be, but I don't want to risk it. There's already too much at stake.

"Are you serious?" she questions.

"Yes! You're stomping."

"I'm not!"

"You kind of are," Cerys chips in. "And you both need to stop sistering while we're running from a murderer."

I roll my eyes, thankful for the darkness because they're not really paying attention to my facial expressions. After adjusting to the lack of lighting, I can spot the silhouette of their bodies, but not really their expressions.

"We're not sistering," Carmen protests, her tone slightly pitching with offense.

Cerys is right, though. We can't keep talking unnecessarily when we're trying to avoid being killed by a madman.

Biting the inside of my cheek, I keep myself in line, refraining from making any comments as Carmen takes off her shoes, holding them in her hands. She's probably clutching them as a defense tool. They're not as effective as a knife, but if a body comes running at us, the impact might slow them down.

Good thinking, sis, I praise her in silence.

Theta house is more difficult to navigate when it's in complete darkness and I'm unfamiliar with the territory. The floor plan is different than Kappa's, I notice, the second I turn left at a corner and end up hitting a wall where there should be an open hallway. Venturing deeper into the house, we cross a room that I guess is some type of games room. Cerys stubs her toe on the leg of a billiard table.

With every step I take, my anxiety rises to a new level. There haven't been any more screams after the second one, which means the killer is probably creeping around, looking for their next victim. I don't know what's worse, the sickening screams or the deathly silence. Is it wrong for me to say I prefer the screams? At least with someone making noise, albeit a horrifying one, I can tell if the murderer is nearby or not.

But with silence? There's nothing but the promise of a threat lingering over our heads. It's only a matter of time before we stumble upon the killer.

What if I'm leading them straight to the murderer?

My entrails grumble with nerves. Maybe I'm putting my loved ones in danger by guiding them in the wrong direction. Perhaps I should've ignored the rule of never heading upstairs. There are rooms to hide in on the second floor.

But what will you do in a room with no alternate exit? Nothing, my common sense reminds me.

It's the only thing keeping me going on the same course instead of rethinking the original plan. It doesn't matter if there are rooms upstairs to hide in because, if the killer finds us in one of them, there's no other way out, no way to escape. It's much worse to be trapped than standing in a hall with open passageways.

"Are we going the right way?" Cerys dares to ask in a barely audible tone, but it's loud enough to be heard under the fast and heavy stomps heading our way.

My heart bangs in my chest, faster as the milliseconds tick by. At my side, I can just about make out Carmen raising a shoe, preparing to throw it. I don't know if she has the arm power to cause anything other than a distraction, and I find myself wishing Danny was here with us. He was a pitcher for the Westbrook baseball team.

The wound in my soul stings at the reminder of him, but I push it away. No, I can't engage with any sad or distressing thoughts.

Danny's fine. He's probably stuck somewhere, hopefully hiding along with the rest. Yes, that must be it. He *has* to be okay.

Even though there's a golden rule about not trusting any romantic interests in slasher films, Danny is different.

The steps slow down as they near us, almost fading to a stop, before a figure springs around the corner, turning a flashlight straight at us. Before I can process who the person is behind the phone, Carmen throws a shoe at the figure, and it hits them straight on the chest. The person stumbles back, tripping over their feet. The fall is louder than it should've been, dramatically blasting across the hall.

Fuck.

I wince, bracing myself for the killer to rush here, but after a beat goes by, there's nothing.

I puff out, emptying my lungs.

It's Leighton.

She remains sprawled on the floor, her phone flashing at the ceiling. The sudden brightness hurts my eyes, and I hold a hand up to cover the harsh LED glare.

"Are you insane, Leighton?" Carmen mutters, picking up her shoe. "Turn that off, right now! You'll get us caught, you dumb cow."

Almost instantly, I elbow Carmen.

While I understand where she's coming from, she's being unnecessarily mean. Leighton is a sweet and sensitive girl. And, yeah, she's a bit dumb, but there's no need to insult her, even though her irresponsibility might get us killed.

Okay, maybe she does deserve it a little, but I still don't want to deal with any emotional tears.

"I'm sorry!" Leighton exclaims, louder than we need.

We shush her.

Leighton grabs her phone and struggles to turn the

flashlight off. In the moment of illumination, I take the opportunity to examine her. She fell, but she's unharmed. Her fair skin is spattered with blood. She was the one standing closest to Elodie when the killer appeared, so it makes sense for her to have Elodie's blood on her. Her eyes remain wide open, pupils dilated with shock. Harsh pink rims her lids, and her mascara has spread over her cheeks, the tears leaving black stains.

"Elodie's dead," she mumbles and begins to sob, reality setting in. Her thumbs hover trembling over the screen, but she still doesn't turn the flashlight off. "And then I lost Bethan . . . I'm just . . . I'm glad to see you girls."

A trace of empathy grows in my chest. I can't even begin to imagine what she must be going through. She just watched her friend get murdered in front of her and has been wandering around lost and panicked, with no one to rely on. Stained with the blood of someone she knew.

I crouch down to her level. Softly, I lay a hand over hers while the other grabs her phone. I need to turn the light off. I feel guilty about using comfort as a tool to get what I want, but she's close to a state of shellshock. Confused and lost.

"I'm sorry about Elodie," I begin to say, pulling the phone into my palm without breaking eye contact. The screen illuminates us, but I don't care to act before I know she's calm. "I know she was your friend."

I wish I could say more to ease her sorrows. I've remained emotionally distanced from this life long before I moved to LA. I'll remember Elodie as a sweet and gentle person. She deserved to live a full life, grow into a confident woman with a bright career. Elodie deserved the chance to explore a future. But, right now, with danger looming over us, I can't bring myself to grieve for her the way Leighton is.

I'm not sure I'll ever be able to.

"She is," she mumbles in agreement.

Her use of the present tense makes my soul twist painfully.

This will be something she won't completely heal from. It doesn't matter how much therapy she has, there's going to be a part of her that will always be trapped in this moment where she witnessed one of her closest friends get brutally murdered.

"We can't stay here on the floor, come on," I tell her, tugging at her hand to encourage her to stand up.

She doesn't have much of a choice. If it had been any other time, I would've let her stay on the floor for as long as she wanted, but we're in a vulnerable position. The corner isn't safe, someone could be hiding against the wall, waiting for the perfect moment to attack. I know because I did a film with Aidan where the killer ends up sneaking up on the group from a corner and then kills someone.

"Elodie's dead," Leighton repeats, withdrawing her phone from my hand. The flashlight is still on. "And you hit me with a shoe." She looks at Carmen like she should be ashamed of herself.

Carmen groans. "I thought you were the killer," she excuses herself.

"Do I look like the killer?" Leighton's voice rises half an octave. "I—*bleurgh!*" Her words get cut off, drowned in her throat.

Because just like in the movie, the killer sneaks from

around the corner and plunges a knife into Leighton's head. The blade disappears through her temple. Her eyes widen, the capillaries in them bursting. Red tears spill from them, mixing with the mascara on her cheeks. Her body spasms, the phone falling from her hands to the floor. The light shining from that angle creates grotesque shadows under her horror-petrified expression.

The killer withdraws the knife and blood—probably some brain matter too—splatters over my face, catching me off guard.

I flinch, staggering back.

And then, when the killer drops Leighton to the ground as the life spills from her, Carmen's shoe flies past my head, hitting him straight in the face.

Chapter 12

THE SHOE THUDS AGAINST CUPID'S MASK. THEN IT FALLS on top of Leighton's body, rolling into the large pool of blood. It feels wrong that it hit her corpse, as if we had somehow defiled it. I'm sure there has to be some sort of exemption for moments like this, though.

Jesus, this would make a really bad horror movie.

I was nine years old when I became interested in the genre. I stumbled upon an incredibly gory splatter film. I knew I wasn't supposed to watch it, but I was too hypnotized by the violence. I couldn't sleep. It didn't matter how hard I tried. Unable to remove an image from my eyes, perpetually burned into my retinas.

It's happening with Leighton's death.

I blink fast, processing Carmen's attack.

Gulping, I lift my gaze to the killer.

Cupid fixes the mask over his face to keep us from seeing his identity. It takes only a few seconds, but Cerys acts fast, pulling me backward through the hall.

"Wait," I mumble, looking at Leighton.

I don't want to leave her alone.

"We have to move. Now!" Carmen pushes me, looking over her shoulder.

"Your shoe, Carmen," Cerys tells her, slowing her pace. "Throw your other shoe at him!"

Carmen looks down at her hand where she's clasping her remaining heel. Turning around, she halts and lobs the shoe at Cupid. It hits him in the chest, makes him startle and trip over Leighton's body. He slips in her blood.

While the shoe doesn't stop him, it slows him down. It's enough to give us a solid head start as we run away. Cupid doesn't immediately come after us. I peek over my shoulder to see him almost skating over Leighton's blood.

My heart speeds up.

We can get away. I know we can.

Gaining distance from him, we run into an open room.

I can't completely make out where we are, but it seems to be a lounge. Something I've always found incredibly weird with Greek houses is how many rooms they have in which to just sit and do nothing. Some have a trophy room where they display the chapter's awards.

"I need a moment," Cerys begs, sucking in big gulps of air. "I feel like I'm gonna throw up."

She's not the only one.

"Over here." Carmen ushers us toward the back of a couch at the far end.

We slide into the hiding spot. It's not the place I would've chosen, but we don't have a lot of options. We still need to find the kitchen and a weapon, now that Carmen has lost both of her shoes, but this is enough to let us catch our breaths.

I press my hands to my chest, feeling the rapid thumping of my heart. The image of Leighton's death flickers back to me. The crunch of her brain being pierced ripples through my skull. I touch my cheek and feel the blood plastered on it.

I want to peel the skin off my face where her blood has begun to dry.

I feel sick.

Saliva pools in my mouth, and I hold my breath. I can't throw up. So I count to twenty and take another deep breath.

Poor Leighton.

She had just found us before her fate turned sideways. I wish we could've done more for her, especially considering we let a shoe drop on her fresh body. *Dios mío*, why did we let that happen?

"Is he coming?" Carmen whispers.

I focus on trying to locate the noise of his steps. The sound travels down the hall, echoing around the walls. I notice every creak in the house, our uneven breaths in the room, the faint hum of Kappa's music. But I don't hear the steps anymore. They've silenced to nothing, and I worry he's doing it on purpose.

It's the one clue I have at the moment: the killer knows how to walk in the house without making any noise, which means he has probably spent a lot of time in Greek Row. He also knew to trap us with the storm shutters. Knew our phone numbers and exactly which names to use to get us to come to Theta house.

It means he knows exactly where to find us. There's no place to hide in here. We can only run and hope he doesn't catch us. The realization falls deep in my stomach like a boulder, spreading a wave of pain through me.

"We have to get those knives," I mutter.

"No shit," Carmen spits back. "How are you planning on getting through Mr. Psychokiller?"

I open my mouth and then close it. I don't really have a plan.

"Maybe we should split up," Cerys suggests in a whisper.

I choke back a groan. "Have I taught you nothing?" I ask. "People die when they split up."

This is one of the golden rules in horror: never split up. If you want to ensure the group's survival or maximize the efforts, you should never part ways with your inner core. Going separate ways means someone ends up dying. It's usually the person who suggests it.

I want both Carmen and Cerys to have the best odds of making it out of here, but not like that.

"People are dying regardless!" Cerys exclaims.

"Lower your voice," Carmen hisses. "You're going to get us killed. Blondes already have a hard time staying alive in horror movies."

Surprise ripples through me. I always rambled on about horror movies at home, but I never thought my sister was actually paying attention to what I said.

"What else can we do, then? At least that way someone can distract the killer and the others follow the plan," Cerys questions, her voice muffled by a sob. I bite the inside of my cheek. When I don't answer, she says, "See? Even you think it's the only option."

I hate that my determination to stay together decreases with every second that passes. A ball of anxiety rolls in my stomach, making my muscles tremble. Splitting up is a stupid idea. While it means someone can stay behind to distract Cupid, it also increases the risk. What if someone else gets hurt? What if he's not working alone?

But Cerys' words drill into my head. It's a stupid plan, but we have nothing else.

I force my spine straight and take a deep breath.

"You guys go together, and I'll distract Cupid."

The nickname rolls off my tongue naturally. They don't seem to notice it, caught off-guard by my statement.

Carmen's hand clasps tightly around my wrist, refusing to let go. Her fingers almost cutting off my blood flow. Almost as if she feared I was going to run away immediately before giving them a chance to think about it. But I wouldn't do that. I know she'd try to follow me. The entire purpose of splitting up is to increase her odds of survival, not the other way around.

"No, you're crazy," she spits out roughly.

"Mabel, no," Cerys says. "*I'll* go. I'll distract him."

"No, I have to do it," I cut her off, shaking my head though I doubt she can see me. "I owe you."

My throat closes up for a second, and I struggle to clear it. This is counterproductive. We can't waste more time bickering about the logistics or my reasoning for splitting up. We simply have to do it.

"What are you talking about? You don't owe me anything."

"We're not splitting up. Both of you, cut it out," Carmen orders us. "We had a plan and we're sticking to it. Find a weapon and a place to hide. We'll do it together."

I want to protest, but Cupid's steps thump down the hall, nearing the doorway. My first instinct is to cover Carmen's mouth with my hand. I feel her breath hitch on my skin, but she doesn't make any noise. Adrenaline pumps at a rapid rate in my system, flushing through my bloodstream and heightening my senses. Time seems to stop as Cupid's steps stop abruptly. The sound too near for comfort.

He's found us.

I can feel Carmen shaking under my hands, her body jolting silently with fear. I just want to hold her and tell her everything is going to be okay. That I'll protect her.

Cupid paces around the room, the floor creaking under his weight. He's close now. His labored breathing hushes behind the mask as he walks slowly. A heartbeat passes by, and he moves away from the couch. The steps fade away. He's leaving.

Before I let Carmen go, I count to fifty to make sure he's not coming back and then let my shoulders sag with relief. By some miracle, we evaded death. I release my sister and sigh, feeling like I can finally breathe again.

"Can we go—" Cerys' words are cut off by her own horrified scream.

From above us, Cupid pulls Cerys' hair, hoisting her to the couch. Screaming, she kicks and tosses, trying to break free from his hold.

Both Carmen and I jump to our feet, springing into action. I check my surroundings to find something I can use to defend Cerys. My hands grab the first thing I can reach, a trophy of sorts, and I swing it at Cupid's head at the same time Carmen tries to smother him with a pillow. The trophy hits the back of Cupid's head, breaking apart, and I hear a muffled *oomph* as he slouches from the impact.

Cerys takes advantage of the attack and manages to wriggle away from Cupid's hold. She falls to the ground, sobbing as she crawls away from the couch.

"Let go!" I yell at Carmen, taking the pillow from her while I try to push it against Cupid's face to keep him distracted. "Take Cerys with you. Now!"

Carmen's bravado shatters in front of me, hesitant to follow my request. Her silence worries me for a second, fearing she will tell Cerys to screw herself. But I know Carmen's heart. She might be a little mean—quite a lot mean, actually—but deep down she cares. There's goodness in her soul, I've seen it. Even if she's not as fond of Cerys as I am, she's aware of how important Cerys is to me.

Because of my loyalty to her, Carmen will follow through.

"Mabby," she mumbles in a little voice that makes my heart ache.

"I'll find you later. I promise." I shouldn't be saying these words, I'm not sure I can keep them. But, for her, I'll try my hardest. Cupid pushes against the pillow, and I struggle to keep him down while I urge Carmen to go.

Carmen grabs Cerys by the hand and tugs her to her feet, despite her cries.

What I'm doing could be considered a suicidal act. I've

never dwelt on thoughts of ending my life, no matter how lonely and hard life got. Not even when all of Westbrook hated me for standing up for Cerys. So this sensation of courting death feels foreign. But I don't want my life to end so soon.

I have unfinished business.

I want to watch them go to safety, but Cupid catches my attention. His knife pierces the pillow between my hands. A yelp escapes from my lips. *Puñeta*. I don't have the strength to keep him down, let alone actually asphyxiate him, yet I put all my weight into it. Every second counts. It means the girls have a better chance of getting away.

The moment is short-lived because Cupid's knife rips through the pillow. The wadding spills between us, showering him with white fluff as he pushes his head between the hole of my arms. Shrieking, I leap backward just in time to avoid his knife. Cupid swings at me again, and I bounce back, startled when the blade misses me by an inch.

I look for the inner final girl I've tried to cultivate throughout my horror filmmakering career. It's not like I'll be a final girl tonight, but it gives me the motivation to slide a fearless mask over my face. A final girl is motivated by fear and adrenaline.

By their desire to live against all the odds.

And I *want* to live.

"Come on then, asshole."

Cupid raises his knife again and I back into a table. An idea springs into my brain. Grabbing the edge of the table, I push it in front of Cupid and then bolt for the door. I hear the rattle of things shattering in the room, but I refuse to look back. The need to put distance between us is bigger than my curiosity to see him struggle.

My chest heaves with every contraction of my lungs. Adrenaline tickles under my skin, buzzing with electricity. I have to keep running. Unsure of which way the girls chose, I run down the hall where Leighton was.

Running has never been my strong suit, yet I don't stop. My lungs churn and I'm gasping for air. I can't let him kill me.

Carmen needs me, I chant to myself. *I promised.*

I keep a hand stretched out to the wall, searching for an opening, an escape. But there's no place to hide. Not when he's following me. I glance over my shoulder and notice Cupid has forgotten about Leighton's body because he slips on her blood again, almost falling.

I don't want to say I'm glad Leighton's dead, but her body is helping me escape.

My hand hits the wedge of a doorknob, and I see my way out. I halt in my tracks, but it's too sudden. I miss the door and have to turn back, struggling to get it open before Cupid catches up with me. His steps get closer. I don't turn to look at him. They're always closer when you turn to look, so I stay focused on opening the door, fidgeting with the knob until I fling it open, slide into the tight space and snag it closed. But it's a fraction too late.

Cupid swings his knife in the air, wedging it between the frame and the door. The tip of the blade almost caresses the skin between my brows, and I choke back a scream. It's a close call. I pull the door harder, using my entire body weight to fight against Cupid's strength.

I don't know if it's the adrenaline or a miracle, but Cupid retracts the knife, and it allows me to close the door. I breathe for a moment, feeling the relief of managing to win this round until I realize this door doesn't have a lock.

I'm still in a vulnerable position here.

Keeping my hold tight on the door handle, I hoist my leg against the wall to form an anchor.

Cupid tries to budge the door open, but I remain strong until he lets go. I stand close to the door, but not near enough for a blade to go through. I've watched too many movies where the character tries to listen through the wood, only to get stabbed in the head.

I would rather keep my head intact.

But still I wait and listen for his steps to move away from the door. It takes a minute, maybe more. Or perhaps less. Time has become a foreign thing since the attack happened, and I've lost all track of how it moves. It's possible it's just been a handful of minutes since Elodie died.

Outside the door, I hear Cupid walking away. I'm tempted to slide it open only a sliver to make sure he's really gone, but I don't. I stay put. It's always when the characters lower their guards that the killer makes a comeback.

I count sheep in my mind as a distraction from what I've witnessed. Every muscle of my body shakes with adrenaline and fear, my senses heightened by the events. Somehow, I survived this chase. Although it's possible he never intended to kill me now. Maybe I'm one of those deaths that occur later in the movie when you've already gotten attached to the character, just when you think they'll make it out alive.

My stomach twists.

I lower my leg to the floor and step backward into the room, meeting its end a moment later. It has to be a closet of some kind. I pull out my phone, pointing the screen around. I don't want to waste the battery when it could be of more use later. There's barely any juice left. I'm guessing it won't be long until I press the on button and it doesn't spark to life.

I'm distracted by the cleaning products and the mop next to me. It's a mistake. The gentle creak of the doorknob twisting vibrates in my ears.

I hold my breath and the door swings open.

Chapter 13

EVERY CELL IN MY BODY STOPS WORKING. ICE CRYSTALIZES in my veins, freezing my muscles, paralyzing me, even though I should shield myself from the imminent danger.

I don't want to die young. But it appears this is my fate. My heart feels heavy. I haven't gotten to unlock my real potential.

I squeeze my eyes shut and brace myself.

But the impact never arrives.

The piercing blade doesn't come anywhere near my body.

Instead, I hear the closet door shutting as someone steps inside. Even with my eyes closed, I sense a bright light flickering on, illuminating the tight space. Fearing that I'll see the blood-stained cupid mask mocking me, I flutter one eye open.

I don't trust the first glimpse I get of the person in front of me. *Puppy eyes.* I'm afraid it's part of a hallucination, something my brain came up with as a coping mechanism to give me a slice of heaven before I meet horror. A lot of people, at least in movies, tend to hallucinate beautiful images before death meets them, so this must be one of those occasions.

It's what my heart desires the most, I guess.

Just some peace of mind before I die.

Sweet caramel staring back at me.

"Mabel."

A sob escapes from my lips before I can hold it back when I hear Danny's voice, confirming I'm not just imagining things. Unless my brain has the cruel capacity to trick me like this. The tears I've been holding back tonight finally spill free, probably washing away the blood staining my face. I throw myself at him, burying my face in the familiar chest as I fall apart into a million pieces.

His intoxicating scent sends a signal to my brain, letting it know I can let my guard down. Just for a moment.

"Oh, baby, are you okay?" he asks, wrapping his arms tightly around my body, so comforting it only makes me want to cry harder.

There's something about feeling safe after spending time guarding myself that makes me feel like I'm a child wanting to be cradled by a parent. I was never the kid who got to be protected by my parents. Not because they were neglectful, but they always considered me to be independent. Call it the oldest-daughter curse. Always having to be the toughest person in the room while also yearning for permission to be vulnerable.

And that's exactly what Danny is offering me when I need it the most.

I press myself harder against his chest, drowning the noises that threaten to come out of me. I don't want to make any sound, so I bite my lips and choke every sob and whimper. Not daring to look at Danny, I remain with my face hidden in his clothes. My tears must be wetting the front of his shirt, but I don't care.

Not right now.

I've seen death, been chased by a maniac with a knife. He almost stabbed me. It's a miracle I managed to find this spot just in time. I got away. Somehow, I got away. I don't know what superior forces are guarding me tonight, but I surely must've been doing something right. When I thought I was meeting my end, I escaped, and it led me to Danny.

God, Danny.

More tears spill from me, but they're not carrying sorrow. Instead, they wash out of me with relief. When Danny didn't make it to the living room when Cupid killed Elodie, I thought the worst. Usually, the first kill doesn't happen when the main group is gathered in a room. No, in films, the first death takes places before the chasing begins. Just a scene or two before, so it can set the mood and tone for what's yet to come.

And I thought . . .

I shake my head, brushing it away from my mind.

It doesn't matter now what I thought when he didn't make it back. Somehow, Danny made it back to me in one piece. That's all it matters.

"I'm so scared," I whisper in a choked voice as I hug him tighter.

The confession drags out of me in a breath, and I'm almost ashamed to verbalize it.

Does it make me weak? A part of me thinks so. If today is anything to go by, I'm not final-girl material. I'm not doing crazy stunts or making badass moves against the killer. I barely even made it into this closet, and even then it was by pure luck, and I'm still not sure it wasn't because Cupid allowed me to. Maybe he was saving me for a more impactful death later on.

"It's okay to be scared, baby," Danny assures me, rubbing circles on my back to calm me down. I don't know if it's because he's the one doing it, but it seems to work. My crying softens to silent tears with only the occasional hiccup shaking my shoulders. "It's more than okay. This is . . . fucked-up."

I almost laugh.

Yeah, fucked-up is one way of describing it.

"I thought he killed you first. When you didn't return—"

"I'm okay. I'm right here," he mumbles and presses a kiss on my hair. "I thought I lost you for a second. I heard the screams when I found the flashlights and by the time I made it back, everyone had left. There was only Elodie . . . And Elodie was . . ."

He can't bring himself to say it. I can't imagine what he must've thought when he ran back to the living room and saw all the blood and Elodie's gutted body. No one else to be found, not even the killer.

"Elodie was dead." We have to say it. Otherwise, she might fade away in the madness of everything that's occurred today. We have to acknowledge she was the first one to fall among us and treat it with the respect she deserves. "He appeared out of nowhere, I swear. One moment we were all arguing about Cerys because Seth was being an asshole. And then we heard the scream, and . . ."

My breath shudders as I sniff through the tears that return, even though I don't want them to. Why am I crying over Elodie? We weren't friends. I looked after her when she was my assigned little sister, but I don't feel overcome with grief. No, this is the shock of every horror I've witnessed tonight. The gruesome deaths and frightful chases.

"What happened after that?"

I lick my lips, thinking about the events.

It's hard to tell what happened first, what to add and what's not worth mentioning. Like all the screaming that unfolded, the panicking, not knowing what to do. It's not really like we were prepared for this situation. Who would be ready to face a killer? Certainly not me, regardless of what people might think. My association with the slasher genre is purely theoretical, so I would take my expertise with a grain of salt.

Especially after I ran away from the killer in a totally pathetic way.

I'm even more sure now that I'm not cut out to be a final girl. Maybe a supporting character who somehow makes it alive to the end, albeit injured. Or one of those characters who doesn't have a confirmed death, and is revealed to be miraculously alive in one of the multiple sequels. I could settle for that.

"I grabbed Carmen and Cerys, got out of there as fast as we could. I think he killed someone else, one of the guys, but we were focused on getting away, so I didn't check. The girls and I had a plan, but then the killer appeared again."

Leighton's frozen expression flashes into my mind. No longer capable of conjuring up distracting thoughts, I relive the experience for the hundredth time. *Dios mío*, will there be a moment in the future where I don't think about Leighton being stabbed in the head? Because I can't imagine it right now.

I'm afraid I'll be stuck in a loop I can't escape from.

I'll need a *lot* of therapy if I ever make it out of this godawful place.

"Who else died?" His voice is low, wavering a little as if he's afraid to know the answer.

"Leighton. He did it in front of us. Stabbed her in the head, I can't . . . I can't stop seeing it . . ." The sobs make my voice crack. My breathing becomes uneven. Violent images slash in my brain, tormenting me as I try to recall what happened. I touch my face, and I grow nauseous again when I feel the speckles of drying blood on my skin. "Her blood . . . I . . ."

Danny grabs a hold of my face, forcing me to look him in the eye.

"Mabel, baby, it's okay. We'll clean this up, okay?" he assures me. One of his hands abandons my face and goes to the front of his shirt. He grabs the hem and uses it to scrub the blood off my face as he says, "I know you're scared, and you've witnessed terrible things tonight, but we'll make it out of this together."

I nod, accepting his sweet words of reassurance.

"Together," I mumble back like a promise.

A vow that, no matter what happens tonight, we'll make it out together.

This is probably a horrible time for me to remember we haven't discussed what's the label for our relationship. But it's nice to know he's making promises. Even if he's only saying it because we're in a life-or-death situation, but I can't stop the butterflies fluttering in my stomach. I hold on to this feeling because it's the only thing keeping me sane tonight. After everything, I can live in this bubble for a minute or two.

It will inevitably shatter soon.

No matter how much I wish for everything to be over by the time we make it out of this closet, I'm realistic. Cupid wouldn't have lured us here together and gone to all this trouble—leaving us without any source of communication, trapping us in the one house that uses storm shutters for parties, shutting down the lights—to get caught within the first hour or so. No, this was meticulously planned. Perhaps over months. Hell, I wouldn't put it past Cupid to have been planning this ever since Brian's murder.

This is Act Two, and by far the longest of every piece of media that follows the three-act story structure. We have at least another hour of footage to go through.

Danny licks the pad of his thumb and rubs it on my left cheek, I assume to scrub off the blood, but I still frown.

"Are you spreading spit all over my face?"

He stops what he's doing, tilting his head.

"Well, you have some dried blood here. It was using my spit or using some of the mop water from the corner. Considering this is Theta and they're not exactly known for their high standards of hygiene, it seemed like the better option," he justifies the train of thought behind his choice.

The laughter that escapes me catches me by surprise.

I didn't think I had it in me to laugh after the night we've had, but holy hell. This is entirely ridiculous. There's a level of stupidity in certain acts and choices tonight. It's hard to think of everything so seriously when there's a bunch of tiny events making everything seem surreal. Like comedic timing purposefully done to cater to an audience that doesn't exist.

Danny joins me, chuckling under his breath as he continues to scrub the blood off my face, simultaneously using his shirt and thumb until I assume I'm all clean. He smooths down his shirt and gives my cheek a gentle and playful squeeze.

"You're all better now," he says, offering me a tight-lipped smile.

I take a moment to stare at him, observing every single detail of his disheveled look now that I have the chance. His pants have traces of blood in them, probably from when he found Elodie's body in the living room, and red stains cover the hem of his shirt from cleaning my face. The golden undertone of his skin is a shade paler, almost as if he's sick. Though, all things considered, we must all look like that. He's just a bit better at keeping it together than I am, and I think he's doing it for my sake. It's in his nature to nurture those around him.

His hair is tousled as if he has been running his fingers through it, unloading the stress from the night. Or it might be from my own fingers when he had his face buried between my thighs earlier tonight. Good grief, how was that merely an hour or so ago? It feels like ages have passed since we kissed in Carmen's room. And did a lot more than that.

A shiver runs down my spine when I remember how good his smooth tongue felt on me. I shouldn't be having inappropriate and horny thoughts about Danny when we're in this situation, when there are bigger things to be worried about right now. Besides, there's another major rule in the how-to-survive-a-slasher handbook: Don't have sex.

Every time a character starts to have sex at any point during the movie, they end up dying, or nearly dying.

I don't want that.

And yet . . .

"Danny," I whisper his name.

"Yes?"

"Would you kiss me?" I feel my cheeks burning as the words roll off my tongue. "Even though my face is covered in your dry spit."

Danny snorts at my comment. I'm glad we manage to find humor in this situation because otherwise I would be going insane. Cracking bad jokes and laughing at moments I shouldn't is the only thing keeping me from losing my mind.

"Of course, baby."

He doesn't wait for my response. His hands carefully cradle my face, the tips of his fingers caress the nape of my neck, and he dives in to press his mouth to mine. I welcome the warmth and softness of his lips. I'm completely submerged into the bliss caused by the kiss. It's exactly what I need to forget everything I've seen tonight. The gentle pressure of his mouth causes sparks to explode in my brain. I melt against his embrace, wrapping my arms around his neck to hold him closer. For a moment, I completely lose myself in the kiss, following his lead as he tastes me once again, parting my lips with his tongue. Quickly, our kiss goes from gentle to passionate, savoring each other while we still can.

Only for a minute.

Reluctant to part from the one thing keeping me going, I break away from his mouth, and his head trails me down, desperate for more. I ache for him. There's nothing I would rather be doing right now, but there are more important things happening.

Because I can't let this go farther than this.

Not when I still need to find Carmen and Cerys.

"We can't," I say against his lips. "We can't stay here all night."

There's nothing else I would rather be doing with my time. Lord knows I would stay here with him, sharing kisses and hugs until the authorities catch this bastard, but I can't.

"I know," he mumbles in acknowledgement.

Still, we don't move immediately. It's possible it might be the last time we get to hold each other.

I need to stop being pessimistic. I might accidentally manifest my death. It's not what I should be doing. But I've never been great at holding my faith in the universe or whatever forces are above us. There's a part of me that believes in something, but I have many conflicting thoughts that overshadow those beliefs.

"Carmen had a plan before. She thought it was best if we tried to find weapons to defend ourselves from the killer, and I think she was right. But Cupid caught up with us and . . . I had to distract him and give them a chance."

Danny frowns.

"You're not doing that again," he snaps in a firm voice.

"What?"

"Sacrificing yourself for everyone else," he clarifies, holding my hands. He squeezes them three times as he says, "I would go out of my mind if anything happened to you, Mabel. I *just* got you back. I refuse to let you sacrifice yourself like that ever again. Do you understand? Promise me you won't do it again."

I hadn't thought about how he would feel. I didn't think about anything other than increasing Carmen's odds. I can't choose between him or Carmen, which means I can't promise him that. If it's between me and Carmen, I'll always choose her. My entire system is wired to ensure her well-being.

"Danny, I can't promise you that," I say.

He shakes his head. "No, you have to."

"Or what?" I dare, arching a brow.

I step back and cross my arms over my chest.

Danny doesn't have an ounce of controlling behavior in his body. He's reacting out of desperation and it's not helping him see things clearly. He knows me better than most people ever will. He knows there's nothing he can say that will make me change my mind.

Not about this.

His shoulders slouch with defeat. "I'm sorry," he apologizes, massaging his neck with his right hand. He lets it drop to his side as he flexes his fingers. "The thought of you becoming a martyr isn't something I can accept easily. I just got you back," he repeats.

My heart breaks for him.

Why can't things be easier for us? I hope there's another timeline where Danny and I get to have a soft and light-hearted college romance and get to spend our lives together without any of the added troubles.

My vocal cords twist into a knot. I grab his hand and kiss every single one of his knuckles. He releases a shuddering breath.

"And I just got *you* back," I agree in a whisper, barely managing not to burst into tears again. "I wish we had more time to discuss this properly, but there's no time to waste. My sister is out there somewhere, hopefully not doing anything stupid, and Cerys is with her."

"Mabs," he calls softly. "I know you will do anything for Carmen, but don't sacrifice yourself without thinking it through. If it's not necessary, don't take the risk. Keeping Carmen alive is important, but so are you. And you have me by your side. No matter what happens, I'll always be there for you. Don't ever forget that."

My throat closes up and I have to blink rapidly to keep the emotions at bay.

Without any words, I rise on my toes and pull him into a kiss.

The kiss doesn't last longer than a second. But it's enough to spread a wave of bliss through my limbs. I need it to prepare for what's to come. Slowly, I pull away from him. The ghost of his hot mouth leaves a tingle vibrating on my lips. I rub the tips of my fingers along my mouth until the otherworldly feeling dissipates. I command my body to settle down.

It's time to burst the bubble.

Danny lets out a small but longing sigh. His expression full of yearning.

Why did tonight have to end up being a fucking slasher plot twist? We should be enjoying this new development in our relationship. Kissing in dark corners because we want privacy and not because we're hiding from a murderer.

"Mabel," he draws my name out as he leans his forehead against mine. One of his thumbs makes its way to my bottom lip, caressing it. "Are you sure I can't convince you to stay here?"

I shake my head. "You know I can't. It's too risky."

"I can protect you. I *will* protect you," he corrects himself, and when he looks at me, I see the desperation plastered in his sweet eyes. "Please. I can protect Carmen too. What if you stay here while I go to look for her?"

"Protect Carmen?" I scoff. "In what universe would Carmen allow you to protect her?" I enquire, arching a brow. The corners of my lips threaten to curve into a smirk. "She barely allows me to. Besides, I don't think she would trust you."

His forehead knits into a frown, seemingly taken aback by my comment.

"Why?"

"Carmen doesn't trust anyone."

It's a truth, nothing personal.

Carmen simply doesn't place her trust in people.

His charming golden-boy persona won't earn him any points with her, especially after she caught us in her room in an inappropriate position. I don't think my sister would choose to voluntarily trust him in this situation regardless.

Hell, she barely even trusts me.

Carmen has always been perceived as cold and aloof. Always keeping the world at arm's length. I've tried to keep her safe, but she has found a way to sharpen her teeth to guard me instead. Whenever anyone said an offhanded comment, she was always there to spray her poison. "Kind" has never been a word used to describe her. And she's distrustful of those who aren't close to her.

Or aren't me.

And Danny isn't me.

I might've talked wonders about him in the past, but he hasn't done anything to earn her trust. Considering there's a murderer going around, the odds aren't in his favor. I don't know how much attention she pays to my horror movie rants, but I've always told her to be wary of any character that seems too perfect. *Especially* if it's the romantic interest.

I glance up to meet Danny's puppy eyes. Something has changed. Maybe it's a twinge of hurt from my statement, or something else I can't quite decipher. The caramel in his irises has darkened slightly. It's there only a fraction of an instant because, when he blinks, it disappears, allowing the familiar softness in.

"I don't like this," he confesses.

"You don't have to like it," I acknowledge. "But you should know I'm either going with you or going alone, so which one do you prefer?"

"You know which one," he mumbles reluctantly. "I don't mean to hold you back, Mabs. Even though I don't like it, it doesn't matter. I understand why it's important for you, so I'll do it."

For me.

Regardless of how he might feel about the idea of us facing this evil together, he's going along with it for me. It means a lot that he's respecting my decision. I appreciate him even more.

"Thank you," I whisper.

Danny squeezes my cheek in a loving manner.

It drags a smile out of me.

"Anything for you, Mabs. I would do *anything* for you. You know that, right?"

Do I?

A part of me still doubts any of this is real. I need to be told this is real in a million ways because good things don't typically happen to me.

Anything good in my career has happened because I've worked hard. I've hustled and busted my ass, doing odd jobs since the moment I could. I took babysitting jobs around the neighborhood. I created this persona that would fit into Kappa for my sister, and it stood strong for years. Everything I've gotten has been because I've earned it through my labor, sweat and tears.

But personally speaking? Great things? Never.

This is what I've yearned for since the moment I met Danny Singh. And, yes, maybe I'm being a little naive to trust him with my fragile heart, yet I don't see any reason not to. Not even when it seems too good to be true.

I hope it isn't.

"Thank you," I repeat, without knowing what else to say.

I need to work on my communication skills. This is something I'll need to talk about with my future therapist. To give them a little bit of regular therapy experience before I dump this shit show on them about how I've seen former acquaintances gutted and stabbed in front of me.

Danny grabs my hand as he glances around the tiny closet.

I take the opportunity to do the same, cursing at myself for not doing it earlier. Clearly, every time I've written a final girl has been worthless. I've been distracted and unfocused when I should have been keeping my senses sharp and using my intellect to come up with solutions to survive. It's a miracle I've made it this far.

There isn't much to see in the closet. Just a bunch of cleaning products that, upon further inspection, are mostly empty. Multiple brooms, a mop, some paint. Items to do clean-ups, but nothing with the potential to be turned into a weapon. I guess we could snap the broom and mop's handles to create stakes, which would be more useful if we were facing vampires and not a homicidal freak.

"Let's follow Carmen's plan," I suggest again. If we meet them, they might have some weapons already, and if we don't, at least we'll find something to defend ourselves with. "Go to the kitchen. Find weapons."

Danny's mouth twitches as if he has something he wants to say, but he suppresses it. I can guess what he's thinking. That I should stay put while he carries out the plan.

A voice in the back of my head begins to question it. Why the insistence on me staying here? It isn't much safer. Cupid already saw me here, and he knows the door doesn't have a lock. It's possible he's waiting for me to let my guard down so he can slide in later and cut my throat, or something even more nefarious.

"I'm not staying here," I establish for the last time, grinding the words out.

Danny nods. "I know, I know."

He turns, grabs the doorknob and leaves his hand lingering on it for a few seconds, only to spin around and hold my face as he pulls me in for a kiss that almost knocks me off my feet. One of his hands travels to my lower back, stabilizing me as he deepens the kiss. His teeth dig into my bottom lip, enticing a whine from the back of my throat. The tip of his tongue swipes across the sting left behind from his bite, easing the soreness away before he breaks apart.

"Sorry," he whispers against my lips. "I had to do it. Just one last time."

The message is loud and clear, even though it's unspoken. *In case we don't get the chance to do it again.* I lick my lips, recovering from the kiss. I feel lightheaded from the sudden emotion overwhelming my senses, but I manage to shake it off.

Danny grabs his phone from one of the shelves, and I notice for the first time that the illumination we've had this entire time was coming from it. A memory assaults me, claiming my attention.

When he left the living room before Cupid appeared, he volunteered to go find flashlights with Ollie. *I'm going to see if I can find some flashlights,* Danny's voice echoes in my skull as I remember what he said.

But he's been using his phone.

If he went to look for flashlights, why is he using his phone?

Chapter 14

SALIVA THICKENS IN MY MOUTH, COATING MY TONGUE WITH its slickness as a second passes by. I hear a clock ticking inside me. Blood runs cold in my veins, but I've yet to become paralyzed. Surely there must be an explanation for this. I've become too distrustful for my own good, but it doesn't stop my heart from speeding like crazy.

"You didn't find the flashlights?" I interrogate as he turns off the light from his phone, leaving us in the dark.

I see the shadow of his head move to the side.

"No, I tried to find them, but these guys aren't like Delta. Theta is fucking messy, especially now that I hear Gideon is president. He doesn't care enough about having supplies like I did. And by the time I was raiding the closets, I heard the screams and . . . You know the rest."

Mentally, I press the snooze button on the alarm blasting

in my head. His reasoning is transparent and logical. His voice never wavers or falls into the nervous pitch he does whenever he's been caught in a lie. There's a sense of calmness in the way he speaks. Either he's become a great liar in the past year or what he's saying is nothing but the truth.

I choose to believe the latter because in no universe is Danny a killer. He wouldn't do this to us—to me.

"Oh," I mutter without masking my disappointment. I would've preferred to have the option to have some source of illumination that didn't require us to waste what's left of our phone batteries. "It would've been good to have some lighting, just in case."

It's not like using a flashlight would be a bright idea, wandering around and giving up our location to the killer, but it would've been helpful. Like when you're stuck in a closet with no way out. It just . . . It would've made everything easier.

But I guess Cupid doesn't like it when we have it easy.

"Yeah. Maybe we'll find some in the kitchen," he supplies with a hopeful tone that lifts my spirits.

Unlike me, always prone to seeing the worst, Danny is an optimist. Somehow, he finds the way to see the glass half full instead of half empty in every situation. Even this one.

"Come on." He cracks the door open a little and the tiniest bit of pink glow sneaks in, allowing me to see him tilt his head. "You okay to go?"

I tap under my chin twice and then my chest. The signal makes him smile.

His fingers find mine and I squeeze his hand as he twists the doorknob, pushing it open just a sliver to check it's all clear. When he confirms it is empty, he pulls me with him back into the hall. But things have changed in the handful of minutes we've been in the closet.

The hollow darkness that was reigning over the halls has been replaced by a soft neon pink glow lining the ceiling. Somehow, the fact that there's more illumination makes my nerves rub together. The more effort Cupid has put into this, the harder it'll be for us to overpower him. He's been preparing for this for who knows how long.

I cling to Danny's hand as we move through the house. Apparently, when I was blindly running from Cupid, I had been going in the opposite direction from where we're headed. Going as far as being near the main living room where Elodie was killed.

Bracing myself to see her gutted body on the floor, I hold my breath as we step into the room. Things have changed in here too. The projector is on now and although there's no sound coming from the speakers, a film plays on a white screen at the end of the room.

I almost roll my eyes when I recognize the scene from the movie.

It's a romantic comedy.

Cupid has a wicked sense of humor because he's playing a romcom while we're being hunted for his pleasure. Nothing screams romance more than seeing entrails and blood splatter.

This isn't the only thing that's changed, though.

While we were in the closet, Cupid decided to redecorate the room. Dozens of photographs lie on the floor and are plastered to the walls, and they're all of Cerys. And they have one thing in common: the eyes are crossed out like they were in the letters. Inspecting them a little closer, I see that there are articles too. The pink light isn't the best for me to read through them, but a name stands out from the headlines: Brian Manders.

I clutch Danny's hand, and he squeezes it back.

"They're all of Cerys," I murmur. Whoever is doing this, they want her. Maybe it explains why Cupid didn't immediately kill her when he found us in the lounge room. A memory flashes in my mind. "The letter."

"What letter?" His voice sounds hollow as his eyes take in the photos.

"Her letter. It said all the deaths would be her fault."

"Do you think they're doing all this for her?"

Danny dares to ask what I haven't wanted to. That somehow, some fucked-up creep decided to orchestrate this entire night to mess with her, or worse.

"Maybe," I mumble.

His expression twists into a confused frown.

"Where's Elodie?" Danny asks, openly looking around the room.

There's a pool of blood near where I remember her being attacked, and a path of red streaking out of the room like she was dragged out of here. Is this what he's doing? Removing the bodies and placing them somewhere else?

I press my tongue to the roof of my mouth as I place a hand over my stomach. I don't even want to ponder the possibilities of what the killer could be doing to the bodies, because they're all too sick and disturbing for me to handle. Even as a horror fanatic, there are limits to what I can witness without feeling ill. Knowing how bad humanity can be, I don't want to imagine. Even in death, I want Elodie and the others to be safe from any harm, especially when there's no one to defend their bodies, not even themselves.

"He takes them," I say. "Cupid."

"Cupid?"

"That's what I've been calling him in my mind. His mask reminds me of a cherub, so it must be Cupid, I think," I explain vaguely. "He must be collecting the bodies like trophies or something."

Putting them in a room somewhere.

I eye him carefully as he takes in the shocking news. His expression wrinkles in a mix of horror and distress, his mouth falling slightly open. The news is shocking to him and the suspicion I had back in the closet fades away.

"That's fucking disturbing," Danny says, shuddering. "He's fucking insane. Should we find them too?"

The bodies.

No, it's too risky. They're already dead and we have to keep surviving. It would be a waste of time and effort. We need to conserve energy because I don't doubt that we'll crash from the constant adrenaline rush. When the effect stops, we'll be too exhausted, and perhaps maimed, so we need to make wise choices.

Being wise has evaded me so far tonight, but maybe I can still redeem myself.

I shake my head. "No. Let's keep going."

We leave the living room behind as we continue on our path.

Now that there's some decent, albeit a bit dim, illumination, it's easier to travel through the house. Granted, Danny's also more knowledgeable about the frat's layout than I am.

Living in Kappa never made much impact on me. It was more a place to sleep than anything else, so I never bothered memorizing every inch of the place. But for Danny, the experience was completely different. Being the president of his fraternity required him to know the ins and outs of the place like the back of his hand.

Holding on to Danny's hand, I allow him to guide me through the building. I focus my senses on staying alert, just in case Cupid approaches us out of nowhere. Danny takes care of the front, and I watch his back.

It's a team effort.

We're nearing our goal when I hear some soft muffled cries coming from the opposite direction.

"Wait, do you hear that?" I question in a low voice. I don't want to be overheard. "Someone's crying."

By the tone, I think it's a girl.

It feels as if an elephant has stepped on my chest, and I can't breathe properly. It rises and falls rhythmically, but my lungs burn and ache like the oxygen isn't coming through.

What if it's Carmen?

"Danny," his name escapes my lips like a plea.

I can't even muster the courage to say the words.

"It's okay. We can check," he reassures me.

To add more comfort, he squeezes my hand three times.

Following the noises, we approach the source. It's coming from an open area that seems to be a lounge room. At first glance, it appears to be empty, but then I spot the small frame hidden behind one of the couches. The corner barely has any space, but it's a hiding spot. It would be a good one, if it weren't for the crying. If she was silent, she would go unnoticed by anyone who wasn't cautiously inspecting every inch of the place, like we are.

As I step closer, I see that the frame doesn't belong to my sister or my best friend. This girl doesn't have Carmen's curls or Cerys' short bob. Instead, straight dark hair clings to a familiar heart-shaped face.

Zelda.

When she catches a glimpse of us, her eyes snap open with terror. It's only there for a second, though, and then she begins to cry with relief.

"Oh God, it's only you two," she says, pressing her hands to her mouth to drown the noises. The pink from the lights messes with my color perception, but I can see dark stains on her hands, caked around the edges of her nails where it's begun to dry. I'm guessing it's blood, but I can't tell where it came from. "I thought he found me again."

Danny kneels down next to her, inspecting her body for wounds. If the cries and blood are a hint, she must be hurt. It takes him ten seconds to find it, as his eyes dart to me and I see fear plastered across them. I lean in, crouching next to him, and I spot what has him so scared.

The blood from Zelda's hands comes from a deep wound in her lower abdomen, near her right hip. The fabric of her dress is torn and shrouded around the gash, lumping on the edges like ground beef. I swear I can see some entrails and organs resembling long sausages sautéed in fresh blood. The inside of her body looks closer to what you would find in the back of a butcher's shop than anything I've seen before.

Blood pours from the open flesh, staining the fabric of her clothes and her pale skin, pooling under her thighs. It's a miracle she hasn't bled out. Danny tries to cover her wound with his hands, but she bats them away, alarmed.

"Don't touch me!"

He lifts his hands in the air in a sign of peace, respecting her request.

"What happened?"

I swear she rolls her eyes at me, even though she's in pain and probably nearing death.

"I got stabbed, you dumb cow," she mutters through gritted teeth. Okay, it seems like our rivalry isn't over, in spite of the fact that I'm trying to help her. It's incredible that she can still gather the strength to be snarky when she's so badly wounded. "It hurts too much for you to be asking stupid questions."

"It's not stupid," Danny intervenes before I can say anything, getting ahead of an impending and immature argument. "Can you tell us what happened?"

"Sophia left me when he attacked us. We saw him dragging El's body to the bathroom and then he came at us. He stabbed me. I don't even know how I made it here. I think he was trying to get Sophia. How dare she leave me like that?"

I can't say I blame Sophia for reacting out of pure survival instinct, but I can understand why Zelda feels betrayed. Her best friend and confidante abandoned her when she was in a life-or-death situation. If they make it out, they'll have a ton of things to discuss, just like Cerys and I do.

"You'll be okay, Zee," Danny calms her. "This is a scary situation for everyone. Do you know if anyone else was attacked?"

She nods. "Ray."

Who the fuck is Ray?

Danny tilts his head, confused by the name as well.

"Refresh my memory, please," he asks, speaking for both of us.

Zelda licks her lips, gasping for air. I worry she might only have minutes left to live and we're here interrogating her when she's using what's left of her strength. Are we being insensitive? Knowing how many of us are left seems like valuable information to have.

She describes Ray as one of the guys who was sitting with them at the beginning of the night. Which means it puts the death count at three. Almost four, if we count Zelda's current state, leaving ten of us around.

"You should stay here," Danny whispers in my direction, turning his head away from Zelda to exclude her from the conversation.

I frown.

"What? No."

Why would I stay here with Zelda? She's four breaths away from dying. *Dios mío*, I might have zero empathy right now, but I don't see the point in staying with her. We've never gotten along; she was among the people who led a witch hunt against my best friend and me last year. It doesn't mean I want her to die alone, yet I can't really come up with another option that doesn't involve leaving her behind. After all, it doesn't look like she can walk or move. I'm not confident she could even make it out of this lounge without passing out or worse.

"We can't leave her."

I look at her from the corner of my eye.

Would it really be that terrible if we did? I must have a reserved spot in hell for even considering it. Danny is too noble to even consider leaving someone behind, especially a person who can't defend herself.

I gulp.

Carajo.

Deep down, I know the right thing to do. It doesn't matter what has happened between Zelda and me in the past because we're in an extraordinary situation. She's an injured person who needs help and company. Maybe she hasn't made the best decisions in life—neither have I—but she doesn't deserve to go out completely alone. It would be cruel, and I don't consider myself a cruel person.

She deserves some mercy.

"Maybe I can go," I offer for the last time, knowing Danny will never go for it.

"Mabel," he groans.

"No, let's think about this logically," I say, and my voice twinges with a hint of desperation.

Do I want to go alone? No.

Do I want to sit here and stay with defenseless Zelda? Also no.

Do I want Danny to go alone? Absolutely not.

There's no scenario where we can all be happy and content. Someone has to make a sacrifice, and I fear that someone will have to be me, because if we're real and think about it logically, Danny is the one who has the better odds of making it to the kitchen, grabbing a weapon, and finding Carmen and Cerys.

"Mabel," he repeats. "I have to go."

I bite the inside of my cheek.

Why does he get to leave?

Why does he insist on doing it?

Why is he right?

For the first time, I get how he must've felt when I stood my ground earlier and decided to come out here again to find my sister. Yet I don't like it one bit. If anything, it sets off the alarm in the back of my brain. Volunteering to go out alone is always a bad idea. Danny must know this. He barely made it back to me when he went to find the flashlights before everything went down. How is he so confident that he will come back to me again? Why is he so adamant about going off alone when he *must* be aware of the risk?

I hate it.

Frustration builds up in my throat, leaving a scratchiness as it rises. I bite the inside of my cheek and try to come up with a different solution. Anything that might give me the chance to turn this around, but nothing comes to mind.

Glancing at Zelda, I debate with my morals again. But they also won't budge. I'm too aware of what's the right thing to do.

Fuck me. Things are too complicated.

"Don't," is all I manage to say.

A thousand silent words tie themselves to that singular plea. The caramel in his eyes softens, his brows lowering and erasing all traces of determination. Instead, there's a sense of validation in the way he nods in a subtle movement. Quietly letting me know he understands exactly what I mean without having to say it.

Danny lifts my hand to his mouth and kisses the back of it. The pure intention behind the action floods my eyes with tears. I blink them away. I've cried enough for one night.

"I'll be quick."

"Swear it," I demand, holding his fingers tightly between mine, unable to let him go.

His eyebrows curve, softening his expression.

"I swear, baby."

Leaning toward me, Danny presses a kiss on my forehead before he stands up. He gifts me a reassuring smile and, quietly, he walks out of the room, leaving me with Zelda.

Although she grimaces from the pain she must be experiencing, her stare is both confused and shocked.

"You're with Danny?"

I roll my eyes.

Gossip right now seems out of place. It's jarring to think she's interrogating me about Danny when she's bleeding out on the floor next to me. What's happened to the world?

"Um . . . I prefer to not say." I don't have a concrete answer either way.

I drop my weight onto the floor, avoiding the blood pooling between me and Zelda. Thirty seconds go by in silence before she speaks again.

"For a moment, I thought it was you."

"What?" I frown, not understanding.

"The killer. I thought it was you," she explains, pressing her hands on her wound. My jaw drops an inch, caught off guard by the sudden accusation. "You've always been so creepy with your horror stuff. I thought you were capable of killing us."

This is probably the most unbelievable theory I'd ever heard, but now that she's brought it up, I have the chance to dig for information. While I adore Danny and I wish he was with me, his presence distracts me. I turn into a different person when he's around, a much softer version of myself. A damsel in distress, when I should be the opposite.

So I take advantage of this borrowed time and take a look at the mental puzzle. It's something productive to do with my time while I wait for Danny to come back. Maybe, if I can figure out Cupid's motive, we'll be able to stop this from going any further. More people can live, Zelda could get the medical help she desperately needs.

"Why would I do that?" I ask, arching a brow in her direction.

Zelda's brows jump a centimeter, acting like the answer is obvious.

"Because your bestie killed Brian?"

"She didn't kill anyone."

"How can you be so sure about that?" she snaps back and winces. It took too much effort snapping at me. "She's not here. For all we know, she is the killer."

Except she's wrong.

Cerys can't be the killer tonight, regardless of what she might think about her involvement in Brian's death.

If we take out the people who are already dead, there are a handful of people whom I distinctively remember arguing in the living room when the spree began. I can vouch for their innocence. Carmen and Cerys are at the top of my list since I got them out of there when Cupid killed Elodie and then he continued to chase us. I distracted him when Carmen and Cerys went off to complete the original plan, so there's no way it can be either of them. Bethan was also present when everything began, and from what Zelda has said, Sophia was chased by the killer as well, which makes her an unlikely suspect too.

Sadly, I also remember Seth's presence in the living room

because I slapped him. We had been arguing when things went to shit, so, unfortunately, I can't pin this mayhem on him. He's a shitty person, but I don't think he has a murderous streak in him.

Then I remember the guy from the party, his disgusting comment echoing in the back of my brain. When I asked Danny about him, he couldn't give me a name, and it didn't seem particularly relevant until now. He was also here when Carmen and I walked in, but I can't place him at all in any of the arguments that unfolded, nor did we see him when shit went down.

"Zelda," I say to her. She hums in response, urging me to speak while still conserving her strength. "Who was that other guy?"

"What guy? Jaden?"

I shrug. "I don't know, is Jaden blond, tall, wore a polo shirt? Kind of a dickhead."

"Oh, you mean Shane," she replies.

Shane. Why doesn't it surprise me that he has a stereotypical name? Although, I can't deny it suits him to a T.

"What was he doing here? Was he with any of you?"

Zelda shakes her head.

"No . . . I don't remember . . . He was here already when Sophia and I came with Ray and Jaden."

With the new pieces of information, I grab my phone and, with the last of the battery, I begin to create a list of every person who was here when the attacks began. The group has no real connections than I can think of, especially since the guys never got letters—except for Danny.

Girls:
Carmen
Cerys
Bethan
~~Elodie~~
~~Leighton~~
Sophia
~~Zelda~~
Me

I feel bad crossing Zelda's name off the list, but, to be fair, she's already wounded badly. The odds of her turning out to be the killer at the end are very slim. Being near her, I can tell she wants to live, and I hope she gets her chance. Moving on from her, I continue with my list.

Guys:
Danny (got a letter)
Seth
Ollie
~~Ray~~
Jaden (came with Sophia and Zelda)
Shane – main suspect

As soon as I type the words, I lock the screen and pocket the phone. I don't want to waste more battery since it's getting dangerously low, and I might need it for an emergency call if I can manage to get some service.

"So he was already here? Is he close to anyone?"

Zelda shakes her head. "Not that I can remember."

So Shane didn't receive a letter, nor can I recall his presence after the lights went out. He remained quiet, hanging out in the background while we argued about who summoned us to Theta. We can't vouch that he even got a text, he was just . . . there.

What was he doing here?

Low whistling cuts through my train of thought before I can begin to form a plausible scenario. Crystals form under my skin, paralyzing my muscles. The killer is announcing his return.

At my side, Zelda's body shivers visibly. Terror widens her eyes as more tears spill over her cheeks. When she starts to sob, I press my hands over her mouth. She slaps my arms, trying to break free from my hold, but I'm stronger and have the upper hand against her weakened state.

Once she gets the message to stay quiet, I take my hands away from her mouth and scoot to the edge of the couch to get a better look. I put my hair behind my ear and focus on listening.

Cupid stomps closer to the archway while whistling a creepy tune, showing who's in control. He's not nervous or afraid of his spree getting interrupted. It's almost as if he's calmly taking us out one by one until there's no one left, until his blood lust is satisfied.

Will he let some of us survive?

A vase falls to the floor, the sound of it shattering echoes around the room. He knows we're here, I realize. He stomps again and I then I hear another object joining the first one, clattering as it hits the floor.

I look at Zelda. Her eyes speak louder than any words could. She's terrified, screaming in silence. She can barely move with her wound. It's highly unlikely she'll be able to stand and shuffle more than a handful of steps, none fast enough to evade Cupid's blade.

Danny's voice comes back to me, pleading for me to not put myself in unnecessary danger. I don't think this is what he had in mind, but if I stay here with Zelda, not only do I risk my life, but I will also see her meet her death in a brutal way. *I'll die*. I don't want that. I promised my sister I would come back for her. All I care about is being alive long enough to find my sister and my friends.

My thoughts must be written all over my face because Zelda immediately shakes her head in response.

"Don't you dare leave me!" she demands, not caring about Cupid hearing us, her hand flying out to grasp my arm. Her manicured nails dig into the fabric of my shirt and I'm grateful to be wearing long sleeves. "Don't be a backstabber now."

"Sorry, but I have to find my sister."

"Oh God. You're homicidal!"

I stop moving altogether when I should be making my escape, taken aback by her words.

"What?"

"It's almost like you want to die or something," she adds, like it's a foreign concept for her.

"I think the word you're looking for is suicidal," I supply.

"That's what I said, idiot!" she grinds the words out.

I give her a final glance before I leave, finding some newfound respect for her snark, even when death's knocking at her door.

Maybe she can redeem herself.

"Stay alive."

She rolls her eyes. "I might, if you get the fuck out of here. Maybe he'll kill you first and forget about me."

I snort.

It's not in her nature to be gentle or kind. Similar to Carmen, but with less bite and more malleable. It's admirable that she's stayed true to herself. Just for that, I hope she manages to hold on long enough to be rescued. The world needs more defiant girls, especially those who look at death like it's an inconvenience. Who knows, maybe Zelda will realize she was standing on the wrong side of history and make amends.

Tú puedes, nena, I hype myself up as I spot a lamp resting nearby on a corner table. I try not to think about the logistics of it, preferring everything to come to me by pure instinct. It's gotten me this far already.

Thankfully, Cupid is facing the other way when I lift my body from the ground, and I grab the lamp. I unplug it and hold the cord around the middle. Moving to the secondary entrance, I throw the lamp at him.

I miss him completely.

The lamp crashes against the wall, the sound reverberating down the hall. Glass shatters as it hits the ground. Pure power invigorates me as my lips stretch into a smirk. *Take that, cabrón.*

The killer doesn't bother to check if there's any other survivors hiding in the room. Instead, he turns to me.

Carajo, I didn't think about what to do next.

The bloody Cupid mask tilts and I speed out of there as fast as my legs allow me.

Adrenaline pumps into my veins, but the rush of having

the upper hand against Cupid doesn't last long. I've got nothing to defend myself with.

Oh, fuck.

And he's coming after me now.

I knew that was the original plan, but I didn't have anything other than that. Danny won't be happy with me.

Danny.

I want to stop and redirect my steps to the kitchen, but it's on the opposite side of the house. To go there, I'd have to get past Cupid.

My only solution is to ditch the plan and create a new one.

Without knowing what to do, I make a left and my body slams directly into another person. Stumbling upon impact, I hold on to the person to keep me balanced.

"Mabel, oh my God!" My sister's voice floods me with relief.

Drums vibrate in my chest as my heart races.

I want to hug her, push her away, warn her that Cupid's coming after me—everything all at once—but I'm unable to do any of those because her eyes widen in terror as she screams, "Watch out!"

Carmen pushes me out of the way. I almost miss the blur coming in my direction. It takes me a split second too long to understand that Cupid was standing right behind me and he was swinging his knife in my direction. Except it didn't reach me.

No, it didn't come anywhere near. Instead, Cupid ends up burying his blade in my sister's shoulder.

True horror ices my veins, making me freeze. I stop breathing, lungs unable to do anything but constrict painfully without letting a breath go through. When I run out of oxygen and I can't exhale, I scream.

Chapter 15

MY THROAT BURNS FROM THE SCREAM. MY HEARTBEAT rushes in my ears, drowning out the noise around me, and while I can't hear her, I know Carmen is screaming too. I feel the vibrations in her chest as her body slumps against my torso. Blood spurts out of her wound, spraying the walls as Cupid retracts his weapon.

Before he can take another swing at us, my hands snap into action, punching him in the throat. The soft tissue bends under my knuckles, the attack catching him off guard. He makes a choked noise and drops the knife as his hands move up to clasp his throat.

I don't waste the opportunity to kick the knife as hard as I can, as far from us as possible. I don't know if he has another weapon hidden under his clothes, but it will definitely buy us more time.

Every second counts.

Carmen's shoulders heave with every sob and groan coming from her lips.

"Come on," I tell her. "We've got to keep moving."

I'm in awe of my sister's resilience as she takes a deep breath and straightens her back enough to turn and steady herself against my body. I wrap an arm around her waist, pushing her along with me. I take a right and then another, looking to put as much distance as I can between us and Cupid.

He's not following us yet.

Either my distraction worked or he chose an easier prey. But that doesn't matter, not now, when all I care about is getting Carmen to safety.

I find a room that opens on to a large set of stairs. These must be the grand stairs at the back of the house that lead up to all the dorm floors. There's access to every wing. In the corner, I spot the elevator used mainly by the maintenance staff. It's not for general use, but every house in Greek Row must have one to comply with Westbrook's accessibility policies.

I glance behind us, seeing the bloody trail left behind. This isn't good. We'll be easily tracked no matter which way we go.

Unless . . .

No, I shouldn't consider it.

Electricity is patchy and I don't want to end up being trapped in a dead end with no escape. I might have a death wish to be the sacrifice every time, but not enough to run directly into a trap where we can easily be killed if

Cupid chooses to wait for the doors to open. It's way too risky.

Right now, all I need is a place to hide with my sister so I can assess her wound and make sure she's not going to die any time soon. Then, we can figure out our next steps.

Between staying on this floor, climbing up the stairs, and taking the elevator, I choose the middle option. I've been all round this house, unable to find a hiding place or a weapon, so maybe it's time to deviate from what we had originally planned.

So, even though this breaks another rule from the how-to-survive-a-slasher handbook, I choose to take the stairs.

"Let's go up," I tell Carmen.

Her head snaps to me. "Up?"

I nod. "We need to hide."

Carmen groans. "Isn't that one of the big no-no's of slashers? Don't go upstairs?"

Choking back a bitter laugh, I hoist us to the stairs, climbing the steps as fast as we can. Carmen is breathless next to me, air coming out ragged through her cracked lips. A knot blocks my throat when I see the pain plastered over her face as she presses one of her hands to her bleeding shoulder.

"Well, I've done a lot of those tonight," I say, imagining Danny's reaction when he finds out about this one. I look at my sister, struggling with the pain. What was she doing roaming the halls alone? "Why were you on your own? Where's Cerys?"

Carmen shakes her head. "I lost her," she mumbles. "We

went to the kitchen, found two knives, but we had to get out of there quickly. That fucker was after us. We had to split ways, and I lost my knife too. I dropped it when he was chasing us. What about you?"

I gulp.

"I found Danny for a little bit. We were going to follow your plan, but then we found Zelda."

"Alive?" she asks.

My lips tremble as I try to come up with an answer. How do I even put it together without immediately saying "*Con un pie más allá que acá*"? It's clear she was more dead than alive, but I can't precisely tell her that. While they were never friends, I don't know what Carmen's reaction will be to another death.

We've never had to deal with major losses in our lives. Death was something we only ever heard of rather than experienced. Perhaps that's what drew me to the horror genre. I was attracted to something I'd never been near to.

Now? I want to get as far away from it as possible.

"She was hurt," I say, skipping over the gruesome details. "Did you see anyone else?"

Another shake of her curls. "No. There was some blood around, but God knows who it belonged to."

It's harder to tell when you consider Cupid has been moving the bodies around. I share this detail with her and Carmen recoils but says nothing.

"I need a moment," she pleads once we make it to the second floor.

We move a few meters away from the stairs, and Carmen rests her back against a wall. She gasps for air, grimacing as her bloody fingers trace the two-inch stab wound on her shoulder. I begin to worry that it's not the innocent sort of injury that the movies would have us believe. I hope to God it didn't hit any major arteries, because I can't watch my baby sister die.

I refuse to let her die.

Why the hell did she get in the way? She should've let Cupid stab me and get it over with. I would very much rather die than live in a world where Carmen isn't with me. Even with all our fighting and bickering, I'd be nothing without her.

"Sit down for a minute," I order.

For once, she doesn't put up a fight and slides to the floor without saying a word. I kneel next to her and check her wound. She's still bleeding, but not as heavily as before.

What can I do to help? I have no access to any emergency kits, nor do I know how to sew a wound. Frankly, I think I would pass out if I had to put a needle through Carmen's skin with no anesthetics. There has to be another way to stop the bleeding. I could check in the rooms to see if there's anything we could use as a bandage. Though I wouldn't trust any Theta clothes. They don't seem remotely hygienic.

I rub my hands on my pants, attempting to clean off the blood sticking to my fingers, when I remember the clothing in my back pocket.

She'll hate me for this, but oh well.

I grab it and press it on her shoulder to help stop the bleeding.

"Is that your bra?" Carmen questions, her voice pitching in distress. "Ew, get it away from my wound! You'll give me an infection!"

"It's this or some guy's dirty sheets—which one would you prefer?" I snap back, using a firm tone.

I press the bra harder to her shoulder, rendering her immobile. Pouting like a little kid, Carmen glares at me as she allows me to use the bra to staunch the bleeding. It's better than nothing.

"I can't believe you're putting your boob sweat on my shoulder," she mumbles through gritted teeth.

The ridiculousness of this argument makes me giggle.

"You'll live," I tell her. "Someday this will be a funny story."

Carmen arches a brow in my direction. "You're the only one laughing like a maniac here," she points out.

I purse my lips together.

She's right.

I'm the only one laughing, but it's probably because, if I don't do it, I'll cross the line and slip into hysteria. All I've ever wanted is to keep Carmen safe and free from harm, and now the unthinkable has happened.

"I'm sorry," I whisper.

Carmen bites her bottom lip and shakes her head. "No, I'm the one who's sorry. You were right about the letter; it was a threat, but I didn't want to believe you. We should've left Westbrook when we had the chance."

I stay quiet.

It's true, we could've been on a plane right now, but we still don't know why this is happening. As much as I want to believe we could've avoided all this, something tells me it wouldn't have been possible. Cupid has gone to great lengths to arrange this night, so he must have a motive, something that drives him to commit these atrocities. I just don't know what that motive is.

"It's not your fault," I assure her. "I'm just glad we're together."

Tears crystalize in her brown eyes. My heart aches when I notice her lips trembling the way they did when she was a child.

"I don't want to die, Mabby. I've done bad things, but I don't want to die. I don't deserve to die," she cries. "And I don't want you to die either. What will I do without you? Please, Mabel."

Without letting go of the bra, I press her against my chest.

"I'm right here. I'm not going anywhere," I promise. "Did you see me punch him? Papi will scream when he finds out I finally got to try out his technique to throw a punch."

Carmen lets out a watery laugh that makes my chest lighter.

That's much better.

I don't want to see her sad and thinking the worst, even when we're in the worst possible scenario. It doesn't matter if I'm in pieces, I'll do anything to make my sister keep a smile on her beautiful face.

Carmen lifts her head to look at me, tears carving a path down her cheeks.

"Are you okay?" I ask, examining her.

She moves her head in an affirmative motion.

"Don't get me wrong, being stabbed isn't fun. It hurts like a bitch, but I think I'm okay," she explains.

"No dizziness? Blurry vision? Anything?"

Her response comes in the form of a headshake.

"I even believe I'll survive the infection I'll get from your boob sweat."

A snort comes out of me before I can stop it.

"Come on. We've got to keep moving," I say. She extends her arm, wincing, and I help her get to her feet again.

"What do you have in mind?"

I don't have a solid plan. We're in a vulnerable spot, and I don't know where to go.

All the options we have on this floor are limited to open and common areas where we can't use a locked door to escape from him. To prove my theory, I rattle the rooms' doorknobs in hopes of getting one of them open, but none of them budge. Either the Thetas have gotten the memo to lock their rooms for parties or Cupid is an evil genius.

"The rooms are all locked. Where else is there in this house?"

Carmen knits her brows together as she thinks. "All the houses have similar layouts. Theta, Delta and Kappa are the biggest ones, so they have two wings."

"What else?"

"Each floor must have a common room or lounge area."

None of this is helpful. We don't need another open room where Cupid can chase us. We need a place to hide until everything is over, a place where we won't be found as easily. Like a secret passage, a closet or . . .

"The attic," I mumble. "Did Theta keep the attic while they were doing renovations?"

Carmen's eyes light up with recognition.

"Yes! They love to use it for seven minutes in heaven," she says, her voice shaking with a hint of excitement. Of hope. "You get to it through a storage closet."

This is our chance to gain an advantage. If we can get to the attic without alerting Cupid, I can hide Carmen and then find Cerys and Danny. It might not be enough for us to escape this place, but we just need to stall long enough for people to figure out what's going on in this horror house.

Carmen directs me along the corridor until we reach the lounge room. It's empty and it doesn't look like anyone's been here. Perhaps Cupid hasn't allowed them to get this far into the house, or people haven't thought about it. It doesn't take us long to find the storage closet. It's messy and crowded, but I squeeze in and pull down the ladder to the attic. Unfortunately, we can't keep the ladder down with the door closed.

It doesn't matter.

Not now, when all I care about is making sure Carmen is safely hidden.

"You go first," I say, gesturing to the stairs. "I'll keep watch here."

My sister nods and stops pressing the now soaked bra to her wound, so she can use both arms to climb up the stairs. It takes her longer than it would if she wasn't injured, but I don't rush her, I simply watch her in admiration. I don't know if I could handle a stab wound so stoically.

"These assholes don't clean up here," she complains, coughing as she gets fully into the attic.

I follow her up swiftly until I can stand on the floor as well.

She's not wrong.

Theta uses the attic as if it were another storage room. Full of boxes and crowding the AC units with their clutter. I'm pretty sure it's a violation of the attic regulations in Florida, considering the high temperatures in the summer. I can't complain now when it serves as a better hiding spot for Carmen. At least she can rest against the boxes without having to lie down on the floor, so I'll take it as a blessing in disguise.

"You can pull up the ladder now," Carmen says, pointing at the entrance with her chin.

I feel my throat closing around itself.

"I can't," I say, dropping my gaze to the floor so I won't have to face her expression. "I have to find Danny and Cerys."

Carmen groans out. "Don't do this, Mabel."

"I have to."

"No, you don't," she refutes with a hint of desperation marking her words. "It's stupid to continue to put yourself at risk."

"I owe it to Cerys," I tell her. "You wouldn't understand—"

"You're right," Carmen cuts me off. "I don't understand, because it's idiotic. There's no way you'll come back to me in one piece. I got stabbed while you were running," she reminds me, motioning to her wound. "Do you think you're invincible?"

I shake my head. "I know I'm not," I snap. "But there's a lot you don't know about Cerys. She's been through a lot, and I owe it to her to help her. She's my best friend."

"And you're my sister!" she exclaims as if it trumps my own claim.

In many ways, it does.

I truly understand what she means. If I could, I would stay here in the attic with her, where it's safer. But I can't. There aren't enough words in the dictionary to explain why, and even if there were, I couldn't find an eloquent way to string them together. While I'm a talented screenwriter, I'm not really great with spoken words. They don't come to me clearly on the spot, rather I have to polish them over a series of edits until they can convey the message I want.

I don't have that kind of time or luxury. Especially when it feels like I'm wasting precious minutes that I could be using to find my friends.

Pressing my hands over my eyes, I try to come up with a way to make Carmen understand that I'm not going after Cerys and Danny because I'm some sort of martyr. I don't see my life as something I can easily exchange for them, but my conscience wouldn't let me live if anything happened to Cerys because I was too much of a coward. After everything we've been through, I can't fail her again. I can't abandon her in the midst of this chaos. I don't think she would forgive me if I did. *I* would never forgive myself. So even if it scares me to death, I have to try to find her, because I wouldn't be able to live if I didn't do everything in my power to help the ones I love.

"Carmen," I start, but the words get trapped in my throat. "I have to go, but I promise I'll come back."

Now I feel like a liar, because I can't guarantee I'll make it back to her. Well, I don't need to be in one perfect piece, I simply need to be alive. Just alive. It doesn't matter how bad my condition is as long as I'm breathing and holding on to consciousness.

Danny made the same promise to me earlier, I realize. Was he lying too? Was it something he said because he knew I wouldn't let him go unless he did? Somehow, the words rang true when they came from his lips. Unlike me, Danny isn't unreliable. His nature is always noble, going to any length to keep his word.

I'm sure he meant it when he swore that he would come back to me.

What if he made it back to the room where I left Zelda, looking for me, only to find me gone?

But I made sure not to make a promise I couldn't keep when he asked me to not be a sacrifice. If it's for Carmen or Cerys, there's no other choice.

Slowly, I lift my gaze from the floor to meet my sister's eyes. Her expression is twisted into a snarl, lips curving in disgust.

"You're a bad liar, Mabel."

"I know," I admit. "But I swear I'll do everything in my power to come back to you," I vow, making sure to inject as much sincerity into that statement as I can. To add more weight to my words, I curl my fingers, letting the pinky rise in the air between us. Carmen lets a tear fall down her cheek and she mirrors my actions, linking her pinky with mine. "Now it's an unbreakable promise. You know I'll fight like hell to come back to you."

Carmen throws herself at me, wrapping me into a clumsy one-armed hug. A pained moan is muffled into the crook of my neck as she wishes me good luck on my journey.

I press a kiss on her hair and make sure she's keeping up the pressure on her wound because it has started oozing blood again. The last thing I want is to find her bleeding out when I return, so I don't move until she's doing it. I begin to make my way down the ladder, knowing I'm throwing myself back into danger.

Chapter 16

THE HOUSE IS SILENT WHEN I LEAVE THE ATTIC. NOW THAT Carmen is safe—or as safe as she can be after being stabbed and with a psychokiller running around downstairs—I can focus on finding Danny and Cerys without torturing my brain with dreadful scenarios.

Glancing down at the floor, I make sure there aren't blood traces that could lead to Carmen, and aside from the spot near the staircase, I don't find anything. She might complain, but using the bra to stop the bleeding wasn't a bad idea. Regardless of the boob sweat.

If Carmen hadn't walked in on me almost naked in her room, I wouldn't have shoved my bra into my pocket in my haste to get dressed.

Blessings in disguise.

Riding the high of having the upper hand against Cupid,

I scout the right wing of the second floor. I check every door, attempting to find a way out while I search for my friends.

Where could they be? I haven't seen any traces of Cerys on the ground floor since we last saw each other, and she wasn't with Carmen either. A bundle of nerves clumps in my stomach. I hope she didn't stumble upon Cupid while we were busy. I can only pray that Danny found her, and they're hiding somewhere safe together.

Because the alternative is daunting.

A gruesome image forms in my brain, of Danny's body in a pool of blood, similar to the one that surrounded Zelda when we found her. A shiver runs down my spine. I can't bear the thought of finding his dead body.

Don't think about it, I chastise myself.

Nothing good will come of letting those intrusive thoughts cement themselves in my brain, so I redirect them. Where I've been to, the doors I've checked, listening to see if I hear Cupid's steps. Anything that might give me a hint of where my friends are and where the killer might be—so I can find them and avoid him. I also try to keep a mental note of any possible escape routes.

Cupid has been thorough, but even the greatest minds have been known to make mistakes. I *know* there has to be a weak spot. There's no such thing as a perfect crime, and while so far we've been outsmarted, I'm sure there must be *something*.

I can feel it in my bones.

That's what makes a good slasher. The certainty that the killer always slips up, one way or another. Even when it seems like they've got it all figured out, their motive ends up being part of the reason why they become sloppy. The first kills are great, but after they've been hunting for a while and tiredness and exhaustion begin to take over, they become desperate. I'm sure we're nearing that point after three bodies.

Three bodies—that I'm aware of.

There might be more by now. We still don't know if he managed to catch up with Sophia after he left Zelda to succumb to her injuries alone.

How long has it been since the massacre began? I guess that's the proper term for what's happening now: massacre. It's what they'll call it once it reaches the news outlets and media. They'll use it as a cautionary tale for why you should never join any college's Greek life.

At least someone will end up making a lot of money once they decide to turn it into a movie in the next few years.

The sound of someone panting cuts through my line of thought. I attempt to tread softly to avoid giving up my location. I stop near a corner and spy around it to see who's responsible for the noise.

My heart skips a beat.

On the floor, Jaden lies in a pool of his own blood, his fingers buried in his throat. Gnarly gashes slit across his neck, the lines jagged along the flesh like it went through a kitchen slicer. His mouth, tainted with red, hangs open like he had been trying to scream when the knife cut his throat. Empty, lifeless eyes stare into the void.

A blond man stands with his legs on either side of the body. He's the guy from the party, the one who had no reason to be in this house, the main suspect from my list.

Shane. I recall his name from my conversation with Zelda.

His shoulders heave with his heavy breaths as he steps closer to the body. Leaning over Jaden, he picks up something from the floor. The blade's reflection gives away what it is: a knife. Blood drips from the point, and Shane wipes it on his stained pants.

The weight of the world falls on me when I realize what's happening. I've accidentally discovered who's the killer behind the mask.

I release a shaky breath and, as I back away, the guy spots me. Time stops moving as our gazes connect, sending a panic alert to my brain.

I've seen Cupid without his mask, and now I'm in danger.

A drop of sweat slides down my spine as adrenaline charges through my system. Quick, shallow breaths force my chest to heave. I've faced Cupid before when he was just a faceless killer. It was easier to confront a mask than an actual human being.

Shane lets out a chuckle.

"This isn't what it looks like," he says, lifting his hands in the air, attempting to feign innocence.

I jerk at the movement. It's hard to believe when he's still holding the knife.

"Why don't you tell me what it looks like?" I ask. My wobbly voice betrays the fear rushing through my veins.

Shane looks at Jaden's body and shrugs. The nonchalance of the act doesn't build a strong case in his favor. He doesn't need to be sobbing, but he doesn't appear to even feel respect for the person who died.

"He was dead when I found him," he explains, dropping his hands to his sides.

I stare at his blood-soaked shirt.

If Jaden was dead when Shane found him, why is his shirt covered in blood?

Every cell in my body urges me to run. But I can't. Where would I even go? I can't run back to the attic. It would lead him to Carmen.

I need to come up with a sneakier way to get out of this. *Carajo*, how am I going to survive this? I glance around and notice my only way out—the stairs at the end of the hall. I'm not sure if they're a good choice, but they're all I've got.

I just need to figure out how to get there before Shane does.

"What happened to your shirt?" I ask, because if he's busy explaining himself, then he's not thinking about killing me. I'm so tense, my muscles are struggling not to cramp.

Shane rubs his forehead and unknowingly smears more blood over it. The stain on his face makes him look even more disheveled and scary.

"You're not going to believe this," he starts, laughing once again. Where's the joke? None of this is funny, but he seems to find it hilarious. "I didn't see him at first, and I . . . well, I tripped."

He breaks into loud cackles, and I pretend to join him.

My gaze drops to the knife.

I'm at a huge disadvantage here. I don't know Shane, but he seems to be in great shape. He's tall and lean, athletic given the way his muscles stretch the fabric of his shirt. And he's wielding a knife like it's not a lethal weapon.

"You tripped?" I mumble, my voice sounding pitchy.

Shane tilts his head. "Why? You don't believe me?"

"Yeah," I rasp out, moving my head in a nod to match my words. "I believe you."

He squints at me quizzically.

"You don't sound so convinced about it."

"I am."

"Bullshit," he spits out. "What do you think happened here? That I saw Jaden, waited for the perfect moment, and slashed his throat? Do you realize how insane that sounds? C'mon."

"I didn't say that."

"But that's what you think, isn't it?" There's a note of desperation shaking his words, making them sound more intense, turning my blood to ice. With every second, he becomes more desperate, his eyes moving frantically, losing the little humanity that was there to begin with. Pushed closer to the edge, Shane fidgets with the knife, turning the handle between his fingers. His knuckles pop out with every turn, exposing his firm hold on it.

Saliva dries in my mouth, leaving me unable to swallow, let alone utter another word. My gaze focuses on the blade, knowing he's close to snapping, and I move my body backwards.

Shane takes a step forward, carelessly stomping on Jaden's arm and stumbling. He doesn't fall, but it's enough to give me a head start. I take a left, running down the hall as swiftly as I can to head down the stairs, but Shane recovers fast.

Too fast.

His legs are long, and he's motivated by the fact that I've caught him without the mask. I've become an eyewitness in the case against him.

Shane's hands catch up to me, grabbing a handful of my hair. The sharp tug sears my scalp as he pulls me down to the floor. I fall backwards, my butt taking the first impact as I hit the ground. Pain spreads through my hips, but I ignore it as adrenaline pumps like crazy in my system, pushing me to defend myself from the sudden attack.

Shane's fingers are still twisted in my hair, holding me in place. I shift on the floor and bite his hand as hard as my jaw allows me. A metallic taste floods my mouth as I cut his skin with my teeth. Shane lets out a loud yelp and slaps me across the face with his other hand, releasing me from his hold.

"You bitch!"

White spots dance in my vision as the burn from his slap extends over my cheek. Blinking, I spit out the mouthful of blood and shake my head. It's a battle to clear my senses as I roll on the ground away from him. *The stairs, I need to make it to the stairs*, I tell myself.

"Where the fuck do you think you're going?" he snarls, kicking me.

A muffled moan escapes me when he hits my hip. Panic has taken over me, shielding me from feeling the pain. I'm numb to the touch. I can't feel anything other than the desperate urge to flee. Thrashing and kicking, he struggles to use his knife on me.

He groans at my blows, sounding more inconvenienced than pained. He drops his entire body weight on me, leaving me breathless as he traps me underneath him. He must be at least fifty pounds heavier than me, completely crushing any chance I had of overpowering him.

The knife seems to shine in his hand as he lifts it high in

the air, poised to slam it deep in me. *This is it.* This is where I meet my end. I should close my eyes as I brace myself for the blow, but it never comes, the moment suspended in time.

A hatchet buries itself in his head.

Blood sprays across my face as I lie frozen in place.

Shane's body jerks and twitches, the hatchet lodged deep in his skull, piercing his brain. With a strength usually only seen in movies, he turns to face his attacker, and I scoot from under him, putting as much distance between us as I can, but without tearing my eyes away. I couldn't stop watching, even if I tried.

Cupid stands behind Shane. It's difficult to tell how he feels about someone else wanting to take credit for his kills, but I'm sure Cupid's not happy with Shane. He yanks the hatchet from Shane's head and delivers another blow. The edge of the hatchet sinks into the upper half of Shane's face, splitting it apart.

Nausea rolls in my stomach as I gasp for air.

Taking advantage of the distraction, I push myself off the ground until I stand on wobbly legs. Shane must've hit me harder than I thought because I can't run without feeling like I've pulled a muscle, making me limp down the hall. It takes its toll on my speed, but I'm less than two meters away from the stairs.

I can do this.

Behind me, I hear Cupid drop Shane to the ground and head after me. *Quickly.* His gloved hands reach me before I can get to the first step. His fingers graze my back and when he's about to grab me, he trips and pushes into me instead.

The fall happens in the blink of an eye. Vertigo twists my stomach as I plummet down the stairs, hitting my ribs and back.

My head receives the hardest impact as I roll onto the ground floor. Black dots haze the edges of my sight, swallowing the image of Cupid at the top of the stairs, hatchet held at his side, watching me fall.

I urge my body to move, to do anything other than lie here. But it's pointless.

Darkness spreads in my vision as my mind disconnects with my body until I can't see anything other than a void.

I lose consciousness.

Chapter 17

AN ACHE PULSATES IN MY SKULL, MATCHING THE RHYTHM of my heartbeat. It grows excruciating, awakening me. My senses begin to come back to me one by one, alerting me to what's happening around me. I hear an inconsistent splatter hitting the ground. It's close, but not near enough to hit me, or at least from what I can tell.

Although they feel heavy, I force my eyelids to open, to figure out where the sound is coming from. Blurriness coats my vision; I blink in an effort to clear it. I regret doing so the moment I make out the shadows in my line of sight. My throat dries and I choke in a gag as I stare in horror at Shane's body hanging upside down from the banister like a fish on a hook. The hatchet buried in his eye socket, splitting the upper half of his face apart. A mixture of blood and goo drips from it, sliding down his forehead to the floor below.

My stomach feels queasy, and I breathe through my mouth to block out the rusty scent of blood.

I was wrong. Shane wasn't Cupid, he wasn't the masked killer, but there was a darkness within him that pushed him to almost murder me. If Cupid hadn't shown up at the exact right time, I wouldn't be here staring at Shane's corpse. I would be dead.

A wave of cold washes over me. I can't be relieved that Cupid murdered Shane. I can't say it was to save me, but his actions did save my life, and I don't know how to cope with it. A whimper slides from my lips, drowning the splattering noise in the background.

I turn my head away from Shane as tears slide from the corners of my eyes.

My breath hitches when I notice Cupid's black combat boots standing in front of me. This is the first time I've been so close to him, and I can't help but notice how tall he is. Maybe it's the imposing stance, secure and confident behind the mask, as he watches me cautiously.

He tilts his head. The mask seems focused on me, watching me like a hawk tracks its prey.

Even if I wanted to, I don't think I could move. The pounding headache is debilitating, softening my muscles when I should be up and running. My brain is aware that this would be the moment in a film where the audience screams at the character to stand the fuck up and stop whining, but I can't help it. After falling down the stairs, hitting my head and passing out, I'm only just slowly coming to myself.

I know I will spring into action, but it's taking me longer than it would in the movies. It doesn't help that I'm being observed by the killer. Fear is a weird thing. Sometimes it gives you the courage to run or to fight. But this time? It does nothing but paralyze me.

I'm unable to do anything but stare back at Cupid.

Why is he not killing me?

Or torturing me?

Although, he hasn't tortured his victims so far. At least from what I've seen. Cupid is straightforward with his killing. Most of the time, he aims for the head.

Like with Leighton.

And Shane.

Slowly, like he's trying not to disturb me, Cupid eases down to his knees until he's almost straddling my legs, but not quite. He doesn't let his weight fall on me. If anything, he's delicate in the way he approaches me, gentle as he crawls over my body without touching me. The fabric of his robe is the only thing grazing me.

Tiny whimpers escape from my trembling lips as I fight the sobs wanting to break free, wanting to give in to the fear reigning over my body. I shake under him, muscles spasming.

Cupid doesn't make a sound. He takes his time to explore my body, analyzing every inch as he crawls over me until he stops at my waist. Leaning back, he pulls out a dagger from his clothes where there must be a hidden pocket. This is a new one, untainted by anyone's blood.

Patiently, Cupid begins to drag the tip of the blade over my pants. I tense and close my eyes tightly, not wanting to witness what could happen if he decides to rip the fabric and have his way with me. There's only ever been one instance where I've felt this helpless before, where every inch of my body betrays me and stays still when I should be getting the hell out of there. Tears sneak past my closed lids, escaping away like I wish I could do.

I'm not a religious person. Most of the time, I'm unsure if I even believe in anything, but in this brief moment, I say a silent prayer.

Cupid doesn't seem to be interested in stripping me of my clothes as he drags the dagger over my pants until he reaches the waistband. My body jerks when the cold blade touches the sensitive skin of my navel. He stops at the button and twists the point of the dagger around it, threatening to pop it open. The scrape of metal grinding against metal makes my teeth ache.

But he doesn't open it.

He's . . . teasing.

Letting go of the air trapped in my lungs, I flicker my eyes open to meet his mask.

Cupid leans forward and supports his weight with the hand he's holding the dagger with, and brings the free one to my face, caressing the edge of my jaw with the tip of his fingers. His hands are covered by the leather of his gloves, so his touch feels cold and detached, but it doesn't make it any less nauseating.

Bile rises from my stomach to the back of my throat, warning me that I'm close to my limit. If I let this go any further, I'll be unable to stop myself from throwing up.

Under him, I shake uncontrollably. Panic seizes my muscles as I begin to awaken my body to respond to all my commands. I shed more tears when Cupid presses his body against mine and buries his mask in the crook of my neck.

His labored breathing comes out full of want and desire. Slowly, he draws an invisible path from the curve of my neck to the edge of my ear. I can almost feel the warmth of his breath as he rocks his hips, and . . . *Fuck no.* The protuberance of his boner can be felt through the layers of clothing as he presses it against my hip. It twitches and he lets out a soft groan that makes my skin shrivel.

Cupid is turned on. He's getting off on this, the desire apparent in the way he continues to rock his hips on me.

I need to break free from this.

If I don't . . . I don't even want to think about what will happen. Desperation increases in my chest as I try to order my limbs to push Cupid off me, but they don't respond. There's a disconnect between my mind and my body, making it impossible to do anything while I swallow my tears and bile. I urge the nerves in my body to respond, to do something other than send shuddering signals to my brain.

Anything, please.

I can't stay here. He's going to do much worse than kill me. I would prefer it a thousand times if Cupid simply dug his knife in and left me to bleed out on the flood, like an animal for slaughter. I would accept my death that way rather than have to endure him taking away what's left of my broken dignity.

The shields I've kept in the dark corners of my memory threaten to break under the pressure. No. If I let those paralyzing memories resurface, I'll never make it out of here.

I breathe in short puffs of air, becoming more lightheaded with every passing second. The only thing that's too aware of everything is my head.

My head.

If I'm unable to move my arms or legs, I know something that will work.

Without giving it a second thought, I gather all the strength in my body and slam my forehead as hard as I can into Cupid's face, aiming for his nose under the mask.

There's a loud *crack* and I'm not sure if it comes from the plastic of his mask breaking, or if I successfully smashed the bridge of his nose. Cupid lifts himself off me, groaning in pain as he covers his mask with his hands. The pained groan is almost familiar to my ears.

A *clang* catches my attention, and I stop watching Cupid to witness the dagger falling to the ground near me. I know what I must do. The opportunity has been presented to me on a golden platter, I'd be an idiot to pass it up.

It's now or never.

Regaining control over my body, I hoist myself from the floor and grab the dagger. Cupid is too distracted by my attack to notice me escaping. I'm lightheaded as I limp back up the stairs. Shaking my head to disperse the dark haze clouding my sight, I keep moving, holding the hilt of the dagger tightly.

I have a weapon now. I don't let the triumph spread through me because I'm still in danger. I stagger across the second floor, barely missing Jaden's body as I step over him to cross the hall and go down a path I hadn't explored before. Anxiety mixes with the adrenaline buzzing in my bloodstream.

Frantic thoughts rush through my brain in flashes. Instinct guides me as I roam the corridor. The soles of my shoes are sticky from Jaden's blood.

I'm disoriented thanks to the dull ache in my skull. I'm still not a hundred percent recovered from what I've just gone through.

I barely made it out of Cupid's hold.

This is a dire situation. I'm slowly becoming that character who's so close to surviving but dies regardless. That character who ends up generating multiple discourses online because the viewers believe they should've become a final girl.

But I wouldn't say I'm final-girl material.

In my most vulnerable position, I froze when I should've fought, fear completely taking over me.

Where is a good spot to hide?

I try to recall what Shane told me before he was killed. He said he'd stumbled across Jaden's body, but where was he before that? Cupid seems to dispose of the bodies quick enough, so either Shane was roaming the halls or he was hiding somewhere nearby.

I take a right at the end of the hall and continue trying all the doors. Cupid has been ahead of us every time, making sure the spots to hide are limited to the common areas.

Common areas . . .

The lounge room is out of the question. It wouldn't make sense for someone as tall as Shane to hide in a public and exposed area.

Maybe he's a Theta? Shit, I didn't think about that possibility before. He could've been hiding in his room the entire time. It would definitely explain what he was doing here.

Could that be it? I carry on checking the doors until I spot it: a door with a bloody knob and a partial handprint on the edge of the frame, showing it's been opened by someone recently.

Silently pleading that I won't find Cupid's secret lair, I twist the knob. The door opens with a quiet *click*. I look over my shoulder to make sure Cupid hasn't followed me.

The threat of his attack is still too fresh in my brain, causing goosebumps to erupt over my skin. I push the thoughts away.

I swiftly slip into the room. Closing the door behind me, I attempt to find a lock but there's nothing. Why isn't there a lock?

Simple white tiles flash in front of me when a light is turned on. I swirl around, stunned by the room's sudden brightness. Two sets of eyes stare back at me.

Eyes belonging to the people I've been desperate to find.

Danny and Cerys.

Chapter 18

"MABEL?" DANNY'S VOICE IS A SOOTHING BALM TO MY hysteria, silencing the blood rushing in my ears until there's nothing but a faint hum. There's a hint of confusion in his voice and, when I spot him, he's frozen in place as his eyes move frantically over my figure, examining every inch of my body. I haven't gotten the chance to glimpse my reflection, but I must look like a mess. Even though I can't see it, I know it. Covered in blood, sweaty from the physical activity and the adrenaline, with a puffy face from the attacks and tears. Not a pretty sight. "Mabel, are you okay?" His question pierces through my thoughts, and I drift back to reality for an instant, only to slip back again into the ocean of darkness in my brain.

How could I even begin to express what I've been through? Minimizing my response to a simple, single word seems too shallow. It wouldn't even begin to cover the emotions weighing my spirit down.

Scared shitless? Too vague.

In shock that I managed to escape from Cupid after discovering murder and nonconsensual touching turns him on? Too triggering.

The words become prisoners in my throat, unwillingly trapped when I should force them out as I stare back at Danny, sight solely focused on him while I will my body to stop shaking like an anxious chihuahua. He is a beacon of light in this twisted reality, keeping me grounded in a positive horizon, even though there's no certainty that there will be one. After what seems like forever, but is only a handful of seconds, I glance around to try to take in my surroundings.

I'm in a communal bathroom. Danny kneels by a toilet where Cerys is sitting on the closed seat, eyes flickering between us like he can't figure out what to do. Thanks to the two flashlights illuminating the room, I notice when a third participant hovers in the background, walking from the sinks with something in her hands. Copper hair shines as she moves past the lights, and I finally identify who it is.

Bethan.

She had been completely absent from my mind since the second we got separated. How has she managed to stay alive? Zelda didn't mention her before, and Carmen hadn't seen her either. Could it be that she's been hiding here since the beginning?

I narrow my gaze, focusing on the details of her appearance. She's more disheveled than I've ever seen her, which is saying a lot since we lived in the same sorority for years; I've seen what she looks like in the morning. Her red hair is messy, matted in places where it has tangled, with sweat plastered along her hairline. Streaks of mascara chisel her cheeks, revealing she's been crying. Although her clothes are dirty and her pale legs have some bruises forming around the knees and shins, she doesn't appear to be hurt.

But her worn-out appearance isn't what catches my attention.

My eyes remain locked on the towel in her hands. White fabric stained by red.

Blood.

My heart drops to the pit of my stomach, leaving me dizzy as I piece together that someone here is injured.

And it's not Bethan.

I squeeze my eyes shut as I press the backs of my hands to them to avoid shedding more tears. Why is it that every time I come close to feeling any sort of relief, it's quickly turned to ashes by a dreadful event? Hope is a fragile thing in this place, so easily crushed.

It's stupid of me to believe anything good can come out of this when I know what the odds are for surviving a slasher. Most of us will not make it. But I have a harder time facing the fact that the people I care about can and will inevitably be hurt.

Like Carmen was.

Like someone here is now.

"Who's injured?" I ask, my voice barely a whisper, even though I think I know the answer.

I just need to hear it.

The lingering silence tells me more than any verbal response could.

Opening my eyes, I focus on them all. Danny and Bethan turn to Cerys.

He's on his knees, pressing his hands against the side of Cerys' torso where blood is leaking from between his fingers. There's a first-aid kit open at their feet on the floor. He gestures to Bethan with his head, and she approaches with the towel, putting it over his hands until he moves them from underneath so she can apply pressure to the wound. They're taking it in turns to try to stop the bleeding.

Cerys' whimpers become muffled as she covers her mouth and nose with her hand. Tears spring from her blue eyes as she closes them, trying to endure the pain.

"What can I do?" I question, burying the memories of what I've just lived through, swallowing down the trauma so I can give all my energy to Cerys.

If I focus on one task at a time, I can stay solid, even though my bravery and sanity have been chipped and scarred by the events I've endured alone.

I kneel down between Danny and my friend, setting the dagger on the ground for a moment, even though it might be a stupid move that will put me in danger. I don't need it right now. While I can't see her wound, I can tell she's badly injured. Worse than Carmen, not as badly as Zelda, yet it doesn't mean she doesn't need medical attention. Sweat beads crown her hairline and she's paler than usual, accentuating the dark circles under her eyes. She looks feverish.

My entrails twinge with worry.

This isn't good.

Fuck, this is so *not good*, I confirm a little louder in my mind.

I run one hand through my hair, pulling on the strands

even though my scalp is sore from Shane's sharp tug. It's a good distraction to prevent me from falling into a pit of hysteria.

This isn't how things were supposed to go tonight.

I had promised not to come back to Westbrook until Carmen graduated, but I did it to ensure nothing bad would happen to my sister. Then, when I found out about my best friend's arrival, I added her to the mission to keep them safe. When the horrors started, all I cared about was making sure that Carmen and Cerys walked out of this without a hair out of place. That's all I've wanted.

Now I've failed at keeping them from harm. They're both hurt and I can't do anything to help them.

I dread to think about what will happen next, considering we haven't reached the climax of this slasher story just yet, but we're getting close. So close my gums ache from clenching my jaw.

Cerys extends her hand to me, and I take it in both of mine. Her fingers are cold to the touch, possibly from the pain she's enduring. I don't want to think about anything other than the pain. As long as she feels something, she's not dying, right? There's no scientific logic behind the thought. I just need to convince myself that she's going to be okay.

"What happened?" I ask, even though I'm afraid to know the answer.

I can't bear to hear how I've failed to protect her, but staying informed is also important. That's the only way we'll be able to figure out Cupid's motive.

"After you left—" Cerys starts retelling her version of the events, but she's struggling with the words as Bethan applies more pressure. The clasp on my fingers tightens until my knuckles turn white. "Carmen and I went to the kitchen and found the knives. Then we went to find you, but the killer appeared, and we got separated. I wandered around alone for a while, and then I found Bethan in the laundry room. We tried to find a way out, or one of you, until Danny found us."

Danny stops searching for supplies in the kit and glances at me.

"I was looking for you."

I wish it was bright enough that I could see his eyes. The words make his voice hoarse with intensity and it tells me everything I need to know. If he weren't focused on helping Cerys, he would be scolding me for abandoning my place. While it wasn't a promise I actually made, he's still holding me accountable.

"We tried to find you and Carmen," Bethan continues as Danny begins to bandage the wound. "He came out of nowhere, stabbed Cerys, and moved on. It happened so fast that, if Cerys hadn't screamed, we wouldn't have noticed."

Wait, what?

I blink as I process what they're saying.

"He didn't try to attack you two?" I question, pointing at Danny and Bethan.

They shake their heads.

"That's the thing, he could've killed me," Cerys adds through gritted teeth. "There was plenty of time to do it. Instead, he simply . . . left."

I frown, confusion slithering under my skin.

Every time I've seen Cupid—or almost every time—he's been consistent with the way he hurts people. The only times he's attacked without killing have been because his targets got away, like Carmen and I did when he stabbed her. Otherwise, his lethal blows are delivered with speed. He did it with Elodie, Leighton, and even Shane. Going straight for the kill without wasting time with torture. From what I can infer, he did the same thing with Ray, the guy Zelda mentioned.

But what they're implying is that for some reason Cupid only cared about hurting Cerys without necessarily killing her. The question is *why*.

Why go out of his way to change his M.O. for Cerys?

Unless she's a part of his end game.

Unless she's the target . . .

Killing her too early would be a waste for him when she's designed to be the last victim.

If she's the goal, then what's the motive?

I'm lost in my thoughts as I watch Danny bandage Cerys' wound like an expert. I'm in awe of how calmly he deals with everything that's been occurring, because I can barely keep it together.

I wonder now how I managed to treat Carmen's injury myself. Although I didn't do much, other than find something to use to press on the wound and soak up the blood. If I had been Danny, I would've remembered that the bathrooms are always stocked with first-aid kits. It would've been a massive help to me when I was trying to figure out what to do.

"What about you?" Danny asks, pulling me back to reality. "You weren't where I left you."

I pick up on what he's not saying when his eyes roam my face and body, still checking for wounds. Unlike Cerys, I'm not bleeding. Or at least I think I'm not bleeding. It's hard to tell when my shirt has gotten splattered by blood and gore throughout the night.

Danny lets go of Cerys and stands, gesturing me to follow him to the sinks. There isn't much privacy here with Cerys and Bethan listening to our every word. Considering Cerys' history, I don't feel comfortable mentioning everything that happened to me. Especially what Cupid was trying to do before I managed to evade him; what could've happened if I hadn't head-butted him.

I gulp.

A montage of horrible images fast-forwards in my brain, reminding me of what I've been through since I left Zelda in the lounge. Finding Carmen, witnessing her getting stabbed, Shane . . . A cold shock hits the base of my spine as I remember the way he attacked me.

He tried to kill me.

Somehow, it feels worse to think about him murdering me because I wasn't expecting to die, or come close to dying, by the hand of someone who wasn't Cupid. When I got a bad feeling about him earlier tonight, I never thought he was capable of murder. Though, should I truly be that surprised? He already viewed me as less than a person by the way he expressed himself, wishing I'd been the one Brian raped instead of Cerys.

"Baby," Danny calls softly, lifting my chin with his index finger, bringing me back to the present. Concern is visible in the lines of his face. "What happened?"

I shake my head.

Not now, I want to say.

I don't know if I can even speak about what happened

with Cupid without feeling like I want to scratch my skin off to erase all trace of him.

"I'm sorry." It's all I can muster.

He shakes his head. "You warned me that you couldn't keep that promise, but I never thought you would sacrifice yourself for Zelda."

I think it was meant to come out as a lighthearted joke, but I can tell there's truth underlying his words. He hasn't fully gotten over it.

Cerys' head snaps in our direction, no longer pretending she's not listening in to our conversation.

"For Zelda? What?" Surprise increases the pitch in her tone.

I know it must come as a shock to her, considering everything that I've said about Zelda in the past. She could be both irrationally mean and drastically bitchy. And that's before we even get to the obvious reason why I don't like her: the stance she took to defend a rapist.

Even so, I still find myself feeling empathy toward her. That might make me seem like an idiot, but I still hope she survives and sees the error of her ways.

"We found Zelda a little while ago. She was badly injured, so I left Mabel with her while I looked for Carmen and you," Danny explains to Cerys and Bethan as he turns the faucet on in one of the sinks.

A wrinkle creases my forehead.

He didn't leave to find Carmen. His main reason was to find the knives in the kitchen and then follow the rest of the plan after he returned to me. Apparently, neither of us can keep a promise.

Instead of arguing, I bite the tip of my tongue and watch what he's doing as he leans over the sink with the water running. I think he's doing it to wash Cerys' blood off his hands, but then he pulls me closer and starts to tenderly wipe away the blood speckles on my face, erasing every trace.

A sting burns in my eyes as tears gather behind my lids. How can he be so gentle and caring with me? What did I do to deserve this treatment from him? I haven't been the best to him. We spent so long apart because I was stubborn and mean, and yet here he is, tenderly cleaning the blood off my face, even though he's not happy with me and my tendency to play the martyr.

Thank you, I mouth, unable to make a sound, and to add more weight to it, I tap under my chin and then my chest.

"I didn't know if you wanted me to use spit again," he teases, signaling back with a gentle smile. Inevitably, my lips curve upwards. Turning to Cerys, he continues, "When I returned, Zelda was alone, and she told me that Mabel decided to become the sacrificial lamb."

Zelda was alive after Cupid stabbed Carmen. It's a relief to know she hadn't given up the fight. I don't know how long she has left in her before she loses the battle, but I'm hoping it's enough for her to hold on until she's rescued.

Huh. Who'd have thought—at the start of the night I didn't care whether she lived or died, and now I'm rooting for her to survive.

"That's not what happened," I defend myself to Danny. "Cupid was in the room with us. If I'd stayed there, you would've found both of our corpses."

It's unfair of him to be mad about my actions when it was

what kept me alive. The world may never know what would've happened if I hadn't fled, but I very much doubt there would've been a positive outcome. At least this way I'm alive. Bruised and beaten, with future nightmares stored up in my memory, but alive.

It's all that matters.

Danny purses his lips in discontent.

"That's not how Zelda described it."

"Are you going to believe her over me?" I grit out. Closing my eyes, I press my lips together as I regain some control over myself. I didn't mean to snap at him or turn this into an argument. There's no need for us to engage in one when our time together is precious. "She's probably feverish and hallucinating—"

"Guys!" Bethan interrupts us before we can continue bickering about trivial stuff.

It doesn't matter whether I kept my promise or put myself at risk. The truth is that there's nowhere safe in this place as long as we continue roaming the halls. Cupid will catch up with us if we don't figure out a way to leave the house or get enough service to call for help.

"So, after you left me with Zelda, I heard Cupid coming," I continue, focusing on the story instead.

"How did you know it was him?" Bethan interrogates, crossing her arms.

I swallow, licking my lips as I recall the small ways that I've memorized to identify Cupid without having to look at him. It's not a foolproof method, but it has helped me enough.

"His steps. He walks funny, like he's making sure to step as hard as he can to announce his presence before you can even tell he's there," I explain, unsure if it makes sense or if I'm just sounding like a mad woman. "He's deliberate about it, though. When Leighton died, he was swift and silent."

Cerys nods in agreement. "You're right. It was the same when he attacked us in the room and when he stabbed me."

"I noticed that too," Danny says, as he continues cleaning the blood off my face.

Even though he's not happy with me, his touch on my skin is gentle, never once applying unnecessary pressure or causing me any discomfort. Invisible rope ties itself around my ribs, tightening its hold on me.

"When I heard him," I continue without breaking eye contact, "I knew I could either wait for him to find me there or give myself at least a chance to survive, to keep myself safe, even if he came after me."

"Sacrificial lamb," he mumbles under his breath and shakes his head.

I resist the need to roll my eyes and continue telling the story of how I distracted Cupid and ended up finding my sister. I describe how he stabbed her, omitting the fact that I stemmed her bleeding by using my bra because I didn't think about the first aid-kits in the bathrooms. Clearly, my work under pressure is a bit hit or miss.

"There. Much better." Danny finishes cleaning my face as best he can.

Turning to the mirror, I wince when I see my reflection.

I look . . . horrible.

My hair is messier than Bethan's, strands standing up in odd places where tangles have formed. Red smears disappear into my hairline where blood congeals on my scalp. There's puffiness under my eyes from all the crying I've done tonight. A bruise is forming on my jaw, and I can only guess it's from both Shane's slap and the fall down the stairs. What was once a clean shirt now resembles an abstract painting from all the different blood splashes and sprays, but it covers just enough to hide any other bruises.

I'll look even worse tomorrow—if I make it out.

"Where's Carmen now?" Bethan ask, distracting me.

I turn from the mirror to look at her.

"I hid her."

"Where?"

Defiance swirls on the tip of my tongue. I'm almost tempted to ask why she wants to know where I hid Carmen, but I'm also aware it's part of my rising paranoia.

I have no reason to distrust Bethan right now. After all, from my encounters with Cupid, I know she can't be him. She's too tiny and fragile to fit Cupid's build and have carried out all those atrocities. Besides, it's not like Bethan has anything against Carmen. My sister was always one of her favorite pledges since her first day. Bethan is a sucker for girls who have a backbone, even when hers can be easily swayed.

"The attic," I reveal after a few seconds of silence. "It doesn't seem to be a way out, but it was untouched when we got there. I made sure I wasn't seen leaving and that we didn't leave any hints that there was anyone up there. So, it's safe enough."

"Safe to hide," she murmurs, almost echoing my words. Nodding, she adds, "It could work. Assuming people will leave Kappa to come here within the next hour, I'm guessing we could stay there without problems."

It's almost surprising to me that we agree on something. Not because she's particularly stupid. I've simply lowered the bar for her since she decided to support Brian and his father against Cerys. If she truly thought for herself, she would've stood with her friend. Not with a rapist. But there isn't much we can do about that now.

The past should stay in the past, at least for tonight when we have a bigger common enemy. If we weren't in this scenario, I'd still be holding a grudge.

"Should we go to the attic, then?" Cerys asks.

We all look at her.

Going to the attic could be the difference between her survival and her demise. However, we have to be realistic. She's hurt and might slow us down, both revealing where we're headed and making us vulnerable.

"Do you feel up to it?" I say, tilting my head to her wound.

Slowly, Cerys nods. "I feel like the worst has passed." Her lips curve into a tight smile, and I can tell she's lying to make us feel better. "The pain comes and goes in waves."

In waves, like every time she moves and causes the skin of her torso to stretch itself, which is exactly what will happen when she walks or climbs the ladder up to the attic.

"Cerys—"

"I'm fine," she reassures me before I can get another word in. "I can walk."

"We'll help you," Danny intervenes. "I can carry you."

Even in her current condition, Cerys has the audacity to look offended.

"Nonsense," she chastises him. "I said, *I can walk*."

I lower myself to the ground in front of Cerys so I can meet her eyes.

"Are you sure?"

The blue in her eyes lacks the usual glint. If it weren't for the tears gathered in them, they would look void and empty. It sends an alert to my core. She's not doing well at all and is trying to put on a brave face to avoid holding us back.

"What else can we do? Stay here?" she whispers. "He will find us eventually. I don't want to be the reason you guys end up in danger. I already feel like it's my fault."

Her lips tremble.

I wish I could comfort her and say this is not all on her. While she's not responsible for Cupid's behavior, she does seem to be the reason behind all this. Why else would he stab her but then let her to live to tell the tale? He's had her in his hold twice and hasn't killed her yet. So uncharacteristic of him, unless that's part of his plan. I think back to the letter blaming her for the deaths and the photos plastered on the walls. It might not be her fault, but someone is targeting her.

"He did this, not you," I remind her, taking her hands in mine. "Everything that's happened tonight... *He's* responsible."

Cerys shakes her head. "His letter said that every death would be my fault. I did what he asked, I came back here, yet he's still killing." Her voice cracks as she reaches the point of no return, caving under the pressure of her injury and all the trauma that has unfolded tonight. "Why is he doing this?"

Without knowing what else to say, I throw my arms around her, wrapping her in a gentle hug, careful not to hurt her. She doesn't seem to mind or care, because she presses herself tighter against my chest and then suddenly the dam breaks. Heartbreaking sobs wrack her body, making her shoulders heave with every breath she takes.

I don't know what to tell her.

I can't share the theories I've come up with because it would only make her feel worse.

Begging for help, I look to Danny, silently asking him to waltz in with his charm to save the day.

Thankfully, he gets the message and approaches us with one of his radiant smiles, the one that can light up an entire room. The corners of his eyes crease with emotion. I watch in wonder at how he manages to be a beacon of light even in the darkest situations.

"Cerys, it's not your fault," he reassures her. "We all received letters that put blame on us. We all did what was asked of us, and it was pointless because he had all this planned. We would've been here regardless."

"I mean, *some* people didn't do what was asked," I point out, looking at Bethan.

I remember her venting about it before we discovered there were other letters. She was told to quit her role as president of Kappa, which is something she failed to do.

Guilt flashes in her eyes. "I'm sorry."

I wave a hand to her, minimizing the importance.

"Like Danny said, he would've done this regardless."

With this level of preparation, Cupid must have been sure that we would be here. The threats were only meant to keep us on our toes, make sure the ones who were out of town came back, and to keep the ones who were already here in place. This spree was bound to happen.

Even if we had ignored the messages, he would've found a way to drag us here.

I wouldn't put it past him to go as far as drugging and kidnapping us. I find it almost too sickening to think my brain has adapted to this reality with such ease. How I could go from being too scared to even think about the possibilities to being able to try to figure out all the possible scenarios.

I should be disgusted with myself.

This isn't a movie plot I'm reviewing, but after everything, my brain is trying to find a coping strategy to come to terms with what's happened. If it means seeing everything from a filmmaker's point of view, then so be it.

To distract myself, I rub Cerys' back in circles to calm her down. After a minute, her cries subside to shaky sniffles every few seconds.

"I don't want anyone else to get hurt," she says. "I know what you guys are saying is true, but I can't shake off the feeling that this is all because of last year; because of me. Do you really think this is Brian's killer messing with us, Mabel?"

When I first came up with that theory, I only had the letters, and it seemed like a logical assumption. The messages were threatening to kill, so it made sense at the time to think of the person who had murdered before. However, I'm not so sure anymore. Brian's killer seemed to be on our side. They called him out for being a rapist. It's the reason why most of campus believed Cerys had killed him.

This feels different.

If it's the same person, maybe he felt like Cerys owed him something. He killed her biggest threat, only for her to leave campus. Perhaps Cupid feels abandoned.

While I like this theory, there's also the possibility that Brian's killer and Cupid are two separate individuals with different agendas.

It explains why the other one seems like he wants to torture her. All the articles and photographs plastered over the house point back to her. Targeting her more than once in the house and letting her go—it's a twisted game he's playing with her.

The only thing both killers would have in common is that they're both using Cerys for their motivation.

"Maybe, but we can't waste time theorizing about it." I redirect the attention back to what we can control. "We have to get to the attic, if you're still feeling up to it," I add, empathizing with her condition.

Cerys looks down at herself and then nods. "Yes, let's do this."

"Wait, the attic," Danny mumbles as if he has remembered something important.

"What about it?" I ask.

"This is Florida," he says as if we're meant to catch what he means. "Attics aren't like the ones up north, they need proper ventilation, or the high temperatures will fuck the roof up."

Ventilation.

Understanding washes over me.

"There's a way out," I say. "Through the vents."

Danny nods. "It might be too small for me, but I'm sure you girls could squeeze out, even if it's only one of you."

We just need one person to get out, then they could call for help. Granted, it leads to the roof, and whoever goes out there would still need to figure out how to get down to the ground; but maybe the phones would work from there since it wouldn't be inside the house.

"You're a genius."

Danny's cheeks pinken as he scratches the back of his neck. "Let's not get our hopes up just yet. We don't know in what condition Theta has kept the vents. It might be a dead end."

I shake my head. "It won't be."

We need this little grain of hope to get us by, to help us endure whatever is ahead of us.

This *has* to work.

Chapter 19

DANNY'S CARAMEL EYES GLINT WITH HOPE, ELATION growing between us now that we have a clear mission. It's not only about having a place to hide, but a way to escape as well.

I glance at Danny, who offers me his warm hand to help me stand up. Giving his hand a light squeeze, I offer him a tight smile. It's the best I can come up with. I wish we had more time to sit and talk. There's nothing I would like better than to discuss my theories with him, since he's the one who has believed every crazy thought that I've had today. Starting from the moment I told him about Brian's killer being the one who sent the letters too.

Together, we help Cerys to her feet. She groans a little from the effort it takes her but manages to remain standing in spite of the stab wound to her side. It's impressive to see how strong she is. I don't know if I would have the same courage to do what she's doing. Once she's on her feet, I pick up the dagger from the floor before I forget about it.

Bethan takes over helping Cerys, pulling her arm over her shoulders to support her weight.

"I'll make sure the coast is clear," Danny offers, heading to the door.

I follow him. Bethan and Cerys stay behind, waiting for the confirmation that it's safe to go.

His hand stalls when he reaches the knob, almost like he's reconsidering his actions. A few seconds go by in which he does nothing but stand there.

I touch his arm softly, barely caressing the skin with the tips of my fingers. Conflict shadows his expression, wrinkling his forehead as a million thoughts gather behind his eyes. Danny looks at me like he has something important to say. His gaze travels over my face, staring at my lips while his hands fidget with the edge of the doorknob. He seems to be at odds with himself, battling with something I can't quite figure out.

I'm about to ask if he's okay when he speaks first.

"Oh, fuck it," he whispers under his breath.

Taking a step forward, he cradles my face with his hands and presses his mouth against mine. For the first time, he kisses me in front of others, fully claiming ownership of my lips as he presses me closer against him. The kiss isn't passionate, just a light peck, but even so it ignites sparks in my stomach. Yearning grows in me, spreading through my limbs as I mold myself to fit in the space against his chest.

In a movie, this would be the intimate moment that makes the viewer swoon. Accompanied by dim lighting, vibrant emotions run high, appearing on the skin in the form of goosebumps. Melting into each other, sharing one last moment before reality has to set in. From a director's point of view, this kiss would require a close-up to encapsulate the passion and longing pouring from our lips.

Bethan clears her throat loudly, snapping us out of our moment.

Heat rises to my cheeks, coloring the skin of my face with a tint of embarrassment.

Part of me wants to tell her to mind her own business, but we don't have any more time to lose. Her presence is a reality check. We've already wasted enough time with this. It would be a major risk to stay here sharing kisses when we should be getting Cerys to a safe location.

The other part of me . . . well, it feels childish to admit, but I guess I'm just shocked to have been shown a public demonstration of affection like that. I never thought there would be a day where that would happen.

"Cute moment and all, but we're on a tight schedule," Bethan comments, brows twitching with impatience.

The warmth from my cheeks spreads to my neck. I stare at my shoes, contemplating the blood crusting on them as I collect myself. By this point of the night, I can't tell whose blood is on my shoes. Might be Leighton's or Zelda's. Then there's some of Carmen's from when she got stabbed, and I'm sure I have some of Shane and Jaden's too. And now Cerys' as well, probably. I carry a bit of every victim with me as I continue my journey through this madhouse.

I plead to any force above that I won't have to carry anyone else's blood with me.

The amount of therapy I'll need after tonight is insane. I've successfully been able to push back a lot of my struggles and traumas, but I draw the line at witnessing mass murder while trying to stay alive. It'll take me years to unpack this night.

Danny recovers faster than me, opening the door a sliver to check if the coast is clear. When he's sure there's no movement outside, he holds a finger up to signal to wait a second and slips into the hall.

Time seems to stall as we wait for Danny to come back. None of us says a word, only the slight hush of our breathing blows over the silence. I've always been comfortable in quiet places, but this one is unnerving, making each strand of hair stand on end. The tension increases, swirling around us in a thick rope of anxiety.

I decide to count to thirty in my head in an effort to dispel the anxiety clouding my judgment. I've just made it to twenty-one when Danny pops his head through the gap between the door and the frame and offers us a sharp nod.

The signal to get going.

Somehow, leaving the bathroom is easier than sneaking in. Danny, guiding our steps, motions us to come out one by one. I go first, keeping the dagger firmly in my hand as I eye the end of the corridor across from Danny while Bethan helps Cerys. When we're all in the hall and Danny closes the door, he pivots on his heel to look at me.

"You go first," Danny orders, pointing at the dagger with his chin. "I'll stay at the back."

Silently, I get his message that I should lead the group. If anything were to happen from this end, I would be able to protect them since I'm the one with a weapon.

Bethan and Cerys remain in the middle of our group, closely followed by Danny. The floorboards creak. Louder than I would've liked.

Anxiety transforms into a rope tightening around my ribs, and my spine straightens. Worry triggers itself in my system, striking new flames of paranoia in my entrails.

This is a bad idea.

When has a plan in this house ever gone right? Everything we've accomplished has been by sheer luck. Perhaps we should've considered staying in the bathroom for a little longer since we'd have better odds that way.

I don't share my anxious thoughts with the group. After all, that's the last thing they need. They're motivated by the hope Danny and I gave them.

I swallow the sourness coating my tongue and focus on leading the group. While my sense of direction is off-kilter, it should be easy to locate our route considering Jaden's body was lying in the hall.

"Wait." I stop the group, tightening my hold on the dagger.

There's no body. Just two pools of blood soaking the floorboards to indicate the murders. I wasn't expecting to see Shane, but Jaden? He was still there when I crossed the hall not too long ago.

In the time that we were in the bathroom, Cupid must have taken Jaden's body and disposed of it. How did it happen so quickly?

He was right here. Did Cupid follow me when I escaped? Maybe not as far as the bathroom, but he could have started to come after me but then decided to move Jaden's body.

A chill travels down my spine.

There's a bad omen shadowing us, creeping up my skin.

"What's up?" Bethan asks, her tone strained by what seems to be a mix of fear and impatience.

They're going to hate what I have to say.

Maybe we should've found a different route to find the attic, but it's too late now. Danger is closing in on us as we stand here whispering to each other.

"He already took Jaden's body," I tell them.

Bethan's eyes widen and Cerys' breath hitches.

"Jaden's dead?" Bethan asks at the same time as Cerys says, "He takes the bodies?"

I nod, unable to say anything else.

There's no point in recounting how I discovered that Cupid hid the bodies. My stomach rebels against me, almost making me gag when I picture all the corpses laid together in a room as if they were prized collections. By now, considering he's murdered five or six people, he probably has a favorite kill.

That's a very high number, considering what it means for the next part. The stakes are getting higher and the killer is top of the leaderboard. Act Three is approaching fast, and I'm terrified, because that's when the final killing spree will happen.

The knot in my throat blocks me from gulping the acid in my mouth.

"The body was here when I went to the bathroom," I tell the group, shifting my position slightly to be able to watch them and the end of the hall at the same time. "If he's gone—"

"It means Cupid was here recently," Danny finishes, catching on to what has me so shaken.

An ominous silence spreads among us. I hold my breath until the tissue in my lungs starts to scorch. When I let it go, slowly, I spot a shadow moving at the top of the stairs. I hear a floorboard as it creaks under pressure, and I know the noise isn't coming from where we are.

It comes from *over there*.

"And now he's back," I confirm in a whisper, though my voice carries through the hall.

Another creak, followed by a stomp, slashes the tense atmosphere, confirming my words.

"Cerys," Danny calls in a barely audible tone.

"Yeah?" Her voice is small and fearful, sounding frail.

"Can you run?"

It's the most important question. She's at a disadvantage with the stab wound affecting her speed.

Still, she moves her head in a barely perceptible nod. "I'll run."

At this point, it's not a matter of whether she can run or not. She *has* to because the alternative is to stay here and die. Cerys must know we would do our best to help her fight her odds, but it puts all of us at risk. I don't know if Bethan feels bad enough for how she treated Cerys to sacrifice herself for her in an act of redemption, but I know Danny and I would.

"Get ready," Danny warns. "You too, Mabel."

I furrow my brows.

What does that even mean?

Are we not all running?

My eyes narrow on him, spotting the way his muscles

tighten under his shirt as if he were preparing to face someone. Arming himself with courage and determination to fight. I flicker my gaze between him and the end of the corridor where he's looking.

Distrust scratches the walls of my throat.

"Danny," I pronounce in a hoarse tone.

"Mabel, don't fight me on this one, *please*."

His voice wavers on the last word, begging like he has something stuck in his throat and is trying to remain strong. There's something about his tone that sounds off. He's holding back from saying what he wants to say, or he's trying to prevent me from getting what his plan is, but it doesn't take a genius to figure it out.

From the way he's bracing himself, tensing his muscles against a possible attack, I can guess he's going to try to stall Cupid to give us a chance to run to the attic.

But he doesn't realize there's a fault in his logic.

We can't simply stall Cupid, we have to lead him as far away as possible to give the girls a fair chance to get safely to the attic without being followed. Otherwise, we're simply putting them at risk. Our entire plan to use the vents to escape will be worthless if Cupid gets to the attic before we can even attempt to check them.

Cupid takes a step forward, out from the shadows. He stands there and tilts his head like he's waiting for us to make the first move. At first, his confident stance, legs planted apart and arms behind his back, seems almost harmless without a weapon in sight.

He just watches us like we're having a staring contest and he knows he's going to win it.

My chest rises and falls with short gasps of air, even before we start running. Adrenaline pumps in my veins, igniting a new conviction in me. There's no way in hell I'm going to run and let Danny stay behind with Cupid. The killer might not have a weapon at the moment, but I remember how easily he pulled out the dagger from under his clothes. He has ways to hurt us that we're not aware of.

This is all a sick, twisted game to him, watching us run and attempt to fight.

There's no way in hell he doesn't have a way to kill us under his robes, especially when he's outnumbered by our group.

It's almost like Cupid reads my mind. Although I can't see his face behind the mask, I swear he smirks triumphantly as he brings out one of his hands from behind him and shows us the long machete he's been hiding. The sharp edge almost mocks us, shining through the dim hall.

He has the upper hand now; he's had it all along.

Behind me, Bethan lets out a frightened whimper.

"Daniel," I use his full name, a stronger tone this time.

I clasp my fingers around the dagger's hilt until I fear it might break. God, the small blade has nothing on that machete. He will cut our arms off before we even have a chance to get near him.

Why would we even try in the first place?

Cerys sniffles, almost as if the universe itself wanted me to remember why it's important to put up a fight. My best friend, who has been through hell and back and still hasn't gotten her happy ending, deserves a chance at survival. She has earned her right to make it out of here and live a better life than all of us combined.

I owe her this much. I'll pay my debt to her because, this time, she won't be the one carrying the burden.

"Baby, please," Danny begs, and I know he can sense that I'm making up my mind about what I'm about to do next.

But, really, was there even a choice?

He's out of his fucking mind if he thinks that I'll leave him behind. I don't know if I could say I would die if something happened to Danny because I left. If Carmen survives this and he died, I know I would do my best to live, but my soul would be shattered.

Without him, I'd be a ghost wandering without any purpose.

I shake my head.

"You don't get to be the sacrificial lamb alone," I tell him and turn to face Bethan. I thrust the handle of the dagger into her hand without giving her a chance to think about it. "On the count of three, you run like hell. Don't look back."

Like Mami always said, *Para atrás ni pa' coger impulso*. You should never go backwards, not even to gain momentum.

Bethan's eyes cloud for a moment before they clear up and she gives me a sharp nod. They should go and forget we're even coming. Carmen will have a hard time understanding it, but it's our best chance we have if at least some of us are to survive.

It might be stupid for me to leave the dagger with them when it's something we'll need, but Carmen is locked in the attic with no weapon. They need it more than we do. After all, the plan is to distract Cupid and lead him away from the attic.

We can do that without a weapon.

Cerys unwraps her arm from Bethan's shoulders and holds on to her bicep instead so that she still gains some support from her, but not enough to slow her down. Her forehead twitches with the effort. Pride swells in my chest. *She will make an awesome final girl.*

Because even in this moment where death seems so near, her strength and power are admirable.

I stretch my hand out to Danny and ask, "Together?"

His lips tremble but he offers me a short nod. Lacing our fingers together, he stands firmly next to me, expanding his chest to prepare himself for the worst.

"Together."

We exchange looks with Cupid and I nod firmly.

"One," I whisper to the girls.

"Two."

A beat passes.

My heart speeds up.

Danny squeezes my hand three times.

"Three!"

Let the games begin.

Chapter 20

TO BE TRUTHFUL, I HAVE NO IDEA HOW SPRINTING AND racing actually works. The only time I've ever participated in a race it was one *Carrera del pavo* and even then I missed the countdown. I've never known if we're mean to start on *three* or a beat after.

However, as my heart speeds to my last count, I don't hesitate.

When I reach *three*, Danny and I move in unison, cohesively taking a step forward, directing our bodies toward Cupid. Fast and sudden but perfectly matching the girls' pacing. It's quick enough to give them a head start in the opposite direction, heading to the corner where the halls meet. They know what they need to do and so do we.

As Danny and I move, Cupid does too, mirroring our movements. He lunges forward, swinging the machete.

A warning that he's ready to chop our limbs off if we continue down this path.

But there's no option other than to keep moving forward.

We move together, as if our minds were working as one, directing our bodies in synchronized steps through the dim hall.

Seemingly annoyed by our determination to keep going, Cupid grunts and runs straight at us, lifting the machete in the air.

"Get down!" Danny exclaims and snaps into action as he finishes speaking.

His arm pushes me down to the floor, forcing my body to bend in half, just in time to avoid Cupid's machete. Behind me, the sharp blade meets the wall where my head was a second ago, scraping itself along the dry wall. Pieces of dust fall over my shoulders and I gasp out a choked sound.

Danny doesn't stall from the shock like I do, instead he pushes Cupid away while I get up onto my unsteady feet, giving me an opportunity to recover.

The killer stumbles, losing balance for a split second. His body clumsily stumbles, but not enough to fall. It would be too good to be true in this Murphy's Law horror house. We can only hope for brief instances of salvation. Cupid recovers quickly, almost impossibly fast. For a moment, I wonder if he did some drugs to prepare for this night or if he's simply incredibly agile, powered by anger or adrenaline—or both—as he leaps at us, jabbing the machete at Danny.

But my boy has strong reflexes, avoiding the blade by a few inches. The tip of the blade cuts into the dry wall next to his elbow.

I jerk backwards as I evade the swing that comes for me. I lower my body near to the ground and notice the girls are nowhere to be seen. A joyful rush spreads through my limbs, and a wave of power runs through my veins.

With Cupid focused on us, we can move from here with the reassurance that he won't follow them. He has no idea where they're going.

Anger spills out of him in grunts as he brandishes the machete.

Behind the mask, he puffs for air, his chest raising and falling at a rapid rate. Temptation rolls in my system, wanting to goad him to cause a bigger distraction. The chances that he'll follow us increase the angrier he gets.

The words slip from my lips before I can consider if this is a good idea.

"Can you even breathe in that mask, or are you carrying an oxygen tank under those robes?" Snark drips from my tone. "It would explain why you're so fucking slow."

Danny lets out a choked snort, completely caught off guard.

I'm too committed to distracting Cupid.

There's nothing that triggers a killer's temper more than sassy remarks and an attitude. While I don't have the physical strength to fight him off or acute reflexes like Danny, I've been trained by a mean little sister. Learning how to deliver punches with my words has been a skill I've developed over time, cautiously picking up on her sarcasm and brutal sassiness.

Cupid halts for a split second, only to react a moment later, kicking me in the knees.

I buckle forward, and if it weren't for Danny, I would fall on my face. His hands wrap around my arms, hoisting me up to prevent Cupid from taking advantage of my vulnerability. I realize a second later that if I had fallen, I would've been in the perfect position for a beheading.

Acid overflows in my mouth, mixing with thick saliva. It's a struggle to gulp it down to prevent it from taking over.

"Stairs," I mumble at Danny.

He turns his head to the side, eyeing the end of the corridor where the stairs begin, and he nods.

Without waiting to think about it or starting a new countdown, he pulls me by the arm along with him as he sprints in that direction. My legs struggle to keep up with his long strides. His days of baseball glory show in the way he runs fast and lightly, but I manage to hold my own, maintaining a constant rhythm.

I have no other choice because Cupid stomps behind us.

"We need a weapon," I tell Danny, holding on to the banister to prevent myself from falling as I reach the steps.

He moves his head in agreement.

"Kitchen?"

"Kitchen," I concur.

Keeping up the pace as we go down the stairs is hard, especially when we stumble upon Jaden and Shane. Both of their bodies are now hanging off the ledge of the banister.

Nausea bubbles in my mouth, and I have to urge the contents of my stomach to stay in place as I make it through. Danny's hand tightens its hold on me when he sees the bodies, but he manages to keep it together, going past them without any reaction. Since he manages to ignore it, so do I.

My hesitation could mean my death.

Or, even worse, Danny's death.

We pick up the pace when we reach the ground floor. This time, we don't stop to check the corners because the killer is at our heels.

Although my lungs scream at me to gasp for air, I run like hell with Danny. Not slowing down even though my thighs burn and ache like hell. I don't want to end up impaled on Cupid's machete.

I bet it would made a nice addition to his killing collection. More than a game, it seems to be an art for him, and he's planning on turning us into his next bloody masterpiece.

"We're almost there, baby," Danny huffs out.

Clearly, my lack of physical activity is showing because I feel faint from the run and he's noticed it. I force myself to keep going as we go through the archway into the kitchen.

Holy fuck.

I'm slightly taken aback by the huge, fancy kitchen. It seems like Theta put all their renovation money into the kitchen and forgot to spread the budget evenly through the house. If I wasn't being chased by a psycho, I would sit back and admire the refined and sleek aesthetic of the room.

But there's no time. Only an instant long enough to run to

the cabinets and open the drawers in search of what I need. Spoons, forks, butter knives . . .

"Where the fuck do they keep the carving knives?"

"Keep looking!" Danny exclaims and, before I can process it, he runs straight for Cupid, misdirecting the machete away from me.

"*Puñeta*," I gasp in shock, my eyes wide.

If it weren't for my knight in bloody shirt, I'd be suffering from a horrible injury.

Loss of a limb, probably.

Maybe even my head.

Cupid is determined on having my head, by the looks of it.

"Mabel!" Danny yells at me, forcing me back into motion.

I can't waste time when every second is invaluable.

Nodding along, I continue rummaging through the drawers until I find what I need. A row of knives neatly put together. I don't waste any more time, grabbing the hilt of the biggest knife I can find.

Game fucking on.

Let's even out the playing field. This time, it's two against one, and Danny is holding the fort, wrestling with Cupid for the machete while trying his hardest not to get cut. Cupid kicks Danny in the gut and then pushes him hard, knocking the air out of him. Danny stumbles against the kitchen island and lets out a pained groan.

I need to act quickly.

Led by pure instinct and the thrill of revenge, I bury the knife in Cupid's shoulder. The same way he did with Carmen. The flesh makes a *thwack* as the blade carves a sheath in the shoulder. Stabbing requires an amount of strength I wasn't ready for. I have to force the knife through the layers of clothing, skin and muscles, pushing the hilt with my palm further into his body.

I don't care about stabbing him when he's done far worse things. Hunting us for fun, killing all those people. This ends now.

He's going to be the last victim.

A shriek escapes his lips, in a higher pitch than I was expecting. Blood gushes over us as I pull the knife out, squirting me with red. I realize he's not as tall as he seemed. If anything, he's around my height now. Did I make him taller in my mind because I was terrified? Maybe now that I'm high on the power I'm perceiving him as shorter.

Behind me, I hear Danny rummaging for another knife.

I brace myself, giving in to the darkness in me as I get ready to stab Cupid again. This time, I'm going for the torso.

Gathering momentum, Cupid throws his head back and then headbutts me before I can plunge the knife into him.

Pain spreads through my face, blindsiding me for a second as it pulses under my skin.

"Mabel!" Danny's voice reaches me just as the machete slashes my arm.

I don't feel the blade cutting me until the burn spreads through the gash. It's a miracle I don't drop the knife, but it definitely weakens my hold on it. An animal noise reverberates in the kitchen, and it takes me a second to realize it comes from me.

I'm the wounded animal.

Danny's hands pull me backward through the kitchen.

I let him lead me away from Cupid just in time to prevent another slash. As we move, Cupid does too, making sure to swing the machete from side to side, forcing us back until we hit a half-open door. He pushes it wider and shoves us inside. The space feels colder here, and I'm not sure if it's because I'm entering a state of shock from the recent injury, or if there's an actual temperature change.

Then, all of a sudden, Cupid stops attacking.

He simply waves his machete in the air like he's saying goodbye, and slams the door shut. Danny jumps, moving to the door and smacking his hands against it.

"Hey!" he screams. "No, no, no."

Pressing my free hand on my bleeding arm, I glance around the room. It's a tight space, slightly bigger than the closet we hid in earlier. It's dark in here, and I struggle to make out the shadows of items around us that fill the metal shelves on each side of the room. My body trembles from the drop in temperature, making the beads of sweat on my skin feel cold.

It's a freezer, I realize.

These assholes from Theta have a fucking walk-in freezer.

Which one of their rich daddies paid for this?

Danny continues yelling at Cupid or anyone to open the door, but it's pointless. The door is tightly shut, and Cupid must've locked it from the outside. If there's something we can assume, it's that the freezer has layers of insulation that will drown out our calls for help.

Besides, who would hear us anyway?

Carmen, Cerys and Bethan should be two floors above us now, safely hidden in the attic, trying to find a way out of here through the vents. Who else is there? Zelda? Too injured to move, if she's not dead already. There are some unaccounted-for people, like Sophia and Ollie, but what are the odds they're alive to help us? We haven't caught sight of them since we split up.

"It's no use," I tell Danny.

I hate to be the voice of reason in this situation, but it's a waste of time and energy for him to bang on the inside of the door, hoping for something that will not come.

We're not getting out of here. Not unless Cupid himself wants us out, and who is to say he won't leave us here, turn the full power back on and put the freezer settings on blast so we can have a slow death. Leaving us to die of hypothermia could be another nice addition to his collection of kills. Perhaps not as bloody as the other options, and odd for a slasher who has been brutally murdering people, but it's surely creative enough to stand out.

We're the tragic romance. Some might even call it a homage to a popular movie, with the difference that, in this story, there's no door-space to debate about.

In this story, both lovers die.

After all, this night was never intended to be a romance. It was always meant to be a horror.

Danny's loud sigh echoes in the emptiness of the freezer. He presses his forehead to the door, shoulders slouching in defeat. I've never seen him so lost before and it breaks my heart that he fought so hard tonight only for it to end like this.

"This can't be it," he laments, his voice sounding broken. "For a moment, I really thought we had him."

His words hit me right in the gut, provoking a sudden

surge of emotion in my body. My lips tremble, and I press them together to prevent any noise from coming out.

"So did I," I admit, sharing the sentiment.

When I stabbed him, I got a rush of power, I truly thought we had the upper hand there, with Cupid wounded and submitting to the edge of my blade. I thought we were going to win without having to go through another horrible spree, without having to worry about my sister anymore.

I believed Cupid would be the last one to die tonight.

But he wasn't.

He's still out there, roaming the halls, looking for his next victim. Wounded, but not fatally. Instead of stabbing him in the shoulder, I should've gone for the head or neck. Something that would inflict more harm.

I walk to the back of the freezer, and press my back against the wall so I can slide to the floor. The humidity gathered on it helps me drop to my butt faster, hitting my coccyx on the way down, but I can barely recall the pain when other emotions are clouding my sensors.

The disappointment of our failure is stronger than the pain from the gash on my arm.

The certainty of death is bigger than everything combined.

In the darkness, I spot Danny's shadow approaching me until he sits next to me.

"Are you okay?"

I mumble an affirmation. Sadly, hoping to die from the wound on my arm would be too much to ask for, considering our circumstances.

He riffles around, pulling an item from his pocket, and

turns on the flashlight from his phone. I didn't even notice when he retrieved it from the bathroom. I can't even recall him turning it off as we abandoned that place, but it's here now.

The brightness makes my eyeballs hurt for a second, forcing me to close my lids until the sharpness of it dulls. I blink a few times, slowly getting used to the illumination. I've spent most of tonight trapped in dark places or dimly lit halls with pink neon lights. Great to create a scary atmosphere, but not so much to get good visibility.

I open my eyes just in time to catch Danny slicing off part of the hem of his shirt. Once he has a long strip of fabric, he moves to me and begins to wrap it around my arm, improvising a tight bandage to stop the bleeding. It doesn't need to be as tight as a tourniquet, just enough to slow the flow and help the blood clot.

"Does it hurt?" he asks as he ties the ends of bandage together.

Always gentle and caring, even when death is a door away.

My sweet Danny.

Why did I waste so much time being stubborn when I could've gotten to experience this for the past year?

"We're going to die." I say the words out loud, testing them in the hope that they'll sound fake, or he'll deny them.

Neither of those things happen, and it feels as if a heavy stone has dropped in my stomach.

"I know," Danny whispers in return.

A piece of my heart chips away.

I know.

A confirmation I didn't expect to hear from his lips. I guess a part of me was expecting Danny to have a plan, to hold on to hope when it seems like we've reached a dead end. He's been so good at staying calm, positive and collected through the persistent horrors, I didn't expect him to give up. But he has, and it makes the muscles of my heart contract.

"We still have time," I say, forcing myself to be the optimistic one now. "The power was out for a while. It doesn't feel as cold in here as it could be. Someone might still find us."

A pack of lies.

Danny's glance tells me as much.

"There's no one left to help us, Mabel," he concludes with an edge of defeat that makes me want to burst into tears.

He's right. We might have some time left, but how long? No one knows we're here. Even if the girls make it out, would they even think to check the freezer? The cops would search in every room in the house before they think of this. We'll likely die from hypothermia if we're not found in the next couple of hours.

Hopeless.

That's the word I'm looking for to describe how I feel—everything seems hopeless right now. This is the moment I've been dreading since the night began. I've always known that the chances of survival were low, but I never thought I'd have a slow death where I could contemplate every single moment I've lived through tonight.

After escaping Cupid's mortal blade multiple times, dying in a freezer seems like a lame joke.

Not even heroic or iconic.

Just . . . *bland*.

Of course I would have a bland death instead of an iconic one after busting my ass to stay alive.

"Well, at least we tried," I mumble, attempting to sound optimistic or even ironic, but my voice is frail and tiny.

I bite the inside of my cheek, commanding my body to behave and keep the tears at bay. Crying is the last thing I want to do. It means things are more serious and dreadful than we're pretending they are. If I manage to keep it together, maybe I can enjoy these last moments with Danny.

I turn to look at him, hoping to remember every detail, immortalizing his appearance and beautiful face in my brain.

His brown hair is slightly wet from the sweat and blood layered along his hairline. Unlike me, his face is free from any blood smears or splatters, the gold of his skin contrasting with the slight stubble that has grown a little since I first saw him today, back when we were ignorant of what the night had in store for us. The front of his shirt stained with blood is a map of the victims we've met tonight. *At least some of them.*

While he wasn't hurt physically, his eyes are no longer warm and bright. They've been clouded and darkened by a mask of pain in them. That's the biggest change I notice in him because I've always found warmth and comfort in his sweet puppy eyes. Now, he simply appears lost and disheartened.

"Yeah," he mumbles, his voice unable to hide the pain. "We tried."

I put my hand over his, can't find the words to make his pain any lighter. At least we can share it. Pain is always a bit easier to carry when there's someone helping you lift the weight.

"I hope the girls made it to the attic," I say, giving his cold hand a light squeeze. "We bought them some time, so hopefully they can escape."

He just nods.

A moment of silence passes, and then he returns the squeeze.

Followed by two more.

Squeezing my hand three times the same way he did when we decided to face Cupid together. I might be delusional at this point, but it almost feels like it means something to him.

Too purposeful to be coincidental.

"Danny."

"Mabs," he replies, moving his free hand to my chin, grasping it tenderly. His eyes roam over my face as if he's trying to memorize every inch of it. The caramel of his irises melting like he's adoring me through his gaze. "You're so beautiful."

My heart skips a beat.

"Even when I'm covered in blood?" I joke, unable to accept the compliment.

Danny simply smiles. For a second, the glint in his eye returns, and I wish I had a million more jokes up my sleeve.

"Even then," he says. His smile fades a second later, replaced by a slight frown. "I'm sorry I ever made you think you weren't."

I vaguely remember asking him if he thought I was ugly earlier tonight. Why does that seem like it happened ages ago? The memory of saying those words feels strange, like they belong to an entirely different person.

"You didn't," I assure him. "I was just . . . too caught up

in my head and insecure to understand what was happening. I guess I told myself I wasn't your type and you were out of my league because it made it easier for me to cope with what had happened. But then my ego also got in the way, so I mostly felt embarrassed."

Danny blinks a couple of times as if he were processing.

"It pains me to know you put yourself down when I should've tried harder."

Guilt is in his expression, furrowing his brows and lips. It seems like it was ages ago that we talked about The Incident. Too much has changed in those hours. Crazy how time twists itself when your mind is operating in survival mode. I don't want to sit here and talk about the *what ifs* or consider what we should've done differently.

Reality is, we could've both done things extremely differently. There were a million opportunities for us to be honest with each other, yet we weren't. Instead of facing our fears, we simply assumed the worst, allowed embarrassment and shame to govern us, and so lost time.

Valuable time we're never going to get back.

Time we no longer have.

Time we keep wasting.

"Maybe," I mumble. "Then again, I could've also tried harder to talk to you and discuss what happened, take accountability for kissing you. What I'm trying to say here is that it doesn't matter now, Danny. We're dying. I don't want to spend our last moments thinking about everything we did wrong. We have to let it go."

Danny's chest inflates as he takes a deep breath.

"That's the thing, I can't let it go," he says, shaking his

head. "I can't let it go because I was a fucking coward before."

I frown, a bit lost by his sudden urge to think it was his fault.

"Danny, it's okay."

"No, it isn't." His Adam's apple bobs as he gulps. He scratches the back of his neck, the nervous tic returning. "I'm screwing this up again."

"I don't . . . I don't follow," I confess, confusion twisting inside me.

Danny scrubs his forehead with his hand and sighs.

"Let me start over, please. I have to get this off my chest because I'm afraid you'll die before I can get this out. And I need to say it."

"Okay."

"I wish we reconnected under different circumstances so I could properly tell you how much of a fool I've been. I wish I hadn't let fear take over whenever I wanted to message you so I could find a way back to you, because I messed up big time." There's a pause in which he breathes. His thumb caresses my trembling chin, soothing the skin with his touch. "When you kissed me that night, I felt so conflicted and ashamed, not just because you were drunk when you did it. I know that I appear confident and straightforward, but I'm just a stupid fool for you, one who can't seem to say the right thing or make the correct move, so I just couldn't think of a scenario where you'd want to kiss me without being intoxicated. I thought you only kissed me because you were drunk, but I kissed you back because I was in love with you."

My breath hitches, stuck in my airways.

Because I was in love with you.

Danny was in love with me. I think back to the nights we would sit on the roof, sharing conversations when no one was there to see us. All that time thinking he didn't like me, while he was harboring love for me, and I never noticed. Before all the hurt and heartache, he was in love with me. Somehow, in the moments of deep conversations, inside jokes and stolen glances, he fell in love with the girl I used to be.

But the sad truth is I'm no longer that girl.

And not just because I live a different life on the other side of the country.

This world has broken me on levels I can't even begin to describe, since long before tonight happened. Loneliness and trauma carve deep scars into a person's soul until there's nothing left but scar tissue. That's how I feel. Like I'm damaged goods, unable to experience anything other than hurt and pain, creating walls with spikes on them to prevent the sharp world from harming me anymore.

Finding out he loved me for who I was hurts more than the gash on my arm.

He'll never get the opportunity to see if he can love the woman I currently am, the bolter.

"You were?"

Danny doesn't answer my question, his eyes unfocused.

"You left," he whispers, sounding broken. "I was so in love with you, and you slipped away from me before I got the chance to make things right. For the past year, I've told myself to move on and let go. I buried my feelings deep until I no longer felt them, but then . . ." His voice trails off, silence extending with his breaths.

"Then what?" I prompt, even though I'm unsure if I want to hear more about how he used to love me, and I left. He needs this more than I do.

If this is the peace of mind he desperately needs before dying, then I can handle the hurt and discomfort.

I'd do anything for him.

His gaze wanders over my face as if he's trying to soak in every detail before focusing on my eyes.

"Then I saw you today and everything came rushing back to me. I fell in love with the girl I knew and fell even harder for the woman you are now. I'm still in love with you—deeply, madly in love with you."

Everything stops. My heartbeat, the oxygen flowing in my lungs, the blood rushing in my veins. I lose all sensation along my skin as the words echo in my brain, repeating the confession over and over again until my body no longer vibrates with emotion, and I can speak without shattering into tears.

It's my turn to confess.

"When I left Westbrook, I told myself just about every lie in the book so I could move on, but nothing worked. It felt like a chapter I couldn't finish, no matter how hard I tried. If there's one thing I've learned today, after everything we've been through, it's that I couldn't move on because I love you, Daniel Singh."

"I love you," he repeats, squeezing my hand as he says each word.

Realization slams into me like a massive wave of emotions flooding my chest.

Three words.

I love you.

Three squeezes.

I . . . love . . . you.

My heart flutters as I finally understand what he's been confessing all night, silently telling me he loves me while I thought he was simply comforting me.

Unable to utter more words, I put a hand on the back of his neck and pull him into me, pressing my mouth on his. Danny melts into my embrace, kissing me back and moaning as I bury my fingers in his hair.

"I hate that we lost so much time," he mumbles against my lips.

I sigh and press my forehead against his.

"Honestly, how dramatic of us to wait to admit our feelings until literal death is knocking on our door," I say to lighten the mood before we get lost in that spiral.

Thinking about the time we've wasted is too depressing to think about right now.

Danny snorts.

"At least we got to say it," he says. "I can't even imagine what I would've done if something had happened to you before I could say it—"

I press my fingers over his lips. "Shh, we said it. That's all that matters."

"We did," he agrees.

His arm wraps around my shoulders and gently, making sure he's not hurting my arm, he pulls me closer to him. His hug is warm as the temperature drops a degree or two. I welcome it, resting my head on his chest where I can hear the steady beat of his heart, finding comfort in it.

In the silence that covers us, I take the opportunity to

look at the interior of the freezer, now that we have the phone's flashlight on. The metal shelves are full of different boxes and packages, frozen food for the frat guys.

"I can't believe Theta has a fucking walk-in freezer," I comment.

Laughter rumbles in Danny's chest.

"Fucking rich people."

"They're fucking insane. How much money did they spend here?"

Danny hums. "A lot more than we could ever afford. It's pocket change to their rich daddies, though."

"Ugh, you're so right."

With the tips of his fingers, Danny begins to draw an invisible path down my back. When he reaches the end of my shirt, he climbs back, never touching the sliver of skin between my shirt and pants. Each caress sends shivers down my spine, making my hair stand on end. It's such an intimate thing, sitting here huddled together, enjoying our last hours together, soaking in every touch and caress.

"Mabel?"

"Hmm?"

"What part of the horror movie would this be?"

His question is interesting, although I can't pretend it's something that hasn't crossed my mind this evening. I've kept drawing parallels between the events of the massacre and my horror knowledge.

"Near the end of the second act," I respond. "Moments away from the climax, when everything is still for a second before the shit hits the fan with the killer reveal. It's shitty I won't be there for that moment."

"Do you have any theories about who it might be?"

I shake my head.

"Not anymore. I thought it was Shane, that shady guy from the party, the one who was also here, but while he turned out to be a creep regardless, he wasn't the killer. I saw Cupid kill him."

"Well, shit. I was hoping you had some idea."

A chuckle bubbles out of me.

"Trusting me as a horror connoisseur to know who the killer is?"

"Of course. If you can't figure it out, there's no hope for the rest of the casuals like me."

His humor lightens the mood, softening my tense muscles.

"I think Cerys is the final girl," I confess, and I feel his body clam up around me. "I didn't want to say it in the bathroom, but I believe the killer is doing it for her."

"For her?"

I wince.

"Maybe not *for* her now, but it started out that way. If it began with Brian's body, the killer empathized with her in some way."

"Why do you say so?"

"He wrote *rapist* on Brian's chest. Left him there for everyone in Greek Row to see," I remind him. "Don't take my word on this, but I think maybe the killer did it for her at the beginning, but then it didn't turn out how he expected. Maybe she didn't give him the attention he wanted, so now he's punishing her."

Danny takes a second to respond.

"That's fucked-up," he whispers.

"I just hope Carmen manages to survive. There's always two or three characters that survive the story, and since that won't be us, I hope it's them," I say.

"I hope they make it out too."

This time, since I can't reach his hands from this position, I settle for squeezing his thigh three times. His fingers stop caressing my back, and I raise my head from his chest to look at him for a second before I drop to his mouth. The bow of his lips draws me in like a moth to a flame, and before I can stop myself, I kiss him.

Danny returns the kiss immediately, as if his brain is wired to respond to my lips the instant they make contact. His soft mouth becomes ambrosia for me. I shouldn't be greedy, but I grow desperate for more of him, slipping the tip of my tongue in his parted mouth.

He groans as his tongue plays with mine, licking the tip before he sucks on it, eliciting a moan from me. I arch my back to press my chest closer to him. Getting bold, I shift our position and straddle him, hips rocking ever so slightly as the pressure in my lower abdomen begins to boil, spreading a wave of desire through my body.

Laying his hand on my lower back, he pulls me tighter to him.

It's not enough.

Raw greed thaws in me, turning me into a needy woman.

However, Danny doesn't seem to mind as he hoists me closer so I can get better access to him. I'm shaking on top of him as I lower myself onto the front of his pants, feeling the bulge growing under his clothes.

I gasp loudly when I feel it pulse against my core, and I pull away to meet his eyes.

There's a playful glint in them.

"Since we're going to die," he comments lightheartedly, "is having sex still considered a horror-movie sin?"

Chapter 21

IS HAVING SEX STILL CONSIDERED A HORROR MOVIE SIN?

His words create a loop in my brain as I process what he's saying. It's mostly a joke. There's a playful and lighthearted tone in his voice as he says it, yet there's something in his eyes, a tinge of intensity, that lets me know he's serious. Instead of pressuring me into it, he's letting me make up my own mind.

A joke or a proposition; it's up to me to decide.

If I say it's still a sin, Danny will take the rejection like the gentleman he is.

But if I say it isn't . . .

I swallow, attempting to quench the thirst drying out my throat.

My mind pulls out the memory of our moment together in Carmen's room. How his control snapped. How he transformed from the sweet guy I've grown to love into a man with no purpose other than pleasuring me. Kissing me as if I was the air he needed to survive, teasing my body, touching me in places that would elicit moans, begging to have a taste of me . . .

I shudder at the memory of how he gave me a delicious, mind-shattering orgasm.

Holding my breath, I force myself to think even while the oxygen isn't flowing in my system.

The choice should be so easy to make. We're dying, for fuck's sake, what do I have to lose? This is our last opportunity to finish what we started earlier, to get to experience everything with someone who cares about me as much as I care about him. I want this, being on his lap, feeling his hard dick pulsing for me. I didn't get a chance to see him earlier, let alone touch him. Now I'm desperate to do so. To strip his clothes off him and see what he's been keeping from me for so long.

I need this.

I need *him*.

"Mabs, it's okay," he says gently, caressing my cheek with the back of his fingers. "It's perfectly fine if it's still a sin."

I want to smile at his gentle reassurance. He wouldn't be my Danny if he didn't make sure he had my full consent. But my hesitation doesn't really come from a place of consent. He can do whatever he wishes with me because I'm all his for the taking—heart, body and soul.

Every single bit of me belongs to him for as long as he'll have me.

Until death comes for us.

"Will you let me speak?" I ask, arching a brow inquiringly.

My tone makes him snap his mouth shut, although his lips curve into a wide smile, enjoying every second of it. "I don't think it's a sin."

His brows quirk with interest.

"No?"

I tilt my head and fight the instinct to roll my hips and grind against him like I desperately want to. "Well, *I don't care* if it's a sin or not. I've already broken all the how-to-survive-a-slasher handbook rules, so what's one more?"

"But?"

Wetting my lips with the tip of my tongue, I gather the courage to admit the truth.

"My experience is *very* limited." The words come out fast and hushed, slipping through my teeth as I feel my cheeks heating, even though it's becoming progressively colder in this place. "I've never actually done this before."

His expression changes completely as realization sets in. Brows rising on his forehead, lips parted slightly as understanding crosses his face.

"It'd be your first time?"

I open my mouth then hesitate for a second. My mind has an answer, but my body has another. A knot forms in my throat. So I simply offer him a nod in response.

"Do you mind?"

Danny shakes his head. "No, I just really wish we weren't in a fucking freezer for it."

"It's not really the place that matters but the person you're with," I state, staring deep into his eyes.

I notice when the haze of worry dissipates, allowing for the softness to return. Danny pushes a few strands of my hair away from my face and caresses the edge of my jaw without breaking eye contact.

"You're so beautiful, baby." I roll my eyes, unfamiliar with receiving compliments so openly and casually, but I can't help smiling through it. "It would be an honor to share this first experience with you, if that's what you want."

"I want this," I say, leaning in to brush my nose against his, our breaths mixing as I inevitably grind myself on him.

The hard bulge of his dick presses against the seam of my jeans, rubbing on my core. Wetness pools in my panties and it provides the most delicious friction against my clit. Sensations explode in me, fluttering my eyes closed as I feel the sparks striking a match in my system. I moan in delight and take a bite of Danny's bottom lip, tugging on it ever so slightly to push him over the edge of control.

Danny buries his fingers in my hair, tugging on the strands as he kisses me deeply. His lips moving at a commanding pace, releasing the accumulated passion pouring from him until I'm drowning in the thousand sensations evoked by his body.

"Wait, I don't have any protection. I know we're dying soon, but if we survive by any chance—"

"I have an IUD," I cut him off before he can continue. "And clear scans."

His forehead creases slightly, but it's only there for a split second, like a passing thought that made him doubt. It fades instantly.

"I'm all clear too."

When he kisses me this time, he doesn't stop. Hands roam over my body, touching my back and traveling down my thighs. Caressing me over the fabric, making me yearn for the actual sensation of his warm skin over mine. As I arch my back, his hands slip under my shirt as they climb a feather-light path to my chest. Pebbled nipples greet his palms when he gives my breasts a gentle squeeze, ready for the attention they've been craving.

His fingers pinch the hard peaks, eliciting another moan from me.

"Please," I beg in a whimper. "I need you."

I've never felt this close to losing control, not even when he was kneeling between my thighs. Perhaps it's that we're on borrowed time, only having this suspended moment to show our love and devotion.

We've already lost so much, I need to have this one memory with him before I die.

"I wish we could take our time," he mumbles, biting my bottom lip. His teeth scratch, leaving behind a slight sting that he soothes with his tongue a moment later. "You deserve to be worshipped, Mabel."

One of his hands moves lower, abandoning my nipples to unbutton my pants skillfully. Wasting no time, his hand squeezes in the space between the layers of clothes and my skin. Anticipation and arousal build in my system in slow pulses, spreading with every breath I take waiting for him to touch me where I need it the most.

Slowly, his fingers venture south, tracing the slit of my pussy, finding me already wet for him.

Danny's mouth parts, amusement highlights on his face.

"Fuck, you're so wet," he muses, his voice hoarse and raspy, sending shivers down my spine. "Is this for me?"

His fingers spread my lips, creating a *V* that rubs the sides of my bundle of nerves as he moves them up and down. Pleasure tingles across my body and I can barely contain the sounds slipping from my lips.

"Only for you," I moan.

Danny's mouth curves into a lopsided grin that makes my legs feel weak.

Fingertips circle my entrance, playing with the slick wetness before he buries two of them as deep as the angle allows him. My walls clench around his fingers as he stretches me open, the heel of his palm brushing my clit. Trembling against him, I let out a shaky breath, getting used to the electric sensations spreading along my skin.

"You're so tight."

I lean in until my lips caress the spot between his ear and jaw.

"Imagine how tight I'll feel around your dick," I whisper, teasing him as his dick twitches.

His hand moves faster, his fingers sliding in and out of me in a come-hither motion. White spots dance in my vision, completely overtaken by the wave of delight.

"If only we had more time together," he says in my ear, and the shakiness in his tone doesn't come from melancholy but from desire. "I can think of a thousand different ways I want to fuck you. Make you feel good and lick your pretty pussy, bend you over and see your perfect ass bounce when I bury my cock deep inside you. Pull your hair and make you come over and over again until you can't take it anymore."

My breath hitches, mixing with a moan, as I picture the scenarios he's describing.

Dios mío, when did he go from being my sweet golden boy to this dominating sexual man? Last time, I met a guy devoted to my pleasure, and I loved every second of it. But now? It's a different side of him, one driven by lust, but it's only a fraction of what I'd already discovered. He's not promising to be overly rough with me for his pleasure, instead he's talking about giving me endless orgasms.

His satisfaction comes from mine.

Now I wish I could turn back time and urge myself to get my shit together earlier.

"What else?" I ask, wanting to hear more, hanging on to every word.

The rawness of his voice scratches an itch in my system, stimulating areas of my body that his fingers can't reach. The searing flames pulse in me, building pressure in my lower abdomen.

"I want you to sit on my face and ride my tongue," he carries on between pants as his fingers continue sliding deliciously inside me. "Fuck, your pussy is getting tighter."

Wordlessly, I nod.

My muscles begin to stiffen as I inch closer to the orgasm.

"I . . . I . . . *I'm so close*," I want to warn him, but I'm unable to form the words.

Every time I breathe, a moan rasps out of me, scratching the back of my throat.

"Are you going to come for me?" Another nod from my part. "What if I stopped?"

It would be torture to even think about being left on the edge when I'm so close I can almost taste it.

"No."

Danny smirks. "No? Why don't you ask nicely?"

So bossy.

"Please," I plead.

"I love it when you beg," he croons. "Come for me, baby."

Beads of sweat drip down my spine, in spite of the cold air around us. I lean in to kiss him, digging my teeth into his lip as I get closer and closer, hanging off the ledge until the tether snaps. Bliss swarms me, the devastating orgasm spreading through me in pulses, and I clench around his fingers. My sight goes blurry as I roll my eyes, shuddering through the pleasure until my pussy stops contracting around him.

Danny withdraws his fingers, and I can see them glistening from my wetness. Keeping his gaze locked on mine, he licks his fingers clean, the image so erotic I tremble again.

"Fuck me."

Even though I just came, I need him more than ever, though it's not just about pleasure. I want him to wash away the unwanted ghosts from the past. I need to feel him. I crave this moment of intimacy, to be together with him, as close as two bodies can be, skin to skin, heart to heart.

"Are you sure?" he asks, and, for a second, his voice goes back to the familiar gentleness. "I'm perfectly happy pleasuring you like this."

"I'm sure."

He kisses me for a brief instance before he pulls away from me, shifting our positions. Gently, he moves my body until I'm no longer on top of him but lying on the cold floor. He doesn't remove my shirt, only lifting it enough to uncover my breasts and sucking on the hard nipples.

I bury my fingers in his hair, tugging on his scalp.

"Stop teasing," I grit out.

Danny chuckles against my sensitive skin and nibbles on one of my nipples, stealing my voice.

"I'm not teasing, I'm enjoying you, baby," he comments, defending himself. "You're my last meal on death row, Mabel. I want to savor you," he adds, kissing his way down my abdomen. His light stubble prickles against my skin, raising goosebumps as he travels south. "Every. Single. Bit." He accentuates each word with a kiss.

When he reaches my unbuttoned pants, he presses his lips on my hips and hooks his fingers in the waistband of my jeans. His eyes search for mine and I nod, giving him permission

This time when he pulls my pants down, he takes my underwear with them, baring me completely for him at once. Although, like before, he has to stop to remove my shoes, dropping them somewhere, I don't care where. For the first time, I'm entirely naked from the waist down for him, and I feel the urge to keep my knees together to preserve some shed of dignity.

"Don't get shy around me now," he begs, placing his hands on my knees. "Let me see you, please."

There's something in his voice; a twinge of vulnerability that makes me want to give him everything. So, I allow him to part my knees and settle between them. His hands caress my thighs, kneading the skin as he hisses like he can't believe his eyes.

"You're so beautiful. I'm truly not worthy of you."

I shake my head.

"You are. Only you are worthy."

Danny lets out a moan and unfastens his pants, lowering

them to free his hard dick. A choked noise comes out of the back of my throat when I get a good look at him. He's even bigger than I imagined.

Good lord, I might've overestimated my body and its abilities because how on earth will that fit inside me?

He seems to read my mind because he sketches a cocky grin.

"Don't worry, I'll stretch you out," he promises, trailing a hand to my pussy where he wets his fingers and strokes his hard shaft, lubricating himself. It's an erotic sight and, suddenly, I'm no longer worried. I'm just eager to feel him inside me.

He rubs my clit with his thumb, and I arch my back off the floor, giving in to the pleasure.

"Danny."

"What do you want, baby?"

"Fuck me. Please."

"Anything for you."

Spreading my legs farther apart, he positions his dick on my clit, rubbing the sensitive spot with the tip a couple of times, preparing me and making me eager for him. My inner walls clench around nothing, desperate to feel him. I've never been good at waiting patiently for things, which makes me greedy and needy, but I can't help it. Slowly, I feel Danny's dick at my entrance, and he crawls over me, placing his hands on the floor next to my head and kisses me. I can barely focus on the kiss, sloppily licking his tongue when his dick begins to slide into me.

I wince when I stretch around him, and it stings a little. Not enough to hurt, but not precisely comfortable either. It's not exactly an intrusion, I've given him the consent to do this, yet I can't help the instinct to tense.

Danny stills his movements.

"Are you okay? Do you need me to stop?"

I shake my head, closing my eyes as I breathe through my nose to calm down. While I'm trapped in a dark room illuminated by a tiny light, it doesn't mean I can't put a stop to this. I know Danny will stop if I say the word.

I'm safe with him.

In short huffs, I let out the air in my lungs.

I'm safe, I'm with Danny, I repeat like a mantra.

"I just need a moment, please."

A minute until I get used to feeling him spreading me open, until the stretch is no longer uncomfortable, and I feel confident he can move without hurting me.

"I can pull out," he offers.

My hands fly to his hips, keeping him in place as I say, "No. I just need to get used to your humongous dick."

Danny snorts.

"Don't make me laugh when I'm inside you and you don't want me to move, please."

This instance of silliness reminds me that this is Danny.

He's the same guy who brought me green apple candy after finishing a big assignment. The same person with whom I share a lot of inside jokes. The man I'm in love with, who brings me comfort and joy, even in moments of terror.

When I open my eyes, his kind eyes meet my gaze, and I know I've never been safer than I am in his arms.

"I'm okay."

"You sure?"

"Yes, keep moving, please."

Slowly, Danny rocks his hips and drives himself an inch deeper into me, stealing a gasp from me when the head of his dick rubs a sensitive spot. Withdrawing a little to do it all over again, he begins to pick up the pace. Deep and slow, trembling whenever I inevitably clench around him.

"You feel so tight," he grunts.

"How tight?"

"Deliciously tight. You'll make me come too fast."

"I want you to."

A moan escapes me as I curve my body flush against his torso. I'm overwhelmed by the rush of sensations blasting in my system. The hot flares boiling under my skin clashing with the cold freezer air, the tightness in my lower abdomen, the slight sting mixed with new pleasure with each thrust. It's all too much and not enough at the same time. I wrap my arms around him, digging my nails in his back, as he fucks me, faster and faster. Through the blood pumping in my ears, I hear a combination of our pants and moans echoing in the freezer. Skin slaps against skin, raw and naughty.

For a moment, we stop existing in this nightmare, linking together as one. His heart rapidly beating against mine when his thrusts drive deeper into me. Satisfaction stings behind my eyelids. I slide a hand between our bodies so I can rub my clit in tight, quick circles, pushing myself closer to the edge.

"Tell me you love me," Danny asks.

I moan, on the brink of my orgasm.

"I love you," I whisper.

"Again," he pleads.

"I . . . lo . . . love you." My voice breaks as I reach my climax, convulsing under him.

The pleasure blindsides me, white spots dancing in my vision as I clench around Danny's hard dick. It's almost too much to handle. I can't stop shuddering as he fucks me through the orgasm, thrusting his hips, chasing his own pleasure.

"Mabel," he groans my name, and it comes out shaky and desperate, like he can barely keep it together.

"I love you."

He drops his head in the curve of my neck, his labored breathing brushing my skin as he pumps faster into me until he breaks apart, grunting. His orgasm hits hard and fast, and I'm taken aback by the sensation of his dick pulsating inside me for what feels like forever, but it can't be longer than a handful of seconds.

Danny melts over me, pressing me to the floor with his weight as he recovers. I can barely breathe, but I don't dare to complain, afraid he'll move away too soon when all I crave is to be in his arms.

"Holy shit," he mumbles a minute later.

"From one to ten, I'd give you a ten," I comment, using his rating system from our first encounter.

He cracks up, laughing as he kisses my temple.

"I love you."

I hum with delight.

Slowly, almost as if he were scared of hurting me, Danny pulls out. A second later, I feel his seed dripping out of me.

"That's so fucking hot," he groans, staring between my legs.

Biting his bottom lip, he moves a hand to my pussy and shoves his fingers inside. He pumps them in two times, using our fluids as lube.

I shiver, both from the cold and the overwhelming sensations. I'm too sensitive to be touched right now.

"Should I stop?"

I nod. "Please. It's too much."

Immediately, without trying to even convince me to engage in something else with him, he stops. Because I asked him to.

A lump of emotions clogs my airways for a second.

Breathe.

And I do.

This moment couldn't have been more perfect. Well, I can think of a few improvements, like preferably not while we're in a near-death situation, but I wouldn't change anything about him.

Having sex with Danny was the perfect real first-time experience.

It should feel awkward to get dressed afterward, but it doesn't. It's not like when we got caught by Carmen and had to rapidly pull clothes on our bodies. We take our time. Danny aids me, not because we have somewhere to be, but because it's getting colder.

Now that our horniness has died down, it's easier to tell the temperature has changed completely, dropping a few degrees since we got locked inside. My blood-soaked shirt feels frigid. I'm sensitive to the cold; being from the Caribbean has ill prepared me for whenever temperatures change, and it sends a hint of worry to my brain.

Danny wraps an arm around my body, pulling me into a tight hug that spreads some warmth. We stay there, holding on to each other for a minute, maybe more. I pull him closer and focus on the sound of his heart beating until he laughs out of nowhere.

"What is it?" I ask, craning my head to look at him.

Danny shakes his head.

"Nothing. I just thought of a movie scene."

That piques my interest. Although I talked a lot about movies during the duration of our friendship, it was rare for him to do so. I'm interested to know if it's something he watched back then or if it's something new.

"Anything I've watched?"

"Most definitely," he confirms with a nod.

"Which one?"

He waves his hand dismissively. "It's not really important."

I frown a little.

Why is he suddenly being cagey about it? He's not the type of person to get shy over something so trivial as a film.

"Danny."

He presses his lips together, but caves in.

"I just thought that, after everything we've been through, all we've done . . ." He pauses and glances at me with a hint of the devil in his eyes. "Wouldn't it be funny if I was the killer?"

Chapter 22

THE WORLD STOPS SPINNING ON ITS AXIS. HIS WORDS FALL over my shoulders like a bucket of ice-cold water. My lungs fail to allow the oxygen to flow and bring me a sense of relief. I'm unable to do anything but stare at him.

Why would he say that?

Danny's eyes crease around the corners. His lips stretch into a grin, finding humor in the comment. Shadows cross his face, darkening his expression in a way that seems almost sinister. He lets out a soft chuckle, scratching the back of his neck the way he does when he's nervous.

Or maybe I've always misread it as a nervous tic when it meant something else entirely.

"What?" I mumble.

Danny's grin remains plastered on his face.

"It's just a joke, Mabs."

Under much different circumstances, I would've appreciated the joke. I'm sure there's a funny aspect to it, but after the horrible things I've witnessed, his joke falls flat. Borderline tactless and insensitive. Especially when we've just shared a very intimate and vulnerable moment.

Acid bubbles in my stomach, threatening to rise at an alarmingly fast rate. The seed of doubt plants itself in the pit of my stomach.

I press my tongue to the roof of my mouth, urging my body to calm down.

It's just a joke.

Although it's not particularly amusing to me, I let out a shaky giggle, putting on the best performance I can.

But what if it isn't a joke?

The main suspect of every slasher is always the romantic interest. It's one of the first rules of slashers because the person you trust the most is always the one who can hurt you.

And I've been blindly trusting Danny tonight. Only because I've harbored feelings for him.

He disarmed me with his puppy eyes and kind smile, but was any of it real? There have been serial killers who seemed charming—until the bodies buried in their backyards were discovered. All this could've been one big performance, and I've stupidly fallen for it like a fucking fool.

My eyes ache from the held-back tears, but I force myself to smile. Gazing around the room, I spot the place where I left my knife. It's barely a meter away.

Would I be able to fight Danny if it came down to it? He's a tall man, and while he's not bulky, he's not lanky either. It would be fairly easy for him to overpower me. If he were really intending to, he could kill me without effort. And I don't know how to defend myself from him because my heart doesn't want him to be the villain of this story.

He can't be the man who has orchestrated this torment for all of us.

Yet, sadly, he seems to be the one with the most opportunity to do it.

A loud clank interrupts my thoughts. I can't tell what's going on, but it seems like someone is unlocking the freezer door. My heart drums inside my chest. I glance at Danny from the corner of my eye and then I stare at the abandoned knife on the floor. He has a knife of his own, but I can't spot where he left it after bandaging my arm.

Could he really be Cupid?

No, it makes no sense, right? We met Cupid together when we came up with the plan to go to the attic. Together we distracted the killer. Before he managed to lock us in here, I stabbed him. Cupid, not Danny.

But what if Cupid isn't just one person?

While in reality it's hard to find a murder buddy, this night is a slasher film. Starting with the letters, locking us in here, and all the murders. It's not uncommon for slashers to have two killers. Cupid might be a costume worn by two different people.

The one I stabbed, and someone else . . .

Someone like Danny.

If I'm right about this, then maybe I was correct when I theorized that Cupid and Brian's killer may not be the same person. It's possible they could be collaborating. But what is the motive linking them? There's always a common factor, whether it's power or revenge or both.

The clang repeats, followed by the suction noise of the door dislodging from the seal. I move to the corner where my knife rests, wrapping my fingers around the hilt with precision. I rise to my feet, stepping back into the farthest corner of the freezer, careful not to clumsily slip on the icy floor.

If I'm right about Danny, I stand no chance of fighting them both off at the same time. Alternating between staring at the door and the man standing next to me, I tighten my grip on the knife and take another step back, my butt hits a shelf as I do.

Danny moves in front of me like a shield. He raises his own knife with the tip directed to the door.

Why would Danny be the killer when he has tried so hard to protect me? He could've simply allowed Cupid to have his way with me. My brain hurts, almost as if it were being split in half. What should I do? Trust Danny, or shield myself from him before he can hurt me?

The door opens fully, and I force my eyes to stay open, not wanting to miss Cupid's appearance. However, it doesn't happen. I'm met with a familiar and annoying face.

"Whoa! Dude, what the fuck? Were you going to kill me?" The alarm in Seth's voice makes it ring louder, almost to the point of squeaky, like a dog's broken toy. He lifts his hands in the air as he stares at the knife in Danny's hold.

Danny lowers his blade and places a hand on his chest, whistling with relief. His shoulders and back slouch slightly, letting his guard down. How can he be sure that Seth isn't the killer?

Why is he trusting him?

"What are you doing here?" Danny asks. "How are you even alive?"

Seth shrugs. "After that psycho killed Ellie . . ."

"Elodie," Danny corrects him.

Seth scoffs in return.

"Bro, do you think I care about her name?" he quips. "Anyway, after what's-her-face got killed, I ran upstairs and hid. It was going fine when all the screaming was happening downstairs, but now it's coming from upstairs, so I decided to change locations."

My breath hitches.

If he was on the second floor and there was screaming coming from upstairs, it means it must've come from the attic. The place where my little sister was supposed to be safe.

"Upstairs?" Danny echoes.

"Yeah, are you not following the story? I decided to use the freezer as a hiding place, because who would be dumb enough to hide in a freezer, right? It's the perfect spot," he concludes, putting his hands on his hips. "I mean, you guys clearly thought about it."

"We didn't, actually. The killer locked us in here."

Seth's brows lift on his forehead, almost meeting his hairline. "Ah, that explains why she looks like she crawled out of a circle of hell." He points his chin at me.

Danny cleaned the blood off my face before we left the bathroom, so I must have some of Cupid's on me from when

I stabbed him. My dark brown hair feels tangled, even more so than when I looked in the mirror after having Danny's hands ruffling it—never mind the friction from when he was thrusting into me—and part of my shirt got ripped by Cupid's machete. The makeshift bandage is still tied around my bicep.

"And you look oddly clean," Danny points out with a hint of suspicion in his voice.

"It's not my fault I'm the smartest one here. *Obviously.*"

The smartest, the luckiest, or the guiltiest.

Clearly, I'm not very good at reading people, considering I might've unknowingly fucked the killer, but it's very unlikely Seth has spent the past couple of hours hiding without being caught up in any sort of skirmish. Even Bethan, who was one of the least hurt among us, had some scrapes and bruises.

The only two people who seem to be free of injury are the men standing here in the freezer with me.

"You said you heard screaming?" I ask, directing the conversation to what interests me the most.

I don't care if he has been hiding in a corner all night. If what he's saying is true and he heard the screams from above him, it means the girls might be in danger. Bethan, Cerys, my sister. Anxiety inserts its claws under my skin, refusing to let me go.

"Yeah, sounded like someone was getting murdered."

A whimper escapes me.

Is it horrible of me that I hope the screaming came from someone else? I don't think any of us has deserved what happened tonight, except maybe Seth, for running in the same circle as Brian, and Shane, for trying to murder me when there was no reason for it.

Danny grabs my free hand and draws soothing circles with the pad of his thumb.

"It might not be them," he says.

I pull away from his hold, not wanting to be touched by him or anyone. The phantom of his touch leaves a trail of tingles in the spots he caressed. I shiver, overstimulated by the blend of emotions clouding my senses.

The doubt, my suspicions about Danny, the fear rumbling in my veins.

It's too much to handle all at once.

"You can't know that. There's barely anyone left."

The night started out with fourteen of us. Elodie, Ray, Leighton, Jaden and Shane are all dead. While Zelda, Carmen and Cerys are all injured in various ways and in different locations. Zelda in a room on the first floor, hidden behind a couch. Carmen tucked away in the attic, and Cerys almost dragged around by Bethan to head to the attic as well.

Mentally, I count off the names, tapping the tip of each finger as I add a number.

Nine.

Nine out of fourteen, so it means there are five left to count.

Considering Danny, Seth and I are all in the freezer, it leaves only two people unaccounted for: Sophia and Ollie.

According to Zelda, Sophia ran away after her friend got viciously attacked by Cupid, and she hasn't been seen since.

It's hard to tell if she is still alive and hiding, or was killed at some point during the night without us knowing, especially with Cupid's predisposition for hiding the bodies, making it more difficult for us to keep track.

"We should go to the attic," Danny announces.

Seth tilts his head.

"Uh, I don't know about that. That's where the screaming was coming from."

I grind my molars, anguish adhering itself to my insides.

"Right, because hiding in the freezer is such a great idea now," Danny spits out. "The killer locked us in here. What makes you think he won't come back for us and find you instead? Have fun dying."

"You two always ruin things."

"If you want to stay here and die, be my guest," Danny points to the back of the freezer. "We're going to the attic."

My brain blocks out their bickering, barely conscious of the way I step out of the freezer with the knife in my shaking hand.

Dread deepens in my stomach as I walk ahead of the guys, their steps following me, though not as quietly as I would've liked them to be.

How could Cupid have known the girls were hiding in the attic?

I look at Danny as we begin to take the stairs.

Doubt spreads its roots deeper into me as I evaluate tonight's events from an entirely different perspective.

Starting from the moment the power went out. He volunteered to find the flashlights, refused my company, and made me stay with the girls. He wasn't in the room the first time Cupid killed someone. Then, he just *happened* to find me in that closet after I was chased by Cupid. I had been too distressed and lovestruck to look at the clues that were laid out before me.

He had blood on his shirt when we met in the closet. It never crossed my mind to think about the possibility that he got his clothes stained because he had been the one committing the kills.

There's also the fact that Cupid showed up only a few minutes after Danny left me in the room with Zelda. Leaving enough time for him to fetch the cupid costume and grab his weapon.

While he was *allegedly* with Bethan and Cerys when I got harassed by Cupid, it doesn't absolve him from guilt. After all, having an accomplice is part of my theory.

And, in the kitchen, Danny was the one who got close enough to Cupid without hurting him. Maybe because he was telling his accomplice about the girls' hiding spot, pretending to fight him off.

I count Cupid's victims and the unaccounted people.

There's someone who has been missing since the beginning of the night. I was so focused on the flashlights that I never stopped to wonder.

"Where's Ollie?" I ask, stopping mid-step.

I don't even care about our exposed position in the middle of the stairs. I can't lead the killer to Carmen, even if he already knows where she is.

Both Danny and Seth turn to look at me, confused by my sudden question and decision to stop walking.

"What do you mean?" Danny questions, cocking his head to the side.

Twisting the knife's hilt in my hand, I look him dead in the eye, hoping to catch a glimpse of guilt. A hint that he's been caught. But I find nothing other than a cloud of confusion.

He could be a great actor, the voice in the back of my brain whispers. Maybe I never really knew him at all.

"You volunteered to find the flashlights after the lights went off, and you took Ollie with you, so where is he? I haven't seen him all night, and you haven't mentioned him either."

Danny's eyes get a bewildered flicker.

"Why are you asking me this?"

"Why aren't you answering?" I rebuke in a desperate tone.

"Mabel," his voice wavers with a hint of pain.

He attempts to take a step toward me, his hand extended between us. Instinctively, before I can consider if it's a wise choice or not, I raise the knife in front of me. A silent warning of what will happen if he chooses to move again without my consent.

I won't be fooled by his trickery anymore.

"Is it such a difficult question or are you hiding something?"

His expression drops, brows sunken and lips parted, visibly heartbroken by my accusation.

"I don't know where he is," he responds to the original question, his words sounding gentle, though they have an edge that wasn't there before. Anger? No, it's too dull to be anger. "We went together to find the flashlights, but he started to freak out once he heard all the screaming. By the time we found Elodie, he bolted and ran. I lost him. I tried to find him, I swear I did, but . . . I was trying to find you too. I hope he's alive and safe. I truly do," his voice trembles with uncertainty.

I'm afraid he's not being truthful.

Despite the threat of my blade, Danny extends an arm to touch me, but I flinch and draw away from him again.

"Danny, I . . ."

What is there to say when all the words in the world fail to convey what I'm feeling? Nothing can knit together the perfect combination to encapsulate this moment of betrayal between us. It's almost like the ground has opened under our feet, creating an abyss between us that can't be put together by something as trivial as saying *I'm sorry*.

Because apologizing for not trusting him is not something I can afford to do. He's supposed to be the person I trust the most, the man I'm blindly in love with. I trusted him with every single bit of my soul, even putting myself in danger because the thought of his sacrifice was unbearable.

But now?

Now that I have a new perspective, I notice how he's always had the perfect excuse for everything. It's like I've been blinded by his good looks and charming personality, irrationally believing every single one of his excuses. Always too perfectly constructed, almost rehearsed. All the lies that have abandoned his lips today form a chain in my mind.

From the second he gave me that story about the letter. His reasoning for Cerys wanting to come to Westbrook.

Before, his reasoning made sense to me because I know my friend is a kind person.

But she wouldn't have come back if Danny hadn't encouraged her.

I think he might've taken advantage of that to manipulate her into this. And Cerys fell helplessly for his lies.

Who would ever distrust Daniel Singh? Golden boy, natural and selfless leader who created a legacy at Delta. Always there with a charming smile and kind words.

Tears sting my eyes, covering my sight with a layer of blurriness that makes it difficult to see Danny's heartbroken expression. *Good.* I don't want to witness his pity act when my heart is chipping apart.

"Wait," Seth says, eyeing us carefully like he's just catching on to what's happening. "You weren't in the room when that psycho killed Elanie."

I'm so close to breaking down in tears, but I still want to roll my eyes at his stupidity.

How has it taken him so long to figure it out? He doesn't even need to put the pieces together when I've already laid and glued them together for everyone to see.

"Shut the fuck up, Seth," Danny snarls. The anger in his tone is almost out of character for him. Like he's so betrayed and frustrated by my inability to trust him that he can't handle someone parroting the obvious to his face.

"Oh shit. You're the killer!"

"If you don't shut your mouth," Danny warns, craning his neck to look at Seth in complete disbelief, his brows furrowed and nose flared.

But Seth doesn't stop.

"You killed Ollie and then went and murdered Elsie!" he yells.

If he doesn't stop saying her name wrong . . .

Besides, it's possible Ollie isn't dead and has been Danny's accomplice. It'd explain why he hasn't been around. I wish I could remember if Ollie's build matches the Cupid I hurt back in the kitchen, but the images come back blurry.

"Seth," I mumble as a warning.

It's not wise to rile up a killer, especially when he has a knife in his hand. Like being stupid enough to bleed in a shark tank and hope you won't get eaten.

"Shut up!" Danny exclaims, stepping closer to Seth, almost getting in his face.

But Seth doesn't back away. His hands fly to Danny's knife, trying to snatch it from him. In his anger, Danny must've kept a hard grip on the hilt because even though Seth has a larger frame than him, he's not able to wrestle it out of his hold. Instead, they barely manage to keep the blade between them.

"Don't just stand there, stab him!" Seth shouts at me.

But I can't move, I back away, climbing a step to put some distance between them and me. I scream at them to stop. This isn't good. We're not in any position to be wasting time like this, especially not on the stairs, where so many things can go wrong. Running my fingers through the tangled strands of my hair, I debate what to do.

I don't want to give my knife to Seth, because I know what will happen to Danny. I'm almost sure he's one of the killers, but I still can't bring myself to be a part of his demise. Not like this. Especially not without being a hundred percent sure about his involvement.

Because if I'm wrong, by any chance, then it would mean I killed him. Maybe not with my own hand, but by supplying the murder weapon, and that's not something I can live with.

They tumble against the banister and one of them loses their footing, dragging the other along as they fall down the flight of stairs. The knife slips out of Danny's hand, and I hear it clank on the ground. Both Danny and Seth come to rest with their backs on the floor—right in front of a pair of black combat boots.

Ones shadowed by black robes and an axe.

Cupid.

"Look out!"

Before I can shield my eyes or even blink, Cupid holds his axe high in the air and then brings it down on Seth's neck. The loud *thwack* reverberates through the house as he hacks off his head, followed by my horrified shriek. Spreading the flesh with the edge of the axe to break through the bones, Cupid swats Seth's head, making it roll along the floor.

Then, he lifts the axe again in Danny's direction.

I scream his name, but fortunately Danny's reflexes kick in and he rolls out of the axe's path just in time to avoid the same ending as Seth. He shuffles backward, out of range of Cupid's killing weapon, evading the axe swings as he tries to reach for the knife.

"Mabel, run!"

Regret spreads through my body, leaving me breathless and gasping for air.

If I hadn't distrusted him and questioned all his actions, Danny wouldn't be in this position. We would've made it to the second floor. Seth would probably still be alive, but he's not the one I care about.

I care about Danny.

The gentle guy I know doesn't have the heart of a killer. I've always known this. He doesn't have the capacity to inflict hurt, it's not in his nature to be mean and ruthless. Deep down, I've always been aware of this. It's why it took me so long to question him about Ollie, why I believed every excuse, because he wasn't lying to me.

I let all my insecurities control me; it didn't allow me to see the real picture. Too focused on trying to find reasons to find him guilty, I stopped thinking about the guy I'm madly in love with. I went as far as telling myself a different version of what I've lived through tonight to fit the narrative of him being the villain. Building a wall to protect myself from the vulnerability I feel around him.

But being vulnerable wasn't a weakness.

My feelings for Danny were what held me together throughout this nightmare. They brought me comfort in the moments where I felt like I couldn't continue, giving me a purpose, even when I felt death was a touch away.

My love for Danny made me stronger, but I chose to ignore it because the fear of being betrayed by someone I love was more powerful.

"I can't leave you," I say, shaking my head.

Tears abandon my eyes, rolling down my cheeks.

"Run," he orders firmly, standing up to meet Cupid. "Stick to the plan. They need you."

Our gazes lock for a split second.

How can I let him know how sorry I am for not trusting

him? I should've done better. My trauma response urges me to run away and isolate myself to avoid getting hurt. I'll always be the one who bails.

Like I must do now after committing the worst mistake of my life.

Run, he mouths at me silently.

So I run, taking the rest of the stairs as fast as I can. I can't look back now. More tears flow out of me. I run until I find the closet that leads to the attic, only to find the door already open.

My throat burns with anxiety.

When Seth mentioned he switched hiding spots because he heard screaming coming from above, a part of me refused to believe it was because my sister was in danger. But it must've been the truth.

Nausea settles in my stomach. Without Danny, I don't have the courage to face the horrors awaiting me in the attic. But I must carry on, even as I'm being crushed by regret. I can't let Danny's sacrifice be in vain. If I freeze now, I'd be failing him, and I've already betrayed him enough to last a lifetime.

Rushing to the closet, I waste no time climbing the steps to the attic, noticing the blood smeared over them. I gulp down the knot of tears in my throat and continue crawling up the ladder until I get to the hatch. On my knees, I hoist myself into the attic, searching for my sister.

I spot Bethan first, sitting on the floor with her hands pressed to her bleeding thigh. Next to her, perched on a box, is Cerys. The bandages that Danny had put together for her are now shredded at her feet, her hands pressing over her wound.

A choked noise erupts from my chest when I find my

sister. Her beautiful face is framed by smudged make-up and tear streaks. But that's not what makes my knees buckle. It's the blade pressed to the base of her throat by a man with familiar blue eyes.

"Hi, stranger. Took you long enough to make it to the killer reveal."

Chapter 23

"AIDAN?" THE NAME COMES OUT IN A RAGGED BREATH full of disbelief.

My eyes widen, doing a double-take to process the scene before me. Aidan has an arm snaked around Carmen's upper body, pressing the forearm against her chest to keep her steady, while with the other hand he holds a knife to her delicate neck. His tall body is curved to loom over her small height. As he stares at me, his lips curl into a mischievous grin that sends chills down my body.

I blink. I must be imagining things, confusing Aidan's complexion with someone else's. Perhaps I got a concussion when I fell down the stairs after Shane's death and now I'm hallucinating. But the dull ache from when I hit my head is barely there. Not strong enough to be the cause of what I'm witnessing.

This isn't real. It's not happening, I tell myself, but as I continue to stare at the man threatening my sister, the more reality descends over me. My gut instinct wasn't wrong when I was convinced Cupid was someone close enough to hurt me, I just never expected it would be one of my closest friends.

I've been an idiot, too focused on surviving and trying to protect the people I love to see the full picture. I begin to unravel the puzzle of this mystery.

Not only does Aidan fit Cupid's description, with the right height and build as the one who molested me. But who else would have the capacity to orchestrate the perfect slasher scenario other than him? He's the son of a prolific horror mastermind, a film student obsessed with slashers.

Getting flashbacks of tonight's events, it's so fucking obvious. I don't know why I didn't see it sooner, perhaps because he was smart enough to keep himself out of the equation until the moment it was right for the big reveal. He's one of the few people who have my address in LA and of my workplace, because I went to him when I asked if I could have his father's letter of recommendation. He infiltrated himself in the Greek Row life by becoming a part of Delta. He even killed Leighton by sneaking up on her from around a corner, paying homage to the short film we did together.

Who else would understand the reference? Why didn't I see it sooner? It was too symbolic to be a coincidence.

Aidan set the perfect foundation for this to work. He executed a solid pre-production for his biggest project, except this isn't a movie project.

This is real life. Between him and his accomplice, they've killed six people. And for what?

What is the motive behind this?

Fame? He can easily gain that. Getting his daddy's blessing by proving he deserves his horror praises as well? It's highly doubtful that his father will appreciate it. Unless Aidan actually believes he can get away with this.

I squint at him. If there's a glimpse of the fun and supportive friend I knew, maybe I can somehow crack through his madness. Except, I get nothing back when I meet his gaze. The blue irises are shinier than ever, but the darkness in his pupils is as dense as a black hole.

There's not a trace left of the guy I used to know.

"Why don't you put the knife down, Mabel?" he suggests, tilting his head to point at Carmen with his chin, subtly letting me know what he plans to do if I'm not as docile as a gothic damsel in distress. "You don't want her to get hurt, do you? Though she's always been such a pain in the ass to you, it'd be fair if she got a little punishment for all the sacrifices you've made for her."

"No, don't hurt her," I mutter rapidly, without thinking twice. Then I add, "Please."

I lift one hand as if I were swinging a white flag as I lower my body to deposit the knife on the floor. I carefully rise back to my full height without taking my eyes off them, ensuring he hasn't moved an inch.

"Kick the knife down the hatch," he orders.

Puñeta. I glance at the entrance to the attic. We're losing our chances for defending ourselves. But with Carmen in his hold and the threat he presents, I have no other option. I've already lost too much tonight. I wouldn't be able to tolerate it if she got hurt because I chose to act stupid.

With my foot, I push the knife down, and it clangs once it meets the floor.

"Good girl," Aidan praises.

The encouragement almost makes me gag, but I manage to hold it back. Approaching a devious killer by pissing him off isn't the brightest idea. Especially when my sister's life depends on appeasing him. This time, instead of choosing between fight or flight, I pick fawn.

If I keep him happy enough, we might have time to figure out if there's a way to escape from him, maybe trick him long enough to trap him.

Or kill him, my subconscious supplies.

There's no coming out of here without getting our hands dirty. Survival is directly linked to doing whatever it takes to stay alive, and if Aidan gets between that and my sister's life, then I'll kill him.

If that's what it takes, I'll take his life as if it means nothing. Compared to my sister, he means nothing to me. I can live without a friend, especially one who has taken it upon himself to hunt and traumatize me for whatever motive, but I can't imagine even living in a world without Carmen.

"See?" he says in a soft voice, like it wasn't a complicated task to complete. "It's not so bad when I'm in charge."

Biting my tongue to prevent my lips from curling into a snarl, I recall our encounter earlier tonight when he alluded to having a project he wanted my help with. If this is the project he meant, I want no part in it.

"Let her go, please."

Aidan hums like he's considering it, only to snort like the request amuses him.

"You don't call the shots, sweetie. *I* do," he reminds me, pressing the blade harder against Carmen's neck.

Carmen's chest inflates with air as she arches her back toward him and rises on her toes to avoid the sharp edge of the blade.

My breath hitches in horror, and Aidan lets out a loud cackle, throwing his head back. He has completely lost the plot. How did I never see he was fucking crazy when we were friends? Even tonight, he seemed like the guy I used to know, the one who was my friend, who I shared so many good moments with on set. Where did that guy go? Did he ever even exist? Because he's certainly not this psycho in front of me holding my sister hostage.

"You're too tense," he growls at Carmen, clicking his tongue with a firm shake of his head, rolling his eyes as he lessens the pressure of the blade on her neck.

"Why are you doing this?" I question through gritted teeth.

His forehead furrows, and he tilts his head.

"Isn't it obvious? I did it for you."

Aidan's words fall over me like a splash of cold water, leaving me breathless and gaping like a fish.

"W-What?" is all I manage to utter in a broken syllable.

"I thought you would love this, getting to live your own slasher movie, becoming the perfect final girl. This is my gift to you."

Becoming the perfect final girl.

Oh, I had it so wrong, right from the start.

The letters were the clue all along. I couldn't connect the dots at the beginning because I thought they were related to Cerys, but they were meant for me. My sister's letter had my photograph. While Danny's photograph had Cerys' image, I was the in the picture too. Even my own letter had nothing to do with Cerys. He used Carmen, the only person I'd come back to Westbrook for.

They were meant for *me*.

When I woke up to Cupid touching me, getting turned on, it wasn't because he was having a physical reaction to my unconscious state. Or at least not completely. He was turned on because it was *me*.

All along, I've been the key to everything.

But I don't understand what compelled him to ever think this is what I desire. In what world would I want people to die for me in such a brutal and grotesque way?

"Why would I love this?"

Rolling his eyes, Aidan shoves Carmen to the floor, and though her body drops harshly against the wooden floorboards, I can't fight the small seed of relief planted in my system. At least she's out of his grip. That gives me the vaguest sense of hope.

Maybe I can talk to him long enough for someone, *anyone* to come to our aid.

Who am I kidding? No one is coming to the rescue. The only person who has saved me tonight has been Danny, and I doubt he's even still alive. Not after I left him on his own to defend himself from the second Cupid.

"Come on, you're not stupid," he says calmly. "This is

what we always talked about when we worked together. How would we create our perfect slasher?"

"In fiction!" I exclaim, the words escaping me before I can hold them back. "Have you lost your goddamn mind?"

His expression darkens. Pupils dilating to the point where the void in them seems to swallow the clarity of his blue irises.

"Don't be fucking ungrateful, Mabel. All of this has been a present for you."

I bury my hands in my hair, tugging on the scalp to see if I can grasp some sense of what he's saying. What is he even talking about?

I exchange glances with Carmen, who appears just as lost as I am with Aidan's crazy statements. My sister shrugs her shoulders slightly, almost imperceptibly, and shoots me a glare that screams at me to continue talking to Aidan for a little while longer.

I need to keep my cool.

Although it's one of the hardest things I've ever done in my life when he's spewing such vile nonsense, I fill my lungs with air and hold it for a couple of seconds before letting go. I repeat the process two more times, easing the tension in my muscles so I can tolerate his words.

"I'm getting rid of all your enemies one by one." As he finishes talking, he deliberately steps on Bethan's wound, ripping a deafening scream from her lips.

The sound pierces my eardrums and I want to press my hands on each side of my head to drown the noise, but instead I remain locked on what's unfolding. The merciless actions causing Bethan more harm and pain than I've ever seen someone withstand.

It's torture.

"My enemies? What are you even talking about? I don't have enemies."

Not anymore.

There was only one person in the world whom I considered to be a real enemy to me, but he hasn't been alive in a year.

Aidan quirks a brow in my direction.

"No?" he dares. "What about this bitch who threatened to kick you out of Kappa after Cerys dropped out, huh? How did she put it? Ah, yes, she said she would put your ass on the streets if you ever mentioned Cerys' name in the house again."

Bethan's face, reddened by the pain, constricts with a hint of shame. Tears spring from the corners of her eyes while she looks at Cerys.

"I'm sorry," she whispers to her old friend.

Aidan's expression darkens as he grabs her by the neck.

Bethan's eyes go wide, her hands flying up to undo Aidan's fingers, but it's useless. With strength I didn't know he had, Aidan lifts Bethan by the neck, forcing her to her feet, even though she's clearly struggling to stand with her injured thigh. The blush under her skin intensifies with the lack of oxygen.

"Or what about the time you made it against the rules for anyone to talk to Mabel because you said she was a liar? It lasted two weeks."

Has he been keeping track of every bad interaction I had during those horrible months, while I relied on his friendship to finish my days in Westbrook? If he did so with the intention of avenging me, then Theta should've been filled with more people than the ones he chose tonight, because I'm sure there were more, especially since there were people here whom I barely recognized.

"Stop," I tell him, seeing how the lack of oxygen transforms Bethan's face transforms from a shade of red to a purple hue, the fear in her eyes.

He's going to kill her with his bare hands.

"I believe you owe Mabel an apology, not Cerys," he corrects her through gritted teeth. "She wasn't strong enough to stick around and withstand the hate that was directed at Mabel. The hate *you* kept spreading in your sorority."

Bethan moves her lips, but no sound comes out.

"She can't breathe, stop it!" I yell, my voice pleading.

Fortunately, Aidan seems to listen to my request and weakens his hold. A second later, he releases her neck, letting his hand swing by his side. Bethan bends over, coughing and gagging as she tries to recover her breath. The purple tint under her skin starts to fade as she gasps for air.

"I want her to apologize to you."

"I'm sorry, Mabel," she rasps in a barely audible tone.

Aidan slaps her with the back of his hand.

"Say it like you mean it, bitch."

"I'm so sorry. I let everyone control me and didn't think about how it would affect you," she sobs. "I regret it all. If I had the opportunity, I would go back and make better choices. I swear. I'm sorry."

"It's okay," I tell her.

I don't care about an apology.

I've built a better life away from all the Greek Row

nonsense. What happened in Kappa was horrible, but insignificant compared to what's happened tonight. Besides, forced regret does nothing for me.

"Hmm," he muses, moving his knife around. "Did that sound honest to any of you?"

"Yes!" I rush to say abruptly, fearing what will happen if I don't appear to be satisfied by Bethan's apology.

Blood flows in my veins so fast I begin to feel lightheaded.

He wrinkles his nose and then presses his lips into a toothless smile.

"You're too kind, Mabel," he praises. "However, you've never been a particularly great actress. I can see right through that lie. But don't worry. You won't have to pretend for much longer. After all, I promised I would take care of your enemies."

Aidan plunges his knife in Bethan's lower abdomen. He grabs the hilt and guts her like a fish. Entrails, thick and gooey, fall to her feet. Her intestines slush and gurgle in the air as they slip to the floorboards.

Carmen scoots away from the danger zone, brown eyes wide with disgust and terror as some of Bethan's entrails stick to her dress. Cerys shrieks in horror at the sight of her former friend being brutally gutted. Her shoulders curve as she gags, vomiting over the boxes around her.

The blend of scents is pungent and nauseating. The metallic smell of blood mixed with the acid from Cerys' vomit stings my eyes. I press the back of my hand to my face, covering my mouth and nose.

Bethan's body thumps to the ground. A choked noise

comes from my throat as her lifeless eyes stare at nothing, empty pupils framed by burst capillaries.

Aidan wipes the blade on his clothes and turns to look at me with a triumphant grin.

"Her apology wasn't very sincere, was it?" he comments, resting a hand on his hip. "Oh, sweetie, don't cry."

I want to recoil as Aidan steps toward me. He extends a gloved hand to my face, caressing my cheeks with the bloody leather. Almost like he doesn't even realize that he's smearing Bethan's blood over my skin.

"I didn't want this. I never wanted to live this nightmare," I mumble to him.

His eyebrows twitch with a hint of confusion.

"You're just not seeing the big picture, Mabs," he insists, letting go of my face to walk around the attic as he speaks. "Just imagine how big this will be once we come out as the survivors of a homicidal freak. It will make national news, and that's when the studios will hit us up, wanting to buy our movie rights. Of course, we could negotiate the directing and scriptwriting roles. No offense, but you were always a better writer than a director. Sometimes your artistic vision lacked depth."

Oh my God. Is this asshole fucking for real?

"Who will believe that?" I question.

Aidan shakes his head, lifting his knife again as if to prove a point.

"Everyone! I have it all planned. It took me about a year to figure out the logistics, but I created the perfect plan. Or should I say the perfect *crime*?" He laughs at his own joke, looming his knife over both Carmen and Cerys, but without hurting either of them. "With the rest of them dead, everyone will believe our version of the events. Just imagine it, the two of us together like we've always wanted. Being *the* iconic couple of horror. We'll be legends, Mabel. As a gift, not only am I getting rid of all your enemies, but I'm also turning you into a star."

My chin trembles with disbelief.

Ay, Dios mío. He's fucking insane if he believes that's ever going to happen. Does he truly believe I would love him after he tortured and terrorized my loved ones? After killing them?

"Do you really think I would let you get away with killing my sister and my best friend?" I rebuke him, the tears in my voice making it sound thicker and choked. "You don't know me at all if you think that's what I would do."

Aidan purses his lips together, deep in thought for a minute, and then he shrugs nonchalantly.

"Well, I'm open to some slight plot changes. Many good slashers have a group of people who survive. Five is a good number of survivors."

I look at Carmen and Cerys, counting how many people he's referring to.

There's one missing.

"Five?" I ask.

Steps echo on the floor below us and my muscles clench into stone. *His partner.* Aidan's hand wraps around my arm, pulling me with him to the middle of the attic where I have a wide view of the hatch.

"My partner has to survive, don't you think?" he whispers in my ear, the words brushing my lobe.

Someone begins to climb the attic steps, and I hold my breath, waiting for the reveal to come. Who else did I get wrong in this? Familiar dark hair makes an appearance through the hatch, followed by the adorable puppy eyes I'm so fond of.

My heart plummets to my feet as a sob drags out of me painfully, leaving my throat sore and my chest aching.

Did he truly fool me? Has he been working with Aidan all along?

Danny hoists his body up into the attic, and I see the blood soaking his shirt. A big gash spreads across the side of his torso, the torn fabric glued to the gnarly open wound. He trips clumsily and wraps an arm over his abdomen to apply pressure to the wound.

"Danny," I whisper faintly, my heart splintering into a million pieces.

Someone else comes up the ladder behind him, someone who hooks the head of an axe on the curve of his neck, not quite hurting him, but establishing that they will if he does anything stupid.

He's not Cupid.

The wave of relief barely lasts a split second.

If Danny isn't the accomplice, then who is it?

There's only two people left unaccounted for: Ollie and Sophia.

The second Cupid walks out of Danny's shadow and uses a hand to push the mask away from their features.

I feel Aidan's smile in the curve of my neck.

"Don't you love a shocking killer reveal?" he muses.

My lips part in utter disbelief when I recognize the face

behind the mask. The person I fought off in the kitchen wasn't Ollie. Nor Sophia.

"What the fuck?" I mutter in shock.

The last person I was expecting stands next to Danny, holding the axe that cut off Seth's head.

"Why don't you say hi to my partner, Elodie?"

Chapter 24

A PINK FLUSH RISES IN ELODIE'S ROUND CHEEKS WHEN Aidan introduces her. With her lips stretched into a victorious smile, she lifts her chin in my direction. One of her brows arches in a smug expression. The meek and kind girl I saw today is overshadowed by this sinister version, carrying herself with a confidence she didn't have when she was being ordered around by Zelda and Sophia.

"What happened, Mabby?" Elodie pronounces my nickname with a hint of mockery and then furrows her lips in a fake pout of disappointment. "Are you surprised about my reveal?"

Surprised is an understatement.

While Aidan's reveal caught me off guard, Elodie is the one I can't believe. I never once saw a flicker of a backbone in that girl before. I constantly wondered what she was doing in a place like Kappa, where she would go unnoticed half of the time. Nice enough to blend in, but not charismatic enough to stand out. But it seemed to be all an act, because there's nothing meek or shy about her now as she keeps her axe at Danny's side.

A boulder drops in my stomach when I realize that as well as being the one I fought in the kitchen, she was the one who killed Seth.

How did they trick us?

"You died," I point out, confused.

I saw her gruesome death, the way Cupid stabbed her—*Aidan*, I correct myself—Aidan stabbed her multiple times. I remember the way the blood projectiled out of her mouth as her body spasmed, meeting death. Danny mentioned seeing her corpse right after she died. So she must've laid there in a pool of . . . fake blood? Until Aidan gave her the green light to switch into her killer costume.

Elodie throws her head back and snorts.

"Come on," she singsongs. "As someone who spent a *lot* of time asking for my help to test the perfect recipe for fake blood, you should know how easy it is to fake a death."

The memory flashes in my brain.

I was a sophomore when Elodie became my appointed younger sister in Kappa, but that year was also the beginning of my self-produced horror shorts. I spent a lot of time researching low-budget effects and resources, like Hollywood's recipes for fake blood, and Elodie was more than willing to help me with it all. At least until she made friends of her own.

"Corn syrup, water, non-dairy creamer, red food coloring,

and a hint of blue to bring out the perfect shade," I recite from memory.

Elodie's smile widens as she dips her chin into a nod of affirmation.

"So you *do* remember."

Vaguely, if I'm truthful.

The memory is barely a blip in the timeline of everything I did when I was in Westbrook. Insignificant after meeting Aidan's father and learning better practical effects from Aaron Ledger himself.

"Aidan and I thought of different scenarios for my big reveal," Elodie comments with enthusiasm. "Originally, I was going to be a part of your group, but it meant he would get *all* the fun."

Aidan chuckles, his mischievous undertone sending goosebumps along my skin, spreading a tremor down my spine.

"Elodie had the brilliant idea to fake her death. If everyone, especially you, thought she was dead, it would be easier to move around the house and get rid of the enemies."

The enemies.

"What enemies?"

"Everyone who has done you wrong, like that Bethan bitch," he grunts and unwraps his arm from my body, taking a step forwards to point at her body.

"What about Shane?" I mumble.

He doesn't fit the victim profile. I never interacted with him prior to the Smash or Pass event, and he wasn't a part of the original plan. Hell, no one even knew why he was at the house. Unlike Ray and Jaden, who were brought in by

Zelda and Sophia, without knowing they would meet their deaths.

Aidan's expression darkens as he snaps his jaw shut, grinding his molars.

"He shouldn't have approached you tonight," he mutters, rage coating his words. "I saw how uncomfortable he made you."

"You killed him because it looked like he made me uncomfortable at the party?"

Aidan blinks like it makes perfect sense for him.

"Mabel, you don't get it, you looked beyond uncomfortable. You were freaked out by whatever he told you. I wasn't going to allow that." He shakes his head with discontent. "Besides, I was right about him needing to go. He almost killed you tonight, sweetie."

My vocal cords become knotted, preventing me from pronouncing even the smallest of sounds.

"That was a risky last-minute move," Elodie supplies, sounding almost annoyed.

"But it all worked out at the end, didn't it?" Aidan chirps back. "*And* we even have our perfect cover-up," he points at Danny with the tip of his knife.

Elodie moves the axe onto Danny's shoulder, walking around him to press it against his neck. Danny struggles to keep his back straight, his breathing coming out in heavy puffs of air. Blood drips from his fingers, creating a small crimson pool next to his shoes. He squeezes his eyes shut, groaning in a barely audible tone.

Worry grows between my ribs.

His wound doesn't look good. The golden tone of his skin

has lost its hue, replaced by an ashy, sickly pallor. Beads of sweat roll down his temples, wetting his hairline one drop at a time.

And if we take into consideration what Aidan said, only five of us will survive. He said he was amendable to keeping Carmen and Cerys alive, but he never said anything about Danny.

"Your cover-up?" I ask, arching my brows.

"Well, *someone* has to be the killer," he reminds me. "If we don't want to end up being the suspects, someone else has to carry that responsibility. Precious golden boy here will do just fine."

I can't help it, I laugh.

"Who would believe that?"

The answer is no one.

Danny Singh has a stellar reputation in Westbrook. He graduated with an almost perfect GPA, was a great baseball player, and the president of Delta. His legacy and records are impeccable, getting him into one of the top law school programs in the country.

What possible reason could he have to snap and choose to murder a group of his former acquaintances?

None.

Aidan cocks his head.

"Everyone will," he says, sounding sure about it like there's no space for doubt in his logic. "When we tell them how Danny used to be a close friend of Brian Manders."

"What?" Danny croaks out.

"Shut the fuck up," Elodie spits out, applying more pressure to Danny's neck.

"After finding out who killed his *innocent* best friend, Danny decided to get rid of every person who was involved in Brian's tragic downfall. But, most importantly, he chose to get revenge on his friend's murderer." Aidan spins on his heel, clasping his hands together, keeping the knife between them as he stares at me. "You, Mabel."

Everyone's head turns to me, shocked and bewildered by the accusation.

My throat dries.

What is he even talking about?

I didn't have anything to do with Brian Manders's death, no matter how much I wanted to get rid of the guy. It would've been foolish of me to murder him when Cerys hadn't gotten her justice yet. His death only made her look guilty, and people hated her even more, which made her drop out of college. Why would I ruin her future like that? No matter how much I hated him, I wouldn't do that.

Silence lingers around the attic, waiting for my reaction.

But I don't know what to say.

You got the wrong person, sorry? It's not like they will believe me either way when Aidan has been putting forward a compelling case against me.

"I didn't kill him," I say, frowning.

If they think I was the one who murdered Brian, it means neither of the cupids were responsible for Brian's death. It leaves Cerys still unable to clear her name against people's accusations and stigma. Cupid and Brian's killer have always been different people. Of course, now it's much clearer to see. Cupid's identity and motive spin around me, while Brian's killer defended Cerys' accusation.

Aidan clicks his tongue and pouts his lips as he approaches me.

"Oh, sweetie," he croons. "It's okay. You don't have to lie anymore. You're safe to confess the truth here."

"What truth?" I snap. "I. Didn't. Kill. Brian." I enunciate every word clearly, pausing between them like they will make any difference.

"Sweetie," he repeats the pet name in a tone that's meant to be endearing but only makes me want to spit in his face. "I know you better than anyone else in the world. You trusted me with your secret."

My heart jumps a handful of beats, almost leaping out of my chest when he says those words. Alarms blast in my brain, making me see red. Shivers vibrate in my body, and I shoot a glance to Cerys, who seems almost as shocked as me.

"What secret?"

It's not possible that he's referring to what I *think* he's referring to. There's only *one* person in the world who knows that secret, and it's Cerys. She never would've ratted on me to anyone, let alone Aidan. Even when her world crumbled around her, she still kept my secret. Even when it could've helped her, she chose not to betray my trust.

Aidan touches my hair, twirling a strand around his gloved finger.

"That Brian hurt you too," he reveals in a gentle voice. "He raped you months before he touched Cerys, and you didn't tell a soul."

Shame drops in me like a heavy rock, crushing me under its weight. I lower my gaze to the floor, my sight blurring with unshed tears. I feel naked in front of everyone, exposed and vulnerable. I try not to cry, but my chin trembles, warning me that the dam is about to break. A sob rips out of me, echoing around the walls of the attic.

"H-how do you know that?" I question through my tears.

I've never told anyone that before, only Cerys when she told me about Brian.

I guess a part of me never wanted to fully accept what had happened to me that night almost two years ago when Brian Manders spiked my drink at the last party of junior year.

The events of that night are hazy, with some mental lagoons appearing from time to time. Sometimes I get flashes of what happened whenever I get a whiff of the cologne he wore when he raped me, or when I taste beer. My trauma comes tied to my senses, not my memory.

I don't remember how everything started. I have a vague recollection of talking to him briefly that night when we played Beer Pong, then everything gets blurry. I remember feeling woozy and thinking it was due to the game. I've always been a bit of a lightweight when it comes to alcohol, so playing any drinking game gets me drunk pretty fast, but I didn't drink much. He offered to take me to his room to catch my breath, and I don't remember ever agreeing. All I know is that one minute I was next to the Beer Pong table, and the next he was undressing and climbing on top of me. The worst part about the drug is that I couldn't move. I'm always great at bolting out of places, but I couldn't do it then. I couldn't do anything, not even close my eyes to avoid seeing how he took advantage of me, not even when the pain and burn were overwhelming.

And I never told anyone this.

Only Cerys, and only after she went through the same thing.

How could he have known about it?

"You told me, Mabel. Don't you remember?"

No, I don't.

After Cerys told me about her rape and I went with her to get the rape kit done, I went down a self-destruction spiral for days. Drinking too much, barely getting any sleep at night because I would remember Brian's eyes as he pounded inside me.

"I-I don't know."

Aidan caresses the edge of my jaw, wiping the tears hanging from it. I move my head to the side, not wanting to feel his touch, and I end up meeting Danny's eye.

I shy away from him, avoiding his expression. Fear scratches my open wounds, my heart aching with vulnerability. I'm too terrified to see his reaction. I don't want him to think differently of me now that he knows the truth.

"It was after Cerys came forward," Aidan continues, refreshing my memory. "You told me you felt guilty for failing her because you backed out of filing your own complaint against Brian, leaving her to stand up to him on her own."

I close my eyes, getting flashes and pieces of that conversation now that he pulls the memory from the deepest crevices of my brain. I was horribly drunk when I confessed my truth in front of the fountain where Brian's corpse was found months later.

God, I felt horrible for backing out when Cerys asked for my support. She has always had my undying loyalty, but I was too scared about what would happen to me if I did. Cerys' parents weren't as rich as Brian's, but they live comfortably. They could afford lawyers and supported their daughter in every way she needed. I couldn't imagine making my family stand against Senator Manders' legal team and dirty money. We barely had enough to scrape by growing up. They would've crushed us completely and I didn't want to be responsible for ruining my parents' lives too.

It was enough knowing Brian had already taken something very important from me. So I pretended to be strong, especially for Carmen. I never wanted her to see me like this; broken and scarred.

I meet her gaze and my heart aches when I see the tears sliding down her cheeks. I want to wipe them and tell her to stop crying, that I'm okay, but I can't. I'm not okay, and she must know it because her eyes harden with hatred when she focuses on Aidan. "Oh, Mabel," Aidan says sweetly. "That night, you showed me you trust me more than anyone else in the world. I knew I would do anything to keep you safe, which is why I never said anything when you killed Brian."

"But I didn't kill him," I repeat. "You guys believe me, right?" I ask, glancing at Carmen and Cerys.

And then my gaze focuses on Danny. His expression springs a new wave of tears from my eyes. Brows arched, lips slightly parted, eyes glossy. He looks utterly devastated and lost. My chest tightens.

Aidan grabs my jaw and forces me to look at him instead.

"You don't have to lie anymore. There was nothing else you could've done. Going to the authorities would've been a complete failure, I get it. Especially after everything Cerys was going through with the case and the way her name was getting smeared all over. He would've wrecked you," he concludes like it's reason enough for me to murder someone, like this ridiculous theory makes perfect sense in his mind. "You never told me the logistics of it, but I think it's pretty obvious the rage won. You needed justice for yourself, for your best friend. You killed him in the same place you confessed to me, and that's how I knew. But don't worry, sweetie. It was the right thing to do."

"Is that why you chose to murder my friends?" I dare to ask.

He tilts his head.

"Well, most of them weren't your friends."

Like that excuses what he's done, the lives he has ended in my name. I don't want to carry that weight on my shoulders, yet he's putting it on me regardless. Just because he carries a warped sense of vengeance for me.

"Cerys? Carmen? Danny?" I supply. "They had nothing to do with that!"

Most of them didn't even know about it until he exposed my secret just now for everyone to hear.

"Collateral damage. They wouldn't understand why you killed Brian. Besides, someone has to take the fall for everything."

"Why Danny? Why not Seth, who was a complete asshole?"

Why attack the only guy in the world who has ever made me feel safe and secure?

Aidan laughs and lifts a finger in the air like he needs a moment.

"No, no, you don't get to make me look like the toxic one

here, sweetheart," he excuses himself. "You know I'm right about them not understanding why you did it. It's not like everyone believed Cerys, right?"

I grind my molars, hoping I'm able to turn them into dust.

Then, Carmen breaks into laughter. Her loud cackles reverberate in my chest as she shakes her head, trying to catch her breath. Tears sprout from the corners of her eyes, and, with one finger, she wipes them away, smudging her make-up even more than it already is.

"What a joke," she scoffs at Aidan's logic. "You really think Mabel has a murderous bone in her body?"

His expression grows serious. "I know she did it."

Carmen cackles again.

"Oh, you dumb freak. She didn't kill anyone."

"How are you so sure about that?"

My sister blows a sharp breath, her expression losing the humor as she lifts her chin defiantly.

"Because it was me," Carmen confesses with a proud smile on her face. "I killed Brian Manders."

Chapter 25

SILENCE REIGNS. MY SISTER'S EXPRESSION REMAINS impassive after her confession. When her gaze meets mine, I search for a hint that she's fabricated the perfect lie to throw them off course, but I find nothing. Her face shows no artifice or remorse for what she has done.

For a moment, the glint in her eyes dims.

"I heard you talking to Cerys the night after she filed her complaint," she says to me, keeping her words vague like she's trying to give me a shred of privacy in this vulnerable moment.

She doesn't have to say any more, I know exactly what she's referring to.

That night has haunted me this past year because it was the moment that changed everything for my best friend. Cerys had hopes that things would go in her favor, especially since Westbrook had been promoting safer and more proactive policies regarding assault and harassment on campus. But no one in the administration wanted to take any action against Brian and his father, considering Senator Manders was a benefactor of the university. Cerys' spirit broke that night because not only did things not go how she expected, but I had reduced the weight of her statement by not joining her.

If we had gone together, maybe things would've been different for her. They would've chosen me as an easier target. Being a minority and from a lower-class family, I wouldn't have her privilege or the resources to be able to put up a fight against the Manders' power and influence. They would've crushed me like a bug.

I felt horrible for letting her down, I still do, but I was too scared to come forward.

Look at what happened to her, even with her privilege and money. So for the sake of my parents and to protect Carmen's future career, I chose silence against my abuser.

And as selfish as it may sound, I believed that if I never spoke about what happened, then I could still play pretend. I could act like I had the opportunity to redo all the first times he took away from me without my permission.

I just . . . I wanted it to go away. I desperately wanted the ghost of his touch to vanish from my memory.

Somewhere along the line, when I was trying my hardest to forget, my baby sister chose to act with violence to defend me.

"Carmen," I whisper her name, my voice betraying me when it breaks.

A part of me still expects her to sneakily hint that she's lying. But she doesn't. Her expression remains without an ounce of regret, like she would do it all over again if she had to.

"When I heard what he did to you, how scared and helpless it made you, I knew I had to do something about it," she reveals, anger filling her words. "I've always had a darkness in me, and I felt it when I found out what happened to you. And I let it win. I planned my revenge. It was unfair that he got to live a normal life, while you were being eaten away by what he put you through. I made sure he never got to live again."

"Carmen," I repeat, without knowing what to say.

How does anyone react when you find out your little sister, the most precious person in your life, has decided to get her hands bloody on your behalf?

"I made my choice, Mabby. I decided to kill Brian, and I don't regret it one bit." She turns to look at Cerys with a hint of apology in her curved brows. "I'm sorry you never got a chance to clear your name, Cerys, but the motherfucker needed to die."

The confession lingers in the air, shock plastering every inch and surface of the attic, thickening the tension around us.

My mind reels with a plague of thoughts. The memory of Brian's butchered body returns to the front of my brain. The way he was killed sent a clear message to everyone about who he was.

And it was Carmen who did it.

"Is this why you distanced yourself from me?" I ask. "So I wouldn't find out about it?"

Her curls shake.

"No, it wasn't about you finding out. I wanted to tell you the truth. Keeping it from you was the hardest thing I've ever done, but if anything came out, I never wanted you to suffer the consequences. What I did to him should never have affected you. The less you knew, the better. Especially if the cops ever caught on with evidence. I didn't want you to be a suspect." She glances at Cerys. "No offense."

"None taken."

"When you left this place, I was so relieved because it meant you would be far away from all the hellfire if anyone discovered something about the case."

"Wait, so you were really the one who killed Brian?" Aidan interrupts, standing between us.

"Don't you feel stupid now? Murdering a bunch of people because you believed Mabel was capable of killing someone?" Carmen taunts him.

He shakes his head, but it's not a response to her jibe. He's having second thoughts about what he has done. This entire scenario was based on his interpretation of something that never even happened.

"It doesn't matter," Aidan grits out. "It'll be you and me at the end, sweetie. I will get the girl, and this inconvenient asshole will die." He points at Danny with his knife.

Elodie groans out loud, charged with annoyance.

"Oh, shut the fuck up, Aidan!" she shouts, stopping him in his tracks. "You won't get a chance to ride off into the sunset with Mabel like homicidal losers."

"What are you—"

The gunshot blasts in my ears, and I scream as I lower to the ground, watching as Aidan's corpse falls in the middle of the room, spreading a crimson pool around his head. Or what's left of it. The bullet burst through his eye socket, leaving clumps of flesh around his face.

The instinct to run pulses in me, but I glance at my loved ones instead to make sure they're free of harm. Or free of any bullet holes, since they're all injured and losing blood already.

Danny's gash is still ebbing blood with every minute that passes by since he's unable to stop the bleeding with just his palms pressing against the wound. His chest heaves with shallow breaths, and when our gazes meet, I notice the shock and sorrow swirling in his eyes. I force myself to look away. Still sitting on a box, Cerys is pale and shivering, her lips cracked as she struggles to remain perched there. Across from me, maroon streams flow from Carmen's shoulder wound, soaking her dress.

Elodie is the only one standing.

"Great, now we have another homicidal loser," Carmen mutters under her breath, but it comes out louder than she had intended.

"Shut up!" Elodie screams, pointing the gun at her. My breath hitches, fearing the worst, but she doesn't fire. Her finger abandons the trigger, and she leans her head to the side, observing us. "I should kill you right now for what you did, but I think I'll leave you for the end."

Elodie shoves the gun in her clothes and tightens her hold on the axe's handle, pulling Danny's body to the side as the sharp edge presses against the side of his neck.

"Why are you even doing this?" Cerys interrogates in a frail voice. "We never did anything to you."

Although Cerys voices what we're all thinking here,

they're the wrong words to say because madness flares in Elodie's eyes. Pure rage in the form of a flush spreads over her skin, coating her face in a shade of deep red.

"Nothing? You did everything," she growls.

"What are you even talking about?" I press, almost begging for some clarity.

Her head turns to me, a wicked smile carved in her face.

"Aidan was in love with you," she says, completely ignoring my question. "The stupid fool really thought he'd be able to get away with this and gain your love," she tells me, twisting the axe handle. Danny lets out a choked whimper. "What a fucking creep, if you ask me. He clearly couldn't see he had bigger competition."

The more she talks, the more confusion grows in my system. If she didn't join Aidan's plot to create an elaborate slasher film, what's her reason? People don't just randomly wake up one day and choose to collaborate in a carefully curated massacre. Especially when she planned to eliminate her partner all along.

I'm missing the last part of the puzzle.

Elodie is a piece that doesn't fit in with the rest of the characters in the picture.

"Yeah, he was a delusional idiot," I agree, following her train of thought. If she's talking, she can reveal her intentions. After all, there's nothing a killer enjoys more in a film than explaining why they're murdering people. "Why did you help him?"

She wrinkles her nose.

"Help him? You've got this all wrong. He was helping *me*."

"Why?"

"Because you took everything from me with your lies."

Revenge? She's doing this because she wants revenge?

I frown and look in Carmen's direction. She shrugs in confusion.

"Lies?" I cock my head. "What lies?"

"About Brian, you slut!" she shouts. Losing her control of the axe for a second, she knicks Danny's neck and my heart summersaults. "You're all responsible for his death."

Somehow, it all leads back to him.

Aidan used Brian's actions to create this night of horror as a fucked-up grand gesture of love for me. And Elodie is seeking revenge in his name.

Two twisted sides of the same coin.

"Brian brought it on himself. We never lied about anything," I spit out, the flush of anger heating my skin. "And why do you care so much about his rapist ass?"

Elodie's nostrils flare as she glares at me.

"He was the love of my life," she reveals. "Brian was my boyfriend. I loved him. He loved me."

I crane my neck in her direction.

This is the first time I've heard about it, because Brian Manders never had girlfriends. He enjoyed having his freedom, fucking anyone who crossed his path, even the ones who didn't consent to it. He was like any other basic frat boy. Loved to drink and party, never caring about his future or career because his rich daddy would get him the perfect job after graduation. If there was something Brian adored, it was his fuckboy life.

He was far from what Elodie seems to think he was.

"All of you took him from me," she carries on, her voice

cracking with emotion. "With your false accusations and lies, kicking him out of his frat home, slandering his name. You're all guilty, especially *you*," she determines, staring at Carmen. "You'll pay for this."

And my sister does the worst thing anyone can do when a killer is exposing their motive: she laughs. A full belly-laugh like someone is tickling her ribs.

"Carmen Lucía," I grit out.

"I'm sorry, it's just..." She snorts, laughing again. Carmen shoots me a look like she's trying to get me to understand something.

"What are you laughing at?"

"At you." Carmen's gaze flickers to Elodie's axe.

I frown.

What is she playing at?

"At me?" presses Elodie, her wide eyes twitching. Her jaw tightens, as she spews, "I'm going to have so much fun killing you, you little bitch. It'll be a slow death, so you really suffer."

"Do it," Carmen taunts her. "I bet it'll be longer than your fake relationship with Brian."

"Shut the fuck up! You don't know what you're talking about."

Elodie's grip on the axe loosens as her muscles shake with anger, and for a moment I'm afraid Elodie will whip out her gun and just shoot Carmen. She takes a small step forward and stops pressing the axe against Danny's neck.

I finally understand what Carmen's doing. She's distracting Elodie.

"Did Brian even know you guys were dating?" Carmen taunts her with a mean smirk.

"Knowing Brian, I doubt he even knew her name," I say, adding salt to the wound. My eyes flicker to Danny and then to the pocket in Elodie's robes where she hid the gun. His brows twitch for a second, but as his eyes track mine, he gets the message, giving me the tiniest nod. "She's as delusional as Aidan. Actually, more than Aidan. At least I remembered his existence. Can't say the same for Brian remembering her."

Filled with rage, Elodie lets out a guttural scream, her hand flying to her robes. But Danny is faster than her. He elbows her in the gut and knocks the gun out of her pocket.

Elodie is caught off guard, but she's too angry to focus on him. Unable to find the gun, she hoists the axe over her shoulder and swings.

"Watch out!" I yell at Carmen, dropping to the ground as Elodie tries to take my head off with the axe.

Thankfully for us, the fury in her makes her movements clumsy and unprecise.

"You're all liars! He *loved* me. Brian was in a relationship with me, why would he want to go with someone else? You probably made up those lies because he rejected both of you. Since you couldn't trap him, you chose to hurt him instead."

"He probably used you because you were an easy fuck," Carmen throws back at her.

"News flash for you—Brian didn't like accessible girls," I add.

"That's not true. He was loyal to me."

"Is that why his favorite hobby was to drug girls and rape them in his shitty twin-sized bed?" Carmen quips.

"He didn't do that! Stop lying!" she shrieks with her eyes

closed, throwing the axe in my sister's direction in an attempt to get her to shut up.

The axe is too big for her to throw precisely, missing Carmen's body by a mile.

She lets out a visceral scream and moves frantically in a circle, searching for something.

The gun.

I can't let her grab it. Without giving it a second thought, I lunge at her. I dig my fingers into the place where I know I stabbed her. Elodie shrieks in agony when I push her and she loses her balance. Her arms fling around, trying to find something to grasp on to.

And that something is . . . me.

She grabs handfuls of my hair, tugging on my scalp as we both fall through the hatch. I hit my hip hard on the ladder's steps and let out a moan. My body slams on the floor. Adrenaline pumps in my veins, allowing me to recover faster than I had anticipated. The pain is barely a dull ache as I spot a knife lying a few meters away.

Por fin.

Crawling on the floor, I reach for the knife. Elodie bites the back of my arm before I can wrap my fingers around the hilt, and I scream. Elbowing her in the face to push her off me, I grab the knife and stagger to my feet.

Elodie stands too, her nose dripping blood over her mouth as she bares her teeth, looking almost animalistic. She slams her body against mine and tries to wrestle the knife out of my grasp.

While we have similar body types and strength, she's fueled by raw and visceral madness. I know she needs to die.

If I want to protect the ones I love, I have to kill Elodie.

I slam my face against hers, hitting her nose and it cracks. More blood gushes out of her, but she's unstoppable, kicking her legs, trying to get me down. We hit the banister at the top of the stairs and I push her against it, hearing it crack.

Her eyes widen in fear.

Taking a step back, I slam my body against hers as hard as I possibly can. The banister breaks under the force and we fall.

There's a bigger distance between the first and second floor, almost a story and a half. Probably close to fifteen feet. The air is knocked out of my lungs, the fall harder than the one from the attic. My fall is broken by Elodie's body. I almost feel my ribs crack as I lie parallel on top of her. My abdomen radiates overwhelming flames of pain through my system.

I place my hands by the sides of Elodie's head and push to sit up, moving to a straddling position. Looking down to the spot where our bodies are still linked, I see that Elodie's hand is wrapped around the hilt of a knife that is buried in my stomach.

She stabbed me.

I gasp for air, shock permeating my skin as I clasp my thighs at the sides of her body, keeping her locked in place.

La cabrona stabbed me.

My sight gets blurry at the edges, and I don't know if it's thanks to the pain and the blood flowing out of me, or the adrenaline vibrating under my skin. I shake my head, hoping to clear it as I grab the hilt of the knife.

Elodie's eyes grow in shock, her jaw slackening as I slap

her hands away from it. With my chest heaving, I do something I probably shouldn't. I'm not a doctor. The very sparse medical experience I have is limited to watching hospital dramas on TV and creating horror wounds on film, but I do know you should never remove any type of weapons or foreign objects embedded in your body.

Yet it's what I do.

I pull the knife out of my gut. Warm blood gushes out of me, coating both of our bodies, and I smile at Elodie's horrified expression. The animalistic glow in her eyes is long gone, turning her from a predator into meek prey.

Like she always was.

"Now it's your turn to die, you fucking bitch," I grit out.

Before she can respond, I bury the knife in her chest, using every bit of strength I have. The blade pierces through layers of clothing, skin and muscle, hitting bone as I cut through her. I retrieve the blade and plunge it in her again, her flesh making a gooey *thwack* noise.

Thwack.

Thwack.

Thwack.

Thwack.

Blood sprays over me as Elodie's screams blast in my ears. Or am I the one screaming as I stab her? I feel my vocal cords vibrating, but I can't hear my voice. I don't know anymore. My body is in overdrive. Depositing all the adrenaline, trauma and pain into killing the person who has caused us so much torment tonight. Especially because I know that, beyond everything Aidan did, Elodie was the one who hurt Carmen and Cerys.

She hurt the people I love the most.

She almost killed Danny.

She deserves a horrific death too.

So I stab her over and over again until she stops screaming. I don't stop piercing her body with the knife until she stops thrashing and the only movement that comes from her is caused by me stabbing her. I plunge the knife in her chest one last time and leave it buried there where it belongs as I admire the gruesome image of the violence I created.

Her robes are torn and shredded from the wounds, flesh split open in so many places that there are holes in spots where I stabbed her twice. Empty eyes stare at the ceiling, lips bloody, as she lies lifeless on the floor.

Rattled breathing comes out of me in puffs as I roll off her, resting my back on the floor. Adrenaline ebbs from my wound, disappearing from my body. I've grown numb. A tingling sensation radiates from me as I lie there. Shivering pain comes in waves from my abdomen, and it's then I notice the movie projecting on the wall across from me.

The romantic comedy that was barely starting when Danny and I left the closet. As people count down to midnight, Harry runs to meet Sally to confess his harbored feelings. I've seen it enough times to know the lines, even though I can't hear the dialogue. I'm unsure if it's because I'm losing my ability to hear as consciousness slips out of my grasp or if the audio never played.

Has it only been an hour and a half since then?

Time moves in weird waves.

I shift my head, staring at the ceiling.

"Mabel!" Carmen's voice sounds miles away, but she's

nearer than I can process as I catch the faint movement as she kneels next to me. "Danny, do something!"

"You don't get to do this, Mabel." Danny holds my face, turning it to the side so I can see him, but he's a blur. "You don't get to be the sacrificial lamb."

The sacrificial lamb.

Aidan thought he was turning me into the perfect final girl, but all along I was just the sacrificial lamb. The character who dies for the sake of others. At least my death will mean something.

At least I got to keep them safe.

Dark spots dance at the edge of my vision.

And, like any film script reaching its end, I fade out.

Chapter 26

The Aftermath

ONE THING'S FOR SURE, I'M NOT NEARLY AS DEAD AS I thought I was. Either that or heaven—or hell—looks a lot like the interior of a hospital room. I blink a few times, getting used to the brightness as the world around me fades into view. The room looks sterile and clean, with white walls and floor. I think I'm alone, until I spot my sister sitting next to me. She has her feet hoisted on a cushion as she scrolls on her phone.

I notice she's no longer wearing her bloody dress. Instead, her body is clad in a pair of gray leggings and a Westbrook navy-blue hoodie. Her eyes peer at me for a second and she immediately locks the phone as she rises to her feet.

"Hey there," Carmen says in a soft tone. Her fingers caress my arm where an IV line is stuck in. My throat feels dry, my tongue sticking to the roof of my mouth as I try to swallow. "Do you want a sip of water?"

Slowly, I nod. I don't think I can speak until I hydrate my burning throat. I watch her walk around the bed to reach for the jug of water on the table. She fills a cup and comes back to my side, carefully lifting the cup to my lips.

"Small sips. Try not to spit it all over me like the last time," she warns.

I frown, confused by her words. Have I woken up before this? The concern is washed away as the water slides down my throat, quenching the fire. I sigh with bliss. It's refreshing. I ask for another sip and it's even better than the first one.

"Last time?" I croak out, testing my voice. It sounds hoarse and scratchy, but it's better than I expected.

Carmen hums an affirmative response.

"You've woken up like five times in the past couple of hours. Those pain meds are *strong*," she says. Well, that explains why I feel like I'm lying on a puffy cloud when I'm sure the lower half of my body is torn to shreds. "You were freaking out the first two times and high as a kite the next three. Mumbling nonsense about Danny's tight ass," she tells me, wrinkling her nose.

Dios mío.

I want to crawl into a ball and hide under the bed, but even the *thought* of moving an inch is painful.

"Is Danny okay?"

"Relax, your man candy is more than fine. He got stitched up. Crazy Elodie missed all the important organs when she whacked him with the axe," she says. "He actually just went to grab some coffee and to check on Cerys."

"She's okay too?"

Carmen nods. "She had to get some minor surgery."

I feel my face blanching.

"The stab wound?"

Her lips quirk. "No, she was fine from that. Turns out getting stabbed helped the doctors know her appendix was about to give up on her."

"Her appendix?" I mumble. "She got stabbed and had to get surgery, not because she had a knife in her gut, but because she had appendicitis?"

"Yup."

"That is . . ."

"Ridiculous?" Carmen supplies when I fail to come up with the word. "I know, trust me. Imagine how it must feel for me when I haven't slept in twenty-six hours, and they pumped me full of meds to stitch my shoulder."

I snort.

"What happened after?"

"After you passed out?" I nod. "The TL;DR version: Danny lost his mind, found Elodie's axe, used it to smash the front door, called for help. He turned into a whole movie hero there. I'm still a bit shocked. Never thought there would be a day he would seem attractive. All bloody and manly, carrying you out of the house, even with his own injuries," she says, fanning herself in a dramatic way. "He really loves you."

My cheeks heat up.

"This is not the *too long; didn't read* version," I remind her.

Carmen sighs but gets back on topic.

"After what seemed like forever, the whole emergency department showed up. We got an ambulance for you and

Cerys. The police found all the bodies in one of the rooms, Ollie was among them. Sophia had been hiding in the elevator, she was freaked out, but fine. Zelda is now known as Kappa's Jesus for still being miraculously alive after everything."

"Kappa's Jesus? I'm sure a few people would find that massively disrespectful, including Abuela."

"Well, Abuela isn't here, and I'm allowed some dark jokes after last night."

"Fair," I grant.

Being told what happened after I passed out is almost like hearing her comment on a movie she saw and not something we actually lived through. But it did happen. We survived two murderers and a night full of horrors that could never compare to anything I've ever written.

"Yeah, I know it's a lot," she mumbles, toning down her frantic storytelling when I stay silent for a minute. Her hands hold my fingers and, when she looks up at me, her eyes are full of tears. "I'm sorry."

"It's okay," I whisper.

If I wasn't so full of drugs, I would be crying as well, but the meds keep my emotions dull and faint. Like they're behind a crystal wall where I can see them but not experience them to the fullest.

"No, I caused all of this. If I hadn't . . ."

"Don't blame yourself," I interrupt her before she can admit to something that will get her in trouble. "The ones responsible for this are Aidan, Elodie and Brian. No one else."

"But if I hadn't . . . *done that,*" she emphasizes, sobbing. "I was so scared you were going to die, Mabby, and it was all my fault."

I shake my head, opening my arms so she can lean against my chest. My little sister wastes no time, hugging me tightly. I bite the inside of my cheek when a sharp pain cuts through my abdomen as she presses her weight against me, but I swallow it down. My only priority is comforting my sister.

"I think we've all done things we're not proud of," I say, rubbing a hand on her back to ease her sobs.

After all, my hands are also stained with blood. Maybe it wasn't as premeditated as Carmen's murder, but I still took a life in a brutal way. I remember how many times I stabbed Elodie, even when her body was no longer fighting back or struggling to get away from me. I've tasted rage and darkness, and I'm still waiting for the pang of guilt to consume me, but it never comes. I don't regret killing Elodie any less than Carmen regrets killing Brian. In a way, I could say Carmen and I are two sides of the same coin. Both clawing our way through the world, having to take violent routes to ensure our survival.

While I can't excuse what she's done, I also can't blame her.

"I put you at risk," she says.

As I rub her back, I look for the right words to ease her fears.

"Maybe," I concede. It's a fact. Her actions were a gateway for two fucked-up persons to come up with a twisted plan of their own. Carmen's shoulders tense. "But you know what? I don't care."

She lifts her head to look at me. "You don't?"

I gently push a curl behind her ear.

"No, because I would've done the exact same thing for you," I confess.

I *did* the same thing when I killed Elodie.

Carmen sobs into my chest. "I love you," she whispers. "I love you so much."

I squeeze my arms around her, despite the pain that shoots up my spine.

"I love you too. More than you can imagine," I tell her.

A soft knock at the door catches my attention, and Carmen pulls away from me, wiping her tears with the sleeve of her hoodie. The door opens a sliver before Danny pops his head through, his warm eyes glinting when he catches a glimpse of me. A smile spreads over his face, so wide I can almost see his molars.

"You're awake," he points out brightly, his voice full of relief and joy.

Carmen looks between us.

"I'm going to give Ma a call," she tells me, excusing herself. Though I can guess she's only doing it so Danny and I can have a moment to talk. "She went home to shower and grab some stuff."

"Carmen." Danny stops her before she can leave the room. "I spoke to Cerys."

She frowns. "About?"

"About Aidan's confession." I tilt my head. What is he even talking about? "That he murdered Brian and lied to Elodie about Mabel being the killer to get her on his side."

Carmen remains frozen in place, processing his words.

Since my brain is fuzzy from whatever they've put in my

IV, it also takes me a moment to get what he's saying. Once I do, my heart melts. He's protecting her, giving me a chance to keep the most important person in my life while still clearing Cerys' name.

Carmen gets to walk free, and Cerys gets to have a fresh start.

"Thank you," Carmen mumbles, her voice soft with appreciation. But it only lasts a moment because she adds, "Just for that, I'm willing to forgive you for getting my sister naked in my bed."

Danny chuckles. "Are we even?"

She nods. "Yeah, golden boy, we're even."

More than even, I'd say, but that's for them to discuss.

Carmen turns on her heel and slips out of the room, closing the door behind her to leave me alone with Danny. My heart swells when he steps closer to the bed, sitting on the edge.

"Should you be walking around?" I ask him, looking at his torso, remembering the wound Elodie left behind.

He cocks his head.

"Plot armor, baby," he responds.

I snort, laughing for a second before I have to catch my breath.

"Thank you," I say, extending a hand to him. He holds it, lacing our fingers together. "For keeping Carmen's secret."

"She doesn't deserve to go down for getting rid of scum. That's not justice."

"I wonder what your father would say about that," I comment.

Danny shrugs. "I don't know. He was too stunned to speak

when I called him to say I was in the hospital after surviving a killer and I want to specialize in sports law."

"Oh, buddy," I whistle under my breath.

"I surely choose the best moments to drop news, right?" he jokes. "Dadi almost had a heart attack when she heard what happened. Said she needed to buy more chili and lemon for the Nazar Battu she's making me. And that she's going to bake more *nankhatai* for you."

My stomach almost growls. I can't remember the last time I ate, and I would kill for one of his grandmother's cookies right now.

"That's nice of her."

"You deserve it."

I smile.

I squeeze his hand three times.

"I'm sorry I didn't trust you."

He draws soothing circles with his thumb.

"It's okay. I won't hold it against you, what happened in the house. Besides, you kind of made up for it when you turned into a final girl and took down the killer," he points out.

Danny's not entirely wrong. What happened in the house was horrible and nightmare-inducing, but I can count a few memories I would like to keep. I hope he's not wanting to walk away from me now that the adrenaline has run out. Especially now that he knows the truth about what happened to me. The secrets I had held on to, the grittiest and rawest parts of myself.

"Danny." He cocks his head, waiting for me to continue. "What Aidan said about Brian . . ." My voice breaks, crushed by the weight of the lump in my throat.

Danny squeezes my hand, his eyes clouding.

"I'm so sorry, Mabel," he says in a soft whisper. "I'm so sorry he did that to you."

While the meds keep me from crying, I've never felt this raw and vulnerable before. An ache presses against my vocal cords, and I struggle to find the words to express myself. I can only sit in silence for a minute.

"You don't have to say anything," Danny continues, giving me a comforting look. "It was your story to tell and it's so unfair that Aidan felt like he had the right to use it against you. They both took advantage of you in ways that I can't truly imagine, and I'm very sorry. You went through that alone and I wish I could've helped you more."

I shake my head.

"I didn't want anyone to know," I confess. "I just wanted to forget it ever happened."

He frowns with concern.

"Mabel, have you talked to someone about this?" he asks in a gentle tone. "A professional, someone who can help you?"

I drop my gaze to my hands, biting the inside of my cheek.

"No," I admit.

I hear him take a deep breath. "Is it something you would like?"

Would I? I spent so long trying to keep the memories locked in the back of my brain where they couldn't reach or hurt me. But it didn't help. It just delayed my reaction, looking for coping mechanisms that prevented me from strengthening the relationships around me. I never allowed myself to get the support that I need.

"I think so," I mumble.

"Would you let me be there for you through that process and everything else?" The vulnerability and genuine concern in his voice make my chest tighten with emotion. A tear slides down my face as I nod in response. Carefully, Danny wipes it away, his eyes softening with adoration. "You're the bravest woman I've ever met, Mabel. And I'm so proud of you."

My heart flutters at his compliment.

I love him so much it almost hurts.

"I'm certain I'm also the most stubborn woman you've met too." I try to make a joke to lighten the mood.

Danny rolls his eyes, but he can't hide the smile spreading across his lips.

"That too. Especially when you're trying to sacrifice yourself in horrible circumstances," he says, but there's not an ounce of seriousness in his voice. He's matching the humor in my tone.

I lick my lips.

"What about our love confession? Were those horrible circumstances?" I ask.

He leans in and kisses my forehead.

"As fucked-up as it sounds, those were the best moments of my life."

Happiness pulses in my veins, and I would worry it's caused by the IV line if it weren't that Danny's words make my insides tingly.

"I would agree with you, but let me tell you, these drugs are kicking your ass," I joke.

Danny laughs and caresses my face with gentle fingers.

"You're high as fuck."

I nod, humming with contentment. The cloud that is my bed shifts as he scoots to get closer, resting his back next to me.

"Very."

I turn my head to look at him and find him already staring back.

"Would it be weird if I said I'm madly in love with you now?" he questions.

I shake my head. "No, because I love you too," I say, resting a hand on his neck to pull him in for a brief kiss. "Are we ready to begin a long-distance relationship?"

His brows almost touch his hairline.

"Long distance?"

"With me living in LA and you in New York?"

His thumb rubs the edge of my jaw.

"Baby, I've already spent a year away from you. I almost lost you," he reminds me, his voice wavering for a second. "I'm never going to be away from you again, even if I have to pack all my stuff and move across the country for you."

My mouth dries.

"You would uproot your life for me?" I rasp, feeling close to breaking down in tears, even more than I did when Carmen was crying over me.

Danny nods.

"There's nothing I wouldn't do for you, baby," he promises. "If you want me, of course."

I search his face for any hint that he's only saying it because we're still on edge from what happened in Theta, but all I see is devotion and love in his eyes when he looks at me. He doesn't scratch his neck with nervousness or quirk his mouth like he does when he's feeling unsure about something.

I move my hand from his neck to his cheek, touching the slight stubble on his face. With him so close to me, I feel more secure than I've ever felt in my life. I don't want this feeling to ever end.

"I do, I do want you," I say immediately. "But you don't have to move. I will."

"Mabs—"

Placing my fingers over his mouth, I silence his words before he can protest.

"I've spent my entire life running away from things, leaving people behind to protect myself from ever being hurt, and I almost died in the process. You almost died," I remind him, the image of Cupid standing over him with the axe as he told me to run flashing into my brain. Closing my eyes, I push it away. "I don't ever want to leave you behind again."

"I love you."

"I love you," I say back, kissing his lips for a moment. "Also, I'm thinking I should make a career switch. Horror and slashers are kind of ruined for me now."

"What will you do instead?"

For once in my life, I don't know the answer to that.

"I guess I'll have to figure it out."

He presses his lips to my forehead, and I rest against him.

"It's okay. We can figure it out . . ."

"Together?" I ask.

Danny squeezes my shoulder three times.

"Yes, baby. Together."

Epilogue

A year later

ATTEMPTING TO GET A CAT INTO A CHRISTMAS SWEATER IS quite frankly the hardest thing I've ever done in my life. Which is saying a lot, considering I've faced two killers. Mauricio, the chubby cat I rescued from an alley, claws at me as I try to fit one of his paws through the tiny sleeve.

"Mauricio, *ya para*," I groan, forcing him into the ugly green sweater that, if I'm honest, clashes with his orange fur. Whoever said redheads look amazing in green clearly hasn't seen my cat, but I don't have the heart to tell Danny after he brought the sweater home with an excited look on his face. "I know we hate the sweater, but you've got to make your dad happy, okay?"

Mauricio hisses at me, and I'm tempted to hiss back.

I rescued him after I got my current job at XYZ Network. He was a scrawny little thing, meowing from an alley when I found him and decided to bring him home. Danny had a lot to say about it when I texted him that I had added a new member to our family, but he fell in love with him the moment he walked through the door.

"Are you fighting with the cat again?"

Mauricio takes advantage of my distraction and jumps off the bed, running out of the bedroom now that the door is open.

I rest my hurt hands on my hips and stare at my boyfriend's beautiful face, unable to stay mad at him for letting the cat out after I had the hardest time trapping him with treats.

My knees grow weak at the sight of Danny.

He leans against the door frame with his hands in the pockets of his black slacks. A white collared shirt peeks out of the red knitted sweater. His sleeves folded up to his elbows, showing off a gold watch strapped around his wrist.

He looks utterly delicious.

If we weren't hosting Christmas at the apartment we just leased, and our guests weren't due at any minute, I would suggest we have another quickie. I don't know if it's because I'm head over heels in love with him or because he gives me mind-blowing orgasms, but I'm insatiable when it comes to him.

"Stop it," he warns me.

I lift my brows and pout, feigning innocence.

"Stop what?"

"Stop looking at me like you want me to bend you over the bed and have my way with you."

My core clenches around nothing.

Well, I wasn't thinking of that specific scenario, but now that he's planted the seed in my brain . . .

"Hmm . . ." I muse as I step toward him.

He sucks in a breath and lets it out in a sigh.

"Sorry, baby," he mumbles when I pull him closer by his belt loops. "Cerys called a few minutes ago saying her plane just landed from Boston, and your sister is already on her way with your family. There's no time."

I arch a brow.

Although his warning is clear, I'm not as easily persuaded. Cerys is staying in our guest bedroom for a few days, as she's finally getting a break from her first semester of law school, and it will mean that we'll be too busy giving her the tourist treatment to have any time for ourselves. These are our last minutes alone before we're swamped, and I'm more than eager to make the most of them.

"Is that a challenge?"

The thrill of knowing we could be interrupted at any moment is exciting.

"Did you finish your script?" he asks, changing the subject without giving me a response.

Challenge accepted.

I reach up and wrap a hand around Danny's neck, my fingers toying with the ends of his hair.

"Yes," I whisper in his ear, brushing my lips against the sensitive spot between his neck and earlobe. "Last night."

Danny sighs.

"Are you finally going to tell me about it?"

I got thousands of offers to participate in podcasts and tell my story about what happened the night of the Greek Row massacre, as the media has called it, but I've refused all of them. Including the offer to write the script of my own version of the events for a major production house, as Aidan predicted would happen. But working in horror only makes me feel sick, so I took a break from the genre. For the past couple of months, after deciding to refocus my career in a different direction, I've been silently working on something new, keeping it a secret from everyone, including Danny.

He's been dying to know what I've been working on, but he's been respectful of my muse. Keeping the story close to my chest has been a pivotal aspect of getting it finished.

I hum against his skin, pressing a kiss on his sweet spot.

He trembles.

As I smile triumphantly at him shedding a layer of control, I press my body against his, feeling a hard bulge.

"You're eager . . . for someone so against having a quickie," I tease, leading a hand to it, except my fingers meet something harder than a boner.

I frown, craning my neck to meet his gaze, and find his eyes are wide. His hands fly to the spot I'm touching, and he pushes my touch away.

"Shit," Danny mumbles.

"Wait, what is that?"

He stares at me, his eyes conflicted before he lets out a long sigh of defeat.

"I should've known you would find a way to mess with my plans," he mumbles under his breath, but his lips are curved into a gentle smile.

What is he even talking about?

Danny places his hands on my arms and slowly moves me to the middle of the room. Then, he shoves his hand in his pocket and withdraws a black box.

A black jewelry box.

A small one.

Just big enough for a . . .

Danny drops to one knee, keeping his back straight as he raises the box in front of me. Then he flicks the lid open, showing the most perfect emerald-cut ring. The pavé-style platinum band sparkles under the room lights.

Tears sting behind my lids as I gape at the ring, too stunned to know how to act.

"You're a frustrating woman, you know?" he comments.

"Is this the speech you rehearsed?" I choke out.

"Oh, not at all. You just ruined the whole proposal I had originally planned and took me by surprise yet again," he says. "Mabel Marie Rivera."

"Yes, Daniel Singh?" I croak out through the lump in my throat.

"I've been yours since the moment we first met. I've loved you through happiness, sadness and fear. I've loved you in the face of death and in our shared home. I loved you even though you brought home a flea-infested cat." A watery laugh escapes from me and tears roll down my cheeks. "And I love you as you ruin the perfect speech I carefully curated for months while I waited for the perfect moment to ask you to spend the rest of your life with me."

"Yes."

"I haven't asked the question yet."

"You don't need to ask, the answer is yes."

Danny tilts his head.

"Mabel, will you marry me?"

"Yes," I repeat, kneeling in front of him. "I love you. Yes."

Drawing the ring from the box, Danny slides it onto my shaky finger. I waste no time, wrapping my arms around his neck and kissing him fiercely.

"Thank you," he mumbles against my lips.

"What for?"

"For making me the happiest man on earth," he says, merging his mouth with mine once again. "So, do I get to know what your script is about? As your future husband, I should get some intel."

A laugh rips from me and I shake my head in disbelief.

I lean into him until my mouth is next to his ear and whisper, "It's a romance."

Just like ours.

Acknowledgments

Slash or Pass was written from a place of love and appreciation for various things: the horror genre, filmmaking, romance, friendships, and sisterly bonds. I haven't put this much of myself in a story in a long time, to the point where writing Mabel felt as natural as breathing. And while the act of writing itself can be a lonely process full of sleep-depravation, questionable eating habits, and mumbling incoherently about characters, it wouldn't be possible without a constant support system.

A huge, colossal thank you to my wonderful editor, Soraya, for always going above and beyond for me and this story. Thank you for trusting my instinct, for putting up with my unhinged emails, and for tolerating my incredibly stubborn little sister behavior. Working with you has truly been an honor.

To the team at Headline Eternal, thank you for giving this story a home.

To my parents who always told me *el cielo es el límite* and encouraged me to pursue every single one of my dreams.

To my sister, I hope I made you proud with the way I wrote Mabel as an older sister. I might never fully understand what it takes to be one, but I had you as an example. Strong and independent, fiercely protective over your little sister (me), and always spoiling me. *Te amo*. Also, I hope you don't read the acknowledgments first like you always do with my books.

To Sav, for being my best friend. You've been there through every moment of this process, listening to me, being my personal dictionary and thesaurus, because why would I use one when I can just message you "What's the word for this?", right? I love you more than words can express. I hope you love your new stepchildren.

To all my friends. *Las nenas* for the weekend getaways, the venting conversations and *las crisis de mayo*. Amanda, for always teaching me about horror and giving me the best movie recs. *Las Chanels*, I don't know what I would do without our group chat.

A very special thank you to my boyfriend, who was there for me on FaceTime through every writing and editing session. For our first Valentine's Day together, you wrote me a love letter, and then I told you that my love letter to you was yet to be written. Well, I kind of lied about that. I used to write about romance before because I craved it, and now I write it because you make me feel it. This is my love letter to you.

ACKNOWLEDGMENTS

And to all the readers absolutely third wheeling the previous paragraph, thank you for giving this story a chance and for witnessing a romantic grand gesture from the author (sorry about the PDA). I hope it was to your liking (the story, not the third wheeling).

RAISING READERS
Books Build Bright Futures

Dear Reader,

We'd love your attention for one more page to tell you about the crisis in children's reading, and what we can all do.

Studies have shown that reading for fun is the **single biggest predictor of a child's future life chances** – more than family circumstance, parents' educational background or income. It improves academic results, mental health, wealth, communication skills, ambition and happiness.[1]

The number of children reading for fun is in rapid decline. Young people have a lot of competition for their time. In 2024, 1 in 10 children and young people in the UK aged 5 to 18 did not own a single book at home.[2]

Hachette works extensively with schools, libraries and literacy charities, but here are some ways we can all raise more readers:

- Reading to children for just 10 minutes a day makes a difference
- Don't give up if children aren't regular readers – there will be books for them!
- Visit bookshops and libraries to get recommendations
- Encourage them to listen to audiobooks
- Support school libraries
- Give books as gifts

There's a lot more information about how to encourage children to read on our website: **www.RaisingReaders.co.uk**

Thank you for reading.

hachette UK

---

[1] OECD, '21st-Century Readers: Developing Literacy Skills in a Digital World', 2021, https://www.oecd.org/en/publications/21st-century-readers_a83d84cb-en.html

[2] National Literacy Trust, 'Book Ownership in 2024', November 2024, https://literacytrust.org.uk/research-services/research-reports/book-ownership-in-2024

HEADLINE ETERNAL

FIND YOUR HEART'S DESIRE...

VISIT OUR WEBSITE: www.headlineeternal.com
FIND US ON FACEBOOK: facebook.com/eternalromance
CONNECT WITH US ON X: @eternal_books
FOLLOW US ON INSTAGRAM: @headlineeternal
EMAIL US: eternalromance@headline.co.uk